# the love you win

## PIPER HALE

*For Jennica and Ashley. Because I would have given up so many times if not for you two.*

*Thanks for being my besties. Throuple forever.*

# a note from piper

While I have tried to stay as true to the rules and realities of professional hockey as I can, I may change or adapt some things to better serve the story. Please also note that while the story takes place in actual towns and cities, the vast majority of the places and businesses described are fictional. My hope with doing this is that you won't be pulled out of the story if you read it five years from now. If the places and businesses are fictional, they can't change or disappear.

Ultimately, this is a work of fiction, and I hope it will provide a temporary escape from the real world. And a new book boyfriend to swoon over.

Happy reading!

*one*

ISLA

I WONDER HOW MANY DONUTS I CAN EAT BEFORE I feel sick?

My phone buzzes beside me on the couch for the third time.

This Boston Cream is *really* good. I can't believe Alex didn't like Boston Creams. Looking back, that should have been a dead giveaway that he's a soulless asshat. And maybe foreshadowing that he wasn't into eating *creamy* things. Honestly, I should have seen all of this coming the first time he went for a powdered cake donut back in high school. Who actually likes those? I think the only flavor more boring than powdered cake is plain cake. His second favorite flavor.

Shocker.

But *ugh*. The way he'd make that *smacking* sound with his lips as he tried to lick all the powdered sugar off them?

*Gag.*

They always say love is blind. Apparently, mine was deaf, too.

My phone buzzes again. This time, it doesn't cut off after the short two-burst vibration alerting me to a text message.

Who the hell is *calling* me right now? What kind of actual barbarian does something like that? For the love of god, we're not living in the twentieth century. Text messages are clearly superior because I can pretend I didn't see them right away.

I groan as Jess's name lights up in big block letters. I want to send her to voicemail, but that would be a mistake.

*Here we go.*

"Isla's den of donuts. How can I help you?" A pause on the other end makes me grin.

"Have you showered today?"

Well, okay then. Going right in for the kill. "Hi to you too."

"Yeah, yeah. Seriously, Isla. Have you showered today?"

I consider how to answer. I could lie, but... "I showered myself in donut crumbs. Does that count?"

"Yep," my best friend says to someone, her voice growing muffled. "You were right. She probably hasn't changed her underwear in days."

Jesus. You forget to change your clothes for a few days when your life blows up, and your friends never let you forget it. Being unceremoniously dumped by your fiancé two weeks before your wedding for no real reason other than you're suddenly *not good enough* should give you a pass for things like forgetting to change your clothes.

And I've been doing fine. Until last week. When Alex

and I were supposed to take our honeymoon. The one we scheduled for summer vacation so I wouldn't have to take time off during the school year. The bastard still went to Cabo. Without me. "Um, rude. I totally changed my panties today. I think." I tug on the stretchy waistband of my grease-stained leggings to check the color of my undies. Navy blue.

Well, crap.

"Okay, so I changed them yesterday. Whatever. I'm not going anywhere today." I was doing so well when I had teaching and my students to distract me. Sure, I was depressed, but with all the end-of-year testing and general craziness, I never had time to wallow in it. Summer though? I don't have built-in distractions to keep me from spiraling about the honeymoon that should have been. Now, I'm this weird combination of depressed and pissed. I planned that whole damned honeymoon. But Alex paid for it, so he's the one that got to enjoy the sun and sand.

Fucking typical.

Two sets of groans float through the speaker. "We're coming over. Please take a shower and change your clothes. Don't make me douse you in Febreze."

"You know that stuff makes me sneeze," I reply, offended. I don't smell bad. A little ripe, maybe, but nothing a quick rub-down with deodorant can't fix.

"You have half an hour," Nevaeh pipes up.

"Seriously? You two are ganging up on me right now?"

Nevaeh's smooth chuckle floats through the speaker. "That's what best friends are for. Now drag your cute little butt into the shower, get clean and dressed in clothes you haven't already worn this week, and brush your teeth. We'll be there soon."

I groan, but what my two best friends can't see is the smile overtaking my face. Which is probably a good thing because I'm *pretty* sure I have chocolate frosting on my teeth. "Give me forty-five minutes."

Jess sighs. "Forty-five minutes and not a second more. And shave your legs. We're taking you out."

Dammit. I haven't shaved my legs in at least a month. This might be a two-razor job.

---

"WHERE ARE WE GOING?" I ASK MY FRIENDS AS they force me to stand in front of my bathroom mirror. I apply a coat of mascara and a few swipes of blush. After staring at my pasty face for a minute, I can acknowledge I need it. Normally, I've got some color in my otherwise-translucent skin, but I've been looking more and more ghostly with every month that goes by P.B.

It's how I measure time now. B.B. and P.B. Before Breakup and Post Breakup.

Before Breakup Isla always had her fiery red hair curled in loose waves that cascaded gracefully down the middle of her back. Before Breakup Isla had rosy cheeks that softened the smattering of freckles that dusted her face. She wore light makeup but always looked like she'd spent an hour getting ready. She smiled. Well, sometimes. B.B. Isla may not have had the perfect relationship—who does?—but she knew her place in the world and had someone to share it with.

Post Breakup Isla is a mess. She rocks stringy hair that air-dries in tangled, asymmetrical waves, pale skin that highlights dark under-eye circles and the freckles across her upturned nose, and nary a smile to be seen.

Nary's a weird word.

Maybe I do need to get out of this slump. My thoughts sound too much like the Regency-era romances I've been binging. And those women aren't allowed to get any until their wedding night. Even then, I doubt the sex was anything to write home about, so I definitely don't want to live in their world. Hell, I'd be considered an old maid back in Jane Austen's day. A spinster. A crone.

Even with the blush and mascara, I still look haggard.

Whatever. If my appearance screams *bog creature* or *old crone* and scares all the men away, then good-fucking-riddance. That's what I want, after all. No more men for me. I'm determined to focus on my career and myself. When I started teaching, I had these big dreams of making a difference and empowering my students to pursue their passions. I was going to build them up. But after everything with Alex, I lost sight of that for a while. No more. If this breakup has taught me anything, it's the importance of an unflinching support system.

I study my reflection for a moment and shrug. This is as good as it's going to get.

My best friends give me a last once-over before turning to one another. Nevaeh's full lips twist to the side, her springy curls bobbing as her head tilts at an angle. "Yeah. We've got our work cut out for us. I think you're right. We should make her an appointment with Louise."

I turn slowly to face them. "And *why* exactly do I need an appointment with Louise? I don't need her brand of torture. No one's petting my kitty anytime soon, so there's no need to groom her."

Nevaeh chuckles, and her rich umber eyes sparkle. Her straight, white teeth practically glow against her warm brown skin.

"We're going out," Jess replies. As if that explains anything. "We have a surprise for you."

Her gray eyes narrow when my gaze slides her way, looking stunning and sharp against her deep golden skin. They're up to something. I don't like it. Especially not when her thin lips twitch with a failed attempt to keep a smile off her face. Jess brushes a strand of raven hair behind her ear and raises a perfectly shaped eyebrow in challenge.

"You know I don't like surprises."

Nevaeh squeezes my hand, and her expression softens. "You used to."

I did. I liked surprises once. But not anymore. No, I've had enough surprises to last me a lifetime, thank you very much. Something about being dumped two weeks before my wedding—*SURPRISE!*—sorta sucked the fun out of being caught off guard. Still, my protests are weak as they drag me out of my apartment.

We pile into Nevaeh's car, and I stare out the window as she and Jessica chatter about their jobs, the disastrous dates they've gone on with guys from dating apps, and the latest gossip about their coworkers. I don't say much of anything.

Being the center of Alex's attention was thrilling. He was so confident and driven; he made me feel special and rare when he showered me with love and affection. But when that affection turned into annoyance and his attention became cruel? His words were weapons, and he was an expert at cutting me down.

Why did I let him get in my head?

I'm trying to figure out where I went wrong when we park in front of a cute dress shop that is *way* outside of my budget. That's when the first swirl of discomfort hits me. My friends both have glamorous jobs with equally glamorous paychecks. Me? I'm a high school English teacher in an inner-city school. The closest I ever come to high-end fashion is when I splurge on a dress from Zara rather than Target. A place like this? It would gobble up so much of my paycheck that I'd be eating Ramen for weeks.

Nevaeh and Jess hop out, their faces bright and excited. They don't even give me a moment to regret my life decisions before yanking the car door open and tugging on my hands.

"What are we doing here?"

Jess smiles brightly. It makes me twitchy. "You're going to have a *Pretty Woman* moment."

I frown. "You're pimping me out?"

To Nevaeh's credit, she tries to hide her laughter behind a coughing fit, but it only earns a glare from Jessica.

"No. Chris Hemsworth on a cracker. You're going shopping. With my black card. Whatever you want, you get. As long as one of those things is a super-hot dress that shows off those toned thighs of yours and your killer rack." She tilts her head and hums, eyes glazing over. "We should probably get you some sunless tanner, too. I've seen your legs recently. You could blind a person with those things."

"Gee," I say, following her into the fancy shop. "Thanks."

Racks of beautiful clothes give pops of color to the otherwise monochromatic shop, and I eye them with distrust. "As sweet as it is that you want to step up and be my sugar-mama, why exactly are we here?"

Jess flicks her hand in the air dismissively. "Do I need a reason to treat my bestie to a day of shopping and fun?"

"Yes."

My friend clutches her chest. "Don't you trust us?"

"Are you really asking me that right now?" I let my fingers trail across silky fabric as I arch an eyebrow at her. "The last time you bought me clothes was at Halloween. You promised you wouldn't pick out anything too racy and then showed up at my apartment with a slutty nurse costume that didn't even cover my butt cheeks."

Nevaeh laughs. "I warned her you'd be pissed about that."

"Well, I was," I retort. "Thank god I had those Cookie Monster onesie pajamas."

"Oh, come on," Jess says with a roll of her eyes. "You would have been such a hot slutty nurse. You just need to have some confidence in yourself, babe. Now try this on." She pushes a crimson bodycon dress against my chest, forcing me to grab it. A silky off-white number with spaghetti straps and a flared skirt follows quickly behind it. "And this."

"You still haven't told me why we're here."

"Sweetie, it's been five months since you and Alex broke up. I know you thought you'd be spending your life with him. We know it's been hard, and without teaching to distract you this summer, you've been struggling. But it's time to put yourself out there again." Nevaeh squeezes my shoulder. "It's time to move on."

Sure. *Move on.* She makes it sound so *easy.* She's not the one who had to call and email every single one of her friends and family members two weeks before her wedding date to tell them it was off. She's not the one who had to return wedding gifts and smile at words of sympathy while scrambling to renew a lease she'd already let lapse, keep it together for her students while feeling like a worthless failure, or lose—in one day—an entire group of friends she'd had since high school because they were her ex's friends first.

"I've moved on."

They both shoot me incredulous looks.

"What? I have. I totally don't think about Alex anymore." Ok, that's a bit of an exaggeration, but I don't cry myself to sleep anymore. And I haven't sat on the couch to Netflix and chill with my thumb hovering over his name in my contacts list for at *least* two months. I'm over him. I am.

Jess turns to Nevaeh. "Did you see the photo Alex posted last week with his new hair? Can you believe he bleached it? He looks like early 2000's Justin Timberlake. Total ramen hair."

"He didn't dye his hair last week," I say with a frown. "He just posted a photo yesterday, and it's totally still brown." My friends stop sifting through the racks and stare at me with raised brows.

Dammit. Busted.

In my defense, I'm not stalking Alex's socials because I'm still in love with him. I'm looking for some sign that he regrets dumping me, so when he comes crawling back, I'm ready to put on a revenge dress and tell him to kiss my ass.

Mostly.

Sometimes, I'm just a glutton for punishment.

I let my head hang in shame. "Fine. So maybe I need to

move on. I still don't see what that has to do with us buying dresses that cost a third of my paycheck." They practically shove me into a dressing room, demanding I start with the red bodycon dress.

"You need something hot to wear on dates," Jess says as I wiggle into the skin-tight dress. Jesus. It looks like I painted it on.

"Oh, no." Nevaeh's nose crinkles. "I think the slutty nurse costume was less provocative."

I snort, closing myself back into the dressing room and trying on a little blue number with a halter neckline and a low-cut front. "I have plenty of clothes," I tell them as I open the door to model this new option. It's not a winner, either.

"New clothes, new you," Jess sings. "Besides, you tend to dress for comfort."

Pulling on a yellow dress that does nothing for my complexion, I grunt. "And what's wrong with that?"

"No," Jess says when I swing the door open dramatically. I immediately swing it closed. "And there's nothing wrong with dressing for comfort. When you're at home or teaching your students. But when you're out on a date? Dress to get what you want."

I roll my eyes as I pull a slinky black dress over my head. The fabric is shimmery, and it has a scoop neckline, thick straps, and a hemline that falls mid-thigh. I stare at myself as I ask, "And what, exactly, do I want?"

Nevaeh's throaty chuckle filters through the thin changing room door. "To get dicked-down real good by a hot professional athlete."

I choke on a laugh. "That may be what *you* want. I've never been the girl that falls all over herself for a jock."

Besides, I haven't had sex since Alex. I need someone who's the sexual equivalent of a bike with training wheels. Average, unassuming, and reliable enough to get me across the finish line. Even if the ride isn't exciting. Some hot jock with a string of sated women in his rearview mirror is more like a motorcycle. Sure, it could be the best ride of your life, but you could also end up going too fast, falling, and finding yourself covered in road-rash for your troubles.

Road rash being an STI.

"Then you don't know what you're missing," she replies. "Big, strong hands, nimble fingers, and muscles that you'll want to li—" She falls silent when I step out of the changing room. She and Jess stare at me as I do a little spin—because I'm feeling myself in this dress—before turning to each other with matching mischievous grins.

"Oh, that's the one. That dress will bring monsoon season to your Sahara." Jess waves vaguely toward my crotch. "Now we *really* need to get her an appointment with Louise."

"Seriously, you guys, I do not need an appointment to get waxed. I don't even have any dating prospects, let alone professional athlete prospects." I pull a face. Besides, aren't all athletes notorious for sleeping with anything with boobs? The last thing I need is chlamydia.

Jessica shrugs. "But if you had a potential date, you'd go?"

"I guess so."

"And if you happened to land a date with a sports star, you'd go to that too?"

That makes me laugh. And maybe tomorrow, pigs will

gain the ability to fly. "Sure. If I landed a date with some famous jock, I'd go on that too."

Easy enough to agree to. It'll never happen.

Jessica's beautiful face breaks into a smile I don't like. It's her *I'm up to no good* smile that reminds me of the Grinch when he's about to steal Christmas, and I feel like I'm about to wake up to a tree without presents. "Nevaeh, make that appointment with Louise."

"Um, no, do not." I point to myself. "Dateless, remember?"

"Actually," Jess exchanges a look with Nevaeh, "you have a date this Saturday night. With Maddox Graves."

Maddox Graves. I know that name. How do I know that name?

I stare out the window of the dress shop, my mind trying to place where I've heard of him. A bus idles at the stoplight with a massive photo of one of the Minnesota Rogues players on the side. He's ridiculously hot with his tousled black hair and five-o'clock shadow that accentuates his sharply-cut jaw. The color of his eyes is warm brown, flecked with amber, but his expression is hard and sexy, and he holds his hockey stick like he's ready for a fight.

Okay, I wouldn't mind going out with a guy that hot, even if he was a cocky athlete. "Who in the hell is Maddox Graves?"

Jess laughs. "You seriously don't know?"

"No," I reply, irritated. "I seriously don't know."

Jessica leans forward, lifting her arm and pointing at the idling bus before it pulls forward. "*That*, my sweet Isla, is Maddox Graves. And come Saturday evening, He will be *your* date."

My eyes must be round as saucers as I turn to her and splutter, "Bullshit!"

Anticipating my response, Nevaeh holds up her phone, the screen confirming what Jess just told me. "Not bullshit, babes. And there's no getting out of this because you swore."

I stare at the larger-than-life photo of Maddox Graves as the bus drives away. His piercing gaze seems to linger on me. As if making a silent promise to upend my life in the most catastrophic way.

But maybe my life could do with some upending. Maybe Jess and Nev are right. It's time to get over Alex. To focus on my students and get ready to start the new school year off with a bang. I *will* walk into Center High with my chin up and a renewed determination to be the best damned teacher I can be.

And if my best friends think going on a date with a broody hockey player might help me get my groove back, I guess that's what I'll do.

# *two*

<br>

ONE WEEK PRIOR

## MADDOX

"Settle down, assholes," Coach Cross shouts over the din of the locker room. We've all changed out of our workout gear and have been waiting impatiently for this meeting to start. It's Friday night, and everyone has plans. Griffin Wright, Sebastian Navarro, Logan Byrne, and I are going to our favorite bar. Beer, hot women, and live music that never disappoints. Wright and Byrne go for the women, Navarro for the music, and I go for the beer.

"As all of you know, the off-season is the time of year when the Rogues do our annual charity event." Some guys grumble, others are excited, but Coach ignores them all. "We've had some great successes over the past few years, so our marketing and community outreach teams have gotten creative this year to top our past events."

"Please don't be some exhausting meet and greet," Navarro murmurs from my left. He runs a tan hand through his jet-black hair, mussing it up.

"I hope there's food," Wright pipes up from my right, hazel eyes wide and excited.

"I just hope there are women," Byrne offers from Wright's other side. The guy's the consummate lady's man. Even after a hard practice, he looks put together. His dark blond hair is smoothed back, his gray eyes are sharp, and the stubble along his sharp jaw is perfectly groomed and purposeful.

"Shut up and listen," I tell them all with a roll of my eyes.

Wright snickers. "Yes, sir, Captain, sir."

Jesus. Like herding cats.

"This year," Coach says, shooting a glare our way, "the team will host a silent auction. It's a two-part event. There will be a dinner where guests can bid on prizes and experiences, as well as mingle with each of you."

That doesn't sound too bad. Not my idea of a good time, but survivable.

"We expect everyone to participate. You'll all sign jerseys, sticks, photos… all the normal stuff."

"Easy enough," I mumble.

"But the big draw will be dates with some of our players. People will bid on those online, and the dates will occur prior to the silent auction dinner." Everyone starts talking over each other while Navarro and I exchange horrified looks. "Anyone who wants to volunteer, see me after this meeting, and we'll get you signed up."

A few of the younger players look excited at the prospect of going on dates with rich women who've paid for the pleasure of their company like glorified escorts. They're the new blood. The guys that don't have puck bunnies lining up to blow them the way the seasoned players do. They crave the fame and recognition most of us old guys could live without.

"This is a great chance to show our team in a positive light, so there will be no sleeping with the women who win you," Coach says to the *boos* of a few. "You want to screw them, end the date and ask them on another one, even if it's five minutes later. You're not hookers, you're hockey players."

Wright chuckles, nudging me with his elbow. "They're called sex workers, Coach. Hooker is a derogatory term. And these guys aren't pretty enough to be sex workers. Me, on the other hand..."

"Jesus," I groan.

"One last thing," Coach says as my teammates stand to leave. He completely ignores Wright's comment. "Graves, you'll be taking part in the date auction, too." The locker room falls completely silent as all eyes turn my way.

"No. No fucking way, Coach. Absolutely not." The last thing I want—the very last thing—is to be forced into a dinner date with some vapid woman who's probably fifteen years older than me, married, and looking for someone exciting to cheat with. Or worse, a jersey chaser my age who thinks she can use a forced date with me to wiggle her way into my life. After all, I don't date anymore. Not after everything that happened. So what better way to bag the white whale of professional hockey?

"It's not a request, Graves. Not only will you draw enough interest to raise some serious money for our charities, but you've got an image problem. We're going to use this as a controlled way to fix that."

My friends chuckle under their breath. I elbow Wright, and it makes him laugh louder.

"I don't have an image problem," I scoff. "I'm one of the league's scoring leaders. I'm not off starting brawls, and you'll never see an article about how I was sloppy drunk in a single magazine or blog."

Coach shakes his head. The few streaks of gray in his dirty blond hair glint in the locker room lights. His mouth pulls into something between a grimace and a smile. "They call you the Gravedigger. Which would be great if they were just referring to your performance on the ice and not the way you brutally break up with every woman you've ever dated and bury her heart six feet under. You know I don't give a shit about any of that, but the public does."

I wince. I hate that name. It doesn't matter that the stories that spawned it are lies. The cursed moniker's still stuck. "Oh, come on, Coach. My dating life has nothing to do with the team."

"It does when your jilted girlfriends sell their stories to whatever gossip rag they can. Do you think it's just your name that gets dragged through the mud, then? Because it's not. The team's name is right there being dragged along with you."

Pinching the bridge of my nose, I try to ignore the amused stares of my teammates. They must think this is hilarious. At least someone does because I'm about to blow a gasket. "And how is some awkward date with a desperate rich woman going to help my image?"

"This is going to backfire," the rookie, Ryder Hanson, mutters.

"Because there will be photographers and reporters waiting to interview everyone after their dates. You'll take whoever wins the night with you out, treat her like a queen, make her feel special, and then she'll gush to the reporters about how wonderful you are." He crosses his arms over his chest. He's annoyed that he has to have this conversation with me. Well, guess what? I'm annoyed too. And I'm the one who's never going to hear the end of this tonight at the bar.

Coach shakes his head. "Prove that you're more than a heartless bastard, and it'll do wonders for your image and the team's. Hell, you might even find some of those endorsements you've been negotiating close a little easier."

Dammit.

"You're doing this, Graves. End of story."

"Whatever you say, Coach." He side-eyes me for my tone, but come on. This is so far from my idea of a good time. I don't date jersey chasers. I'll take them home for a few hours of fun when I have an itch that demands to be scratched, but that's it. They're not good for anything serious. They're all fake, simpering gold diggers. Candace hammered that lesson home when she sold a false story to the tabloids about how I used her after our breakup. Even though it was the other way around. She painted me as the bad guy when I let her down gently. Dragged my reputation through the mud to make a quick buck and prolong her fifteen minutes of fame.

Jersey chasers don't care about the men they chase. They care about the lifestyle. The money. The cameras pointed at their pretty, Botox-ed faces. I've been in this game too long to find them anything other than repugnant.

Coach pins me with his best *take no shit* stare before clapping his hands together. "All right, that's it. You're all dismissed. I expect everyone in the weight room by ten a.m. tomorrow."

There's a chorus of *Yes, Coach*, and he strides out of the locker room without a look back. I stare at his retreating form, at a loss for words. I'm so focused on Coach disappearing that I jump when Byrne claps a hand on my shoulder.

"Looks like our boy here could use that drink. Meet you all at Chasers in fifteen."

I grunt my agreement and fume the entire drive. I'm so irritated by the whole thing that I've got a perpetual scowl etched into my face, even when a few patrons cheer at my entrance and clap me on the back.

"Lighten up, man," Wright says when I head back to our table in the corner. "You look like your dog just died. Or maybe like you've got a turd prairie-dogging it, and you're struggling to keep it contained."

Navarro turns to look at Wright with a raised brow and curled lip. "Classy, Griffin."

Griffin Wright shrugs. "You're all thinking it."

"I can tell you we weren't," Byrne says with a laugh. He slides a foamy pint across the table to me. "Drinks are on me tonight."

The beer is cold, and it goes down smooth, but the flavor's tainted by the knowledge that, in just a couple of weeks, I'll have to sit at some fancy restaurant in one of my best game-day suits and try to make a strange woman feel like I enjoy her company. "Thanks, Logan."

Byrne nods. "So, a date auction, huh? That should be fun."

Right. *Fun.* "I'd rather have second-degree sunburn on my balls."

"Are you going to sign up to go on a date?" Navarro asks Byrne, ignoring me.

"You know there'd be a bidding war for a date with *the* Logan Byrne." He puffs out his chest and does that douchey thing where he smooths his fingers over his eyebrows. "I'd hate to overshadow Madds's big day."

"Oh, jump off a cliff," I grumble. Even so, it's a struggle to smother the smile trying to twitch its way onto my face.

Wright and Byrne start talking about the women at the bar and who they want to bring home, and Navarro leans toward me. "Seriously, man. You okay?"

*No.*

"I'm fine. It's just crap."

Navarro nods, and his expression is so solemn I know he's not just humoring me. He knows the whole story behind the exposés. He knows how they affected me, my sister, and my mom. I've worked hard to get where I am for them, and those women I dated almost blew all of it to hell. I won't make that mistake again, which is why being forced into this date is such a slap in the face. I don't have room for relationships in my life outside of the guys on my team and my family. They're what matters and the reason I strive to be the very best.

"Maybe it'll be better than you expect," he says before taking a swig of his IPA. "Who knows, maybe she'll be smart and pretty, and you'll fall madly in love."

I hold his dark gaze for a few beats before we both burst out into raucous laughter.

Right. Maybe she'll be my soulmate.

And maybe tomorrow I'll be crowned the King of England.

# *three*

## ISLA

This is a terrible idea.

"I'm sick," I say as I open the door for my two overly-excited besties. I do my best to look absolutely pathetic. A little shoulder hunching, a few coughs straight out of the finest production of *Oliver Twist*, and my hair looks like a rat's nest. Though, that's just because I haven't combed it yet today. It's Saturday and summer. I don't have students or fellow teachers to fool into thinking I have my life together, and I'm embracing the mess.

*Be the mess you want to see in the world.* Gandhi said that, right?

In they come: a tornado of snacks, makeup cases, and massive smiles. Jess boops me on the nose as she passes me by. "Nice try."

"I am," I say, trying to make my voice sound raspy. I'm not a good actress. It doesn't work. "I'm so sick, Jess. Guess one of you will have to go on this date with Mr. Hockey."

Nevaeh arches one eyebrow as she grabs my cheeks with one hand, squeezing my lips open like a fish. There's a thermometer in my mouth before I can even register what she's doing.

"If your temperature isn't above one hundred degrees, you're going, missy." She ignores the sputtering sounds I make around the thermometer. Turning to Jess, she rolls her eyes. "Told you she'd pull a stunt like this."

"That you did," Jess says. "Dinner's on me tonight."

Did they make a bet on me? "Not cool," I mumble.

"No talking, or I'll have to take your temperature again, young lady." Nevaeh has the mom-glare down. I swear, she's even more terrifying than my mother sometimes.

When the thermometer beeps, it's no surprise it reads 98.5. Damn. It's hard to spin that. So I cough a few more times. "I don't have a fever, but my throat... I think I have strep."

Jessica grabs me by my shoulders and gives me a little shake. "You. Are. Going. You're going to get all glammed-up, have a free fancy dinner, ogle a hot hockey player, and at the end, you'll take a selfie which you can post on social media."

"Why?"

She rolls her eyes. "To rub how great you're doing in Alex's face. He's going to see you looking hot on the arm of a broody hockey god and think, *man, I done fucked up.*"

I look down at myself. There's a coffee stain on my right boob in the shape of Ohio, my sweatpants have holes in them, and I definitely have a wedgie. "Yeah. I'm doing so great."

"He doesn't need to know the truth," Nevaeh says. "This is for social media. Nothing on there is true. He just needs to think you've moved on to greener pastures and bigger dicks."

"Wouldn't be hard," I grumble.

"Honestly," Jess says, tugging me toward my bathroom and starting the shower, "I know you thought you were in love with Alex, but did you *ever* orgasm during sex with him?"

"Only if I helped myself along."

"He couldn't even lend a helping hand to make up for his pinkie-sized manhood?" Jess shakes her head, and the two of them start to undress me like I'm some errant toddler who'll fight them on getting into the shower. I mean, I will, but can't they even give me a chance to prove them wrong?

"Nope." Alex was all quick, frantic thrusts and weird, animalistic grunts. And when he'd come, he always made this high-pitched noise that sounded like a bad impersonation of Michael Jackson singing *'hee-hee.'* A real two-pump chump. For him to lend a hand, he would have had to last longer than two minutes.

Jess looks wistfully into the distance. "I bet Maddox Graves has a dick the size of my forearm."

I wrinkle my nose as they shove me into the shower. "Would he be able to skate with something like that shoved in his pants?"

Jess shrugs. "Probably not. Now wash your hair twice before you condition it. You don't want stringy hair on your date."

"Rude," I grunt, but do as she says.

"Did you leave the house this week?" Nevaeh asks, hopping on my vanity where she sits guard. Are they seriously not going to let me shower alone?

"Yes, actually. I checked in on one of my students. He lost his dad toward the end of last school year." It had been a heavy week. One that will always be burned into my brain. "I don't know if I ever told you guys about it. They called him into the guidance counselor's office in the middle of the day to tell him. I could hear his sobs from down the hall."

"Oh, god." Nevaeh covers her mouth. "Do they know what happened?"

I nod. "He worked at a warehouse, and there was a forklift accident. The driver was rushing and bumped into a tower of pallets stacked way too high, and it crushed him. Apparently, he survived until they took the last palette off. It had been staunching the worst of his internal bleeding." My voice catches. I'll never forget the sound of my student's cries as they echoed down the empty hallways.

"Jesus. I can't even imagine." Jess's eyes are glassy. She knows some of the struggles my kids go through. Like any city school, we have kids that span a wide spectrum of affluence and situations. Some live in nice, big houses in the older part of town. Some live in cramped little apartments where they share a room with two other siblings. A few even live in shelters. But no matter what their home lives might be like, my students are amazing.

They're the reason I get out of bed in the morning. And, as trite as it sounds, after Alex and I broke up, I used to remind myself that if my kids who live in a shelter could get up, take public transit to school at an ungodly hour of the morning, and still show up every day and do their best, then so could I.

They keep me going, and I want to be the person who

encourages them to keep going, too. I just wish there was more I could do to bring some encouragement to their lives. It's why I've checked in on my student and his mom a few times this summer. I've brought them groceries, given hugs, and just tried to be there for them. Even though anything I do feels utterly inadequate.

It makes going on this date feel icky. I don't know how much Nevaeh and Jess spent on winning this dinner, but it was probably enough to buy groceries for a week for half of my students and their families.

"Hey," Nevaeh says, tapping on the glass shower door. "Just because some of your students are struggling doesn't mean you're not allowed to have fun and do something extravagant."

"I know."

"Do you? Because you're always looking out for everyone else, Isla. You put the people you care about before yourself—and that can be great and all—but who puts you first? Not Alex. He was happy to let you support him throughout law school, but did he support you in the same way when you took a job in the city making less money?"

No. He didn't. He never understood why I'd choose to work in a district with more issues and less pay. Money is king to Alex. That's his passion. Mine is making kids believe they can do whatever they put their minds to if they work hard enough and persevere.

Nevaeh takes my silence as the answer it is. "Well, we're putting you first. We're going to do nice things for you until you remember what you knew back in high school when we met. That you're Isla Harding. You're smart, and funny, and kind. You're one of the most confident women I know. You have a killer body, your laugh is the best sound ever, and any man would be lucky to spend even an hour in your presence."

Silence stretches between us when she's done speaking. Only the patter of water on the tiled shower floor fills the bathroom. I wish it were as easy as all that. If someone came up with some magic pill that restored all the confidence to your soul that some evil ex stole, I'd be the first in line to buy it. But it's not that easy, and I don't know if I'll ever be that woman again.

"What do I even say to some famous hockey player?" I need to change the subject. "I know nothing about hockey. I've never watched a game in my life."

Jess shrugs. "You don't have to talk about hockey. Talk about movies or your favorite foods. Ask him questions. Treat him like a normal person. He'll probably like that more, anyway."

"Besides," Nevaeh adds as I run conditioner through my hair, "he's a public figure. He's probably great at making conversation with people he doesn't know."

God, I hope so. "I really don't want to do this."

"We know." Jess unpacks makeup from her kit and sets it out on the counter beside Nevaeh. "But seriously, babes, this is the perfect way to get back in the game. I swear. You get to have a pressure-free first date with a hot, attentive man and rebuild your confidence. He's not someone you're trying to start a relationship with—hell, he's not even someone you probably have anything in common with— so it doesn't matter if you blow it. And since you know it doesn't matter if you blow it, you won't feel pressured to be the perfect date. It'll let you relax and enjoy yourself."

Nevaeh nods. "Exactly. And then when we create a

profile for you on some dating sites, you won't feel nearly as out of your depth as you would have."

"Whoa, whoa, whoa. I never agreed to dating sites."

"Not yet, you haven't," Jess says. "But you will."

"I just want to focus on me for a while. Alex and I were together for so long, I don't even know who I am without him." Probably because he wore me down with his snide comments and backhanded compliments. "Besides, maybe I just want to stay single."

"Forever?" Jess's face is comical. She can't believe I'd say something like that.

I shrug because who knows? I'm just talking out of my ass. "Maybe. Are men really worth the trouble?"

"Oh, sweetie, Alex wasn't worth the trouble. But that doesn't mean there isn't a man out there who is." Nevaeh's voice is soft as she continues. "We know you're scared. It's hard to put yourself out there after getting your heart broken. Especially after something like what happened to you. But you can do this. I know you're strong enough to open yourself up again."

I'm not sure I am. Don't get me wrong, I *want* to be strong enough. And I really am fine on my own. But when I lie in bed at night, too tired to be anything but honest with myself, I do hope I find someone to share my life with. Someone who will look at me and truly *see* me. Who'll love me more than his money or his status or his career.

"But what if I'm not strong enough? What if this is my life now? What if I wasted all of my best years on a man who never really loved me?"

"I'm sure he loved you, Isla."

I finish washing off, making sure my legs are smooth

and my pits aren't hairy. "That's the thing, Jess. The more I think about it, the more I'm sure he didn't. Alex never loved *me.* He loved being loved. He loved having someone around who would stroke his ego and support his dreams. I was a tool to further his own happiness, and at least at first, I fit the image he wanted to project. Whatever he felt for me, it was selfish. I can see that now."

I only wish I'd recognized it sooner.

"Maybe," Jess says. "But I can tell you one thing for sure. You did not waste your best years on Alex Jones. Not by a long shot. You're only twenty-six, you're a badass teacher, you're smart and successful, and girl, look at you. I'm looking at your naked body right now, and it is *bangin'.*"

"Oh. My. God. Stop being weird, and stop looking at my nakedness!"

"Then hurry and finish showering, already. We have to get our pretty princess ready for the ball."

I cringe as I turn off the water and wrap myself in a towel. If this is a ball, why do I have the feeling I'm going to end the night amidst a wrecked magical carriage with a missing shoe and pumpkin guts plastered to my ass?

## ISLA

THIS PLACE IS *FANCY*.

"I'm so jealous you get to eat here," Jess whines. "The waitlist to get a reservation is like six months long."

I could never afford dinner somewhere like this. I have no idea how long their waitlist is because places like this aren't even on my radar. Every once in a while, Nevaeh and Jess will try to talk me into letting them take me out somewhere fancy, but I always decline. I'm a simple girl. I like good books, pizza, movie nights in, and driving far enough outside of the city that I can find a nice trail to hike. It's not that money makes me *uncomfortable*, it's just that it's never mattered all that much to me. As long as I can pay my bills and the stress of being broke doesn't eat me alive, I'm happy. I grew up solidly middle class. We never went on extravagant vacations or had brand-new cars, but we also never went without the necessities.

I don't need more than that. In fact, I've seen too much

money turn people into miserly, unhappy shadows of themselves.

No, thanks.

"Are you ready for this?" Nevaeh peers back at me from the driver's seat. They insisted on taking me to the restaurant. Apparently, they didn't trust me to drive myself. They said I would be more likely to take my e-reader and park in some random parking lot and pretend to go on the date than actually show up at this place.

For the record, I *wasn't* planning on doing that.

I was going to read on my phone.

"I think I have the bubonic plague." I dab at my tear ducts. "Am I crying blood yet? Pretty sure that's one of the symptoms."

"Oh, for the love of Chris Hemsworth." Jess must really be irritated if she's invoking her sex god's name. It's a silly thing she started back in college, and it's stuck. She climbs out of the passenger seat, opens my door, and drags me out by my wrists. "Get your gorgeous butt in there and let yourself have some fun for once." She cocks her head to the side. "You remember what that is, right? Fun?"

Rolling my eyes, I let my head fall back. I say a little prayer to Chris that the sky will open up and swallow me whole. He doesn't answer. "Yes. Fun. Because all of this screams *Isla's idea of fun*."

"If you stop being so uptight, maybe the night will end in some fun screaming." She waggles her eyebrows at me.

"Sure." Listen, I'm happy with how I look today. My hair falls in sleek, shiny waves around my shoulders and down to my mid back. My makeup is perfect thanks to my friends, and this dress does wonders for my body. I feel beautiful.

But I'm not the kind of woman men like Maddox Graves go for. I'm not supermodel tall and leggy. I'm petite and a little too curvy outside of my flat butt. My face is pretty, but there's nothing all that special about my features. I'm the girl you date in high school. The one you think back on fondly and wonder where she is and what she's doing when you hit the end of your thirties. I'm not the woman you plan your dreams around. And if you do, one day you wake up and realize you could do better, and you call those plans off.

"Hey." Jess gives my hand a quick squeeze. "It's just a date. Let yourself have fun. Give him a chance. But if it's terrible, walk."

"But you guys paid so much money…"

"To help you get out of your head. Not to force you into spending an entire night with a guy if he's an asshole. Get your selfie, pretend you had fun, then bolt if you want."

My chest deflates, and some of the anxiety that's been giving me heartburn all day eases. "You guys really wouldn't be mad?"

"No way," Nevaeh says from the car. "But you owe it to yourself to give it a genuine chance. Promise?"

"Promise." I can do that. I can give this a chance. Who knows, maybe it'll be fun, even though it's never going to lead to anything. And you know what? That's okay. This could be the start of a new Isla. One that can be flirty and casual and not care what a guy thinks about her or whether he could see her being *the one*.

"Good. Now get in there and make a hockey player fall for you."

My spine straightens and I stick out my boobs a bit. I'm under no delusions that he'll fall for me, but wouldn't it be fun if he wanted me a little? "Keep your phones on you?"

"Always," Jess promises. She hugs me before pushing me toward the double doors leading into the restaurant. A mama bird shoving her baby out of the nest.

"Have fun," Nevaeh calls. "Don't do anything I wouldn't do!"

Considering she once slept with a waiter in a restaurant's walk-in cooler, that's not promising much. I give them both one last wave, suck in a deep breath, square my shoulders, and head inside.

"Good evening." A pretty young woman greets me from a large mahogany hostess stand. "Do you have a reservation?"

I could say no and bolt. Except Jess and Nevaeh are still sitting in their car out front, idling at the curb. They give me little waves that say they know exactly what I was just thinking. Sucking in a deep breath, I tuck a strand of hair behind my ear. "Uh, yeah. Hi, my name is Isla Harding. I'm supposed to be meeting—"

"Oh, of course!" The hostess's eyes light up. "I know exactly who you are. Right this way, Miss Harding." She extends a hand, gesturing for me to follow her. It feels like every eye in the room is on me as we wend our way around candle-lit tables and shoulder-height walls that create private little dining nooks. It's stunning.

I don't belong here.

"I hope you don't mind, but I just have to say that I am so jealous of you right now. Mr. Graves is already seated, and ohmygod, he's even better looking in person."

There's supposed to be a smile on my face, but I have a feeling it looks more like a grimace. "Uh, yeah. It's crazy."

The hostess glances back at me and gives me an encouraging smile. "You're going to have so much fun. Anything you need, just ask. My name is Kacey."

*Can you bring me a Xanax? Because I'm pretty sure I'm about to have a panic attack.*

"Thanks, Kacey. I appreciate that."

She leads me to the back corner of the restaurant, where there's a gorgeous table covered with candles and flowers. It's not in a private nook like I'd hoped—nothing like the threat of public humiliation to help set the mood —but there is ample open space around it. Hopefully, that means we won't have people eavesdropping. The last thing I need is some superfan posting play-by-plays of my horrendously awkward first-date conversation on social media for all the world to see.

And it will be awkward. Because Kacey is right. Maddox Graves is positively panty-melting in person.

I take a moment to study him before we're introduced. He leans back in his chair, long legs extended out to the side. His maroon suit pants fight a valiant battle to contain his muscular thighs. His jacket hangs on a coat rack against the wall, and he's rolled his shirtsleeves up to just below his elbows. Muscular forearms ripple as he types away on his phone, a deep scowl on his chiseled face. If the ticking of his jaw is any indication, whatever he's looking at on the screen isn't good news. That, or he's just as unhappy about being here as I am.

There's no way in hell I'll get through this dinner without making a fool of myself. Maddox Graves is completely out of my league. He oozes confidence, and mine evaporates out of my very pores with every step toward him I take. I can feel my spine softening and my shoulders curling.

"Here you are, Miss Harding," Kasey says as she pulls out the seat across from Maddox. "If you need anything, just let me know. Have a lovely evening." And with that, she gives me a subtle wink, and I'm left alone with a gorgeous, brooding stranger.

A stranger who doesn't even bother to stand and shake my hand. He just sits there, his eyes making a lazy perusal of my body as I try not to fidget like a spider monkey on ecstasy. His eyes flare for a moment with what I swear is interest, but it's gone in another instant, and they turn glacial again. I wait for him to speak, but when it's obvious that won't happen, I clear my throat and re-tuck my hair behind my ear.

"Um, hi." I wave like I'm riding on a float in a parade. Smooth. "I'm Isla. You must be Maddox?"

He grunts. "Yup."

*Okaaaay.* What an ass.

Chewing on my bottom lip, I sink into the seat across from him. If I'm lucky, this place will be haunted, and I'll be swallowed whole by a cursed chair. A woman can hope. "This place is nice," I stammer.

Here we go. An uncomfortable Isla is an awkward Isla.

He shifts in his chair. "It's fine."

"My friends have been dying to eat here, but apparently, it's next to impossible to get a reservation. I wonder how they were able to fit us in?"

One dark eyebrow arches. "I'm the captain of the Minnesota Rogues. I'm sure they were more than happy about the publicity they'll get by having us do this here." He thinks I'm an idiot.

"Right," I say, forcing out a fake, breathy laugh. "Of course."

We fall silent, and I wrack my brain for something to say. Luckily, a middle-aged gentleman glides up to our table in a black suit. There's a white towel draped over his forearm, and he carries a bottle of expensive champagne.

"Good evening. Welcome to Rêveur. My name is Gregory, and I will be taking care of you tonight. Can I pour you both a glass of champagne?" He looks at Maddox first, who waves his hand over the champagne flute as if he can't be bothered to utter the word *yes*. He picks up his phone and types something on it as Gregory looks my way. "Champagne, miss?"

"Yes, please," I murmur, ducking my head. I want to tell him to leave the whole bottle because the only way I'm getting through this dinner is by turning it into a drinking game.

Maddox grunts? Drink.

He rolls his eyes? Drink.

Looks at his phone? Drink.

Answers a question with a single word in his best caveman impression? You guessed it. Drink.

Gregory pours us both a glass as he recites the specials, but I hardly hear them. My ears roar with static, and my gut fills with acid. All-too-familiar feelings of inadequacy writhe like snakes in the pit of my stomach. Can Maddox tell I'm nothing more than a broke English teacher who doesn't belong here? Jess and Nevaeh claimed I cleaned up well, but apparently not well enough. Do I smell poor or something?

What would poor even smell like? Ramen noodles and student loan debt?

"I'll give you both a few moments to look over the rest of the menu," Gregory says. And then he's gone, leaving me alone with Captain Grump-ass.

I steal a look at my phone before setting my purse by my feet. I've only been here for five minutes, and it feels like an eternity.

I'm tempted to text the girls and tell them to turn around and come get me. I didn't ask them to spend thousands on this stupid dinner. But I swore I'd give this a chance. Besides, if I leave now, I won't have anything to show for it.

That selfie I've been promised at the end of the night better make Alex so jealous he loses the power of speech.

THE PAINFULNESS RAMPS UP AFTER GREGORY TAKES our order.

"So," I say with an awkward giggle. "Do you auction off dates often?"

Maddox Graves looks up from his phone with raised brows. "No."

"Right. That would be weird. How would you even set something like that up? You'd need an assistant to handle everything. Or a website where women could bid. Or men. I'm sure there are plenty of men out there who would want to date you, too. But I guess if you ever need some quick cash, you've got options." Sweet baby Chris Hemsworth, someone stop me.

My date looks at me like I've grown a second head. He doesn't dignify my verbal vomit with any kind of response, and I think that's worse than if he just came right out and called me an idiot.

"But then again, you're Maddox Graves," I say a little too loudly. "You probably have plenty of money."

I know this isn't a real date and I should be happy my brain has picked this moment to get all the weird out, but holy hell, this is mortifying. If I was actually trying to impress this guy, I would have already slunk out of the restaurant on my belly like some kind of pathetic slug.

"Maddox Graves?" a feminine voice squeals. "Oh my god, I thought that was you."

I glance up to see a very excited teenage girl standing a few feet away from our table. I must have said his name a little too loudly. She's looking back at an older couple who must be her parents.

"See, Dad? I told you it was him." The girl has heart-eyes when she returns her attention to Maddox. "Could I get a photo with you? And an autograph?"

Maddox barely spares me a glance to gauge my reaction. Which is probably a good thing, because my heart is sinking into my stomach. His face transforms in an instant from one of bored disdain to a bright smile. He sits a little taller in his seat, and gives the girl his full attention.

That smile is an iceberg, and that it's so easy for him to pull it out for anyone but me scrapes along the hull of my heart. I'm the Titanic, and I'm going down. Cue the orchestra.

*"This dinner is important for my career, Isla. The least you can do is stop babbling on like a bimbo every time you get nervous." Alex's grip on my upper arm bites into my skin. He hisses the words in my ear so none of his colleagues can*

*hear. It takes all of my effort to keep tears from pooling in my eyes.*

*"You put me on the spot, Alex. You know this kind of thing isn't as easy for me as it is for you."*

*His scowl makes me wither. The way he looks at me makes my heart hurt. A man in an expensive-looking suit approaches and Alex's scowl instantly morphs into one of the charming smiles that drew me to him back in high school. The kind of smile that makes you feel you're the only one in the room.*

*The kind of smile that seems to be reserved for everyone but me.*

I shake my head, dislodging the intrusive memory as Maddox's voice rolls across my skin like thunder along the plains.

"Of course, I'd be happy to take a photo with you."

"Honey," the woman who must be her mom says, "don't interrupt them. It looks like they're on a date."

Maddox waves his hand dismissively. "It's fine. You're not interrupting anything. I've always got time for my fans."

*Ouch.*

The girl barely spares me a glance as she jumps up and down, drawing attention to us. When she leans down to snap a photo with Maddox, people look more closely at what's going on, and I can hear the murmurs starting. These people might all have money, but there's a genuine celebrity in their midst. The women get hungry looks in their eyes, and the men are excited that one of their sports idols is sitting a few tables over.

None of them seem to register the red-haired woman sinking lower and lower into her chair.

After they take a photo, Maddox signs a piece of paper she scrounged up somewhere.

"Oh my god, thank you. I am *such* a huge fan. You're so hot."

Maddox chuckles as the girl scurries back to her parents' table. The dad gives him a nod of thanks, which Maddox returns with a smile. And suddenly we're surrounded by five more women batting their eyelashes at him and asking for photos.

Gregory rushes up to our table with an apology. "I am so sorry. This should never have happened." He shoos the women away, but Maddox stops him with a chuckle.

"It's all right, Greg. They just want a couple of photos. I don't mind at all." Never once does Maddox glance my way to see if *I* mind. And I probably wouldn't, if he'd asked. Or spoken more than a few words to me. Or made me feel more than an inch tall.

The waiter shoots me an apologetic look, which I return with a shrug. What am I going to say? That Maddox can't take photos and sign autographs for his fans? I have zero claim on the man. Heck, I didn't even want to come tonight. It shouldn't bother me in the least.

But after the fourth selfie and autograph, the line to greet tall, hot, and dickish shows no sign of dying, and I *am* feeling bothered. Bothered that Maddox has been such an absolute prick when I've done nothing but try to be nice. Bothered that he saw right through the expensive dress and the perfect makeup and decided from the first moment that I wasn't good enough for him. But most of all? I'm bothered that I've let all of this get to me. Even a little.

A selfie for my socials isn't worth this.

I don't say a word as I grab my purse and get to my feet. I don't spare a backward glance for Maddox or his adoring fans. Lifting my chin even though I feel like crying, I silently make my way to the door. Screw this. Screw my stupid ex, and asshole, Maddox. I may fight back tears, but a new determination fills me. I'm moving on. Kacey, the sweet hostess, frowns when I approach the exit.

"Miss Harding? Are you okay?"

"Oh, of course. I just had something come up." I'm sure my eyes are glassy, which is why she turns to look at Maddox and his entourage of adoring female fans. Her frown deepens.

The hostess returns her attention to me. "You know what? Maybe he's not that good-looking."

A watery laugh bubbles out of me. "Right?"

"Have a better rest of your night, Miss Harding." She offers me a conspiratorial smile that I return, then I push my way out of Rêveur.

Once I'm standing on the sidewalk, I suck in a few deep breaths and fish my phone out of my purse with a shaky hand. Jess and Nevaeh are going to be disappointed. They had such high hopes that tonight would remind me that dating can be fun. Unfortunately, it seems to have had the opposite effect.

I'm more certain than ever that I don't need a guy to make me happy. I need my friends, my job, and my books.

Because arrogant assholes are only attractive in works of fiction.

# *five*

MADDOX

I HATE THAT SHE'S BEAUTIFUL.

This would have been so much simpler if she was significantly older than me and unbearably rude. It would have been easier if she didn't have stunning, delicate features, soft, inviting eyes, and freckles I want to count while we're naked in bed after a night of epic sex. And her curves. God damn, her curves are perfect.

I like a woman who's soft. Whose body gives a little when you press into her.

So I breathed a sigh of relief when her adorable rambling caught the attention of the other diners. If I can distract myself with autographs and photos with fans, she won't be able to lull me into some twisted attraction. It's a dick move, but I'm in more danger than I thought I'd be. She may not reek of desperation like some of these other jersey chasers, but I can't forget she used her money to buy a way into my life. Even if it's just for one dinner date.

And if I stare into her ocean-blue eyes for too long, I very well may lose all sense of reason.

Coach is going to kick my ass for being rude to her. Hell, I want to kick my own ass. I can tell she's nervous and I've hurt her feelings with my gruff answers and bored demeanor. But it has to be done. She has to understand this isn't a real date. She doesn't have a chance with me, no matter how beautiful she is.

Still, I don't enjoy the way she flinches, as though I've struck her, when I tell the teenage girl asking for my autograph she isn't interrupting anything.

Not my proudest moment.

It also doesn't mean I enjoy watching some of the sparkle in her eyes dull when I agree to sign autographs rather than choosing to converse with her.

I'll just sign a couple more, then I'll have made my point. Once it's clear she has no future with me, we can make small talk and end this night quickly and on a more positive note. As long as she doesn't forget the crux of it all.

This isn't a real date, and I'm only here because I have to be.

One autograph has turned into two, then three, then four, and I'm starting to feel guilty. I'm sure my date well and truly understands the reality of this night now. I sneak a peek at Isla to gauge her reaction. Except she's not in her seat.

Frowning, I glance beneath the table to see if her purse is still there. It's not. But when I look up, I catch a flash of long, red hair and a shimmery black dress walking out of the restaurant. That, and the hostess is giving me a dirty look.

*Shit.* The photo-op at the end of the night. The one Coach told me was meant to reform my image of being an asshole to women. I snort at the irony of it all because this won't be the first time the press calls me a dick. But it will be the first time it's true. It won't look great if the reporter shows up to snap a few pictures and get a few soundbites and my date isn't even here.

"Excuse me," I say to the woman leaning over to flash me her cleavage. Rising from my chair, I slide past the line of fawning admirers. I need to catch Isla before she can call an Uber or get in her car. Crap. What if she already has? The hostess glares at me as I race out the double doors.

*Yeah, I know. Trust me. I hate myself, too.*

I'm prepared to search for Isla and comb the surrounding blocks, but there's no need. I nearly stumble into her back. She doesn't turn when my footsteps slap against the pavement, so I take a moment to study her before making my presence known. She's probably about to call her friends and tell them she wasted her money. How disappointing I am. That all her plans to land a rich hockey player were foiled.

Except she doesn't do any of that.

My stomach roils when I notice her hand shaking as she holds her phone. Her chest rises and falls too quickly as she sucks in a shuddering breath.

Have I made her cry? Dammit. I have. Isla sniffles and uses the back of her hand to wipe her eyes.

The Gravedigger, indeed. Maybe I deserve the nickname after today.

"Isla?" I lightly brush her shoulder with my fingers to get her attention. She jerks away from my touch as though

I've burned her. Wide blue eyes skewer me in place. They're glassy, rimmed with red, and she takes a split second too long to change her expression to one of cool indifference. I've hurt her.

"What do you want?" Gone is the awkward, rambling woman I'd met in the restaurant. In her place stands a fiery goddess whose glassy eyes turn hard. I can't decide if I love it or hate it.

I scrub a hand through my hair. "To apologize. I never should have let all those people line up for autographs. That was shitty of me. You paid for my time, and I wasn't respectful of that. Come back inside?"

She stares at me for a beat before snorting out a derisive laugh and turning away from me. "Pass."

Pass? Does the money she spent mean that little to her? She was so desperate to get me on a date that she spent a ridiculous amount of cash, and now she's just going to walk away? Or have I just been that awful to her? I wrap a hand around hers, giving it a tug. "Come on. Let's go finish our date. Give me a chance."

Isla pulls her hand from mine, but she doesn't run away, so that has to be something, right? "Give you a chance?" Her brow furrows, and her lips flatten. She glances down at the phone in her hand, then back up at me. Every word is laced with sarcasm when she says, "Like how you gave me one?"

I deserve her anger. I know I do. And I have to admit, she's pretty convincing. I almost believe she's hurt because I wrote her off from the get-go and not because she's pissed it won't be easy to sink her claws into me. "I'm sorry. I am."

"Guys like you are never sorry. At least not for your

actions. Just that you have to deal with the fallout from them." She shakes her head, and I almost miss the flash of emotion darkening her expression. "I must be a glutton for punishment."

You and me, both, Isla. Because I would love to call time of death on this date right now, but I can't. I genuinely didn't think it would be this hard to get her back into the restaurant. I need to change tactics.

"Come on." I flash her my most charming smile. "We already ordered our food. It's probably ready, and as you said, it's so good they have a six-month waitlist. Hell, I'm pretty sure the guy by the door is just standing there, sniffing the air longingly. He'd probably give his left arm to sit at a table and order whatever he wants in your place."

She hesitates, warring with herself. Her eyes are still glassy, but there's a strength to her spine that wasn't there a few minutes ago. "I *was* excited to try what I ordered."

I fight the smile that wants to crest over my face because I don't think it would help my case, but I've almost got her where I want her. "You ordered the special, right? I almost ordered that myself. I guess if you don't want to eat it, I will."

She gasps. Oh, she hates that idea. I can work with that.

"Actually, you know what? You're right. You should probably go home. I've put you through enough. Not even the best food in the world would be worth spending the evening with me."

The glare Isla levels me with shrivels my balls. "You wouldn't dare eat my dinner."

"I'd hate to let such delicious food go to waste." I shrug.

"You're the worst." She studies me for a few moments

and it's all I can do not to hold my breath. "Fine. I'll go back inside with you. But only because of the food."

My lips twitch as I offer her my arm, but she ignores it and strides back through the doors of Rêveur in front of me. The hostess gifts her a kind smile before turning her nose up at me. Damn the team for putting me through all of this. I just want to go home, turn on a movie, and nurse a cold beer.

I help Isla scoot in her chair like a proper gentleman. Not only because I'm feeling a fair amount of guilt, but I also need her to tell the reporter that she had a good time when the date ends. "I'm sorry again about all of that. I should have turned them away."

"It's fine." She won't make eye contact with me, focusing instead on her glass of champagne, which she nearly downs in one go.

"Is there anything *you* want me to sign?" I rub the back of my neck. I've made this the most awkward date on the planet. Especially when Isla snorts out a laugh into her almost-empty champagne flute.

"I'm good, thanks."

"If you change your mind, just let me know."

She rolls her eyes. "I won't."

*Oof.* Time for some damage control.

"You look really lovely tonight." Lovely doesn't even begin to cover it. Isla is temptation itself. Not that I can tell her that.

She glances up at me through her eyelashes and murmurs a quiet, "Thanks." She chews on her bottom lip for a moment before offering a compliment of her own. "You look handsome, too. I thought for sure they'd Photoshopped your bus photo, but that's all you, isn't it?"

Pink floods her cheeks, and she turns away from me. She might think I'm an asshole, but she's still attracted to me. Hell, she's probably still planning on making her play before the night is over. Jerk or not, I'm still rich and famous enough to provide her with a chance at her fifteen minutes. She'll play at being shy and unsure. Then once we walk out of Rêveur she'll brush her lush tits against my arm, maybe accidentally graze my junk with the back of her hand, and she'll fish for an invitation to my place.

"We won't be having sex tonight," I blurt out. Not the smoothest way I could have dealt with it, but it needs to be said. I might be contractually obligated to go along with this ridiculous farce of a date, and Isla might be gorgeous, but I won't go there.

One auburn eyebrow rises, and Isla's lips twist to the side. She's pissed about that. Well, too bad. She opens her mouth, and I can't wait to hear how she pleads her case.

"The earth is round."

Not what I was expecting. "Sorry, what?"

Her eyes flash with fire and damn me, but my cock hardens at the sight. "Oh, this isn't the *state random obvious facts* part of the date? My bad, I must have misread that."

Well, shit. I shift in my seat. "Look, no need to be offended. I only wanted to make sure we were both on the same page about this evening. I know you paid a lot for this date, and I'm well aware of how appealing it might be to date someone famous..."

The laugh she throws at me is so sharp I should probably excuse myself to the bathroom and check for hidden stab wounds. "Oh, don't worry. I don't think we're on the same page about much, but we are *definitely* on the same page about that. We will most certainly not be having sex."

So many emotions flicker across her delicate features, I might as well be watching a silent film. Irritation, anger, indignation so potent it's like I'm being sucker-punched. But there and gone before she can mask it is something else that makes my stomach twist with a brief pang of guilt. Hurt. She covers it quickly enough with a neutral expression, but I catch it. This is at least the third time I've hurt her tonight.

Her brows furrow and those pretty blue eyes grow unfocused for a moment. I'm bracing myself for another snarky comment. Instead, she mutters something about how she *told them this was a stupid idea* and that *they should know her better than this*. None of it makes any sense to me, but I wish I hadn't opened my big mouth.

"Excuse me," Isla says after she shakes her head. She picks up her purse and pushes back from the table. Her blue eyes flicker to the doors leading out of the restaurant. "I need to use the ladies' room."

She's going to bolt again. *Shit*.

"Wait." I stand, holding my hands out like she's an animal about to spook. I need her to stay. There must be something she wants besides a chance to be the future Mrs. Graves. Jewelry? A date with one of the other guys on the team? She's hot enough that I'm sure I could convince one of them to take her out. "Please stay. I'll make it worth your while."

Her eyes go wide. "Excuse me?"

"Listen, I'm going to be perfectly honest with you. I didn't want to do this. The team forced me, and if you leave now before the reporter shows up at nine o'clock to take our photo, I'm in deep trouble."

"Not sure why you think that's my problem." She scoffs. "I'm not the one being a jerk."

I rub my jaw. "I know, and I'm sorry." Her expression tells me she's not buying it. "Look, if you stay and make it sound like you had a great time tonight, I'll give you whatever you want."

She cocks her head to the side and I feel the need to qualify that offer. "Within reason, of course. I won't go off and marry you or something. But I can buy you jewelry, get you season tickets, introduce you to the rest of the guys on the team... almost anything."

She looks so offended for a moment that I think I've well and truly lost her. But then her eyes spark, and a smile curves across her lips. "Anything?"

"Within reason." Crap. This is going to bite me in the ass. The look on her face is downright devious.

"And you swear you'll follow through? Because if you promise this and then back out..."

"If I back out, you can take the story to the press and skewer me." I hold her gaze. "But I always keep my word. Always."

I don't fidget under Isla's narrowed eyes. She's probably calculating how much a diamond necklace will cost. But Coach is right. If she can help me reform my image, maybe it would help me close that energy drink sponsorship my agent's been negotiating for me.

Her smile is so wide I worry I've gotten myself in too deep. "Okay then, Maddox. Here's what I want from you."

_six_

## ISLA

I CONSIDER THROWING A GLASS OF WATER IN
Maddox's face when he offers to pay me to stay and claim
our date went well. Honestly, it's still on the table. But
then my mind wanders to my students and the hardships
they face. They overcome so many challenges just to show
up each day. And wasn't I just wishing I could do something for them? Something that would encourage them to
keep going? Something to lift their spirits?

Well, Maddox Graves just handed me a blank check
full of possibilities, and I'd sit through this miserable
dinner a thousand times over if he agrees to what I'm
about to ask.

And it doesn't hurt that he looks incredibly nervous. I
swear I can hear him audibly gulp from across the table.
For the first time since I walked into this restaurant, I'm
starting to have fun.

I can't help it. I grin wickedly at him, lean back in my

chair, and chuckle. "You're sweating in your skates, aren't you?"

He doesn't look amused. "I highly doubt you'll ask for anything I haven't heard before. Just know, there will be a monetary limit to what I'm willing to buy for you."

God, he's an ass. He honestly thinks I want him to buy me jewelry or something? As if I'd want to wear a reminder of this date on my body. And also, rude. I'm a grown woman. I can buy my own jewelry.

"I don't want your money." He huffs out a breath but remains silent. Elbows on the table, he waits for my request. "I want your time."

His nose wrinkles. "My time?" I nod. As I open my mouth to explain, he says, "This isn't an offer to coerce me into dating you."

The ego on this guy. I'm not sure how he fit through the double doors of the restaurant.

"It's cute," I drawl, tilting my head to the side, "that you think I'd want a repeat of this night with you." I'd rather make another appointment with Louise to get my snatch waxed. "But that's not what I'm talking about."

His narrowed gaze bores into me. I enjoy making him sweat. Does this guy really have such a shallow view of women that he thinks I'd ask him for something sparkly or more dates? Why? Because he's slightly famous? Ridiculous.

"What, exactly, are you talking about, then?"

"I want you to do a speaking engagement. For free. Maybe bring some shirts or big foam fingers or something." The kids would get such a kick out of that.

He arches one dark eyebrow. "A speaking engagement? Where?"

"At my job. My students would flip out if you came to speak to them. I shouldn't have any trouble talking the principal into setting up an all-school assembly." My mind is whirring with the possibilities. I wonder if I can make it a whole thing? I could approach some local shops and restaurants to see if they'd be willing to cater lunch or sponsor school supplies for the kids. Or even goodie bags full of toiletries and essentials. So many of them go without.

"Your students?"

Why is he repeating everything I say? Did I stutter? "Yeah. My students."

He frowns. "You're a teacher."

"Yup. High school English." We pause our conversation as Gregory delivers our food. The scent is heavenly, and I sigh when I breathe it in. But Maddox? His focus is solely on me. I smile at Gregory. "Thank you."

He gives a slight nod. "Enjoy your dinner."

Oh, I plan to. I spear a green bean smothered in sauce and pop it in my mouth. It's delicious, and I can't help the small moan that falls from my lips.

Maddox clears his throat. "Do you work at one of those fancy private schools in town?"

I let out a huff of laughter. "God, no. Center High."

The wheels turn in his head. He's struggling to compute what I've said. I'm not sure why he'd assume I work at one of the posh private schools in the area. Hard pass. Not because there's anything wrong with posh private schools, but because those kids already have a thousand legs up on mine. And I'm not saying I'm the best teacher in the world because I know I'm not. But I care. A lot. And that's got to count for something.

"Isn't Center High a public school in North Minneapolis?"

I nod. I know what's coming.

His frown deepens. "That area's dangerous."

"You don't have to worry. You'll be totally safe when you come and speak. We have security." I don't tell him that *security* is a sixty-year-old man named Felix who wears coke-bottle glasses and still squints at everything. Doubt that will help ease his mind.

"That's not what I'm worried about," Maddox replies. His voice is gruff, and if he wasn't such a huge jerk, it might even have dampened my panties. But he is a jerk. So my panties stay dry. Mostly. "You don't live in that area, do you?"

What the hell? Why would he even care? "Not sure that's any of your business." This is getting weird. "Anyway. So many of my kids will never get the chance to hear someone important say they're rooting for them. They'll never hear a successful hockey player tell them they can achieve their dreams if they work hard enough. And it doesn't matter how many times I say it to them. For some stupid reason, it'll mean more coming out of your mouth than it ever will from mine." I take a bite of my steak. "So that's what I want you to do for me. I want you to come to my school, look my kids in their eyes, and tell them you're cheering for them. That you believe they can do great things."

His voice is still gruff when he says, "That's all you want from me?"

It feels pretty big to me. It'll feel even bigger to the kids. I cock my head to the side and nod. "That's all I want from you."

He's silent for a moment and I worry he'll go back on his word. Especially since his face is scrunched up like he smells a fart. "I... That's not what I expected."

I scoff. "Yeah, you thought I was going to ask you to buy me jewelry. What the hell, man? What kind of woman would ask some stranger to buy her jewelry? Especially when that stranger has been a total prick." I savor another green bean. "You have a pretty shit view of women."

To his credit, Maddox's cheeks flush. He rubs the back of his neck. For the first time since I sat down across from him, I catch a flash of vulnerability. It's quick, and he hides it well, but I see it. "Maybe I do."

And maybe he and I have more in common than either of us would admit. Doesn't excuse his behavior, though.

"How long have you been teaching?" He only makes the briefest eye contact with me when he asks, focusing on his dinner. I don't blame him. At least his dinner won't scowl at him like I've been doing.

"Not long at all." Even though it can feel like ages. "I worked hard to graduate early. Took classes through the summer and almost killed myself getting my masters in an accelerated timeline. But this is only my second year."

Alex hated how much extra time I spent studying so I could graduate early. It cut into my time with him, and it meant I couldn't always attend the dinners he wanted me to attend. Being in a committed relationship looked good to the partners of the firms he was trying to get into, which meant he loved to parade me around. I spent so many nights apologizing for pursuing my own goals. Because Chris-Hemsworth-forbid he ever had to attend work events alone. Why did I ever apologize for that? I never asked him to put his dreams on hold for me. Never would.

Maddox watches me closely as my mind wanders. I shake my head to clear my thoughts when I notice his attention on me. "I did my student teaching at Center. I fell in love with the kids and practically begged my way into a job. It can be difficult both mentally and emotionally, but it's so worth it."

"You really care about your students." It's a statement, not a question, but I get the sense he's trying to figure me out. That I'm a lowly English teacher seems to have blown his mind.

"I do. They're great kids. I'm lucky I get to be a part of their lives." And I am lucky. I think in the two years I've taught at Center High, I've learned more about tenacity and perseverance from my students than they've learned about Thoreau or Orwell from me.

And while I believe literature is important because it opens our minds to new perspectives and thoughts in a way little else can, I'm not blind to the fact that having the time and freedom to get lost in a book is a privilege some of these kids don't have. So many work part-time jobs after school gets out. Some have to take care of siblings or grandparents. And they do it. Without complaint.

It's humbling. I don't think I was ever that strong at their age.

Maddox nods. "I'd be honored to speak at your school."

"Really?"

"Truly."

Despite my best efforts to control my reaction, I let out a little squeal of happiness. To think, somehow this amazing moment came out of the worst first date I've ever had—maybe the worst date *period*.

So, maybe I'll die alone and sexually unfulfilled. Maybe

I'll never make Alex jealous enough to crawl through pig slop in a bid to beg my forgiveness. Maybe I'm just not built for love. I *was* built to be a fantastic teacher. And right now, that's good enough for me.

I hold out my hand for Maddox to shake, a genuine smile stretching wide across my face. "Then you have a deal."

## *seven*

## MADDOX

I don't know what to make of Isla Harding.

I thought for sure the happy, calculating look she gave me meant she was doing the math on how much money she could get me to spend. Between the cash she forked out for this date and the expensive dress she's wearing, it's clear the woman values money. Or at least has expensive tastes. So finding out that not only is she an English teacher at a school most wealthy women wouldn't step foot in, but she wants to use her favor to get me to speak to her students?

I'm stumped. Utterly confused. And I'm looking at my date in a whole new light.

It will be very inconvenient if she ends up being likable.

"So, are you a big hockey fan?" I need to figure her out.

She chuckles as she pushes her salad around. "I've never watched a hockey game in my life."

"Never?" How did she hear about the auction if she isn't a hockey fan? "Just a hometown sports fan, then?"

"Um, not really. I'd rather read a good book than watch sports. I've never seen the appeal." She wrinkles her nose. "Like, what's so great about watching a bunch of guys who all think their dicks are the biggest in the room play with a ball or slap things around with a stick? Am I supposed to be impressed by that? And then all the guys just sitting around drinking beer while watching think *their* dicks are somehow bigger just for watching it. It's a real sausage fest, isn't it?"

It's clear by her expression that *sausage fest* isn't a compliment. I'm torn between being completely offended at the way she's describing my profession and utterly amused.

"And don't even get me started on the rampant misogyny involved with sports. Women athletes are called all kinds of names by men, and even if you just enjoy watching sports as a woman, you have to prove you're watching it for the *right* reasons. Or that you're an expert on the game. Because if you only casually enjoy watching, you must just like watching men run around in tight pants. As if that's a crime. Or you're a jersey chaser or a ball bunny or some other insulting name that implies any woman at a sports game must be on the prowl for a rich husband. That you're happy to be used as a sexual object because you athletes must have dicks made of twenty-four-carat gold." Her hands gesture wildly by the end of this speech, her eyes are full of fire, and I am more confused than ever.

"Twenty-four-carat gold is actually really soft." That's all I can think of to say. Because I am completely at a loss.

Everything I assumed about Isla seems false, and now I want to know how she and I came to be sitting across this table from each other.

My dumb observation earns a genuine laugh from her, and the sound shoots straight to my cock. It's free and loud and real.

"Exactly. And who wants to chase around after some limp-dicked, egomaniacal man-child? No, thank you."

Man-child? What the hell? "Wow. Good to know how you really feel about me, Isla."

"Oh." A blush steals over her cheeks. "I wasn't talking about *you*."

That has me laughing because that's exactly what I've been acting like. An egomaniacal man-child. She's absolutely describing me, and I deserve it. "You are. And it's okay. I only have myself to blame."

She hums a sound of agreement as she takes another bite of her dinner. "True."

"So if you're not a sports fan and you've never watched a hockey game in your life, do you mind me asking why you'd want to go on a date with me?" I need to know. It's practically a compulsion because I can't make sense of her.

"Um, I didn't." The blush grows brighter as she bends her head so she's looking at her dinner plate instead of me.

"Wait, what? Were you trying to get a date with one of the other players and accidentally clicked on me or something?" Wouldn't that be a kick to the ego?

Isla tucks a strand of hair behind her ear and peeks up at me through the fringe of her long lashes. "Nope. None of this was my idea. I was tricked into it."

Well, that's an even bigger blow than accidentally winning a date with me instead of one of my lesser-known teammates. I clear my throat. "What do you mean, tricked into it?"

"It's... it's a long story," she says, chewing her bottom lip. She makes the briefest moment of eye contact before she goes back to staring at her plate like it's the Mona Lisa and she's trying to decode what made her smile. "But my best friends have been trying to break me out of my shell after a... after a bad breakup. And for some reason, they thought tricking me into agreeing to a date with you would be just the thing I needed."

There's so much to unpack in that statement, I don't even know where to start. Isla's *friends* were the ones who bid on the date? Why? If she isn't into sports, why spend all of that money? And what does she mean, a bad breakup? Did he hurt her?

And now I feel like a real piece of shit. Because *I* hurt her. Shifting in my seat, I study her beautiful face, noting the signs of discomfort. Pursed lips, tense shoulders, and she can't maintain eye contact with me. I don't want to make her even more uncomfortable, but I need to understand. "Why would your friends think a date with me would help?"

She squirms uncomfortably. "It's pathetic."

"I doubt that," I say, making my voice as gentle as possible.

"No, it is. I haven't... I haven't been on a date or even really left my house since my ex ended things with me." Every quiet word is a knife twisting in my gut because I treated this woman like garbage when she was already down. She steals a glance at me. "I guess they figured a date with a guy like you would be the perfect way to get ready to put myself out there again because there wouldn't be any pressure associated with it. I mean, it's not like a date with you would go anywhere." She pushes her food around on her plate with her fork.

"They thought it would be a fun way to practice getting to know a stranger. Then at the end of the night, I could ask you to take a selfie with me to post on social media so my ex doesn't think I've spent the last five months eating too many donuts alone in my apartment like a hermit." She laughs, but it's hollow. Nothing like the free sound that came out of her mouth a minute or two ago. Her blue eyes meet mine. "See? Told you it was pathetic."

I am the biggest asshole on the planet.

She didn't pay a ridiculous amount of money to worm her way into my life. Hell, given her profession, it's unlikely she even has that kind of disposable income. She wasn't trying to trap a rich hockey player. She didn't even want to come tonight, but she did to make her friends happy. Her friends who were trying to help her get over a broken heart by setting her up with a fun night. A night that I ruined by making her feel like she was nothing more than an unwanted obligation.

All she wanted from me was a selfie.

"I don't think it's pathetic," I tell her. "It sounds like your friends care about you very much, and I know how much a bad breakup can mess with your head."

Blue eyes lift to meet mine. "You do?"

All too well. "Yep. Just ask my teammates. There were a few times I lost us games because my head was all fucked up after a breakup."

"I can't picture you as the relationship type," Isla says. A small, mischievous smile tugs at the corner of her lips. "You strike me as a *hit it and quit it* guy."

My answering laugh is loud enough to draw the attention of the tables nearest to us. "I guess I kind of am now."

"Maybe that's what I'll do. Just decide I don't care about being in a relationship and throw myself into a series of hot, meaningless flings."

Something tells me Isla Harding couldn't be a *meaningless fling* girl even if she tried. It's obvious from the way she speaks about her students and friends that she values people and relationships too highly for that. So I offer her a shred of vulnerability. "It's not always as fun as it sounds."

She cocks her head to the side and opens her mouth just as the server approaches the table to check on us and offer dessert. He informs us that the reporter from *Minnesota Sports Monthly* will arrive shortly. And just like that, the moment shatters. I watch as Isla rebuilds her walls, and I know I won't get any more out of her about her friends or former relationship.

And maybe it's stupid, but I want to know. It's been hell resisting her and ignoring her throughout dinner. I want to understand what kind of guy could give her up and hurt her the way her ex did. I want her to let me in, even though I don't deserve it.

I misread her. Completely. And I can't help feeling like I cheated myself by being an ass. Because sure, I cheated her out of the night she deserved, but I also cheated myself out of the chance to get to know a woman who is clearly worth knowing.

"Don't worry," she says, likely mistaking my silence and far-away expression for nervousness about the interview. "I'll tell them you were a perfect gentleman."

"Why would you lie for me?" I sure as hell don't deserve it.

She shrugs. "We didn't get off to a great start, but you agreed to come speak to my students. That's enough to earn a glowing report in my book." I want to reach across the table and tug her lower lip out from between her teeth with my thumb. I want to tell her she should expect more from others. From me. "Do you think we could take a couple of selfies? Would that be okay?"

I give her my most charming smile. "Of course it's okay. I'd love to. And we'll need to exchange phone numbers while you have your phone out."

Her eyes go wide. "We will?"

"Of course." God, she's adorable. "We'll have to hammer out the details about coming to speak at your school."

"Oh." Isla shakes her head softly. "Yeah. Of course. The assembly."

Right. The assembly. I certainly don't want her number for any other reason. Because Isla may be beautiful and kind, but I've sworn off relationships. And she would be a distraction I can't afford at the start of the preseason.

No matter how tempting she may be.

# ISLA

It's midnight, and I'm star-fishing on my bed, trying to make sense of my evening when my phone vibrates.

> **JESS**
>
> Well? How was dinner? You never texted us, so hopefully that means you're naked and breathless in that gorgeous hunk of man-meat's bed.
>
> **NEV**
>
> Is his dick huge? I bet it's huge.

Groaning, I debate ignoring them altogether. But that might just make them show up at my apartment at an ungodly hour tomorrow morning, and I want to sleep in.

ME

I have no idea what size his dick is. We didn't sleep together and never will. He was a pompous asshole for the better part of the night, and I almost left fifteen minutes into the date.

JESS

What? Why? What did he do?

NEV

Do we need to find out where he lives and egg his house?

LOL. Please don't. I'm exhausted. Can we meet for lunch tomorrow and I'll tell you all about it?

NEV

Are you kidding me? How are we supposed to sleep when you haven't told us anything?

I'm sure you'll find a way.

NEV

Rude.

You love me.

JESS

*Sighs* We do. Noon tomorrow at Café Gold?

Perfect. Goodnight. Love you both.

NEV

Love you more.

JESS

Sweet dreams!

Sweet dreams. Doubtful. I'm exhausted, but my mind won't shut up. I keep going round and around with myself, trying to figure out how I feel about Maddox Graves and our date. Because he'd been kind toward the end. And he'd agreed so easily to come speak at my school. It was enough that I didn't feel like a total sellout during the short but awkward interview with the reporter from Minnesota Sports Monthly.

First, the guy looked me up and down so intently it was like he was trying to see through my clothes. Then he'd asked me some weird questions about Maddox. Like whether his nickname was well-earned. Except I don't know a darn thing about Maddox Graves, so I didn't know what he was talking about. Then he asked if I was hoping to go home with Maddox. I almost kneed him in the balls for that one. Luckily, Maddox shut that down and told the reporter he was being rude and inappropriate. The guy seemed genuinely shocked when I told him Maddox was kind and gentlemanly. And he had been, at least at the end, so it wasn't a complete lie.

Still, I've been telling myself not to do a Google deep dive to figure out why Maddox seems to have such an awful reputation. Because it shouldn't matter. I'll see him at the silent auction dinner with the girls if I can't get out of it and then one more time for the assembly. Assuming he follows through on his promise. Then that's it. We'll go back to being utter strangers.

Who cares what his nickname is or why he got it? Who cares why the reporter seemed to find it so unbelievable that Maddox was nice? Not me. I'm above all that gossip and celebrity bullshit.

I stare at my ceiling. Then I grab my phone and unlock

it. My fingers fly across the screen and before I can think better of it, I'm flipping through the photos Maddox took with me before we said good night. He's so tall, the top of my head barely hits his shoulders. His hand rests on my hip in the photos, and I can almost feel the phantom warmth of his palms.

Maddox smiles at the camera in most of the snaps. Except for the last one. In that photo, he's looking down at me while I smile, oblivious. There's almost a wistfulness to his gaze I can't stop staring at.

He was just playing a part. He wanted me to have a good photo to post on my social media accounts. One that would make Alex jealous. That's all it was. Maddox Graves made it very clear from the start that he was not remotely interested in me, and he never would be.

And that's good. Because a guy like him would be way too dangerous for my heart and spirit. Even if he found me interesting enough to go out with once or twice, he'd realize I'm not good enough for him. I'm not the woman you want photographed on your arm. Not when you're an up-and-coming lawyer, and certainly not when you're a successful, high-powered sports star.

That's okay. I'm done with guys like that.

Still, my mind is full of Maddox Graves, and soon I'm typing his name into Google. No one has to know how pathetic I'm being right now. I'm alone in my apartment, and it's not like Maddox has some sort of super-secret spy software alerting him whenever a sad, lonely woman does an internet deep-dive. I sure as hell won't be telling Jess and Nevaeh about this. They'll read way too much into it and decide I'm attracted to him. Which I'm not. At all. Not even a little.

The first few searches bring up his sports stats and information about his hockey career. Even ignorant about the game, I can tell his record is impressive. I watch a few clips of him racing across the ice, stick in hand, as he lines up a shot and slaps it home. The crowd loves him. They chant his name and hold up signs asking him to throw them a puck or to let them have his babies.

Yuck.

But after a bit more digging, I come across articles speculating about Maddox's dating life. They're hardly journalistic masterpieces. Most of them are on gossip sites of questionable repute. But they all say the same thing. Maddox Graves likes to use women up and spit them out as soon as someone younger and prettier comes along. Apparently, he's had a couple of serious girlfriends, but as soon as they bring up marriage and family, he walks away without a second thought.

Or so the women he's dated claim. There are always two sides to every story, but after the night I had with Maddox, I don't have much of a reason to think they're making it up.

It seems a couple of those jilted women even did interviews with a few gossip magazines. Feeling only a little guilty, I click on one with a woman named Candace Peterson. Her photo is prominent at the top of the article, and she's exactly the type of woman I'd imagine a guy like Maddox would go for. Blonde hair bleached to within an inch of its life, lips that look like they're stretched tight with filler, and cleavage for days. Like, I don't know how she's not suffocating from her boobs pressing into her neck kind of cleavage. She stares at the camera with bedroom eyes, and it's enough to make me feel uncomfortable.

If I had even the slightest doubt that Maddox Graves would never be interested in a woman like me, staring at Candace's photo squashes it. Even dressed up in expensive clothes, I'll never give off the sex-pot vibes Maddox's ex does. No wonder he brushed me off so quickly. He probably gave me one look and decided that I must wear granny panties up to my rib cage and suck at giving head.

Needless to say, if *sexual goddess* is Maddox's feminine ideal, I'm not it. Don't get me wrong, I have a healthy sexual appetite. Hell, I read some kinky smut and, if given the chance, I think I'd be pretty damn adventurous in bed. But Alex had his favorite positions and ideas about what sex should be, and most of them involved missionary, lots of grunting, and almost no dirty talk. I haven't exactly had the chance to step into my own *kinky-goddess* era.

Maybe someday.

But I'm getting sidetracked.

The interview starts with Candace talking about how she and Maddox dated for a year. How they met at a bar and had instant sparks. She tells the journalist she was hesitant to date a hockey player because she'd heard they're all players in it for no-strings-attached sex. But Maddox pursued her, and she reluctantly gave him a chance.

I snort at that. Nothing about Candace's photo screams *reluctant*. Am I being judgmental? Probably. Am I wrong? I doubt it.

She paints a pretty picture of a man who wouldn't take no for an answer in his pursuit of her. Telling the writer how, in the beginning, he asked her to go to all of his hockey games and wear his jersey, and how he made her feel like the most special woman on the planet. It was so consuming that she gave up her ambitions to support him.

My chest feels tight. It's a familiar story. Too familiar.

Then one day, it was over. He told her he was done with her. That they didn't have a future. That she wasn't the kind of woman he'd ever tie himself to. She lamented that he'd stolen her heart, made it his, and then buried it in a cold, dark grave.

The writer calls him the Gravedigger.

Rubbing at my sternum, I navigate away from the article. It brings up too many memories, and every word feels like a reminder of how hopelessly naïve I was. I don't know if everything Candace said was truthful. But I do know that I've lived that tragic tale and I'll never put myself in that position again. If I ever reopen my heart, I'll find a nice guy who understands the value of loyalty, love, and family. And I'm going to stay far, far away from men like Maddox Graves.

*nine*

## MADDOX

"There he is!"

It's Monday morning, which means I'm starting the day in the weight room. We have strength training for two hours, followed by conditioning. While it's tempting to slack off during the off-season, none of us do. Hockey seasons are long, grueling, and hell on a body. If you don't want to end up injured, you train all year.

I grunt at Griffin when he greets me with far too much energy. His hazel eyes twinkle with mischief and his floppy blond hair bounces. I swear Griffin Wright has *Monster* flowing through his veins instead of blood. "You're chipper this morning."

He chuckles, slapping me on the back. "Got laid last night. By twins."

Jesus.

"Shouldn't you be a bit *more* chipper? You had that date on Saturday." Griffin looks me up and down as if he can tell just by looking if I had sex. Byrne and Navarro wander over, greeting me with nods and smug smiles. They want to hear about my date, too, apparently.

"Didn't sleep with her." I don't want to talk about this with them. Or anyone. Ever. Saturday night was a disaster. If I tell them about it, I'll have to admit to being a total asshole. I'm sure they'll laugh, but they'll also give me a hard time for the rest of the week.

"Why not?" Byrne asks. "Was she ugly?"

"What? No." Isla definitely wasn't ugly. She was stunning, and that had been the problem.

Bash eyes me speculatively. His dark brown eyes don't miss much. "Then why the hell didn't you sleep with her? Was she a super-fan? Some kind of crazed stalker?"

That makes me chuckle. "Nope. She's never watched a hockey game in her life."

Griffin presses a palm to his chest, mouth falling open comically wide. "Blasphemy."

"I know, right? She told me she'd rather read a book than watch sports."

"I bet she reads some real kinky shit," Griff says as his eyes grow unfocused. "The chicks that read a lot always have the most shocking Kindle history. One time I went out with this quiet, adorably nerdy girl in college because one of my buddies dared me to, and I was *not* prepared. She tied me to her bed and rode me so hard I came in like two minutes. She tried to get me to let her peg me, but I wasn't into it." He sighs. "Best damn sex of my life."

Navarro, Byrne, and I all burst out laughing. Only Griffin Wright could have such a dreamy look on his face while talking about being pegged.

"Pegging, huh?" I chuckle. "I'm surprised you didn't go for it."

Wright shrugs. "I let her finger my prostate a few times, but a strap-on just felt too impersonal."

"Totally," Navarro says with a roll of his eyes before he turns back to me. "So, tell us about it."

"I wasn't there when Wright's girl fingered his asshole."

"Christ." Bash groans. "Tell us about your date, Graves. Stop stalling and spill it."

Loading weights onto a bar, I set up my station and avoid making eye contact with any of them. "It was fine. She was nervous. We ate food, I signed a few autographs. Nothing to write home about."

"Waaait," Sebastian says, drawing out the word. "What do you mean, you signed autographs? Like, you signed merch for her or something?"

I rub the back of my neck. "Uh, no. I didn't actually sign anything for her."

"Then what the hell do you mean you signed a few autographs?" He stares at me, and when I can't meet his gaze, he pinches the bridge of his nose. "Please tell me you didn't sign autographs while you were on a date with the poor woman."

My silence is confession enough, and Navarro groans. "Dude. That's shitty."

"I know," I say a little too loudly. "Trust me, I know. I'm going to be paying for it, too."

All three of them watch me with raised brows, waiting for an explanation. Dammit.

"I had to bribe her to stay until the end of the date and tell the reporter I was a nice guy."

Silence stretches out between us for a beat, then they bend over, shaking with laughter. It earns us looks from the rest of the team, and I hiss at them to shut up. The last thing I need is for Coach to hear about this.

"Yeah, you have to tell the whole story now," Byrne says through bouts of laughter. "And then we're going to go out tonight so I can teach you how to treat a woman."

"Shut up," I grumble. But I tell them everything. Every last embarrassing detail. They howl with laughter again and again, and I'm pissed and red-faced by the end.

"Oh, god," Wright wheezes. "I think that's the best thing I've ever heard. You're lucky she didn't stab you in the dick with her steak knife."

I cup my junk. "Yeah, yeah. I know."

"And here I thought you had at least *some* game," Logan drawls. "Now I'm wondering if you just end up with pity lays."

"I do not need pity lays." I nearly growl. "You guys suck. I never should have told you."

"Do you have a picture of her?" Sebastian asks.

"I do." Not sure I want to show them, though. When I'd taken a few selfies with Isla so she could use them to make her ex jealous, I'd snapped a couple of my own with my phone. I told her I needed it as proof so I could show my coach the night was a success. Truthfully, I just wanted to look at her again. She really was beautiful, and once I pulled my head out of my ass, I enjoyed conversing with her. In the end, I found myself wishing for more time.

Logan cocks an eyebrow at me. "You going to show us, or what?"

With a deep sigh, I tug my phone out of my pocket and open the photo of us. She's small, tucked into my side, and her smile is breathtaking. She's exactly the kind of woman who lights my insides on fire, and my guys know it the moment I flip the phone around to show them.

"Well, shit, Graves." Wright stares at her. "You're a fucking dumbass."

"I know."

"Damn." Navarro gives me a pitying look. "You gonna try to get her number from the team or something? Ask her for a chance to make up for things?"

"I don't need to." I enjoy their looks of confusion. "I have her number."

"How?" they ask in unison.

"I, uh, I kind of bribed her to finish the date by agreeing to speak to her high school students at an assembly."

"She's a teacher?" Wright's eyes gleam. "Hot damn, she can keep me in detention any day."

The smack I give him upside his head rings out in the weight room.

"What the hell, man?"

"Don't be gross," I say.

Bash's mouth goes slack. "You like her. You actually ended up liking her."

Leave it to Navarro to put it all out there, whether or not I want him to. "I misjudged her. I feel bad, that's all."

"Uh-huh. I'm sure that's it."

"It. Is."

"And how many times have you almost texted her?" Bash grins.

"None," I reply. Adding *of your business* in my head. Because yeah, I almost texted her. A few times. Just to say sorry, though. There wasn't any other reason.

"Ho-ly shit." Griffin laughs. "You screwed yourself over good, didn't you?"

I did. I really did. There's no way Isla Harding will want anything to do with me outside of our agreement to speak at her school. I don't stand a chance with the woman after the way I treated her.

"Do you actually want to have a shot with her?" Byrne asks seriously.

Do I? I may. I don't know. All I'm sure of is that I screwed up. I feel terrible about it, and I wish I could make it up to her. Is there a part of me that wonders if we could have had some deep connection had I not sabotaged the evening? Sure. Of course, I do. But what's the likelihood Isla Harding could have been *the one*?

I'm not even sure I believe in all of that soulmate bull-shit. My mom never found hers. My dad was too much of a bastard to care if he found his, and I sure as hell can't look to the guys around me for examples of love and healthy relationships.

"Pretty sure I blew any chance of having a shot with Isla," I say to Logan. "Besides, she probably looked me up the minute she got home and saw all the bullshit Candace and Georgia said about me. Even if she had the slightest interest in me before that, I doubt she does now."

It's so easy for people to buy into their bullshit. It's another reason I haven't dated in a couple of years. If women know about me, they're only interested in casual sex. Nice girls run in the other direction when they see me coming.

The Gravedigger. Jesus.

I shake my head. It doesn't matter what Isla Harding or any other woman thinks about me. I'm done with relationships. It's too hard to tell a woman's intentions when there's money and fame on the line. Hell, the last time I was certain a girl liked me for me was all the way back in high school. I was a different person then.

"So what you're saying is she's fair game and I can ask the team for her number and bang the teacher?" Griffin watches me intently. "Because damn, I'm imagining her in a tight little pencil skirt, a half-unbuttoned blouse, thick-rimmed glasses, and a ruler in her hand. She could bend me over a desk and spank my ass any day of the week."

"Dude," Navarro warns.

I lunge for Wright. He laughs, spinning out of my reach.

"Take it outside, assholes," Coach shouts before my fist can connect with Griff's gut.

"Okay, okay." Wright laughs, his palms up in surrender. "I won't bang your teacher."

"She's not mine," I grumble.

"No," Griffin says with a smirk. "But you want her to be."

And dammit, he's right. I do. Too bad it'll never happen.

# ten

## ISLA

I walk through the week in a daze, but maybe there's an upside to my disastrous date with Maddox Graves. Alex has consumed my thoughts for five months. But this week? He's only popped into my head a few times.

Progress is progress, no matter the cause.

Jess and Nevaeh texted me earlier in the day, demanding a girls' night out. Apparently, staying in on a Saturday night is a crime. They want to get dressed up and meet for dinner and drinks at this posh downtown bar called *Skin and Tonic*. The bar boasts the best cocktails, delicious food, and go-go dancers who sway to the beat in cages that hang from the ceiling.

It's a bit too expensive for my blood, but after roping me into a miserable date, my friends have offered to pay. They feel guilty about the whole thing, but it's fine. I'm over it. And I'm not really in the mood to go out tonight, but they won't take no for an answer.

They're worried about me. I get it. So, to ease their minds, I agree to dinner.

I'm not interested in drawing attention to myself, so I wear a simple black dress that hugs my curves and hits just above my knee. My hair is in loose curls, and I've winged out my eyeliner sharply enough to cut. Jess and Nevaeh draw attention wherever they go, so if I want to blend into the background, I need to look good, but not too good. I fidget with the hem of my dress the whole Uber ride there, checking my phone every few minutes.

Jess texts to say she's running late.

Hopefully Nev is on time.

Skin and Tonic thrums with energy. The girls made a reservation, so I follow the hostess to our table, dodging patrons who laugh and dance. She seats me close to the bar and I settle into the chair facing the door so I can wave to the girls when they arrive. A harried server scurries over to take my drink order, and I try to relax. A few familiar faces dot the crowd—I recognize them as people Jess and Nev work with—but I don't try to initiate small talk.

I'm sipping my passionfruit mojito and alternating between checking the door and my phone when it buzzes with a new text.

NEV

Ladies, I am so sorry. Got roped into an emergency situation at work. I'm not going to make it.

JESS

My boss has been talking my ear off for
the last hour about this promotion. I'm
not sure how late I'll be. Isla, please tell
me you're not already there? I will leave
right now if you are.

My stomach sinks. Of course, this would happen. And I know Jess would walk away from her boss to make sure I'm not alone. Because they're worried about me. But I don't want her to do that. She's been gunning for this promotion, and she's worked so hard for it.

So I lie.

ME

Nope! Couldn't find my keys, so I just
hopped in the Uber. I'll tell her to turn
around. We can do this another time.

JESS

I am so sorry, babes. Are you sure?

Of course. Go get that promotion. Tell me
all about it later.

NEV

Sorry, Isla. We'll make it up to you.

Locking my phone, I sigh. I guess I'm finishing my mojito and heading home. It would be one thing to sit alone at a coffee shop. I could read a book on my phone without looking like a total loser. But here? Nope.

The sound of a throat clearing has me looking up.

A golden-haired man in a very expensive-looking outfit stands less than a foot away from me. He has boyish features and his eyes crinkle in the corner as he offers me a smile, and he must be almost six feet tall. The clothes accentuate a slim but fit build, and his jaw has the faintest hint of stubble. "Hey, Isla, right?"

I fidget in my seat. Have I met this guy? "Um, yes?"

"Blake Carter. You don't know me, but Jessica Martinez's firm does my company's advertising campaigns. I'm the CEO of GoTravel. It's a house-sharing app. Maybe she told you about me?"

"Uh, no. Sorry." How does this guy know who I am? Instantly uncomfortable, I'm trying to think of a way to get away from him when he sits down beside me. Uninvited.

"Well, I hope this doesn't come off as weird, but Jessica had a photo of you and another friend on her desk and she told me all about you. I was actually at her office today and she mentioned something about going out tonight. I didn't realize she meant here. Small world." His gaze rakes over my body in an assessing way. "I have to say, the photo didn't do you justice." He flashes me a wide smile that's probably supposed to be charming, but I feel a bit like Little Red Riding Hood looking down the muzzle of the Big Bad Wolf.

"Oh. Wow." What the hell am I supposed to say to that?

He chuckles. "Jessica is here, isn't she?"

"I'm waiting for her and our other friend. They should be here soon," I lie.

"How 'bout I keep you company until they get here?" He scoots his chair closer.

"You don't have to do that." Unfortunately, I tend to either babble or laugh when I'm nervous, and a strangled laugh claws its way out of my throat.

"I don't mind at all. It's serendipity." He winks. Gag. Not waiting for my acceptance, Blake leans toward me, giving me his whole focus while I try not to crawl out of my skin. "So, Isla, what do you do for a living?"

"Uh, I'm a teacher. English."

He nods his head. "That's right. Jess told me. Center High? That's very altruistic."

*Oh god. She told him where I work?*

"Not really," I say, because this is incredibly awkward, and even though this guy has a baby face and looks like a human Ken doll, he's also sizing me up like he's plotting how to get in my pants. "I get as much out of it as they do. I love teaching."

Blake nods again like he understands, but I know he doesn't. This guy's a CEO of a growing real estate sharing app. I highly doubt he gets what I mean when I say that the kids give me just as much as I give them. "You know, some of our listings offer discounts for teachers."

*Really*? Is he trying to pitch me a vacation I can't afford? What is happening?

"Uh, that's nice."

He looks pleased. "It's a really great platform. Have you ever used it?"

"No. Can't say I have."

"I can get you a great deal." He's giving me bedroom eyes. Does he think offering me a deal on a weekend rental of some rando's house is a flex?

"Thanks...?" Is this really happening? Baby-face Ken looks at me like I'm a sure thing. Like I must be gagging for his CEO dick. Too bad for him. I have no intention of finding out if he's packing an amorphous blob down there like the Ken dolls of my childhood. I'm getting the hell away from him as soon as I get the opportunity.

"So, Isla, Jess mentioned that you recently got out of a

long-term relationship." There's a predatory twinkle in his eye and my spine stiffens.

*What the hell?*

"I'm so sorry to hear that," Blake continues. He either doesn't notice how visibly uncomfortable I am, or he doesn't care. I grit my teeth when he scoots closer to me. So close, our knees touch. I immediately shift in my seat to put some distance between us.

"Yeah, well, shit happens." I scan the bar, searching for an exit or an excuse to bolt, but Blake doesn't seem to catch the tone of my body language, and he trails a finger down the length of my bare arm.

"It's hard to put yourself back out there, isn't it? You just never know if you'll click with someone. If you'll have sexual chemistry."

*Shudder.*

"But when Jessica told me about you, I had a feeling we'd get along."

Oh, he did, did he? Well, unfortunately for him, I'm not interested. At all. In fact, I would rather sleep with Maddox Graves—a man who clearly despises me—than the creep who's pressing further and further into my personal space.

I want to leave. But this guy is just creepy enough that I'm nervous about him following me home. If Jess mentioned where I work, who's to say she didn't also mention what neighborhood I live in? As unlikely as that seems, I'm not willing to risk it.

I need a plan. Or a miracle.

# *eleven*

## MADDOX

"Dude. My balls are *killing* me."

I pinch the bridge of my nose as Griffin plops his ass into the passenger seat of my noir Maserati Levante. I bought the SUV because I end up being the designated driver so often that it didn't make sense to buy a hot little sports car. Plus, this is Minnesota, and the winters are brutal. Still, I love this thing, and they know if they puke in it, they're paying to get it detailed inside and out. "Why the hell are your balls hurting?"

Griffin shifts in the passenger seat, adjusting himself before clicking the seatbelt in. "My waxing lady was in a bad mood today, man. She really went hard on the boys."

Jesus. "Then stop getting your nuts waxed."

Griff shoots me a look that tells me he thinks I've lost it. "I can't ask the ladies to suck the boys if they're all furry." His eyes go all dreamy. "And I love when they just pop 'em all the way into their wet little mouths."

"Sorry I asked." And boy, am I sorry.

"You should go with me sometime," he says. He's way too excited about the idea. "It could be team bonding. Just a bunch of bros getting their short and curlies ripped out."

My balls shrivel up into my body at the mere thought. I roll my eyes as I head toward Navarro's place. Logan's already there, so we can head straight to the bar. "Have you already started drinking?"

Wright looks confused. "No. Why?"

"No reason," I say, shaking my head. He spends the next five minutes trying to convince me that smooth balls are the key to happiness. I've never been more grateful for Bash and Logan than I am when they climb into the back-seat. We're all ready to blow off some steam after an intense week of weight training and conditioning, and Logan suggested a bar none of us have ever been to. Personally, I'd be happy sticking to our normal haunt. The beer is always cold and the women are always hot.

But I suppose it could be fun to try somewhere new.

I hand my keys to the valet with a warning to be careful with my car, and we head inside. It's a cool space, and it has a hell of a lot more character and ambiance than Chasers. This place has black walls with textured damask wallpaper, a huge bar that spans the whole left side of the room, and giant cages hanging from the ceiling where scantily-clad men and women dance.

We head to the bar, where we all order a pint of beer on tap. I'll nurse mine most of the night, but these three? They'll finish the first drink in less than five minutes, which is why we settle in against the bar while scanning the place for an empty table. It's crowded and loud, and when we don't see any open tables, Logan flags down a harried-looking waitress and turns on the charm. She tells him she'll have a booth ready for us within ten minutes.

My eyes wander to a woman in a bikini who writhes and shakes inside the nearest cage. The other guys scan the crowd, looking for women to take home with them. This isn't a sports bar, so there won't be puck bunnies on the prowl for a Rogues player, but that won't stop any of us. We're all dressed in game-day suits, and we're getting plenty of appreciative glances.

"Ho-ly shit," Griffin says beside me. He grabs my wrist and squeezes while bouncing on his toes. "Is that who I think it is?"

"What?"

"Check it out, guys. Is that Madds's TILF?"

Brow raised, I turn to Griffin. "TILF?"

"Yeah, man. Teacher I'd like to fuck." He points, and we all turn our attention to a table close to the bar where a very familiar redhead sits beside a blond guy who's all in her space. She hasn't noticed me or the attention of my teammates, so I'm able to take her in freely. She looks just as beautiful as she did on our date. And even more uncomfortable.

"That's her, right?" Griffin's way too excited about this. I shoot Sebastian a look, asking for backup, which he returns with a nod. He won't let Wright do anything stupid.

"Yeah, that's her."

Griff gives a little *whoop*. "You going to go over there and talk to her? This is your chance, man."

Sure, my chance to be shot down in front of my boys.

"Nah, it looks like she's on a date." An uncomfortable date, but still. Who am I to interrupt her?

Sebastian narrows his eyes while he watches them. "It looks like she's trying to get *out* of a date." He's not wrong. We all quiet down while we watch her, straining to hear any snippet of their conversation over the din of the bar. It's a shitty thing to do, but I've established that I'm a shitty guy when it comes to Isla Harding.

"So," the blond asshole says, drawing out the word as he leans into Isla's space. Space she tries to maintain by leaning away from him. "Teaching can't possibly pay enough to let you afford places like this. But if you find the right man, that's not something you'd have to worry about." He runs his finger down her arm, and Isla visibly shudders. "I make a lot of money with my company. Enough to buy the right woman anything she wants."

Logan grunts beside me. "What an absolute dick."

I agree. And you know it's true when Byrne's the one to say it. Not that he's purposefully a jerk to the women he sees, but he's not exactly warm and fuzzy. More like charming enough to get what he wants. And usually, that's a singular night in bed, then no contact. Though, to his credit, he's always upfront about that when he meets a woman. This tool sitting beside Isla? He's just a jerk with no game.

I recognize the fire that ignites in Isla's piercing blue eyes because I'd earned that same ire on our date last week. Sebastian's hand on my arm makes me realize I've taken an unconscious step toward her. I want to tell this blond prick to fuck off. That money isn't everything, especially to someone like Isla. Someone who cares about other people.

Man, I really read her wrong on our date. How could I ever have thought she was some gold-digging jersey chaser?

"Excuse me?" she spits, wrenching her arm away when he tries to run his fingers down it a second time. "What the hell kind of woman do you take me for?"

The guy's face flushes when curious patrons turn to watch them. I can see him trying to figure out how this went so wrong so quickly. "I just meant that you deserve the best things in life, that's all. You aren't a woman who should have to deny herself what she wants."

He brushes a strand of hair away from her face, using it as an opportunity to drag his knuckles along her collarbone, and way too close to her cleavage. The hand settles at the base of her neck, his thumb resting on her collarbone. "Maybe you just need a man who's happy to provide you with the finer things in life." That fucking thumb of his traces slow circles along her skin, and she's completely tense and visibly uncomfortable.

That's it. I can't watch this anymore. I turn to Navarro, looking at the hand he's still holding me back with. "I'm going in."

"Just don't kick his ass," he commands. "We're not at Chasers."

"Yeah," Griff nods. "We'll drag him outside and kick his ass there. I don't like the way he's treating your TILF."

I shoot him a warning glare. "Stop calling her that."

He grins widely. "You liiiike her. Gravesy's hot for teacher."

"Shut up." I don't bother waiting for his response, already crossing the room toward an increasingly flustered Isla. She's too busy trying to fend off her date's wandering hands to notice my approach. So when I say her name and step up beside her, her eyes go wide. "Isla? Hey, babe, I was just thinking about you."

"M-Maddox?" She stands, seizing her opportunity to get this creep's hands off of her. "Oh my god, I didn't expect to see you here." She fidgets, unsure how to greet me, so I open my arms, inviting her in for a hug with a look that conveys I'm here to save her if she wants it. She only hesitates for a fraction of a second, and then she moves away from her chair and into my arms. It forces blondie to scoot his chair back. He scowls as he watches her press into my chest.

Fuck, she feels good in my arms.

"Hey, beautiful," I murmur against her hair. My voice grows quieter as I whisper, "You look like you could use an assist."

"I'm so happy to see you," she replies. And I think she means it. It does something funny to my chest.

"You look stunning tonight," I tell her. It's what I should have said the moment she walked up to my table at Rêveur. "But then, you always do, don't you?" There, hopefully, she understands.

The pretty pink blush that steals over her cheeks has me hardening. "Thank you." She eyes my royal blue suit and pink tie appreciatively. "You look pretty handsome yourself." She runs a finger along the lapel. "I like this color on you."

Damn, I like hearing that more than I should. Especially since this is an act. I give her the full weight of my attention for a few more seconds before turning to the blond idiot fuming in the chair to my right. My left arm remains wrapped around her waist.

"Hey, man. Maddox Graves, nice to meet you."

His eyes go wide as the name registers, and he gives me a second look. "Maddox Graves? Center for the Minnesota Rogues?"

"Guilty," I reply with a grin.

Blondie stands, taking my hand. He tries to squeeze the hell out of it in some misguided attempt to assert his dominance, but knocks that shit off when I give him a squeeze of my own. He winces. I smile.

"Blake Carter," he says. "CEO of GoTravel. You've probably heard of me."

Je-sus, this guy. "Can't say I have." Isla's body shakes slightly against me, and a glance shows me she's trying desperately not to laugh. Good 'ole Blakey notices, though, and his face twists with anger. Yikes. Glad I interrupted this date, because I've seen that expression on men's faces before, and it never says anything good about them.

"Right." He smooths a hand through his hair. "Well, it was nice meeting you. If you'll excuse us, you've interrupted our date."

I don't miss the way Isla stiffens at my side. She does not like that. I can see her brow furrowing out of the corner of my eye as she tries to come up with an excuse to leave. That won't be necessary. I'll get rid of the asshole and provide the target for his anger. I turn to her with big puppy dog eyes. "I thought when we went out last week we decided not to see other people?" I brush a loose curl away from her face, dragging my fingertips across her forehead and down her cheek. Her breath catches and her eyelids flutter closed for the briefest of moments, and I'm gone. Either Isla Harding is a phenomenal actress, or she's attracted to me too.

"We did," she says, playing along. Her slender fingers grip my lapel as she looks up at me with those big, blue eyes. "This was supposed to be a girl's night. I'm sorry, babe. Please don't be mad."

Blakey-poo splutters some offended-sounding nonsense. He reaches for Isla's wrist, wrapping his hand around it as he demands her attention. "Jess never said you were in a relationship."

A rumble forms in my chest at the same time Navarro, Wright, and Byrne create a wall of muscle behind the pathetic piece of shit pressing his soon-to-be-broken fingers into Isla's wrist. "Get your fuckin' hand off of her. Right. Now."

The man must have a death wish because he doesn't. He glares at Isla, then me. "You'd rather be with some dumb jock than a business owner on Fortune's *40 Under 40* list? I'm going places, Isla. Any woman would be lucky to come along for the ride."

"You're still touching her," Griffin growls behind Blake-the-dead-man. All traces of the goofy man-whore persona Wright wears outside of the rink replaced with the deadly focus of the Rogues' left wing.

Blake finally senses the threat he's facing and drops Isla's wrist. She rubs it with a scowl. He hurt her. He *hurt* her.

"Maddox isn't a dumb jock," she says vehemently. "And this isn't a date. I don't know you, and I don't want to."

His skin pales before flaring red with fury. "Bitch."

"What did you say?" Byrne steps up close enough to bump Blake's back. We're drawing a lot of attention, and the last thing we need is for someone to take a video and plaster it all over social media. Plus, Isla's shaking like a leaf against my chest, and I just want to get her away from this piece of shit.

"Get out," I growl. "Now."

Blake looks like he wants to argue, but a glance at the three angry men at his back makes him change his mind. It's the first smart decision he's made tonight. The little rat scurries out of the bar. There's probably piss running down his leg from the looks my boys are giving him. As soon as he's gone, Isla lets out a shaky breath, takes a step back, and looks up at me.

"Thank you. I was supposed to meet my friends here tonight, but they were both running late, and they felt bad about the idea of me being here alone, but they had important work stuff to finish so I lied and told them I hadn't arrived yet so they wouldn't feel guilty. Then that asshole showed up and somehow knew way too much shit about me like where I work because apparently he saw a photo of me and Jess on her desk at work, and I was trying to find a way to get rid of him, but he was setting my creep-alarm off big time, and I was worried he'd try to follow me home." She's rambling, the words flying out of her mouth so fast I can barely make sense of them. "I just wanted a fun girls' night out with a few drinks and some laughs, and now here I am, shaking like an idiot because some guy got aggressive with me. And I'll go home and worry all night, and I probably won't sleep, and every little sound outside is going to make me wonder if blob-dick-Ken is lurking outside of my windows, and—"

"Blob-dick-Ken?" Griff asks with a burst of laughter.

Isla's cheeks pinken, and she chews on her bottom lip.

"Oh, uh, it's kinda what I was calling him in my head. Because he was boring and conceited and nondescript and he probably has a weird, tiny dick."

Griffin slaps his thigh. "Oh, god, that's great." He turns to me. "I like her. Let's tell the waitress we'll need room for one more at our table."

Isla looks between Griff and me. She's back on the defensive, and even though the end of our dinner date was pleasant, I'm sure she's recalling my initial behavior. "What?"

Griffin Wright can be a pain in my ass and a giant child sometimes, but he's got the right idea tonight. I look down at Isla with a smile. "Why don't you join us? We were just going to hang out, drink some beers, order some food. We're not girls, but it sounds like we had similar plans for the night. Then once you're ready to go, I'll drive you home and the guys and I will check the place over to make sure that asshole isn't lurking somewhere if you're worried he may know where you live. How about that?"

"Oh, no, I couldn't."

"Sure you can," I say. "Do you have other plans?" I want her to agree. She's clearly shaken by the whole exchange with that guy, and I don't want her to be alone. Selfishly, I'd also love a chance to prove I'm not actually an asshole, and I doubt I'll get another opportunity.

She chews her bottom lip some more, and I can't help myself. I reach over and tug it free with my thumb. Her breath catches, but I see the moment she decides to agree. She glances at the guys again before looking up at me. "You sure you don't mind? I don't want to intrude."

That doubt tingeing her voice is my fault. I put it there when I acted like spending time with her was a chore or a burden. And I'm going to fix it. "Mind? Hell, you'd be doing me a favor. Adding some beauty to a table of giant beasts." I motion toward the guys. "Don't leave me alone with them."

The slightest smile twitches on her lips. I've got her.

"Okay, yeah. If you're sure. That would be fun."

# twelve

## ISLA

OF ALL THE WAYS THIS DAY COULD HAVE GONE, I never would have guessed it would end with me sandwiched in a booth with Maddox Graves on my left, his teammate Griffin on my right, and two other giant hockey players named Sebastian and Logan around us. And I definitely wouldn't have thought Maddox would come to my rescue and save me from some creep who seems to know way too much about me after seeing my photo on my best friend's desk.

The world's gone topsy-turvy.

"So, Isla," Griffin says with a twinkle in his hazel eyes. That one's going to be trouble, I just know it. "Heard you had a lovely date with our friend Graves last week."

I arch one eyebrow. "Is that what he told you? Because the way I remember it, the loveliest part of my evening was going home."

All three of Maddox's teammates laugh loudly while he

rubs at the back of his neck. "Yeah, I deserve that. I'm sorry. I really am. And I'll keep apologizing." He looks genuine, but I don't know what to believe right now or which way is up. I'm not even sure how I got here.

"I'm teasing. I forgive you. After all, you did just save me from having to find a way to ditch that creep." I take a sip of the beer I ordered after we all sat down at the corner booth. It's not as yummy as a mixed drink, but it's got a lower alcohol content, and I want to keep my wits about me. "Though I guess I should say I forgive you as long as you're not stalking me or something. You're not, are you?"

Griffin laughs again, but it's Logan that speaks up. "Nah, coming here tonight was my idea. Just a happy coincidence."

"Okay, then I forgive you." Grinning, I playfully elbow Maddox in his side. "So, you guys are all on the Rogues?"

They nod, and Maddox goes down the line, telling me how long they've been on the team and explaining what positions they play, even though he might as well be speaking in tongues. It's all gobbledygook to me.

"Your eyes just glazed over," Maddox teases.

"Yeah, sorry. None of that means anything to me."

Sebastian smirks, the corners of his lips tugging up just slightly. He seems to be the most serious one in the group. "Did you grow up around here?"

I nod. "Yep. Minneapolis born and raised."

"And you've never seen a hockey game? How is that even possible?" He sounds more curious than judgmental, so I answer him honestly.

"My dad's never really been a sports guy. He's an English Lit professor, so he'd rather spend his evenings reading than watching a game. My mom likes baseball, but not enough to sit around and watch it." It's not that I couldn't learn to enjoy hockey or any other sport, it's just that I was never exposed to it. And even though there are tons of badass female athletes, sports are still very much a testosterone-fest. I never found it all that appealing.

It probably didn't help that there were a few guys on our high school football team who harassed me endlessly. Their constant inquiries about whether *the carpet matched the drapes*, and the way they'd dry hump the air every time I walked past them kind of put me off of jocks.

"You should come to one of our matches when the season starts," Sebastian offers. "Even if you don't end up enjoying the game, the atmosphere is like nothing else. It's electric. We can get you seats in the family and friends box."

"Maybe," I say noncommittally. He chuckles, obviously catching the brushoff.

Griffin takes a swig of his beer, stretching his arm out behind my back on the top of the booth. "We'll convince you, eventually."

He says it like it's a foregone conclusion. Like we're friends now, and he's got no doubt in his mind I'll give in. It makes my heart feel funny. And when Maddox swats Griffin's arm away from my back, my ticker feels even funnier.

I don't know what to make of them. Of him. If I wasn't so painfully certain that Maddox Graves is *not* interested in me and I'm definitely not his type, I'd wonder if he's flirting. But the hug and the compliments and the arm around my waist were just part of his *assist*, as he'd called it. And this? Hanging out with him and his friends? That's just guilt for the way he treated me last weekend. Or maybe it's his way of continuing to help keep Blake away.

Whatever it is, I can't read anything into it.

Besides, I'm done with men, I remind myself. Especially rich, cocky ones. They're bad news, and the ambush by Blake only further confirmed it. I may enjoy this time with Maddox and his teammates, but I don't miss the way his friends scan every woman in the bar. I don't miss the flirtatious smiles they give to the more beautiful ones, or the way they track those women like predators stalking their prey.

These guys are players. Both on and off the ice. I'd do well to remember that.

As if confirming my thoughts, Griffin says, "So, d'you have any hot teacher friends? Maybe some real kinky ones who are all buttoned up at work, then you take them home and find out they're a total freak in the sheets?"

Maddox stretches his arm behind me and smacks Griffin upside the head. Then he leaves it there. Resting behind me. "Don't be gross."

Griffin rubs the back of his skull a few times while he shoots Maddox a dirty look. "I was just joking, *Dad*. Geez." Then he turns to me, looking sheepish, and says, "Sorry, Isla."

"That's okay. I actually do have a coworker like that. Her name is Cynthia, and she teaches science. I heard a rumor that she's an actual dominatrix and makes men wear collars and g-strings while they clean her apartment. If they don't do a good enough job, she flogs them, then makes them lick the floor as punishment." Cynthia is also sixty-two, but Griffin doesn't need to know that.

He shivers with his whole body. "Ugh. Who would clean for fun?"

My description of Cynthia prompts Logan to tell a story about the time he went home with a woman after an away game and found himself handcuffed to her headboard, wearing nothing but nipple clamps and his dress socks. I don't think I've laughed so much in months. Hell, maybe even longer.

I try to remember the last time my belly hurt from laughing when I was with Alex. I can't. He was so obsessed with appearing perfect that it bled into our private lives at home. I stopped cracking dirty jokes or telling him anything that might make him scowl at me with that judgmental look of disdain that made my insides wither. At the end, he was a completely different person than the one I'd met. It wore me down, the way he'd tell me every little thing I did wrong every day. Even if it was something as insignificant as laughing at something crass.

The realization that I stopped sharing anything real with Alex years ago hits me hard. Or maybe, worse still, it's not that I stopped sharing things with him so much as I stopped enjoying things. I stopped *living* outside of work and being there for him.

I jump when Maddox's low voice rumbles in my ear. "Hey. You okay?" His eyes are kind and concerned when I look up at him. They search my face, lingering on my frown. Like he actually cares. But that's wishful thinking, because clearly I'm desperate for positive attention.

"Yeah, sorry. I'm good."

He studies me for a moment before nodding. "Let's get you some food. The alcohol's probably hitting, and I suspect you can't knock back as many beers as these idiots can without it affecting you." Without waiting for a response, he raises his hand and waves at our server. I don't correct him because I could eat. And I can't tell him what was actually going through my head because it's too pathetic. That kind of confession would bring this night to a grinding halt, and to my great surprise, I'm actually enjoying myself. And there's a secret part of me that hopes Sebastian's offer to go see a game is genuine because I wouldn't mind doing this again. Hanging out with these guys. With Maddox. Nothing romantic will ever happen between us, but maybe we could be friends.

I could use more friends.

The dark cloud over my head lifts when Maddox puts a plate of assorted appetizers in front of me. I guess I was hungry. It doesn't hurt that he has to slap Griffin's hand away at least five times, which makes all of us laugh.

"Isla," Logan says, "did Madds ever tell you about the time he got locked out of his hotel room in Montreal in nothing but this tiny little hotel towel?"

I almost choke on my panko-encrusted onion ring. "What? No."

"Dude." Maddox gives Logan a look that promises retribution, but his teammate ignores him.

"Yep. We were there for a two-game series, and Wright over there stole all of his clothes while he was in the shower. So Madds is soaking wet, the hotel towel barely covering his whole ass, and he's going from room to room demanding to know who took his stuff. Unfortunately, there were quite a few families on our floor, and this young mother comes storming down the hall and starts yelling at him. She's calling him a pervert and a sicko, and all the shouting draws a crowd." Logan snickers while Maddox has his head in his hands next to me. "At one point, he was so flustered that he started talking with his hands, and the towel fell. He was so shocked that he just stood there, hands mid-gesture, dick swinging in the breeze. His ass almost caused an international incident."

I can't hold back my laughter. "No."

"Oh, yes."

"What did the woman do when his towel dropped?"

Logan chuckles. "She got real quiet for a minute while she made eye contact with his dick and then screamed bloody murder. Bash pulled Maddox into his room and Coach had to talk the chick down from calling the cops."

"Oh, my god." I sneak a glance at Maddox as I struggle, and fail, to hold in my laughter. His cheeks are bright red and his lips press into a thin line, but his eyes sparkle with humor. "You dickmatized that poor woman."

He barks out a laugh. "Dickmatized?"

I nod. My whole body shakes with laughter. "Yep, dickmatized. Like hypnotized or traumatized. Probably a mix of both in your case."

Sebastian throws his head back and howls while Griffin and Logan join in. "God, that's perfect. That's exactly what happened." He raises his beer to me. "We are so going to convince you to come to our games. You're one of us now."

*One of us now.* The words burrow into my heart and make it swell with their easy acceptance. I risk a glance at Maddox to gauge his reaction to Sebastian's proclamation and find him smiling.

*You'll only ever be a friend*, I remind my traitorous heart as it beats a little faster. *You're not his type, and he's not yours.*

Maybe if I say it enough times, I'll actually believe it.

# *thirteen*

## MADDOX

THE GUYS LOVE HER. THEY'RE INSTANTLY protective, can't stop laughing when she cracks jokes at my expense, and they haven't stopped trying to get her to agree to come to at least one of our games. I'm so screwed because the minute we drop her off, they'll be up my ass about trying to win her over. And if I tell them there's not a chance in hell, I suspect Griff will take that as permission to shoot his shot.

As much as I love Griffin, in the time I've known him, he's never been with the same woman for more than three days. Some bullshit about how he's cursed, so why fight fate? Isla deserves better. It's not even that I want her; it's just that I know she's recently been through a nasty breakup, and Griff's not capable of offering a woman more than a few nights of fun.

Isla doesn't strike me as the type of woman who'd be happy with a night or two of no-strings-attached sex. She might try to hide it, but she's got *hopeless romantic* mounted in blinking neon letters above her head.

It's well after midnight, and while my teammates are still going strong, Isla's fading. She's doing these adorable slow blinks and answers half of the questions posed to her with a sleepy '*hmm*?' And with every passing minute, she's melting into my side a little more. That's how I know it's time to bring her home. Because after the asshat from earlier left and there was no more reason to pretend we were together, she hadn't touched me once. In fact, she's been very careful not to. So when her head lolls onto my shoulder, I clear my throat to get the guys' attention.

When Griffin sees her dozing against me, his face breaks into an ultra-wide smile. He takes out his phone and snaps a few photos despite my scowl and turns to Navarro. "For when they get married," he whispers. "We can pull this out and say we were there the night they fell in love." Griff clasps his hands together over his heart and flutters his eyelashes dramatically. He looks ridiculous.

"Shut the fuck up," I grumble.

"Oh, don't worry. I'm texting them to you now." He blows me a kiss, and I sigh, but there's no hiding the smile that twitches across my lips.

"Thanks."

Logan leans across the booth and holds out his palm. "Here, give me the valet ticket and I'll have them pull your car up. I'll also do a quick sweep to make sure that dickless asshole isn't lurking somewhere outside waiting."

My chest squeezes at the thought of him sticking around intending to hurt her, but gratitude for my boys quickly overshadows it. We may all be fuck-ups in our own ways, but there are no better friends. I'm lucky to have them in my corner, and it seems Isla is now lucky, too. I drop the ticket in Byrne's hand with a grateful nod.

"Thanks, man."

"I'll settle up with the bar." Navarro unfolds himself from the booth as Byrne does, and then it's just me and Wright left with a sleeping Isla.

"Help me get her out?" I ask him. He nods, holding her up as I slide out. It's an awkward dance, getting a sleeping woman out of a booth like this, but she's so tired she barely stirs. "Can you grab her purse?"

"Of course, man." Griff grabs her bag and then grins like the cat who caught the canary as I lift Isla, careful to pin her skirt between her legs and my arms so no one sees anything they shouldn't. She mumbles something unintelligible before nestling her face into the crook of my neck and I freeze, so taken aback by her unconscious trust and the realization that I'm tired of being alone, that I'm unable to move.

"She looks right in your arms." Griffin's tone is far more serious than I'm used to hearing when it comes to women. "Don't fuck this up."

Blowing out a slow breath, I meet his gaze. "That seems to be all I ever do." It's happened often enough that I've stopped putting myself out there. I've stopped risking anything and convinced myself I'm happy alone. But am I? Right now, with a beautiful, funny woman in my arms, I can admit I haven't been. It's scary as hell to consider trying again, but ignoring Isla's pull is as impossible for me as it is for the ocean to ignore the call of the moon.

He gives me a knowing look before clapping my free shoulder softly. "You're a good man, Graves. One of the best. The only thing you screwed up before was picking the wrong women." His attention goes to the sleeping woman in my arms. "Seems like Fate finally intervened. Lucky bastard. Don't waste this shot."

Shit. You know you're in deep when Griffin Wright waxes poetic about fate.

We pick our way through the bar and, joined by Navarro, head into the night just as the valet pulls my car up. "Any sign of Ken?"

Byrne shakes his head. "Nope. I think we're good." He opens the passenger door. "Here, put her in front so she's comfortable. The rest of us can cram into the back."

"Dude, that's going to suck," Griff whines. "But I suppose it's the gentlemanly thing to do."

Byrne snorts. "You wouldn't know the gentlemanly thing if it bit you in the ass."

"Ooh, ass play. Kinky." Wright gives him a wink, then climbs into the back seat.

"Can you behave yourself? At least until we get Isla home." Navarro rolls his eyes. They all grunt as he shoves himself into the back with them and they bicker like children as they struggle to find the seat buckles with three massive hockey players jammed so tightly together. I can't help chuckling as I pull Isla's seatbelt across her body and carefully buckle her in. The click, combined with the grumbling in the back of the car, finally has her stirring. She blinks big, sleepy blue eyes at me.

"Hey. What's happening?"

"You fell asleep," I tell her. "We're going to take you home now. Let me climb in, then you can give me your address, okay?"

She hums her agreement, eyes tracking me as I cross in front of the car and climb into the driver's seat.

"Where to?"

She rattles off her address. Once I've typed it into my maps app, we're on our way. "Thanks for driving me home." The shy smile she offers me goes straight to my chest. "And for the assist earlier. I really appreciate it."

"You don't have to thank me," I tell her honestly. "Anyone would have done the same in my position."

Shadows cross her face before she murmurs, "No, not everyone."

It's stupid and irrational, but I want to wipe those shadows from her eyes and make her forget the jerk that put them there. And I want to kick past me's ass for contributing to them last week. "Anyone worth your time," I say instead.

The ten minutes it takes to drive to her apartment go by way too quickly. The neighborhood isn't great, and it causes an irrational surge of protective instincts to flare in my chest. But Isla doesn't seem bothered by it, so I hold my tongue. As soon as I park, she turns, offering us a blinding, if tired, smile. "I had so much fun with you all tonight. Thanks for including me in your guys' night. I'm sorry for crashing it."

Griffin reaches up and ruffles her hair. "Don't apologize, Teach. We had fun with you, too. We'll have even *more* fun when we all go out and celebrate after we win the game you come see."

She chuckles. "That sounds like a plan."

Wright lets out a *whoop* as he turns to me. "Told you we'd convince her."

Hand on the door, Isla chews her bottom lip. I want to reach out and soothe the abused flesh again, but that would be a stupid move. "Okay, well, goodnight. Thanks again."

"Saying goodnight so soon? Why don't you let us walk you to your door? I know that guy freaked you out earlier." I glance at the guys. "Boys." They all climb out of the car. Soon, three hockey players prowl around the parking lot and in front of Isla's building while I stand guard at her side.

"Hockey bodyguards. This is fun. I guess I was pretty freaked out about earlier. Is this car to door service, or do you offer apartment sweeps too? I keep imagining that asshole hiding under my bed," she jokes. Her cheeks grow pink. She's so damned beautiful. "I'm kidding, of course."

"Checking under the bed is part of the package," I reply with a wink. Because she's kidding, but she's not. Even though there's no way that guy is in her apartment, the whole experience unsettled her. I've got a little sister. Unfortunately, I have experience helping a freaked out woman feel safe again. And one way to do that is to make them laugh without minimizing their feelings.

The wind blows a strand of hair in her face, and I reach out to tuck it behind her ear without even thinking. Her blush grows deeper, and my stupid mind conjures images of her flushed and panting beneath me as I move inside her.

Fuck. Now I'm hard.

"Well, I'd be stupid not to get my money's worth." The guys wait for us at the entrance to her apartment building, their visual sweep of the exterior done. She opens the door and motions us in. "Come on, then."

Her apartment is on the third floor at the end of the hallway. It's small but tidy, full of bright colors and vintage furniture. Black and white photos and colorful paintings adorn the space, and floor-to-ceiling bookshelves span the entire wall behind her green velvet couch. It's eclectic and creative, and I drink it all in, savoring this private piece of Isla I never thought I'd see.

She fidgets as she watches us check out her home. Four massive hockey players make the space seem smaller than I'm sure it normally feels. "Can I get you guys drinks or anything?"

"Nah," I say, grinning. "We're okay. We'll just check under your bed and behind the shower curtain as part of our hockey security service, then get out of your way."

Isla laughs. The sweet sound goes straight to my cock. "Uh, feel free to take a look around. And under my bed, I guess. I've seen way too many horror movies to want to look there myself."

The guys chuckle, but even though she's laughing along with them, I see the lingering nerves she's trying to hide. That prick shook her up. And as over the top as all of this is, it will help her sleep better tonight. We'll make her laugh, put on a show of inspecting every dark corner, and help her feel safe. We check out the bedroom and bathroom, making a point to look behind the shower curtain, beneath the bed, and inside her closet. It's overkill, and we crack jokes the whole time, but it does the trick. The tension bleeds out of her posture, and she finally relaxes.

"You good?" I ask her as the guys and I move toward her door. She yawns, obviously tired. As much as some irrational part of me wants to stay, I know we need to let her get some sleep.

"I'm good. Thanks, guys."

"Don't mention it," Navarro says. Wright and Byrne echo his sentiments.

"We'll get out of your hair and let you go to bed." I hesitate, not sure if I should give her a hug or a high five or a kiss on the forehead. Definitely not a high five. I'd never hear the end of it from the guys. In the end, I do nothing. "Night, Isla."

Her sleepy smile is a sucker punch to the heart. "Night, Maddox. Night, guys."

My boys chorus their goodbyes, and I reluctantly follow them out of Isla's apartment. The light inside her place back-lights her as she stands in the doorway, watching us walk down the hall. She gives us a little wave before we hit the stairs. No one speaks until we've hit the first floor, then Navarro claps me on the back.

"It was nice knowing you."

I bark out a laugh. "What?"

He throws me a shit-eating grin. "We all saw that. You're a goner, Graves. Plain and simple."

And damn it all, I think he's right.

# *fourteen*

## ISLA

Last night was… unexpected.

I woke with thoughts of Maddox Graves dancing through my head, and I stare at the ceiling while replaying the evening for the hundredth time. Ending up alone at Skin and Tonic. That asshole, Blake. Maddox and his teammates.

Jess and Nevaeh have both texted me already this morning, but I haven't answered because I don't know what to say. I lied and told them I never made it to the bar, but I can't keep this from them. Jess works with Blake's company. She's bound to hear about our run in. But I'm not sure how much I want to tell them. I need some time to think.

My mind wanders to Maddox and the way he stepped in and gave me an easy out last night. How did he even know to intervene? Did I look as uncomfortable as I felt? And why had he been watching me? It's not like he's interested, so maybe it was morbid curiosity? Or maybe I just looked so much less put together and fancy than I had on our date that he'd been staring at me and thanking his lucky stars he'd never have to date a mess like me again. But if that was the case, why did he jump in and help me? Did his friends ask him to?

My phone buzzes again. Sighing, I unlock the screen. They won't let me ignore them much longer. Except, the text isn't from either of my best friends.

MADDOX

Hey, this is Maddox. I hope it's okay that I'm texting you. I wanted to make sure you were okay after last night.

Confused butterflies take flight in my stomach. They're like delicate bumper cars with wings banging into each other. I'm simultaneously touched and confused. Maddox and I exchanged numbers to set up the assembly, but I never thought he'd text just to check up on me. I... don't know how to feel.

Not letting myself overthink things, I type up a quick reply because it would be rude to ignore him. Plus, after what he did last night, I can't seem to see him as nothing more than the self-absorbed jerk who made me feel like I was worthless. All of this is very confusing.

ME

I'm okay. A little tired, but that's because I slept funny. It could be worse. There could have been monsters under my bed.

I stare at the screen as those three little dots blink to life almost immediately. I didn't expect him to be waiting next to the phone for my reply. And why does that elicit such conflicting feelings in my body? My chest is tight, the way it is any time I'd texted Alex after we split, but those butterflies are still flying winged bumper cars around in my stomach.

Maybe it's because I'm not sure who Maddox Graves actually is.

Is he the selfish man I met on our first date? Is he the white knight riding in to rescue me like he was last night? Or is he something else entirely? Some nebulous mix of the two?

*Get a grip, Isla. This doesn't mean anything. And you don't want it to.*

MADDOX

Thank goodness for that. Sorry the bodyguard service wasn't in time to save you from having to deal with that asshole last night.

ME

Ugh. Yeah. He was the worst.

Two crappy dates in two weeks. I'm sorry. And I want to apologize again for being the reason the first one was so bad.

He wasn't a date. He recognized me from a picture my best friend had on her desk. Creepy, right? And you don't need to keep apologizing. I forgive you. Especially after last night.

I'm startled to realize how true that statement is. I may not know what to think about Maddox, but I have forgiven him. The way he stepped in at Skin and Tonic, the way he carried me out to his car when I fell asleep in the bar, the way he checked out my apartment to make sure it was safe... He's quite a few levels above Alex and Blake in my estimations.

*He carried me out to his car.*

The thought truly hits me for the first time, and a hot flush crawls across my skin. No one has ever carried me somewhere when I fell asleep. Not since I was a little girl. Alex would just poke me on the cheek and tell me I could either walk myself to bed or sleep on the couch. If he woke me at all. More often than not, I'd wake up groggy the next morning with a pinched nerve in my neck and Alex snoring peacefully in our bed. Like he couldn't even be bothered to wake me.

MADDOX

That IS creepy. Are you sure it wasn't a setup?

ME

No, they wouldn't do that to me. Just a weird, unfortunate coincidence.

Well, I'm glad you weren't alone with him long. He was a douche. My friends wanted to kick his ass.

LOL! Yeah, he was the worst. Honestly, part of me would have loved to watch them make him cry.

Got a bit of a violent streak?

IDK. Never thought I did, but then again, I love action movies.

> You should come to one of our games.
> It's like an action movie on ice.

> Sounds cold.

> I'll hook you up with a Rogues hoodie and
> hat. I think we have some branded fleece
> blankets... I'll get you one of those, too.

My heart thrums. He wants me to come to one of their games? He didn't say much last night when his teammates tried to convince me to go. I thought he was indifferent. Now he's offering to buy me warm gear, and I don't know what to make of it.

> ME
> Are you trying to bribe me?

> MADDOX
> Maybe. Is it working?

> Maybe.

There's a pause, that little ellipsis flashing, then disappearing, flashing, then disappearing. For some reason, I'm holding my breath.

> MADDOX
> The guys would be excited if you came to
> a game.

Aaand my stomach twists. Of course, it's not that *he* wants me to go. It's that his friends do. Not that I care. I don't, because Maddox Graves is not the kind of man I need to develop feelings for. Even if he did rescue me and carried me princess-style like I weighed ten pounds.

ME

> It would be fun to see them again. Well, I should go. I have errands to run. Have a good day. Thanks again for last night.

MADDOX

> You don't need to thank me. Have a good day.

Once again, I'm staring at my ceiling, twisted up with confusion. For a few minutes, it seemed like Maddox was flirting with me. Then he invited me to a game because his teammates want me there? That shouldn't bother me, but it does.

I let out a frustrated growl. "Why are men so freaking confusing?"

My only answer is the buzz of my phone. This time it's not Maddox.

JESS

> Hey, girl. We're so sorry about last night.
> Did you end up doing anything fun?

NEV

> Lunch today?

Unable to avoid them any longer, I start typing. My thumbs are about to get a workout.

---

MADDOX

We make it through training before the guys bring her up. Feeling out of sorts, I ask them to skate with me after our time in the weight room. We don't hit the rink often during the off-season, but nothing clears my head like flying over the ice. Usually. It's not as effective as I need it to be today.

"Dude, where's your head at?" Byrne lightly hip checks me after I miss yet another shot. We don't even have anyone manning the goal, so it's even more pathetic than if we were scrimmaging.

"I know," Griffin sings as he skates in circles around us like some annoying ice fairy. "He's thinking about a certain red-haired TILF."

I growl. "I fucking told you not to call her that." I hold my stick out to trip him, but the shithead laughs and hops it.

"Touchy, touchy." Griffin shimmies his shoulders. "Did you spend the rest of the weekend rocking blue balls? Because she's hot, man. I considered rubbing one out to her, but I doubted you'd appreciate me thinking about your woman that way."

"Jesus," Bash says with a shake of his head. "Smooth, Griff."

"She's not my woman." They all look at me funny because I sound put out by that fact. "Isla's not interested in me. I blew any chance of that on our date last week."

Logan side-eyes me. "You sure about that?"

Am I sure? Yes. They didn't see her face that night. The only reason she gave me the time of day at Skin and Tonic was because I helped her out of a sticky situation. Probably didn't hurt that the guys were there, too. They're a good buffer. "Yep."

"I don't know," Bash considers me. "If you really blew it as badly as you think, I doubt she would have hung around with us at the bar."

"She was nervous to leave." I can't let myself think she

was showing any interest. We're about to head into the preseason, and I won't have time for any relationship, let alone a new one. Even if there is something about her.

"She fell asleep on your shoulder."

Pursing my lips, I shake my head at Navarro. "That doesn't mean anything. She was tired."

"She could have dozed off with her head on Griff's shoulder, but she didn't. She fell asleep on yours."

"You're reading into this."

"Maybe," Navarro agrees. "But you are distracted. Are you really trying to convince us it has nothing to do with Isla?"

Yes. That's exactly what I'm trying to do. Because I need to convince myself, too. "It *doesn't* have anything to do with her."

"Uh huh," Griffin sings. He brings his stick to his face and acts like he's making out with it. "Oh, Isla. I'm so glad you gave me another chance. I want to make sweet, sweet love to you. Have my babies. We'd make adorable, grumpy little redheads together." He thrusts his hips against the stick, egged on by Logan and Sebastian's laughter.

"Oh yeah, baby. I love that you don't care that I have a small dick. And that I can only last ten seconds before I blow my load." His hip thrusts become more exaggerated. "That's it, baby. God, you're so hot." He pulls away from the stick, his mouth opening into a look of shock. "Griffin? Why are you crying out his name while I'm buried inside of you? You know what? I don't even care. I know Griff's better than me in every way, so I don't mind if you scream his name while we're naked."

That's it. Putting on a burst of speed, I race toward Griffin and push the annoying bastard down as hard as I can. He lets out a little shout of surprise before he's sprawled out on the ice, stick still clutched in one hand. He guffaws loudly before resting the stick on the ice and humping it.

"Jesus fucking Christ, Wright."

"Nah, man, I wouldn't fuck Jesus. But if you're seriously not going to make a move on Isla, I might try to fuck her."

Navarro shakes his head. "Wrong thing to say."

Before he can react with more than a bark of laughter, I throw myself on top of Griff and throw a few half-hearted hits to his gut. Logan's cracking up, his phone in hand as he records us, and Bash has the exasperated face of a parent whose children are quickly eroding his last nerve.

"Uncle," Griff yells, laughing. "Fucking uncle!" He's still laughing as I extend a hand and help him to his feet. I'm laughing too. It's hard not to when Wright gets going. The man doesn't take much of anything seriously outside of hockey.

"You two done?" Logan taps his phone before stuffing it in his back pocket. We both nod. "Good. Then let's figure out how we can help Graves get the girl."

I scrub a hand through my hair. "What makes you think I want the girl?" I do want her. I just don't *want* to.

I haven't done relationships since Candace sold her fake version of events to that tabloid, and I have no intention of starting now. I'll enjoy a woman for a night when the urge becomes too strong to ignore, but that's all it ever is. One night of mutual pleasure, no strings, no feelings, no expectations.

The thing is, I don't think Isla Harding is a one-nightstand kind of woman. She strikes me as a woman who wants romance, late nights in bed talking, friendship, and depth. That all became clear when she spoke about her job and her students. When I realized I'd read her so wrong. She's not some vain girl chasing someone to pay her way. She's real and beautiful and driven, and she deserves someone else like that.

But I can't be that guy for her. Not that she'd want me to be. I've sworn off relationships, and for good reason.

"Dude, maybe you're fooling yourself into thinking you don't want her," Logan says while rolling his eyes. "But you're sure as hell not fooling us."

"She's pretty," I say. As if that explains it all.

Griffin chuckles. "Yeah. She's also feisty and cool. She's not afraid to put you in your place, and she's funny. She's not some single-minded puck bunny who only cares about snagging a hockey player. In fact, I doubt she's impressed by your job at all. You think we don't realize how attractive that must make her to you?"

When I don't answer, Navarro cuts in. "It's okay to take a chance on someone, man. Not everyone is going to betray you."

He's right, I know he is. The problem is the last two women I let myself feel anything for did just that. Now I worry my ability to pick a good woman is broken. Something in *me* must be broken. If it wasn't, would it have been so easy for Candace and Georgia to sell me out like that?

"I'm not ready to take a chance on anyone."

Bash squeezes my shoulder. "Okay, man. Maybe she could be a friend. Kinda seems like she might need one as much as you do."

"Yeah," Logan says. "What's her story, anyway?"

"She mentioned a bad breakup, but I don't know outside of that. Not even sure when it happened. It's why her friends did the date auction. To get her out of her funk." I shake my head, banishing the intrusive thoughts that start popping up, unbidden. Thoughts of what Isla's lips would taste like. What her body would feel like pressed against mine. What it would be like to wake up next to her every morning. I can't let myself go down the rabbit hole like that with any woman. But especially not one who needs a sensitive, attentive guy who can give her the time and attention she deserves.

I'm not that guy.

"So be her friend, Madds. She's cool, and you could use a reminder that not all women are backstabbing narcissists." Navarro slaps a puck into the goal.

"I don't think all women are like that."

Bash's eyebrows rise. "Your mom and sister don't count."

Well, he's got me there. Not that I'll admit it.

"Why don't you start by inviting her to one of our preseason games?" Logan asks. "It would be a good low-pressure way to spend some time with her. See if there's anything there."

"I kind of already did," I admit. They're all silent for a minute before Griffin speaks.

"What do you mean, kind of?"

"No, I did invite her."

He doesn't look convinced. "What exactly did you say to her?"

I rub the back of my neck. "I told her she should come to one of our games. She said it sounded cold, so I told her

I'd hook her up with some Rogues gear to keep her warm, and I told her you guys would like it if she came."

Three sets of eyes pin me to the ice. Their faces twist in varying expressions of disbelief. Byrne's the first one to speak.

"Hold up. You told Isla that *we* would like it if she came to a game?"

Fuck. I knew they'd pick up on that. I regretted the words the moment they tapped their way out of my fingertips. And when it took Isla longer to respond to that text than the others, I knew I'd screwed up.

"Dude." Griffin shakes his head. "What the hell is wrong with you?"

"You told her *you* wanted her to come too, right?" Sebastian eyes me critically. It's virtually impossible to lie to the guy. He's too perceptive by half, so I don't attempt it.

"Uh, not really."

Logan shakes his head. "You used to have game."

I did. I *do*. Just apparently not with Isla.

Bash shoves Logan to get him to shut up. "You can still fix this."

"There's nothing to fix," I tell him. Frustration bubbles inside of my chest. Frustration with Candace and Georgia for giving me reason to shut myself off from other women, at myself for letting them get the best of me, and at Isla for making me wish I hadn't built such high walls around myself. And even though they don't deserve it, I'm annoyed at the guys for making me confront all of those feelings.

"You don't believe that."

"Come on, Bash, do you actually think she'll want anything to do with me after how I treated her on our date and then said that to her? I blew it, man. It's better if I just accept it."

"Is it, though?"

Crap. I don't even believe that. How can I expect them to?

Closing my eyes, I shut out their incredulous faces. "I don't know how to fix this."

"Good thing you've got us to help you." Logan rubs his hands together. He looks like a cartoon villain plotting world domination. "This will be fun."

# fifteen

## ISLA

I know I shouldn't do it, but my thumb hovers over Alex's username on Instagram and, before I can talk myself out of it, I give it a tap. I'd been doing better at avoiding the temptation to spy on him, but the last couple of weeks have left me feeling raw.

Clearly looking to poke at a healing wound, I click on his most recent post. Brown hair tousled in the wind, his smile is broad and bright, and his blue eyes sparkle in the afternoon sun. He's on a beach—probably Cabo because the asshole went on our honeymoon alone—and he looks so much happier than he ever did with me. Long, blonde hair blows next to him in the breeze, but the owner's face isn't in the photo. My chest tightens sharply. Is he seeing someone? At the end, I suspected he might be cheating, but he'd denied it. Is this her?

. . .

*"I HAVE A WORK DINNER TONIGHT," ALEX INFORMS me as he brushes his teeth. He doesn't even look my way as I shuffle into the bathroom, bleary-eyed and still half asleep.*

*"Oh." I wish he'd told me sooner. I have nothing to wear. "How formal do I need to dress?"*

*"No. You misunderstand." His eyes bounce my way for half a second before turning back to his own reflection. "I'm telling you I won't be home. It's an important dinner, Isla, and I have to impress these people. They have the power to make or break my career. I need to make a good impression."*

*His words crack like a barbed whip across my flesh. I'm instantly awake. Instantly on the defensive. "What exactly are you trying to say, Alex?"*

*He rolls his eyes. His tone is utterly bored as his next words flay my skin again. "These are powerful people, Isla. They have certain standards and expectations. I don't want to make you put on an act with them. You'd just be uncomfortable, and I don't want you to feel inadequate."*

*Inadequate. He doesn't want me to feel* inadequate. *Heat flushes my face and chest, and I know if I looked in the mirror, my fair skin would be mottled with ugly red splotches. It's one of the unfortunate aspects of being a redhead. Even if my facial expressions don't give away my upset, my skin does with its patchy color.*

*"Excuse me? You're acting like I'm some kind of uncultured idiot, and not a teacher with a master's degree in education and a degree in classic literature."*

*Alex waves his hand in the air, dismissing me. "You spend your day with teenagers. No need to make it sound like you're doing something extraordinary. Any idiot can teach."*

*I'm silent for a moment, seething. "Really? Any idiot can teach?"*

*"Oh, come on," he says, rolling his eyes again. "I didn't mean it like that and you know it."*

*Sure. He didn't mean it like that. Of course. That makes it all better. "I know exactly what you meant."*

*"Don't be like that, Isla. We'll both benefit if I get this promotion. Do you really want to jeopardize that?"*

*The painful throbbing in my chest becomes harder to ignore. Alex truly thinks my mere presence at this dinner could negatively impact his ability to get promoted? I'm his fiancée. I supported him every step of the way through law school. I helped him study, cooked him dinners when he was drowning and overwhelmed even though I was working through my own intense course-load. I listened when he vented, held him when he was upset. I've gone to so many stuffy events with him, despite wishing I could be doing anything else, and I've always charmed the people around us. Why is he saying this stuff to me now?*

*"I can't believe you."*

*"Of course, you don't understand." He lifts his eyes as if he's praying for strength. "This really isn't up for discussion. I was simply being courteous and giving you a heads-up that I won't be home tonight. I'll probably just get a room at the hotel where they're holding the event. Don't wait up for me."*

*Tears prick the corner of my eyes as I struggle to maintain my composure. Without another word, I turn and walk away. I lock myself in the guest bathroom and try not to cry as I take an extra-long shower.*

*Alex is gone when I get out.*

. . .

I WASN'T GOOD ENOUGH FOR ALEX, AND WE'D BEEN together for years. Hell, we were going to get married. Maddox immediately dismissed me, and Blake was a douche. The common denominator in all of those interactions?

Me.

Maybe there is something wrong with me.

I click over to my profile, noting the lack of new content. Ever since Alex ended things, my Instagram has been glaringly empty. If my ex were to do a little snooping, he'd rightly assume I've retreated into myself without him. I bet it would bring him immense joy. We can't have that.

Screw it. I tap on the little *plus* icon to post my *fuck you* to Alex Jones. Without overthinking it, I upload the photo of me and Maddox Graves. The one where he's looking at me, not the camera. The one where it almost looks like he finds me interesting and desirable.

I consider what I should write for the caption, then decide to go with something short, sweet, and open-ended. Something I hope will make Alex wonder about me if he sees it.

*Dinner with this guy. Thanks for an unforgettable night, Maddox.*

There. That should make Alex wonder. What was so unforgettable? Did Maddox take me home and ravish me against my apartment door because he couldn't wait the seconds it would take to walk to my bedroom? Have we been dating long? When did we meet? How quickly did I move on? I doubt Alex will suspect it to be memorable for how awful it was and how small it made me feel.

At least there's that.

I suffer a momentary twinge of guilt at using the photo

of me and Maddox. After all, he'd been kind at Skin and Tonic. He'd helped me. But he'd also been an ass when we first met, and this photo was part of the deal. It was one of the reasons I agreed to stay. It's only fair I use it for its intended purpose.

As I tap the button to post it, part of me wonders if Maddox will ever see it. I wonder what he'd think. Would he find me pathetic? Would he even care enough to have an opinion?

*The guys would be excited if you came to a game.*

No, I doubt he'd care enough to have an opinion. And it's probably pathetic to assume Alex thinks about me enough to stalk my socials the way I stalk his. After he broke things off with me, he made this speech about *being adults* and not *making a scene of things*. Which, to him, meant keeping up the appearance of civility. Of being *friends*. Not that we actually are. It just meant he didn't want us to unfollow and block each other all over social media. He claimed it was because it would make us both look bad to our employers, but that's bullshit. Now I realize he's just an asshole.

Why did I go along with that?

Well, I suppose it would be difficult to act like a voyeur in his life if I blocked him. And part of me hopes he'll slip up one day and reveal he's desperately unhappy without me. That he made a mistake and realized the error of his ways.

I wouldn't take him back, I really wouldn't. But it would be nice not to feel so insignificant and easily discarded. It would soothe me in some small way to know that recreating his life without me was just as painful as it was for me.

But Alex is off smiling on what should have been our honeymoon while I'm moping around Minneapolis, feeling sorry for myself. It's clear I was easy to move on from, and easy to forget.

It's high time I do the same. Fuck Alex Jones. I'll give him time to see my photo with Maddox, then I'm blocking his ass. No more moping. No more feeling sorry for myself.

Time to start living again.

*sixteen*

## MADDOX

ANOTHER DAY OF TRAINING, AND I'M MORE exhausted from my teammates' endless meddling than I am from the intense workout. All three of my friends spent the day brainstorming ways I could win Isla over. A few of them were decent, but most of them were ridiculous.

Griffin's favorite suggestion was to rent a horse and ride it to her apartment while carrying three dozen red roses with a Bluetooth speaker playing *In Your Eyes* hooked to the saddle à la Lloyd Dobler in *Say Anything*. But with a Prince Charming twist. When I told him I didn't know how to ride a horse, he just shrugged and said, "*How hard can it be?*"

I still think it's a lost cause, and I'm trying not to dwell on it as I watch ESPN on my comfy couch and drink a beer. I need to relax. To think about anything other than Isla Harding and her fiery eyes and kissable lips.

My phone buzzes in my pocket. I grin when my

younger sister, Mira's name flashes across the screen. It's been a few weeks since we've talked, and I miss her. Maybe I can convince her to ditch Chicago for a weekend and visit me. It'll only get harder to make it work once the season kicks off. I press the *accept* button, put it on speaker, and start to say hello when my sister interrupts me.

"I can't believe you have a new girlfriend and you didn't tell me," she says in lieu of a greeting.

I choke on my beer. "Sorry, what?"

"Seriously, Maddy? Don't play dumb with me. I'm your sister, for god's sake. You know I'll always find someone to spill the tea if you don't." She makes a *tsk*-ing sound. "And she's so gorgeous. Why would you keep her a secret?"

My heart pounds. This wouldn't be the first time some random woman on the internet made claims we were an item, but those women have never fooled my sister. The last thing I need—the very last thing—is for the media to catch wind of this and give a delusional fan a platform to lie about me. I won't be subjected to that again. I try to keep my voice calm and even, even as my head starts spinning.

"Mira, what are you talking about? Who's claiming to be my girlfriend?"

She sighs, and I can imagine her rolling her eyes. "The hot redhead you're making heart-eyes at. You two look ahmazing together."

Hot redhead? She has to be talking about Isla, right? But why would Isla post anything claiming to be my girlfriend? I'm fairly certain she doesn't even like me. "Where did you see this picture?"

"Instagram. Probably wouldn't have seen it if one of

her friends didn't tag you in a comment. She didn't even add a hashtag or anything, so it didn't ping the Google alert I have set up with your name."

The tension in my chest eases. I need to see this post for myself before I flip out. After all, I told her she could take a selfie with me to make her ex jealous. That's probably all this is. "What's her username?"

"Maddox Graves. You don't even know your own girl-friend's Instagram handle? Jesus. Be a better boyfriend."

"Mira," I growl. "She's not my girlfriend. Username. Now."

She rattles it off, and I type it into the app's search function. A black-and-white photo of a smiling Isla pops up in a little circle alongside her handle. My stupid heart speeds up as I tap on it, bringing up her feed.

Sure enough, the last photo she posted is one of us. She smiles brightly while I look at her, a faint grin on my lips. I read the caption—*Dinner with this guy. Thanks for an unforgettable night, Maddox.*—and bark out a laugh. Clever woman. She made it sound like we had some steamy night of passion when in reality, it was unforget-tably awful, not unforgettably wonderful. Win for her, and it covers my ass.

"Well?" my sister prompts, her voice ringing with impatience. "Care to explain? After one of her friends tagged you, it blew up. Everyone's speculating about you two. And about her."

Shit. I doubt Isla will like that, and I'd bet that lack of a tag was intentional. The only person she wanted to see that photo was her ex, so she could make him eat shit. I wonder if she's realized two thousand people have already heart-ed it? I scan the comments, grateful that most of them seem kind and curious, but cringe when I see a few from jealous women speculating all sorts of unkind things about Isla.

"Her friends bid on a date with me in this stupid silent auction the Rogues set up. I treated her like shit because I thought she must have been a gold-digging jersey chaser, but actually, she recently went through a bad breakup. Her friends were trying to get her out of her shell. She was unimpressed with my behavior and left before the reporter who was supposed to interview us got to the restaurant. So I bribed her to finish dinner with me. Taking a photo she could use to make her ex jealous was part of the deal."

My sister is silent for only a moment before she's cracking up. She's nearly wheezing, she's laughing so hard. "Oh. My. God. She's the GOAT. She totally threw shade only you would recognize while making her ex read it the opposite way. Please tell me you turned it around by the end of the night and did some serious groveling so you can take her out again."

I clear my throat. "I may have run into her at a bar with the boys the following weekend and they may have dragged her to our booth to hang out. But I don't think there's any potential there, Mir. She's not my biggest fan."

"Well, make her a fan. I want to meet her."

"Right. Sure. I'll get right on that."

"You better hope Mom doesn't see this."

Dammit. Mom. Despite our father walking out on her shortly after Mira was born and leaving her to raise two kids without help or financial support, despite my abysmal track record with women and assertions that I will never date again, Mom still harbors a not-so-secret hope that I'll find *the one*. She says I've got too much love in my heart not to share it with a good woman.

I think she just wants grandbabies to snuggle since Mira and I are a little too big for that, these days.

"Does mom have a Google alert set up for me too?"

Mira snorts. "Yeah right. As if she'd know how to do something like that."

"Okay good. If she hears about it, please tell her I'm not dating Isla."

"Isla, huh? That's a pretty name."

"Yep."

"She's beautiful. Is she cool?"

"Yeah, she's cool." And gorgeous, funny, and full of fire. And she smells like roses and bergamot. And I've stuck my foot in my mouth every single time I've spoken to her.

Mira laughs. "You like her."

"What?" How in the hell did she get that out of *Yeah, she's cool?*

"Oh, come on, Maddy-Poo. You act like I don't know you. Are you going to see her again?"

I sigh, then tell her all about our agreement to speak at her school. Mira listens as I recount the night at Skin and Tonic. About my disastrous text message telling her the guys would love if she came to a game. Mira nearly pisses herself, she laughs so hard about that. Still, like the guys, she tells me to stop being an idiot and make a move. I tell her I'll think about it, then change the topic.

"It's been a while since you've visited. Think you can squeeze some time in for a brother-weekend before the season starts?"

Mira hums. "I'm not sure. Jared and I are taking a trip

out to California for a couple of weeks. I've got some contacts out there I'd like to pitch in person. But in my downtime, we'll take a few surfing lessons, drink margaritas on the beach, and fuck all night long in our little rental."

"Je-sus." I groan. "I don't need to know that crap, Mi-Mi."

"Sorry." She practically sings the word, so I know she's not sorry. Not in the slightest. "But I can plan a trip during the season. We'll schedule it around some home games or something. Then maybe I can meet Isla, because I'm sure you'll be an item by then."

I chuckle. My sister, the eternal optimist. It works for her, and it's helped her get her business off the ground. Because as optimistic as Mira is, she's just as driven and single-minded. Nothing gets in between her and her goals. We're a lot alike in that regard. My goals are just more literal than hers. And they involve pucks and nets. "*Yeah,* I'm sure we will be. Now, tell me about this guy. Is he good to you? Because if he's not, I'll bring the boys to Chicago and we'll take turns kicking his ass."

"You're so dramatic. He's good to me. I wouldn't have moved in with him if he wasn't. Do you think I'd put up with anything less?"

She wouldn't. Our mom made damn sure of that. "Of course not. But I'd be a pretty shit brother if I didn't offer some vague threat of violence."

"You're ridiculous."

"I know. You love me anyway."

"I guess. So when are you going to ask Isla out?"

Isla's beautiful face stares at me through the phone screen. God, she's stunning. And she felt so good in my arms when I carried her out to the car that night at the bar. But I screwed it all up. She couldn't possibly want anything to do with me, right? But we haven't discussed the assembly, and the silent auction dinner for the team is coming up. Coach said they invited all the winners. I wonder if she's planning to go.

Even if she doesn't want to go out with me, we'll need to talk. I'll just try my hardest not to continue my streak of jamming my foot into my mouth. Because, even though I doubt I stand a chance in hell, I can't stop thinking about her. And clearly, everyone in my life is going to ride my ass until I give it a shot.

The sooner Isla tells me she's not interested, the sooner things can go back to normal.

"Isla won't want to go out with me," I tell my sister. "Even with groveling."

"You never know until you try."

"Sure, Mi-Mi. You just want to see me humiliated."

She's silent for a moment. I expect her to toss a joke back my way, but she doesn't. Instead, her voice is serious when she says, "No, Maddy, I don't. I think you've been humiliated enough, don't you? I want to see you happy."

Well, shit. What can I say to that? I suck in a deep breath, nodding even though my sister can't see it, and make a decision. "I'll shoot my shot. Just don't hold your breath."

My sister releases a little high-pitched squeal. "I believe in you."

I'm glad someone does. Hopefully, for now, that's enough.

seventeen

## MADDOX

Isla's Instagram profile is still on my screen when I hang up with Mira, and I stare at it. There's a battle raging inside my head. Do I Instagram stalk Isla, or do I click out of the app and pretend I never saw her pics? Her profile's public, so I wouldn't be doing anything wrong by looking, but part of me hesitates. Though, maybe that's more because I'm worried whatever I'll see will make me like her more, and less because I think it's crossing some invisible line.

Screw it. I'm curious about her.

There's not much to see from the past year. She's posted a few photos with two women I'm guessing are her best friends. They're all smiling in the snaps, but Isla's doesn't quite meet her eyes. A few photos of sunsets and latte art span several months. Even a few memes get sprinkled in here and there.

As I get to her older posts, it becomes clear when I hit

the pre-breakup photos, even though I don't see any of her ex. The photos have more life to them. More color. Her smile is still tight, but there's light in her eyes. A few months further, and the snapshots become brighter still. I grin when I come across a photo from a year and a half ago. Isla's laughing with her friends. Her head's thrown back, eyes sparkling, her mouth open with what had to have been unfettered laughter. She's even more beautiful like this. Uninhibited and free.

I continue scrolling. She's gorgeous. And fun. And maybe Mira and the guys are right. Maybe I need to figure out some kind of Lloyd Dobler-esque grand gesture if I want a chance to get to know this woman.

There are a few pictures of sunsets and artfully arranged photos of teaching supplies. A photo of an empty classroom filled with posters of book covers and quotes gives me a glimpse into the kind of teacher she is. The room is full of color. It's vibrant and engaging, and I'd bet a lot of the kids in her grade would cite English as their favorite subject.

It makes me excited to speak at her school. I'm not sure what I'll say—and I should probably start thinking about it—but her passion is contagious. There's also a small part of me that hopes doing this will give me an in with Isla. Maybe it will help her see me differently. If she believed I was someone she could trust and rely on, someone who valued her passions and work, maybe it would allow her to open up to me. Even if that's just as friends.

Residual anger bubbles in my chest when I think about that asswipe talking down to her about teaching. When I was a stressed-out, angry teenager, the only adults I had in my corner, besides my mom, were my teachers and coaches. And there were a couple along the way who made a genuine difference in my life and helped me believe I could achieve great things. The world needs more teachers like that. Like Isla.

My fingers move impulsively, swiping out of the Instagram app and into my text messages.

ME

> Is there anything specific you'd like me to speak about at the assembly, or should I just plan something uplifting and encouraging?

I stare at my screen for a minute, but when she doesn't text me back right away, I tap on the Instagram app and pull it back up. Resuming my light stalking, I grin at photos of a rosy-cheeked Isla in a sports bra and leggings. She's looking back over her shoulder as she navigates a hiking trail, and it's the first photo where she looks utterly vibrant and happy. She clutches a water bottle in her left hand, and my brain goes offline when I notice the modestly-sized circular solitaire diamond on her ring finger.

Isla was engaged?

Heart hammering, I flip through a few more photos and realize she must have looked so happy because the hike took place not long after her ex proposed. There are only one or two photos before that where I catch glimpses of her ring. She clearly went through and deleted all the photos with her ex in them, but I can see why she left these. She looks vibrant. Happy.

But now Isla's discomfort with dating makes sense. And I can understand why her friends are worried about her. From the things Isla said, it sounded like they'd been together for years. She thought they were going to get married. Hell, she's probably unsure how to put herself out there anymore because she never thought she'd need to.

An uncomfortable cocktail of shame and protectiveness fills me. I don't know Isla Harding, but it doesn't take a genius to see she's the real deal. She's smart, funny, sassy, and strong as hell. And I want to shield her from being hurt again.

Which is ridiculous and I know it. I have no claim on her. I haven't earned her trust. And I hurt her, too.

My phone buzzes as a text pops up on my screen.

ISLA

Maybe you could tell them a bit about your story. Like how you got into professional hockey, how hard you had to work, and how rewarding it was when that hard work paid off? Then it would be great if you could encourage them and tell them they can achieve greatness, too, if they're willing to put in the work and believe in themselves. They don't all have people in their lives telling them they can be great. I know how discouraging that can be.

She knows from personal experience, or from observing it in her students?

ME

I can definitely talk about all of that. Do you have a date in mind yet?

ISLA

Well, school starts in two weeks at the end of August. I'm not sure what your season and schedule look like.

The preseason starts in the middle of September, so it'll be easier to schedule things prior to that.

Of course. Maybe we could do the second week of school?

That should work. You let me know the day and time and I'll clear it with my coach and make up any training I miss. He won't mind for something like this.

Thanks, Maddox. You have no idea how much the kids will love this.

Don't mention it. It was part of our deal, right?

Yeah. Right, of course.

I kick myself. Dammit, now she thinks I'm only doing this because of our deal. Why do I always stick my foot in my mouth with her?

ME

I've been thinking about it a lot. I'm really looking forward to it. Thanks for giving me the opportunity.

This time that little ellipsis that tells me she's typing flashes, then disappears, flashes, then disappears.

ISLA

To be honest, I worried you'd try to get
out of it.

Yeah. She's got some trust issues. And I deserve that. It's okay, I can be patient. We can work on that if she gives me the chance to earn her friendship.

ME

I may be a lot of things, but one thing you
can count on is that I'm a man of my
word. If I tell you I'm going to do
something, I will always do it. I don't
break promises, Isla.

ISLA

Everyone claims to be a man of their
word. It doesn't mean they are. LOL

My heart pinches. That little *LOL* she throws in at the end doesn't fool me. Whether she realizes it or not, Isla just revealed one of her truths. Determination fuels me to show her that not every man is a liar. I realize that's ironic since I've thought every woman was a liar on more than one occasion after the crap Candace and Georgia pulled on me. Maybe a friendship with Isla could be healing for both of us.

ME

Well, actions always speak louder than
words. I'll just have to show you.

A minute or two passes without a response, and I know I need to change the subject before I lose her entirely. Time to bring this conversation to safer subjects.

ME

> Are you going to the silent auction dinner next week? They invited all the date winners. We could discuss the assembly more then.

ISLA

> I don't know if I'm up for a big, fancy dinner.

> I'd really like you to come. Please? It'll be fun. Promise.

> You'd really like me to come, or your friends would really like me to come?

Well, shit. I deserve that. On the plus side, this gives me a chance to fix my mistake from the other day.

ME

> I'm an ass, aren't I?

ISLA

> No comment.

> I'd really like you to come. To the dinner, and to a game. You're not the only one with a shitty dating history, and I've sort of forgotten how to behave around a woman. Not that I'm saying that excuses my behavior because it doesn't. I'm sorry.

> It's okay. I get it.

> Don't get me wrong, the guys would love to see you, but I'm not asking for them. Please come.

> I'll think about it.

We can take another selfie for your social
media profiles. Really make your ex
jealous.

LOL! That would be a perk.

I'll even put my arm around your waist
and look as smitten as you want.

Smitten?

What?

Nothing…

Come on. Say you'll go.

Well, you did make sure my apartment
was creep-free the other day. I guess I
owe you.

No, you don't owe me anything. But I'd
like to see you.

Do I have to get all fancy?

It's not black tie or anything. Just don't
show up in a stained sweatshirt and I
think you'll be fine.

Do you have a spy cam in my apartment
or something? How'd you know what I
was wearing?

LOL. I was using my own wardrobe as an
example.

I don't buy it. I've seen the photos of you
in your suits. There's no way you own a
stained sweatshirt.

She's been looking at pictures of me? I grin like an idiot because maybe Isla Harding isn't as disinterested as she'd like to appear. Maybe, just maybe, I can convince her to be my friend. Or go on a date with me. A real one, not some awful auction date in a stuffy restaurant with the threat of an interview hanging over our heads. I want to take her somewhere fun and low-pressure. Fancy dinners are great once in a while, but they're not my thing. I'd pick a chill night out almost every time, and something tells me Isla is the same.

I want to see her let her hair down. I want to make her smile the way she did in her older Instagram posts.

With a wide grin, I tap the little camera icon in our text thread, switch it to selfie mode, and point at the stain near the collar of my sweatshirt. It's pizza sauce that never quite came out, but the hoodie is so broken in I can't bring myself to toss it. Why get rid of the most comfortable piece of clothing I own just because of a little sauce stain? That would be madness.

I send the photo and take another sip of my beer. It takes a moment to get anything back from her, but it's worth the wait.

She's fighting laughter in the selfie. She's makeup free, her hair is down and wilder than the two times I've seen her, and her blue eyes sparkle.

Hell, she's beautiful.

When I notice the stain on her hoodie—in almost the same spot as mine—I laugh loudly. The only difference is that hers looks like a red wine stain.

ISLA

Twinning!

ME

Maybe we should wear these to the
auction dinner.

It would certainly make a statement.

So you'll come?

I'll come.

God, I want to make a dirty joke about how I'll make
her come, but I hold myself back. I can't put my foot in my
mouth again. That doesn't stop the mental images of Isla
throwing her head back in a silent scream as she writhes
on my dick from making me hard. I'm always hard when I
think about her.

Guess I know how I'm ending this night. With my dick
in my fist.

ME

I'm going to hold you to that.

ISLA

Well, I wouldn't want to disappoint your
friends.

Well played.

I know.

ESPN is all but forgotten as we text back and forth for
another fifteen minutes. Then I tug down my sweatpants,
imagine Isla's beautiful body naked and kneeling at my
feet, ready to suck me down, and take my cock in my
hand. Using my thumb, I spread the bead of pre-cum
around my head. I wish it was Isla's tongue wetting my
shaft, but this will have to do for now. I'm painfully hard

from our banter, so it's not long before my body tightens with my impending release.

With every tug and stroke of my dick, I picture Isla's pretty little mouth taking me. Her muffled moans would fill the air as I pressed into her throat. Those delicate fingers of hers would clutch my ass, urging me deeper. She'd be greedy for me. Wild for me. A goddess amongst mortals.

My balls tighten seconds before my orgasm rips through me, and hot ropes of cum paint my abs.

If this is how turned on I am after texting this woman, I'm fucked. Doesn't mean I'll stop what I'm doing, though. Like Navarro said: I'm a goner.

# eighteen

*THURSDAY*

MADDOX

Do you think I could get away with
wearing a tracksuit to the auction dinner?

ISLA

Do you even own a tracksuit?

Nah. But I'm bored and doing some
online shopping. Everything 90s is
coming back into style, right? Those
Adidas tracksuits were huge back then.

No. If I have to wear a dress, you have to
wear a suit.

How about I have a tracksuit sent to your
place, too? We can twin for real.

Tempting.

Right? Coach would kill me.

> We don't want that to happen.

Are you saying you'd mourn me if I died in a Coach-related tragedy?

> Of course I would. Who else will take selfies with me and make my ex jealous?

That was cold, Isla.

> *shrugging emoji*

Wow. I see how you are. Gotta go to training. Have a good morning, Isla.

> Have a good training session, Maddox.

## *FRIDAY*

MADDOX

I meant to ask you the other day. Did you tell your friends about that asshole at the bar?

ISLA

> Yeah. They felt terrible about ditching me and flipped when I told them you guys took me home to make sure he hadn't stalked me.

Well, anytime you need someone to check for monsters under your bed, you know who to call.

> Griffin? Yeah, I've been meaning to ask you for his number.

Isla. No.

Kidding, kidding. You'll be the first person
I call.

Good. I mean it, though. If you ever need
something, call me.

Maddox...

Isla.

Fine. If I ever need to change a light bulb I
can't reach, I'll call you.

That's got to be all of them. You're kinda
short.

OMG! Rude. Good night, Maddox.

Night, Short-Stack.

No.

LOL.


## SUNDAY

ISLA

I saw your face on the side of a bus
today.

MADDOX

And you've been thinking about me ever
since?

Yeah. I've been thinking it's probably a
pretty accurate size representation of
your ego.

You wound me.

Someone as short as me couldn't possibly wound someone with a head as big as yours.

Touché, Short-Stack.

OMG. Do not call me that at the dinner next Saturday.

I make no promises.

## *WEDNESDAY*

MADDOX

What's your favorite color?

ISLA

Hi to you too. Emerald green. Why?

Just wondering.

Okaaay…

The guys say hi, BTW.

Hi, guys! Will they be at the dinner?

We'll all be there. Attendance is mandatory.

I guess that makes sense.

GTG. Talk to you later.

## *FRIDAY*

ISLA

Are you sure I have to go to this thing
tomorrow?

MADDOX

Don't tell me you're chickening out. Do I
need to come pick you up?

No, Nevaeh and Jess are coming with
me. I'm just nervous.

Why? You have nothing to be nervous
about.

The rich and powerful aren't really my
crowd. I don't want to embarrass anyone.
Or myself.

What in the world are you talking about?
You won't embarrass anyone.

You don't know that.

You're beautiful, smart, and engaging. I
do know that.

You're just saying that so I don't back out.

I'm saying that because it's the truth.
Who the hell made you worry you'd be an
embarrassment? If your friends said
something like that to you, then you need
new friends.

No, no, it wasn't them. Forget I said
anything. It's stupid.

Did someone say that to you?

No, don't worry. So have you decided what suit you're going to wear? How many suits do you own, anyway?

A lot. I like to change it up for game days. But don't think I'm going to let you change the subject that easily.

What's your favorite suit?

*sigh* Fine. I'll drop it for now. I have different favorites for different occasions.

Tell me more.

Well, I have this black suit with bright orange jack-o'-lanterns on it...

# nineteen

## ISLA

I'M NERVOUS. CHOOSING MY OUTFIT FOR THIS evening was far too big an ordeal. I tried on seven different dresses before settling on a deep peacock green number. It makes my eyes pop, my skin glow, and my hair looks amazing against the rich color. It's pinned in a loose chignon at the base of my head with artfully arranged tendrils escaping the style around my face and neck. My eye makeup is smokey, my skin looks dewy with just enough highlighter to shimmer without looking ridiculous, and my lips are a bright red.

No matter how many times I tell myself I'm worried about looking my best because there will be photographers and reporters at the dinner tonight, I know the truth. Because every time I think about Maddox and the flirty texts he's been sending me all week, my stomach erupts in a flurry of butterflies. He's snuck past my defenses, and that scares the hell out of me. It's exciting, too, but scary.

*He just wants to be friends*, I tell myself. *That's all you should want too*, I say in my head again and again.

I'm a terrible liar.

I'm even more nervous because the photo I posted of Maddox and me went a bit viral. There were thousands of comments on it. Some kind, some not. Some were just downright disgusting. The dumb football players in high school who were obsessed with finding out if my pubes matched my hair are in good company. There are a lot of disgusting men on the internet.

I blocked all the random strangers who started following me because of the photo and set my profile to private. The attention made me uncomfortable, and I'm worried someone will bring it up at dinner tonight.

My vague caption had the desired effect. There is a hell of a lot of speculation about Maddox and me now. It's just a lot of nosey strangers doing the wondering instead of Alex like I'd hoped. Who knows if he's seen the photo?

Or if he'll care.

I'm swiping on one final coat of mascara when my phone buzzes. Nev and Jess are here. I slip into my gold heels, grab my purse and a soft wrap in case the night turns chilly, and head out of my apartment.

"Oh. My. God." Jess squeals when I slide into the car. "You look so stunning. I mean, wow."

"Thanks," I say with a chuckle.

"You really do," Nev agrees, grinning at me from the driver's seat. "Maddox Graves won't know what hit him."

"This isn't for Maddox."

"Suuuuure it's not." Nev winks at me. Whatever. Even I don't believe that. Still, I roll my eyes and don't admit to the truth. They would never shut up about it if I did.

"You guys look hot. Planning on picking up a hockey player?"

Jess laughs. "I wouldn't mind. Have you seen photos of Ryder Hanson? He's a rookie this year, but he already has a huge female following. He's hot. Plus, I hear a few of them are bona fide sex gods."

"Yes," Nevaeh agrees. "Like Griffin Wright? I've heard he's an absolute beast in bed."

That has me laughing. Griffin? The goofy blond with endless jokes and pure golden-retriever energy is a beast in bed? Somehow I can't see it. A good time, sure, but a beast?

"What?" Nev narrows her eyes at me. "Why are you laughing?"

"Nothing, he's just... Griffin's so not your type."

She and Jess exchange a loaded look before pinning me with the full weight of their attention.

"What? Can we just go? We're going to be late."

"Hold on. What do you mean, he's not my type? How would you know that, Isla?"

I shrug. "I told you I hung out with Maddox and some of the guys last Saturday when they rescued me from that awful shithead, Blake. Griffin was there."

Nevaeh squeals as she pulls out of my building's parking lot. "Who else was there?"

"Um, Sebastian and Logan. I think the four of them are good friends. At least, that's the impression I got. They're all really nice, but total players. Well, maybe not Sebastian. He seemed quieter and chill. Less fuckboy." I could see him and Maddox being close. They probably hang out and play video games or sit in the same room and read books while Griffin and Logan are out screwing anything with a half-decent pair of boobs and two brain cells to rub together.

"You have to introduce us," Jess says. "Ohmygod, what if we all ended up with sexy hockey players? We could triple date."

That earns a snort of laughter from me. "Good luck. I don't get the impression that they're the dating type."

Jess considers it for a moment as her brows furrow. "That's okay. How many guys are on the team? Like twenty, right? Plenty of dick to choose from."

"Never pegged you two as jersey chasers."

"Normally we wouldn't be, but after we won that date for you with Maddox, we went on a bunny trail. We spent like three days staring at photos of the team, even watched a couple games online."

"Really?" That surprises me. None of us are all that sporty, and I can't remember the last time either of my friends expressed even the smallest interest in any kind of game.

Jess nods. "Yep. And the whole suits-on-game-day thing?" She fans her face. "Seriously, Isla. Those men wear the hell out of those suits. I mean, damn."

That I could see. They're all tall and muscular, and I've seen Maddox in a suit. Jess is right. Maddox wears the suit. When Alex wore one? The suit wore him. It's the difference between a man and a boy.

"Well, good luck with that. Every other woman in the building will have the same idea, but you two certainly look hot tonight. I'm sure you'll snag one of them." As soon as I say the words, my stomach tightens uncomfortably because I know I'm right.

Most of the women there will be on the prowl, hoping

to catch the players' attention. Maddox has been texting and joking around with me, but will he even look my way when he's surrounded by prettier, more confident women? Probably not. And that's okay. That's fine. Maddox isn't my type, anyway. He just wants to be my friend, and that's all I want, too.

Maybe if I keep telling myself that, I'll finally believe it. Physically, Maddox is everyone's type. But after he agreed to speak at my school and then saved me from a scary jerk, my attraction to him became more than physical.

All too soon, we're stepping out of Nevaeh's car at the valet station. My stomach is a tangle of nerves, and I can't stop fidgeting.

"Come on," Jess says, grabbing my hand. "Let's go have some fun. This is just a fancy night out with the girls. No dates, no pressure, no expectations."

A few photographers snap photos of the important-looking guests as they walk down the red carpet leading into the arena. They shout a few names, ask a few questions, and their cameras flash brightly. At least no one will bother taking photos of me. I'm not rich or important.

"Isla Harding?" a young woman calls out as the girls and I make our way up the carpet. "Is it true you're dating Maddox Graves? Can you tell us how long you've been in a relationship?"

Oh, no. That stupid Instagram post. I stammer, at a loss for words because I never expected any of these people to have seen that photo, let alone ask about it. Cameras flash at us. Jess tugs at my hand.

"Just ignore them," Jess whispers in my ear. "Smile and show them what a babe you are, but ignore the questions."

I try to do as she says, but I'm sure my smile looks

forced and the only color left in my face is the blush I brushed on over my foundation.

"Tell us," that same reporter calls as we pass her, "are you worried that Maddox will break your heart like he's broken his previous girlfriends'?"

My chest tightens as we step into the arena's massive foyer. Am I worried Maddox will break my heart? Of course, I would be. If there was anything between us. But her words, spoken so casually, are like a splinter in my palm I can't quite see. It burrows under my skin and stings. Could she so easily see that I'm the kind of girl who ends up broken-hearted and left in the dust? Are the words *stepping stone* blinking in neon over my head? If my dating life were a horror movie, would the audience know the first moment I stepped onto the screen that I'm not *final girl* material?

"Hey." Nevaeh tugs me over to the side of the coat check so we're not in anyone's way. "Where'd you go?"

"What? I'm fine."

My best friend eyes me skeptically. "You sure?"

"Totally. Should we grab a glass of champagne from one of those servers before heading upstairs?" *Please don't call me on my deflection.*

She and Jess stare at me for another moment before deciding it may be best to let whatever's bothering me go. Hopefully, they assume I'm just overwhelmed by being recognized. Maybe they think I'm panicking that the world is curious about my dating life. And that's all true. But I don't need them to know the core of it. They've been worried enough about my headspace since Alex broke things off with me.

My mind wanders to the strands of blonde hair in his

Instagram post. I never should have looked at his feed. Even if he's not with someone else, it's clear he's moved on. I should move on, too.

The problem is, I'm terrified of being hurt like that again. If anyone asks, I'm happy to list out the myriad reasons I'm not ready to date. They all sound healthy and empowering, and usually, it gets people to back off and stop asking. Which is what I want.

But the real list? The real list has only one reason on it. One paralyzing reason I haven't started dating again.

I can't shake the fear that Alex left me because I'm not enough. Because I'm unlovable. And if he could see that, someday everyone else will, too.

# twenty



WE MAKE OUR WAY UPSTAIRS TO A MASSIVE, OPEN area. It's filled with circular tables covered in ivory table-cloths, hockey-themed centerpieces, and twinkle lights that hang from the ceiling. It's surprisingly beautiful for the inside of a hockey arena. All along the outer edge of the space are long rectangular tables covered in signed paraphernalia, plaques describing services you can bid on, tickets to games, and so much more. People dressed in designer clothes linger before each display. Some scan QR codes with their phones and bid while others window shop.

Jess and Nevaeh *ooh* and *ahh* over everything while I scan the room for Maddox. Or any of the other guys. They should be here, and it'll be nice to see them again. Except, I can't find any of them. There are so many people crowded together. They may be mingling. Or maybe

Maddox changed his mind and isn't coming after all. I inwardly kick myself for how disappointed that thought makes me, and my shoulders sag.

"Who are you looking for?" A deep voice whispers in my ear, so close that the hot brush of his breath on my neck makes me shiver.

I try to hide the massive smile tugging at my lips because the last thing Maddox Graves needs is something else to inflate his already generous ego. "No one," I lie, only turning my head toward him enough to be heard over the hum of the crowd.

"So you're not hoping to spot a devilishly handsome center in an Adidas tracksuit?"

I laugh, turning to take him in, because if he's really wearing a tracksuit, I'm going to demand he go buy me a set, too. Sparkling brown eyes meet mine, and those full lips of his quirk when I look him up and down. I can't decide if I'm more disappointed that he's not wearing a tracksuit, or startled when I notice the color of the tie he's paired with his fitted navy suit. Emerald green. My favorite.

"You look stunning," he murmurs. There's no denying the heated appreciation of his gaze as he takes me in. "Every time I see you, it's like you've become more beautiful."

My cheeks flush hot, and I drop his gaze. I thought I'd gotten over the embarrassment his flirting brings on, but I guess that only applies to text flirting. In the real world, I can't play it cool to save my life. "Thank you. You look pretty handsome yourself."

And he does. God, he does.

He's wearing expensive brown leather dress shoes without socks. On any normal man, I'd think it a strange stylistic choice, but on Maddox? It somehow works. His pants are fitted and slim, hugging every defined muscle of his legs. His shirt is a crisp, bright white, and perfectly tailored. The jacket he's wearing is open, showing off that green tie. Swallowing hard, I do my best to ignore the pulse of desire throbbing between my thighs. When I summon enough courage to look up at him again, he's smiling knowingly. It's not a smug smile, though. No, I'd almost call that smile affectionate.

We stare at each other for a beat longer than could be considered normal before I hear my name being called enthusiastically from a few feet away.

"Damn, Isla, looking good!" Griffin offers me a blinding smile. He jokingly elbows Maddox out of the way so he can steal my attention. Of course, this has my friends turning around. I try not to giggle when Nevaeh's mouth drops open and Jess's eyes widen. Because it's not just Griffin who's wandered over to say hello, it's Sebastian and Logan, too. And while none of them hold a candle to Maddox, I can admit they all look damned good in their suits.

"Oh. My. God," Nev whispers as she stares at Griffin. He grins but has the good sense not to draw attention to her blatant fangirling.

"Hey, Griffin. Hi, guys. You all look pretty good yourselves." I lean in tentatively when Griffin opens his arms to hug me. Maddox makes a disgruntled sound low in his throat, and my stomach flips. Sebastian and Logan don't offer hugs, no doubt sensing their friend's displeasure, but they do offer bright smiles and nods.

"Who are these lovely ladies with you?" Logan asks. "Are these the famous best friends we've heard so much about?"

"Yes, these are my best friends. Guys, meet Jess and Nevaeh." I motion to my besties before pointing at Griffin. "Jess and Nev, this is Griffin, Sebastian, and Logan. And this"—I tug Maddox from behind Griffin—"is Maddox."

They all exchange pleasantries while Logan waves a server over to replace our now-empty champagne flutes with fresh bubbly. The guys are sweet, engaging my friends in animated conversation until they're pulled away to speak with other guests. Maddox rubs his jaw, clearly unhappy about being summoned along with them.

"Would you sit next to me at dinner?"

The breath catches in my lungs, but I manage a nod. "Yeah, of course."

His answering smile is blinding. I'd be lying if I claimed it didn't make me weak in the knees. Then again, I'd challenge any woman even remotely attracted to men not to swoon when he looks at you that way. With another glower toward the teammate I've never met who's calling him over, Maddox runs his gaze up and down my form, lingering on my lips for an extra moment before he excuses himself.

"Holy Chris Hemsworth," Jess hisses. "He's totally into you!"

"He's not," I reply. The denial is reflexive, but even I'm not buying it when Maddox keeps glancing my way. And that's on top of all the text flirting we've been doing.

"Oh, he so is." Nevaeh looks like a kid on Christmas morning, staring at a pile of presents as big as she is. "And you're into him too."

I scoff at that. "Right. I'm into the guy who ignored me on our date."

"No," Jess says, drawing out the word. "You're into the guy who saved you from an obnoxious creep. The guy who's staring at you like he's a starving man and you're his favorite meal." She arches one well-manicured eyebrow at me. "And did he know that shade of green is your favorite color?"

The blush staining my cheeks is answer enough.

"Chris on a cracker." Jess's attention volleys between Maddox and me. "He wore a tie in your favorite color on purpose? Yeah. He wants you."

"It's just a tie." It's not, and I know it. But if I admit how much that small gesture made my heart gallop in my chest, I will no longer be able to float lazily down the river denial.

"And Chris Hemsworth is just a guy." Jess shakes her head at me.

"You're obsessed."

"Duh. Want to know who else is obsessed? Maddox Graves. With you."

And maybe Jess is on to something, because every time I glance at him, he's looking at me. It's like I'm back in high school desperately trying to control myself and my wandering eyes that keep lingering on Mike Menski as he leans against his locker, chatting with the guys in his band. The problem is, the more you think about *not* doing something, the more you want to do it. And as much as I'm loath to admit it, I really want to look at Maddox Graves. I want him to look at me. Hell, every time I catch his eyes on me, there's a voice in my head growing louder and louder that says I want him to devour me.

I shake my head to clear the lusty thoughts because this is the real world, not some bodice-ripper. Men like Maddox don't want to devour women like me.

Right?

The girls and I make small talk with a few people they recognize. We smile and cluster together for photographs, peruse the silent-auction offerings that are way outside of my means, and nibble on finger foods when servers pass by with trays full of spanakopita and bacon-wrapped scallops. I'm staring at a plaque offering a weekend in Vail to the highest bidder and imagining what it would be like to have the money to jet off and do something so extravagant when Griffin sidles up next to me.

"Going to bid on that?"

Hopefully my laugh doesn't sound bitter. I've made choices with my life and I don't regret them. I'm just feeling some FOMO. "God, no. I can barely afford groceries some weeks on my teacher's salary. Pretty sure anything I put on a weekend in Vail would be out-bid in a heartbeat." Squinting at the perfectly retouched photos of smiling skiers, I add, "Plus, I have no idea how to ski. I'd probably break my neck or crash crotch-first into a tree like some uncoordinated cartoon character."

Griffin lets out a guffaw of laughter and cradles his dick. "Ouch. Yeah, maybe no skiing, then."

"The hot air balloon ride over the city is more my speed."

"Oh, yeah?" Griffin looks at the offering beside the weekend in Colorado. It's a romantic balloon ride at sunset with champagne, gourmet dessert, and cozy blankets to keep you warm in the air. "I'm totally afraid of heights. You wouldn't want me to go in something like that. I'd be leaning over the side, puking on some poor sap below within minutes."

I can't help wrinkling my nose at that. "Gross."

"Right?" He shivers. "One time I went on that huge Ferris wheel at Navy Pier in Chicago with the boys and I yacked all over Logan when our car stopped at the top." Griffin stares off into space as though reliving it. "He beat the shit out of me when we got back on the ground. And by that time, everyone was trying hard not to puke too, because it smelled *rank* in that enclosed car." His gaze slides back to me and a massive smile transforms his face into something boyish. "Good times."

That has me laughing. "That's your definition of good times?"

"Hell yeah. Out with my boys, living life, pissing Logan off... On second thought, those weren't just good times, they were the *best* times."

"Whatever you say," I reply, smiling so wide my cheeks hurt. That seems to be a theme around Maddox's golden-haired friend. He doesn't seem to take life very seriously. Thinking of Maddox has me seeking him out in the crowd. I try not to stiffen when I find him in the center of a group of gorgeous women. They're all tall and model-thin, and probably loaded. My smile falters when a leggy blonde laughs, pressing her hand to his chest. Maddox doesn't push the touch away. Of course, he doesn't push her touch away.

"He hates this kind of thing," Griffin says, catching the direction of my gaze, and likely my thoughts. "And he *hates* when women like that fawn all over him." Maddox smiles at one woman when she says something witty and throws her head back in laughter.

"He doesn't look like he hates it."

I can feel Griffin studying me, but I don't look his way. Instead, I continue to torture myself and watch those gorgeous women throw themselves at Maddox. "Look at his hands. See how he keeps clenching his fists?" My attention drops to find Maddox doing just that. He balls his hands into fists, clenches, then releases them, only to repeat the process. "He's trying not to say something rude because Coach would have his ass if he wasn't nice and attentive to everyone wanting a bit of attention from him. Trust me, he's miserable."

Just then, Maddox meets my gaze. Brown eyes search my face, and his brow furrows at whatever he finds. His previous smile slips quickly into a scowl and he shuffles his weight from one foot to the other.

"He just noticed the frown marks between your eyebrows and now he wants to ditch the jersey-chasers and storm over here to make sure I didn't say something stupid to upset you." Griffin laughs gleefully.

We both watch as the blonde woman places her hand on Maddox again. This time, she lightly drags it down his bicep, before letting it rest on his forearm. My frown deepens, and this time Maddox does brush her hand away. "Here he comes in three. Two. One."

And sure enough, by the time Griffin hits *one*, Maddox excuses himself from the crowd of fawning women and crosses the room with a purposeful stride.

"What's wrong? Did Griffin call you a TILF?"

There's a beat of silence as my brain processes that. Then Griffin and I double over with laughter. "TILF? What the hell, Griffin?"

The man shrugs between bouts of laughter. "I meant it

from Maddox's perspective." As Maddox's face grows dark with irritation, Griffin only laughs harder. It's infectious.

"What are you two cackling about?" Maddox turns to me. "And why did you look upset?" He reaches up and smooths the skin between my eyebrows with his thumb, even though I'm too busy laughing to still have frown lines. Maddox's fan club watches our exchange with less-than-lovely glowers, but he's too focused on me to notice. The tightening in my chest loosens.

"I'm fine," I say between gasping breaths. "Griffin didn't say anything to upset me."

"Then why were you frowning?"

I can't tell him the truth. It would be too pathetic. The problem is, I can't seem to think of anything else to say. Which means I'm standing there, mouth open, utterly silent.

"You know how sometimes we're on the road and it's late at night and we're all a little drunk so we turn on those tele-novellas?" Griffin shoots me a wink, silently telling me to go along with whatever he's about to say. "Well, I was doing that. I just made the blonde over there say something ridiculous and Isla was frowning because she was trying to get in character as you."

There's no hiding the *super* graceful snort I let out. "Uh, yep. Just getting in the right headspace to come up with lines for a big grumpy hockey player."

Maddox arches one eyebrow at us both and crosses his arms over his chest. "Is that so?"

"Yep," Griffin says. His smile is utter mischief. It has Maddox rubbing his temples.

"I'm going to regret introducing the two of you, aren't

I?" He doesn't mean it, though. His fond expression makes that clear.

I turn to Maddox. "Is it true Griffin puked all over Logan at the top of a giant Ferris wheel?"

Maddox groans. "Yeah, I'm definitely going to regret it."

# twenty-one

## ISLA

IN NO TIME AT ALL, A HANDFUL OF ADMIRERS surround Jess and Nev. I try to hide my smirk as I hang back. I'd rather grab a snack from a passing server and do some people-watching than wade into the thick of it with my friends. I don't want to spoil it for them. They're in their element.

Neither of my best friends spent their college years in a serious relationship like I did, so they're far more confident and comfortable making small talk and flirting with random men. I'd throw them off their game because they'd feel like they had to talk me up to some guy, and they'd lose the chance to make a connection of their own.

My eyes wander to where Maddox talks to a few men in suits. They're representatives of a company he's trying to nail down for a sponsorship deal. He excused himself with a torn expression about fifteen minutes ago. Even though the conversation sounds important, his gaze still flicks back to me every minute or two.

And that's the other reason I have no desire to flirt with the guys around my friends. I'm too caught up in the flutter of nerves Maddox causes in my belly. Between the flirty texts and the way he's treated me so far tonight, I'm seriously rethinking my no-dating stance. He's already proven he's not like Alex, hasn't he?

Alex never glanced over to check on me when he was deep in a conversation that could further his career. And we'd been engaged. Maddox and I aren't even dating and I instinctively know that if I need him, he'd ditch the sponsorship conversation and make sure I was okay. Not that I'd do that.

My mind whirrs as I overanalyze everything. I'm lost in my head. Which is why I don't hear my name being spoken at first.

"Isla? Hey, I thought that was you. What are you doing here?"

It takes a moment for his voice to register as familiar, but when it does, I'm plunged back into my past with bruising force. I know the owner of that voice all too well. At one point, I'd considered him a close friend. A brother, almost. I slowly turn, bracing myself. What is he doing here? "Jackson, oh my god, hi."

Alex's best friend gives me that signature lopsided smile I once found endearing. Now all I feel is a curdling sense of dread. If Jackson is here, does that mean Alex is, too? Oh, god. No. No, no, no, no, no. Alex is the very last person I want to see. I'll either end up crying or punching him in the dick—probably punching—and neither is socially acceptable in this setting.

My eyes bounce to Jess and Nevaeh for backup and possibly a quick escape, but they're too absorbed in their conversations to realize I'm beginning to panic. Jackson takes a step forward as if to hug me, then thinks better of it. Instead, he runs his hand through his short, dark waves, and his smile morphs into more of a grimace.

"I'm surprised to see you here," he says. "I don't remember you being much of a sports fan. And I definitely wouldn't have pegged you as a hockey fan. Kind of a violent sport, isn't it?" He's fishing for information. No doubt he's already planning his call to Alex. Will he tell Alex that I looked good? Or will they laugh about how I stood alone in a crowded room like the pathetic loser Alex always knew me to be?

Oh, God, this is my nightmare.

"Oh, yeah, I, uh... I have some friends on the team." There. Hopefully, that makes me sound less pathetic. And if the way Jackson's eyebrows hit his hairline is any indication, it does. He wasn't expecting that. Which means Alex must not have seen the photo of Maddox and me. Surely he would have mentioned it to his best friend if he had.

"Really? Who?"

I blow out a breath while wrapping my arms around myself. I don't want to get caught up in conversation with Jackson. The friendship that used to be easy and fun disappeared the day Alex broke up with me. A line was drawn in the sand, and no one ended up on my side of it. "Um, well, Maddox, Griffin, Logan, and Sebastian."

It's not a lie. They called me one of them. They inspected my apartment for creeps and Griffin told me embarrassing stories. They want me to come to one of their games. I'm not claiming anything one of them wouldn't. I hope.

Jackson's eyes go wide and he gives me a more appraising look. I drop my arms to my side and straighten my spine. His perusal communicates his disbelief. He'll probably tell Alex I've lost it and am making up lies about being friends with famous hockey players in some desperate bid to make him jealous. Which is *such* bullshit, even if it was sort of true initially.

My indignation flares. Maybe it's unwarranted, but I'm so sick of feeling *less than*.

Jackson used to be cool. Now he's just a near-stranger who probably knows the woman with the long blonde hair in Alex's beach photos.

"So, how exactly did you meet the four best players on the Minnesota Rogues? This must be a great story." Jackson leans in while taking a sip of whatever he's drinking.

Shit. What am I going to tell him? Not the truth, that's for damned sure.

*Oh, I met Maddox on a blind date because Jess and Nevaeh won it at a date auction. They were worried about how pathetic I've been ever since your bestie left me with a broken heart and thousands of dollars in wedding expenses I'll never recoup. So they literally paid someone to go out with me.*

My gaze jumps to Maddox, only to find him already watching me. He's glaring at Jackson, but when my wide, probably panicked-looking eyes meet his, the muscles in his jaw tick and he excuses himself from his conversation. In no time at all, he's crossed the room, and his hand rests on the small of my back. It's a possessive gesture, and it reminds me of the way he stepped in at Skin and Tonic. But when he rubs his fingers up and down my spine, I wonder if this time it's real. It sure feels that way.

I can't help it. I melt into his touch. The smallest sigh of relief leaves my lips, and Maddox's hand moves to my hip, where he gives me a squeeze.

"I'm sorry," Maddox says as he searches my face. "I didn't mean for that conversation to keep me away as long as it did. No more business tonight, I promise."

Maddox is coming to my rescue again. Maybe he's playing a part, but he said the magic words and my heart thaws. I'm Sleeping Beauty coming back to life after Prince Charming's kiss. Never once did Alex make that kind of promise to me. Never once did he leave a conversation that could have led to more money or new connections just to make sure I was okay.

The walls I've fortified around my heart to keep Maddox Graves out crumble.

"You didn't have to do that. I know that sponsorship is important."

Jackson watches our exchange with a furrowed brow and rapt attention, but Maddox doesn't care. Right now, he's only got eyes for me, and he speaks the next words so gently that he must mean them.

"Isla, I can make an appointment to talk contracts. You're important. I've been looking forward to this dinner with you all week." A mischievous grin lights up his features, and he leans in so only I can hear. "Besides, you're so much more beautiful than Mark is. I'd rather be with you."

Yep. The walls have crumbled, and the little soldier

who guards my heart just rolled out the red carpet for Maddox. God help me if he's only playing a part right now.

We stare at each other for a few beats until a throat clearing brings me back to reality. Jackson. Right. Alex's best friend.

"Oh my god, I'm so sorry," I say, turning to him with an apologetic smile. "Jackson, this is Maddox Graves. Maddox, this is Jackson Campbell. My ex, Alex's best friend."

Maddox's eyes widen for a fraction of a second as all the pieces click into place. He turns to Jackson with a smile I'm coming to recognize as the one he gives fans and strangers. It doesn't quite soften his face the way his genuine smiles do. The skin around his eyes doesn't crinkle adorably, and his lips are tight. He holds out a hand for Jackson to shake. "Nice to meet you."

Jackson looks visibly star-struck but quickly composes himself and grasps Maddox's hand. "Nice to meet you, too. I was just asking Isla here how the two of you met."

Maddox chuckles, giving my hip a reassuring squeeze. "Oh, well, we met at a restaurant and, of course, I was stunned by her beauty. But once I started chatting with her, it became clear she's so much more than just a beautiful face. I practically begged her to have dinner with me. It wasn't easy to convince her, but she eventually took pity on me. Now here we are." His hand snakes up my spine before his fingers tangle in my hair at the nape of my neck. The graze of his fingertips along my skin lights me up in ways I've never experienced.

Jackson tracks the gesture and shifts on his feet. His tone is a bit disbelieving when he speaks. "Wow. That's great. I had no idea you were dating anyone, Isla. You two look really happy together." He turns to me. "I'm glad you're doing well. I'm sure Alex will be glad to hear it, too. He worries about you."

My back stiffens—because what the actual hell?—but before I can even contemplate a retort, Maddox is there.

"He obviously never really knew Isla if he thinks he needs to worry about her." Maddox's fingers massage my scalp and I relax into him again. "I've never met a more badass, capable, stunning woman. Hell, I'm just grateful she's found some enjoyment in spending time with me. I know what gifts her time and attention are."

Jackson clears his throat. "I didn't mean—"

"I'm sure you didn't," Maddox says with a chillier tone than he'd previously used. He presses a kiss to my temple. My heart thunders and my eyes flutter. "But there are so many men out there who take women like Isla for granted. It's pathetic, don't you think?"

The little soldier guarding my heart is throwing a ticker tape parade in Maddox's honor.

It's clear Maddox's insult has hit its mark when Jackson winces. I'm not sure what he thought about how Alex treated me or the way he broke up with me. Jackson is Alex's friend first and foremost, and he always was. But given the flash of shame that plays across his face, I'd hazard a guess that at least some part of him thought Alex's actions were shitty. "For sure. Well, my colleague is waving me over. It really was good to see you, Isla. And nice to meet you, Maddox."

"Enjoy the rest of the night," Maddox says with a nod of his head. Jackson returns the gesture before hurrying off. When he's out of earshot, Maddox faces me, and with just that small action, everyone else in the room ceases to exist. His rich brown eyes are concerned as he studies my features for any signs of distress. His hand slips out from my hair and he grazes his fingers along my cheek. "You okay?"

"Yeah," I reply honestly. "I am. Thanks to you." And I'm relieved to realize it's true. I'm only a bit shaken, but all in all, I'm totally fine.

"Can I hug you?" Maddox asks. His voice is gruff, but his expression is soft.

I nod, trying not to reveal how affected I am by the offer. "I'd like that. A lot." Strong arms wrap around me and press me into a firm chest. I allow myself to melt into his hug and enjoy the sensation of safety that accompanies the embrace. Safety that allows a murmured confession to spill from my lips. "I wasn't expecting to see him here. I worried Alex might have been here, too."

"I figured as much when you looked over at me in a panic." Maddox releases me, but he still stands close enough that the length of our arms touch. If I so much as twitched my fingers, they'd intertwine with his. "I hope I didn't overstep."

"No." I meet his gaze. "You were perfect."

My whole body tingles from the intensity of Maddox's gaze. We're standing so close, and he's looking at me with hooded eyes. Every one of my cells vibrates. They're practically screaming at him to kiss me. Everything else is far away.

But then someone laughs loudly nearby, and the spell shatters. We're not alone. In fact, we're surrounded by people watching Maddox's every move. There's at least one reporter outside who would love to get some juicy gossip about the two of us. Gossip I don't want to have to deal with. This is not the time and place to lose myself to desire. Even if Maddox looks just as eager to get lost as I do.

He clears his throat and looks around. "I think it's almost time for the dinner."

I giggle softly and nod. It's probably safer to change the subject to something innocuous like dinner. But inside, I'm ready to drag Maddox out of this room and somewhere more private so we can devour each other. Dinner be damned.

# twenty-two

## ISLA

There are no assigned seats for dinner, so it feels like the grownup version of musical chairs. As the night wears on, people shift their positions in the room, trying to get closer to whomever they hope to chat with over a long four-course meal.

I don't miss the calculating expressions of several women as they eye Maddox from his post beside me. He hasn't left since coming to my rescue with Jackson. The interaction seemed to flip some switch in him. Hell, it did for me, too. Feeling anything past friendship is a risk, but I can't seem to stop myself. It's impossible to be indifferent. Griffin, Logan, and Sebastian have all spent time talking and laughing with us, though they come and go.

I've heard a few women whispering my name. Apparently, my stupid Instagram post is becoming a hot topic of conversation. They're wondering if Maddox and I are dating. And by the looks I'm getting, none of them are happy that they have to speculate. After all, when they put out the money to attend, Maddox was single and free. Now? They're not sure, and his behavior toward me confirms their suspicions.

Maddox alternates between running his fingers up and down my spine, resting his hand on the small of my back, and brushing my fingers with his. I can barely focus on the conversations I'm supposed to be taking part in. Everywhere his fingers touch, my skin sings with electricity and heat. I shift on my feet as my panties grow more and more damp and I ignore my growing arousal because there are far too many eyes on us.

Actually, maybe this is more like a crowded watering hole in an African desert than a game of musical chairs. It's a lot like that scene in *Mean Girls*. Predatory women eye their prey with hungry expressions. They're on the hunt for big game, and I'm standing between them and their meal. Either way, it's a struggle not to shrink in on myself with every passing moment.

"Are you okay?" Maddox's nose drags along the skin behind my ear as he whispers the word. A pleasant shiver works down my spine. When I look up, I find his body angled toward mine. The sole focus of his attention.

There's no denying we've crossed some invisible line. I can't lie to myself anymore. Maddox Graves doesn't want to be my friend. If his half-lidded eyes are any indication, he wants to make me his. Having the full force of Maddox's attention is heady, and even the insecurities the gorgeous women around me inspire fade away under his gaze. To give whatever this is between us a chance.

"I'm fine," I tell him. "I just…" Do I tell him about the Instagram post and the fact that more people saw it than I ever imagined would? I don't want him to see me as some gold-digger who's only using him for his status.

"You know how we took those selfies so I could make my ex feel like crap?" Maddox nods. His expression is serious, and my chest tightens. "Well, my Instagram wasn't set to private, and I wasn't thinking. I posted one of the pictures and it sort of went a bit viral. I blocked all the random people who followed me and set my account to private, but there was a reporter outside who asked me if we were dating. And now these women are looking at me like I'm public enemy number one, which is really anti-girl-power of them, and I didn't mean to drag you into something like this, and a few of the comments on the photo were super gross guys asking if the carpet matches the drapes which I *hate* more than anything in the world, and I don't like being the center of that kind of attention, and I'm sorry if I embarrassed you…"

"Isla." Maddox's serious expression melts into one of soft amusement. "Take a breath, Short-Stack."

"Don't call me that."

He grins wider. "You didn't embarrass me. I saw the post. Well, my sister did and told me about it. Honestly, I was more worried about how it would affect you to get that kind of attention."

"Really?"

"Really. I've been in the public eye for a while, and I still hate a lot of what comes with it. People think that just because they've seen you play a game or read an interview or seen your social media posts, that they know you. They feel entitled to your life. It's weird and uncomfortable, and I've been on the wrong side of that attention a few times." He grimaces and my mind goes to the interview I read with his ex-girlfriend. "It can be difficult to ignore when people tell lies about you or make unkind comments. You have to remind yourself who you are, and surround yourself with people who care about you and see through the bullshit."

He's got to be talking about fake-tits-Candace. I want to hear his side of the story because the man he's been since pulling his head out of his ass is nothing like the man she described in her tell-all. "Will you tell me about it sometime?"

He considers me with a furrowed brow. "You read her interview."

"I did," I tell him. His face pinches with a flash of hurt, and now it's my turn to be there for him. I rest my hand on his chest. Right over his heart. "I may not know you all that well, but it's easy to see the things she claimed aren't true."

Maddox's eyes widen. He's surprised I don't believe the worst about him? I admit, he worked hard to paint himself as a bastard on our auction date, but I understand now. I'm not the only one throwing up walls to protect myself.

"You don't believe her? Even after the way I treated you when we first met?"

"Oh, you were an asshole at first." I grin, patting his chest again. "But you gave yourself away when you checked for monsters under my bed."

His face fills with light as his frown morphs into a dazzling smile. "Is that so?"

I nod. "Yep. It is."

"Does that mean you'd say yes if I asked you on a date? A real one. No best friends or auctions or awkward interviews afterward." Maddox's eyes sparkle.

"Let's just get through this dinner first. Then we can talk about potential dates." My heart does a pleasant flip, but I remove my hand from his chest when I notice eyes on us. Most of them are women who don't look happy, but Jackson's watching us, too. I wanted Alex to see that photo of Maddox and me when there was no potential for anything between us. That feeling has shifted. Now I don't want Alex to know. Whatever this is, it has nothing to do with him, and I don't want him tainting it.

Maddox's low chuckle rolls over my skin in spine-tingling waves. "Fine. We'll talk about it after dinner. But speaking of potential dates, we need to schedule that assembly. Have you talked to your boss?"

"Oh, yeah. I'm waiting for her to get back to me, but I think the first week of September would work. That's still before your preseason officially starts, right?"

He nods. "Yeah. I mentioned it to Coach, and he thinks it's a great idea. He'll clear whatever date you need that week."

I open my mouth to tell him how much it means to me he hasn't forgotten his promise, but before I can get the words out, someone taps on a microphone. An elegant middle-aged woman stands in front of one of the silent auction tables.

"Good evening, ladies and gentlemen. My name is Tracy Butler, and I'd like to thank you on behalf of the Minnesota Rogues for your incredibly generous donations. You're all doing a world of good in our community, and we're honored to partner with you. Please finish placing any last-minute bids and find a seat. Dinner will be served shortly."

There's a collective inhalation, then everyone is in

motion. They try to move casually to snag seats near their favorite players, but there's a crackle of impatience in the air. Maddox moves with the assurance of a massive, ripped hockey player who knows people will get out of his way as he guides us to a table where Griffin already sits. There's a very excited-looking brunette next to him blinking so rapidly I idly worry she's having a stroke. Maddox pulls out the chair on Griffin's other side for me, then drapes his suit jacket over the back of the seat next to mine.

"I'll be right back," he murmurs in my ear. He watches me until I nod, then strides over toward the tables filled with expensive goods and experiences.

"Having more fun now?" Griffin asks, ignoring the woman beside him as she tries surreptitiously to press her boobs together for maximum cleavage. I grin at him. Not even Jackson's curiosity from the next table over dampens the lightness that's filled my chest since Maddox intervened in our discussion.

"I am," I reply easily. "Are you?"

Griffin grins brightly. "Hell, yeah. My dance card is full for the rest of the week."

I don't bother trying to stifle the snort that comes out with my laughter. Calling his scheduled hookups a dance card is so Griffin. Normally, that kind of talk would piss me off, but I don't get the sense that Maddox's teammate is treating any of these women maliciously. It's more that he doesn't take much seriously. And that includes relationships with the opposite sex. "Is that what we're calling it these days?"

His grin grows wider. "Sounds better than sex roster."

"You're not wrong," I reply with a chuckle.

The girl on Griffin's other side raises her hand. "You

can put me on your sex roster. I can do the splits and put both legs behind my head."

Griffin's eyes widen and he turns to her so slowly it might as well be slow-motion. He holds out a hand. "Hi there. My name's Griffin Wright. What's your name, darlin'?"

There's no holding back my laughter as the two of them discuss their favorite sex positions. Like it's as normal as commenting on the weather. It's utterly ridiculous and hilarious, but there's no denying the way my mind wanders to Maddox and all the kinky positions we could get into. He's so tall and muscular. I bet he could do that thing where the guy holds you up so you're straddling his face while he stands, then eats you out while you've got nothing to hold on to but his hair. Or shower sex that doesn't involve bending over while water drips into your eyes and nose. I know he'd be strong enough to pin me to the wall and pound into me while his fingers dig into my ass as he holds me up.

"Oh, I love anal," the brunette next to Griffin says. It's loud enough that several heads turn in her direction. "I have this super cute butt plug with a fox tail on it. I'll show you if you want."

Griffin hums *What Does the Fox Say* while he nods emphatically. "Oh, Quinoa, I *definitely* want to see that."

I nearly spit out my water and look at Griffin. He meets my wide-eyed gaze with a huge smirk as I mouth *her name is Quinoa?* He just shrugs and stifles a laugh.

Turning back to the ultra-flexible brunette named after a grain, he props his chin on his palm. "What's your stance on cock-rings?"

# twenty-three

## MADDOX

"Miss me?" I ask Isla as I take my seat beside her. She's glowing when she turns my way. A vibrant smile lights her face and her eyes crinkle at the corners. I knew I could trust Wright to make her laugh while I did what I needed to do. I'll have to thank him later.

He's a good friend, and he's got a great heart. Part of me wishes he'd stop wasting it on all these meaningless flings, but Griffin will grow up when he wants to grow up. He got it in his head back in college that he's cursed. Every single one of his relationships ended by their six-month anniversary, and he's taken it as a sign that he's not meant for anything serious. Even though I know the guy is a closet romantic. It's ridiculous, but nothing Sebastian or I have ever said has changed his mind. For now, I'm just happy he and the other guys have accepted Isla so easily and look out for her without being asked. It's a relief for me, but I think it's an even bigger relief for her.

I'm not sure many people look out for Isla outside of her two best friends, who sit across the large circular table, both chatting up Ryder Hanson and some of our other rookie team members. It sure as hell doesn't seem like her ex or their other friends did.

"Oh," Isla says with a chuckle, "were you gone?"

Griffin barks out a laugh, which I ignore, choosing instead to lean in so close to Isla that our noses practically touch. "That hurt my feelings, Short-Stack."

"Aww, I'm sowwy." She scrunches her nose. "Do you need me to make it better?"

I nod. "Heck yeah, I do. You know how you can make it all better, Isla?"

"How?" Her eyes glitter with amusement, but there's heat there, too. It makes my cock hard, and I have to remind myself that popping a stiffy in a crowded room is not ideal.

"There's really only one way. You'll have to kiss it better." Her eyes widen and I grin. I tap my lips with my pointer finger, showing her where she can kiss me.

Isla licks her lips, her attention going to mine for a moment before meeting my gaze again. She wants to kiss me. I know she does. I also know she won't do it. Not in front of all these people. "You carry your feelings in your lips, huh?"

I chuckle and tug playfully at a strand of her hair that's fallen loose. "Doesn't everyone?"

"Pretty sure Griffin carries his in his dick," she retorts, hooking a thumb in Wright's direction. Of course, he hears her.

"I totally do," he pipes up. "It can be hard to contain all of my feelings. They always want to come gushing out."

Isla's nose wrinkles again, this time in mock disgust. She turns her face to glance at my teammate, putting space between us. I instantly miss the heat of her. "Gross, Griffin."

"I thought it was funny," a brown-haired girl with huge boobs and fake lips says.

Griffin winks at me. "Thanks, Quinoa. I knew I could count on you."

"Did he just call that woman Quinoa?" I ask Isla, leaning in close so no one else can hear me.

"Yep." She pops the *p* sound at the end. "She's named after a grain and can put both legs behind her head while wearing a fox-tail butt plug. Clearly, that makes her Griffin's dream girl."

It takes a second for Isla's words to register because I'm lost in her beauty. She's so damned stunning when her face lights up with a huge smile and her eyes dance with mischief. But then my brain catches up. "I'm sorry, *what*?"

"I'm not sure you want to know," she tells me. And I think she's probably right. Besides, if the woman has any special sexual talents, I'll no doubt hear about them with the rest of the guys when Griffin recounts them. She glances at her friends, smiling when she sees them happily flirting away with the rookies.

"Are you having fun?"

She nods. The movement causes one of the curls framing her face to fall out of place, and I don't even think before reaching out and brushing it gently behind her ear. "I'm enjoying this more than I thought I would," she tells me quietly as we stare at each other.

"Me too," I admit. "This would have been miserable if you weren't here."

"Oh, I don't know." Her lips twitch up at the corner. "I'm sure you would have had just as much fun with your fan club."

She couldn't be more wrong. I hate the calculating touches and premeditated attention women like them give me. They don't care about who I am or what I have to say. I could spend twenty minutes going into graphic detail about the time I got a colonoscopy, and they'd titter and laugh like I was the funniest fucker on the planet. Maybe that does it for some guys, but not me. Especially not after everything with Candace and Georgia. Their affection was an act, just like everyone else's here would be—well, everyone except Isla—I was just too young and idealistic to see it, then. I'm not young and idealistic anymore. I'm a grizzled thirty-year-old with plenty of experience being used and betrayed.

What these women don't understand is that every flirtatious look and simpering word they throw my way makes my skin crawl. I don't want a woman who'll treat me like I can do no wrong. The thought of spending my life with a woman who'd rather placate me and ditch her passions in favor of becoming someone she thinks I want is abhorrent.

I was raised by a strong, fiery single mom who never took shit from anyone. After my dad left and she had to become everything to Mira and me, she embraced all the quirks that made her loud and powerful and unique. She became the woman she needed for herself. Not for anyone else. My sister is just as independent and confident, and they're my favorite women on the planet. They're who everyone else has to measure up to.

Which is why I'm so drawn to Isla. She called me on

my shit in the first twenty minutes of knowing me, and she's not afraid to set her boundaries. Granted, I have a feeling quite a lot of those are in response to whatever her ex put her through, but I still love that she doesn't hesitate to enforce them. She's not impressed with my status or money. Isla's the kind of person who's impressed by actions, not a bank account balance. She's a woman I want to know better. And I don't doubt that if my mom and sister ever meet her, they'll want to know her better, too.

Isla chuckles, drawing me out of my thoughts and back to reality. She's stealing glances at a pair of middle-aged women a table over who are making bedroom eyes at me and doing some strangely sexual things to the straws in their drinks. They're beautiful, there's no doubt about that, but they don't hold a candle to the woman on my right. "See? Your fan club would have happily entertained you. I think they're pissed I've been monopolizing your attention tonight."

"You haven't been monopolizing anything. I'd give you all of my attention even if you didn't want it."

She chuckles, her cheeks going adorably pink, but doesn't respond as servers flood the room and place small salads in front of us. Soon, the quiet clinking of silverware fills the room and I almost don't hear her response. "What if I do want it?"

Oh, sweet, beautiful woman. She has no idea of the beast she's just unleashed. I'll still have to play this smart. Isla's been hurt, I know that much. So despite wanting nothing more than to drag her from this cursed, crowded dinner and into my bed, I won't. "Then get ready, beautiful, because you've got it."

Her pink cheeks make the blue of her eyes even more

vibrant as she stares at me from beneath long, dark eyelashes. She wants this. She wants me. But beneath that captivating bravery and bravado, she's also scared. That's okay. I'm scared, too. It's been so long since I've felt this way about a woman, and I barely know her. She's just as likely to hurt me as I am to hurt her, though I doubt she'd believe that.

Neither of us says anything as we take each other's measure. Then her friends ask her a question, and the rest of dinner goes by in a flurry of laughter and conversation, but also stolen touches. My knee brushing hers, my fingers grazing hers, our shoulders touching as I lean over to ask her to pass the salt.

It's the most excruciatingly subtle foreplay I've ever engaged in, and I'm fighting to keep my dick from straining against my pants every moment of it.

"Excuse me, folks," Tracy, the woman who spoke before, says as we all nibble on our desserts. "It's the time you've been so anxiously awaiting. I'm going to read off the winners for the silent auction. We'll have a team of people available to answer any questions you may have at the end of the night, as well as to give you your items if you bid on a physical good."

"I hope I win the yoga retreat," Quinoa tells Griffin. "That resort has some amazing naked Bikram classes. It really opens your whole body." Griffin's eyes grow unfocused. He's probably picturing a room full of Quinoas doing downward dog completely in the nude. I shake my head.

Tracy reads off winner after winner, congratulating them and giving a little description of what they won. Isla fidgets in her seat next to me, clearly bored. It is a rather long list of people.

"Our next winner is none other than our very own Maddox Graves, who has donated a *very* generous amount to win the romantic hot air balloon ride date for two. So if you see a beautifully illuminated balloon floating over the city in the near future, it could be your fearless captain enjoying some romance with the person of his choosing." Tracy shoots me a wink. Every eye is on me now. Especially every female eye. But I only care about one of them.

"Ever been up in a hot air balloon?" I ask Isla.

She's got her lower lip pulled between her teeth again and she's staring at her dessert like it's about to reveal the secrets of the universe. "Uh, no, I haven't."

"Me neither," I reply, leaning in close to her. "I guess it'll be a first for both of us."

Those gorgeous sapphire eyes dart up to meet mine. "What?"

She's so damned adorable when she's flustered. And she is flustered. She doesn't know what to say or how to respond, but there's no hiding the excitement that flashes across her face alongside those other more unpleasant emotions. "I already spoke to the company that runs the dates. They can fit us in next week. Will you go with me? I promise to make it the best first date you've ever been on."

She loses the battle with the smile she's trying to suppress. "Maddox, we already had a first date."

"That doesn't count," I tell her. And I mean it. There's no way we're calling that our first date. "Think of that one like a preseason date. It's just practice. It doesn't count on our record."

This makes her laugh. It's such a beautiful, free sound.

I want to earn that reaction as many times in a day as I can. "A preseason date?"

"Yeah. Just a warmup for the real thing." I grab her hand beneath the table and run my thumb over her delicate fingers. "Let me take you out on a real first date. Just you and me and a balloon pilot. Friday night before sunset." Despite knowing how much she wanted to go up in the balloon, I still hold my breath as I wait for her answer. Because she has to want to go up with *me*.

"Okay, yeah," she says, looking up at me through her lashes again. "Dinner before was only a practice test. It doesn't have to count toward our final grade."

God, she's cute. My cheeks hurt from smiling so widely. "Then it's a date. A real one, this time."

I don't hear any of the other winners they call out. I don't hear any of the chatter around us. Hell, every single person in the room fades away except for the stunning redhead beside me. She's willing to give me a second chance, and I won't blow it.

I'm going to romance the hell out of Isla Harding. And I'm going to make her mine.

# twenty-four

MADDOX

"YOU READY TO HEAD HOME?" ISLA'S FRIEND JESS asks her as the night winds down. Guests say their good-byes and claim their winnings. I'm not ready for the night to end. I'm not ready to let Isla go.

The azure-eyed vixen chews her bottom lip, eyes darting my way before swinging back to her friend. She hums as she shrugs. "Yeah, I guess if you guys are."

She doesn't want to go any more than I want her to. Running my knuckle down her arm, I suck in a deep breath before speaking. "I can bring you home. If you want."

Sapphire irises catch on me and linger. The attention sends zings of desire through my body. Images of those eyes looking up at me through heavy lids as I move inside her, my body braced over hers and caging her in, play in riotous technicolor in my mind.

*Logan in those crusty boxer briefs he wore throughout the*

*postseason last year without washing them. Griffin eating a freeze-dried tarantula on a dare. Bash putting a raw egg in Clamato juice after a night of heavy drinking.* Thinking the un-sexiest thoughts possible, I keep my dick from straining to break free from my suit pants.

Luckily, Isla isn't privy to my scandalous thoughts, and after a moment of consideration and a couple of questioning looks at her friends, she nods. Her pretty red lips curve into a shy smile. "I'd like that. Thanks."

"They're both blushing," Griffin stage-whispers to Sebastian, who shakes his head at our friend. "Isn't that the cutest fucking thing you've ever seen?"

"Okay," Bash says, grabbing Griffin's elbow. "You've had a lot to drink tonight. Let's get you home."

Griffin nods, but then his eyes grow wide. "Wait! Has anyone seen Quinoa?"

Isla's friends share a confused look. Welcome to the club, ladies.

"I didn't get her number. She promised bendy sex," Griffin whines.

Bash rolls his eyes and pats our inebriated teammate on the shoulder. "Sorry, man. I don't see her anywhere. I'll take you to the circus the next time it comes to town. I'm sure you could find a bendy carnie to screw."

Isla tries to stifle a giggle, which has Sebastian giving her a friendly wink. When Griffin's face lights up like a kid on Christmas morning, she can no longer muffle the sound. And when he loudly says, "I actually have banged a carnie. She had a really well-groomed beard. It kinda tickled my balls when she gave me head," she loses it. We *all* lose it.

"Come on, bud. You can tell me all about it on the way

home," Bash says. The tone of his voice is slow and patient, like a kindergarten teacher who has to humor twenty overly excited kids all day.

Isla and her friends laugh and hug as they say good-night. Logan waves from across the room where he's chatting up a leggy brunette. And then I guide Isla to my car with a hand on her lower back. I parked it in the garage reserved exclusively for the players, and when we zip out onto the street and see the gaggle of photographers and reporters still camped out by the main entrance, I pat myself on the back for my foresight. Isla told me about the reporter asking her to comment on our relationship status. She didn't need to say how uncomfortable that made her. It was clear in the stiffness of her posture and the way she worried at her lip as she recounted the moment.

I'll have to do my best to shield her from that kind of attention once we start dating. Because we *will* date. Hopefully, she grows more comfortable with it as time goes on, but I suspect I'll need to be patient with her. I know nothing about her relationship with her ex, but I can tell he messed with her head. Hell, just seeing his best friend sent her into a panic.

"Did you have fun?" Lights play over Isla's pale skin as we drive, illuminating her face in washes of reds, greens, and diffused golden white. She's a work of art, and my right hand reaches out and laces our fingers together. Her high cheekbones round when a smile overtakes her face. She doesn't drop my hand.

"More than I thought I would. That kind of event isn't usually my scene." There's something in the way she says those words that has my ears twitching. She's not letting that douche from the bar get in her head, is she? My mind shouts to find out why her voice dipped and her volume dropped, but I don't. Now's not the time to push her. So I grin and agree with her.

"Mine either. I'd rather be somewhere quiet with a few people I like than surrounded by so many strangers."

Humming low in her throat, Isla gives me her full attention. "Is it weird that everyone knows your name even though you've never met them?"

"Yeah," I admit. "You get used to it after a while, but the more intrusive stuff—like fans thinking they know you and asking personal questions while you're grocery shopping in sweats and sunglasses and just trying to be anonymous—you can't really get used to that."

"I can only imagine." She squeezes my fingers. I feel it all the way to my chest. "I was uncomfortable being recognized by that reporter and that was just one person. And they'll probably forget all about me tomorrow. I'm sure it gets old." Her tone is soft, like she's embarrassed to admit her discomfort, and my chest inflates with protectiveness.

"I'm sorry that happened. I'll make sure no one finds out about our hot air balloon date." I want it to be perfect. That means no nosey reporters.

Isla shifts in her seat and turns those doe-eyes on me. "You were serious about that?"

"Of course I was. I want to take you out on a real date, and what's better than a magical hot air balloon ride?" My thumb traces along her hand. The pretty pink flush of her cheeks makes my cock ache when I steal a glance. But it's not just my dick that responds to her. It's all of me.

When was the last time I felt this way about a woman?

Things with Isla may never work out the way I'd like them to, but I already know she wouldn't sell some bullshit story to the tabloids if it all ended. She's not that type of person. I'm confident about that. My thumb traces along her soft hand. "Are you free Friday night?"

"I don't have much of a life these days," she responds, making a face. "So yeah, pretty sure I'm free." Her shoulders stiffen as her nose scrunches up and her eyes close. "Can we pretend I didn't say that? That sounded sad."

It's impossible to keep the corners of my lips from twitching, but I shrug and keep my eyes on the road. "Say what? All I heard was you're available to go out with me on Friday night."

That earns me a soft laugh. "It must have been hard for you."

I wait for her to finish speaking, but she trails off and I steal a glance at her. "What must have been hard?"

"Pretending to be such an asshole the night we met." She angles her body to face me. "Because you're just a big, slightly grumpy softie, aren't you?"

Her description has me chuckling. I don't know how big of a softie I truly am, and it was easier than I'd like to admit being a jerk that night because I'd been assuming the worst about her, but god, I love that she's giving me the benefit of the doubt. And not because she wants something from me, but because that's just who she is. She's kind and funny and good. Too good for me. Not that it'll stop me from pursuing her. I'm *not* that good.

"Grumpy, yes. Softie? I'm not so sure about that."

"You've come to my rescue a few times now," she says quietly. "Maybe some people don't take the time to see it, but it's pretty obvious you're a good guy."

My throat tightens at the earnestness in her voice, and

my heart thumps away in my chest. "What if I just want you to think that?"

She huffs out a soft laugh. "No, you wanted me to think you were a selfish jerk."

Fair enough. I had. Not anymore, though. Now I want her to see me for who I truly am, and that's a terrifying thought. The only people who fully see me are my mom, sister, and the guys. Back before I started playing professional hockey, I never worried about letting someone see the real me. No more than anyone else worries, at any rate. But that changed as soon as I signed that contract with all those zeros.

Maybe it's naïve, but I don't think Isla gives a damn about my money.

She watches me with a smirk, her hand still in mine.

"And you don't think I'm a selfish jerk?"

She hums and wiggles her head from side to side. "Mmm, you could still prove me wrong, but no. I don't think that's who you are."

"Thanks for giving me a second chance."

"Oh, I wouldn't have," she says with a devious twinkle in her eyes. "But then you almost made what's-his-name at the bar pee himself, and I decided you'd earned it."

My laughter fills the car as we pull into her apartment building lot. Isla shifts in her seat, her gaze pinging between her apartment and me. She's nervous. "Can I walk you to your door?"

That pretty pink stains her cheeks again. "Sure."

I park in an open visitor spot and reluctantly release her hand. I'm around the car and opening her door before she can do it herself, and her blush deepens. Offering her my hand, I help her step out of the SUV, making sure she keeps her balance in her heels. Our fingers intertwine as we make our way to the building entrance. Her hand is so small and warm in mine. Delicate. It makes the caveman part of my brain want to protect her from everything and everyone that might hurt her. It's the part of me that lights up when an opposing team's agitator starts chirping at one of my teammates and gets in their head. The part of me that slams any threat into the boards with forceful precision and zero hesitation.

We walk up to the third floor in silence. Warmth fills me as Isla presses close to my side, her head resting on my shoulder. "Tired?"

She blinks slowly a couple of times and nods. "Yeah. I guess I am."

"Come on then, Short-Stack." I tug at her hand and lead her toward her apartment as she huffs in annoyance at the nickname.

"I'm not that short."

"Compared to me, you are. You're so cute and little." That earns me an elbow to my side, and I laugh. I love riling her up.

"Laugh it up, you giant ogre," she mumbles while fishing her keys out of her purse.

"I *am* giant." I smirk as her eyes widen. This time, her blush goes all the way down to her pale chest. Before she can put her key in the lock, I press her back against the door. One hand goes to her hip, the other tangles in her long red hair at the base of her skull. Isla's breathing picks up as I invade her space, my head dropping so my lips hover over hers. It's a struggle not to push my hips into her as her nipples harden through her dress and brush against my chest with every heaving breath. "See?" I murmur. "So damned cute, and little enough to cover with my body."

Isla's eyes are wide and her lips part with jagged breaths. I bet if I skimmed my fingers up the inside of her creamy thighs and pressed them beneath the fabric of her panties, I'd find her dripping for me. But I won't do that. Not yet. Instead, I lower my lips so they hover millimeters away from hers. Holding her gaze, I silently ask for permission to kiss her. But Isla's the one to bridge the gap between us.

Her mouth is heaven. Soft, full lips move against mine in a sensual dance. When I sweep my tongue along the seam of her mouth, she opens for me with a gasp. She tastes like cherries and champagne, and she's soft everywhere she presses against me. I groan when her breasts rub against my chest, deepening our kiss.

It's intoxicating. The taste of her. The feel of her. My dick is painfully hard, and when I lose myself in the sensation of kissing this gorgeous woman, I forget my efforts to keep from grinding into her. She gasps again as my erection presses against her lower belly and her hips roll.

Holy hell.

A quiet whimper passes from her open mouth to mine and I fist her hair harder, tugging on it just enough to angle her head the way I want to deepen the kiss. This kiss that I never want to end.

Delicate fingers play nimbly over my chest and arms as my own grip her hip. It's torture, being touched by her like this. Because all I want is to demand she open the door and let me in so I can rip her clothes off, spread her out on her bed, and feast on her pussy until she's writhing with so much pleasure she can barely whimper my name.

I loosen my grip on her hip and slow our kiss. I can't screw this up because I'm thinking with my smaller head. I want more than one night of great sex with this woman.

She chases my lips as I pull away, resting my forehead against hers. Our chests brush together as we both suck in great gulps of air. At least I'm not the only one deeply affected, if her grip on my jacket is anything to go by.

The hallway is silent except for our heavy breathing as we stare at one another. She's so beautiful. Flushed cheeks, wide, glassy blue eyes, and lips swollen from our fevered kisses. It's a sight I want to enjoy again and again. And hopefully, I will. If I play my cards right with her.

Straightening, I press a lingering kiss on her forehead and brush my knuckles across her cheek. "Goodnight, beautiful. Call you tomorrow?"

She nods, looking slightly dazed. "Okay. Night, Maddox. Thanks for bringing me home."

I grin, leaning down to steal one last quick kiss before stepping away and tucking my hands in my pants pockets to keep myself from reaching out for her again. "Sweet dreams, Short-Stack."

Her lips twitch. "Sweet dreams, Ogre."

---

## ISLA

Oh. My. God. That kiss.

Sagging against the inside of my apartment door, I run my fingers over my tingling lips. No one has ever kissed me the way Maddox Graves just did. I felt it down to my toes. My whole body still vibrates with shock and arousal.

In a daze, I pad into my bedroom, peel the dress from my body, kick off my heels, and flop down onto my bed with a deep, dreamy sigh in nothing but my black lace bra and matching panties. Phantom echoes of his touch light up my skin, and I groan. Despite the flirting we've been doing over text this past week, I never expected the night to end this way. With Maddox's mouth claiming mine as though it was always meant to be his.

In all the years I spent with Alex, thinking we were destined for each other and believing there was no one else out there for me, I have never been kissed so thoroughly that I lost my wits. I totally get what they mean in romance novels when they talk about being claimed by a man when he kisses the heroine. And oh. My. God. I want more.

My phone buzzes in my purse, and I practically leap off the bed to grab it. What if it's Maddox? Maybe he's still in the parking lot, obsessing about that kiss the same way I am and he wants to come up? Would I say yes? Could I say no? My body sure as hell doesn't want the night to end.

But it's not Maddox's name that flashes across the screen, it's Jess's.

JESS

Are you home? And alone?

Grinning, I reply that I am, and my phone rings almost instantly. I answer, putting it on speakerphone, and both of my best friends pepper me with rapid-fire questions.

"Guys," I nearly shout. "Chill and I'll tell you everything."

And I do. Everything except for the way my heart gets all squishy when I think about Maddox. Everything except for the way I can't stop wondering if meeting him was fate or destiny or some other epic thing that wouldn't normally happen to an English teacher from Minneapolis. They'd never let that go, and I'm not entirely sure I'm ready to let myself go there. Not yet. I was too quick to go all-in with Alex and I won't make that mistake again. I don't want to fall for someone who doesn't actually love me for who I am.

Oh my god. Why am I even thinking about this?

"So, is he a good kisser?" Nev demands.

Now *that* I will talk about. "You guys have no idea."

# twenty-five

## MADDOX

SHE TAKES MY BREATH AWAY. IT DOESN'T MATTER that she's wearing jeans, sneakers, a hoodie, and a jacket in place of a tight-fitting dress. She's no less beautiful with her hair pulled into a high ponytail than she is with it spilling over her shoulders and down her back. In fact, I prefer her this way. This feels like the real Isla. No armor, no pretense, no shiny costume or mask. Her eyes sparkle an even richer blue with the light coat of mascara and nothing else.

"Hi," she says shyly when she opens the door. A twitch of her lips and a pretty flush creeping up her cheeks snap me out of my staring.

Right. I'm being weird. "Hey. You look beautiful."

Isla shifts her weight from one foot to the other. Her fingers fiddle with the strap of her purse. "Thanks."

She doesn't believe me. The realization is a punch in the gut. She doesn't believe she looks beautiful like this.

Screw that. My hands go to her waist, and I tug her toward me. When I lower my face to hers, she sucks in a breath. "You're always beautiful. No matter what you wear. But for what it's worth, I think this look is my favorite so far. I can't wait to see you all bundled up and cheering for me at our games."

Her eyes widen, but a moment later the insecurity evaporates and a hesitant smile rounds her cheekbones. "You're so sure I'm going to go to your games, huh?"

I nod, lowering my face more so our noses touch. "I am. I'm very sure about you, Isla."

Pressing my lips to hers, I swallow her sharp inhalation. The kiss is quick and not nearly as deep as I want it to be, but we're on the clock right now. Tim, the balloon pilot, is waiting for us in the large field outside his company's base a short ride from the city. "As much as I want to keep kissing you, we have to get going. Do you have everything you need?"

She nods, and my chest swells with satisfaction when I notice her hands shaking slightly as she locks her apartment door. Isla Harding is just as affected by me as I am by her.

I ask her about her day as we walk hand in hand down to my car, and she asks about mine. It's mundane and simple and we fall into conversation easily. She listens intently as I tell her about training and seems shocked by how many hours the guys and I spend lifting and conditioning. When I ask her about when school starts, I'm surprised to hear that she's planning to set up her classroom on Monday, and the first day is the following Tuesday. I remember school starting in September, but it seems they go back at the end of August.

Isla starts off reserved as she answers my questions, but ten minutes into the ride, she's animated and excited, talking with her hands as she describes her plans for the year. Her passion is contagious, and soon we're both brainstorming how to make my little speaking engagement even more impactful.

It's not the first time I've thought about it, though, and I have some plans I don't share with Isla. They're not all ready to divulge. A couple are still in the works, but I also want to surprise her. I want to see her face light up like it is right now. She clearly does a lot to support and help other people. Her passion for uplifting her students is plain to see. But I wonder who lifts her up.

I will if she lets me.

That thought has me asking about her family. I realize I don't know much about Isla's actual life. Something I need to remedy.

"So I know you grew up in Minneapolis and that your dad's not a big sports guy, but that's all you've really told me about your family."

She smiles. "I'm an only child. My parents and I are close, but after I got my teaching job, and they felt pretty confident I had my life mostly together, they planned a year-long trip around the world. They've been saving up for it forever. My dad even got the college he teaches at to approve it by doing some guest lecturing at a few universities across Europe."

"Wow," I say. "That sounds cool."

"Yeah." She nods, a fond smile playing across her lips. "They were so excited about it. They almost canceled it when Alex broke our—" She stops herself, but I know what she's going to say. When Alex broke their engagement. But Isla doesn't know I'm aware of that, and if I clue her in, I'll have to admit to spending hours scrolling through her Instagram feed. And yeah. I'm not going to do that. She flashes me a tight smile.

"They almost canceled it when Alex broke up with me three weeks before they were supposed to leave." I reach across the gap between our seats and take her hand. "But I couldn't let them do that, you know? They'd sacrificed so much for me growing up. And I had Jess and Nevaeh. So I told them that if they didn't go, I was moving back home with them and I'd cock-block them at every turn."

The laugh that spills out of me is loud. "You did not."

She nods. "Oh, I did. They've been married a long time, but when I moved into the dorms during college, they kind of fell in love again. It's so cute. And gross. Because they're all over each other like teenagers. If I didn't know my mom had already gone through menopause, I'd be bracing myself for a surprise baby brother or sister. Which would be weird as hell, right?"

Yeah, it would. I can't imagine my mom telling me I was going to be a big brother again well into my twenties. The thought makes my heart pinch because my mom doesn't have someone to fall back in love with. She doesn't have someone to travel around Europe with for a year. But she has Mira and me. And while it's not the same, we take good care of her. Not that she'd ever ask us to do that, but she always made us the priority when my sperm donor disappeared.

She never made us feel like we were a burden. She gave us everything. So one of the first things I did when I signed my first multi-million dollar contract was buy my mom a brand new house so she'd never have to worry about maintaining the older home we'd grown up in. Maybe I should offer to pay for a family trip around Europe next year during the off-season.

"Do you miss them?" I ask her gently.

"Yeah. I do. It's been hard not having them around, but I'm glad they've gotten the chance to do this. And a little jealous, if I'm honest. Someday I would love to trek around Europe. Maybe see Australia and New Zealand. And I've always wanted to go to Japan." She watches the city blur by out her window, the busy streets slowly giving way to suburbs. Soon the manicured neighborhoods will give way to more open land. "When I was in college, I dreamed of taking a month or two after graduation to backpack across the UK, but I didn't want to go by myself, and then Al—" She stops herself again, lips pursing in a thin line. Does she think I'm going to be upset or turned off by her if she speaks his name? She was with him for a significant part of her early adult years. Of course, so many of her stories include him.

"Then Alex what?" I ask in a soft tone.

Isla clears her throat. "He changed his mind about going. Didn't fit with his ambitions."

What. A. Dick.

My sister dated a guy like that back in high school. As soon as I realized what he was doing, I kicked his ass. He left her alone after that. God, Mira had been so pissed at me. But eventually, she realized I'd only done it to protect her.

It doesn't seem like anyone in Isla's life saw the warning signs.

I hate guys like Isla's ex. A strong man isn't threatened

by a strong woman. He thanks his lucky stars she finds him worthy of her affection.

There's still strength in Isla. So much. When she forgets to make herself smaller, it comes spilling out. In unguarded moments, when her temper flares, those banked embers in her burn hot. I'll just have to make sure she knows she's safe with me, so she stops trying to hide it.

"For what it's worth," I say as I make a right turn off of the street and down a long paved drive, "Alex was an idiot. Only a fool would pass up a chance to whisk you off to a foreign land for adventures and travel sex."

That shade of pink. The color flushing her cheeks is quickly becoming my new favorite. She opens her mouth to respond to my slightly inappropriate proclamation, but no words come out. It's clear by the narrowing of her ocean eyes she doesn't quite believe I'm being genuine. No doubt she believes it's some kind of line to get in her pants.

I don't need a line to get in Isla's pants. She wants me just as much as I want her. I can see that now. And I'm going to revel in the feel of her naked body against mine. I'm going to fuck her until her body shakes with pleasure so overwhelming she begs me to stop, to have mercy on her. But I don't need a line because this isn't just about sex. This is about connection.

"We're here," I tell her. Does she notice how rough my voice is? She shifts in her seat. Hooded eyes hold mine. Yeah. She noticed.

Isla doesn't move as I unbuckle and open the car door. She simply watches me. Her eyes track the flex of my biceps, the tight line of my shoulders. Smirking, I shut my door and walk around to hers. She's just turning toward me when I open it up and reach across her to unbuckle her seat belt. My arm brushes against her chest and she sucks in a breath, her eyes fluttering. I can't help myself. I need to touch her.

My fingers skim her jaw, and using the pad of my thumb, I drag her bottom lip open before leaning in and pressing a tortuously slow kiss to her mouth. A needy sound fills the cab of the car as I nip and suck at her lower lip.

"Come on, Short-Stack. If you keep making those little sounds, we'll never make it off the ground. And I have plans to kiss the hell out of you at two thousand feet."

# twenty-six

## ISLA

I'M LIVING IN A FAIRY TALE. MADDOX GUIDES ME TO a large field lit up by hundreds of twinkle lights. They illuminate a massive basket attached to a balloon in the colors of the sunset. It glows against the darkening evening sky. A kind-looking older man with gray hair and thick-rimmed glasses waits for us with a welcoming smile.

"Good evening," the pilot says, offering us a handshake. "My name is Tim, and I'll be your pilot tonight."

"Hey, Tim, good to meet you," Maddox says easily. "I'm Maddox, and this is Isla."

If Tim recognizes my hockey player date, he doesn't show it. It helps squash some of the self-conscious awkwardness filling me since we arrived. I couldn't help wondering if anyone who saw us together would wonder what a guy like Maddox was doing with a woman like me. Now, I breathe deeply and relax my spine.

"Have either of you been up in a balloon before?" Tim asks.

Maddox and I both answer that we haven't, and Tim nods. He runs through a list of facts and precautions before telling us there are drinks and pastries in the basket.

And then Maddox helps me climb into the basket. Tim talks us through what he's doing as he prepares to launch the balloon, giving us some last-minute safety tips and pointing out the parts and mechanisms. Our ascent is smooth, but my heart beats a heavy rhythm in my chest and I clutch the side of the basket with white knuckles.

"Hey," Maddox says in my ear. He presses close to me, the weight of his body grounding and keeps me from panicking. "It's okay. We're safe. Just breathe, beautiful."

I try to suck in a deep breath, but this is so much more nerve-wracking than I thought it would be. I'm not afraid of heights, but floating off the ground beneath a giant balloon while we're braced in an open basket is freaky as hell. It's exhilarating, but it's freaky. And much warmer than I thought it would be. The burner throws off enough heat to remind me of summer evenings spent lounging beside bonfires and roasting marshmallows as a kid. Wind buffets us, twisting my ponytail in an erratic dance as the ground gets further and further away.

It's a symphony of sensation, and I couldn't be more grateful for Maddox's oversized presence at my back.

"This is both amazing and terrifying," I tell him. I have to raise my voice to be heard over the bursts of flame and the hum of the wind.

Maddox wraps one arm around my waist as he grips

the basket with the other. "It really is. The view's stunning, though."

We're so high, everything beneath us looks surreal and miniature. He's right. It's beautiful. I twist around and look at him to agree, but Maddox isn't looking at the shrinking world beneath us. He's not looking at the sky, which is a riot of pinks and oranges. No, Maddox is looking at me. *Me.*

He smiles at my wide-eyed realization. Then he leans down and presses his soft lips to mine in a kiss. It's so reverently gentle I forget all about my fear or the fact that we're floating a thousand feet above the earth. Floating feels natural when Maddox kisses me.

Lips parting, I release my hold on the basket to tangle my fingers in his sweatshirt. He's all the tether and safety I need. The thought should terrify me, and it probably will when I get home and over-analyze every moment of this date, but for now, it feels right. Maddox is right. We're safe. I'm safe. Because he's here.

Our tongues dance, and our lips move together. I'm hyper-aware of every hard inch of him pressed along the length of my body. He's all corded muscles and strength. Maddox Graves is power personified, which makes the gentleness of his kiss such a heady experience. He's the most beautiful contradiction, and I have the passing thought that the women who hurt him are idiots. Who could be with a man like this and not see how lucky they were? Not because of his money or his fame or any of the materialistic things he could give them, but because he is so *good.*

We're both breathing hard when we break apart. And even though we should be drawn to the stunning sunset unfolding before us in vivid hues, our eyes remain glued together. Maddox breaks the spell when his lips twitch into a smile that soon overtakes his face. He's so freaking handsome.

"I can't decide if I'm light-headed because we're so high in the air or if it's because you just kissed all the sense out of me," I blurt.

His eyes crinkle in the corners as he laughs. "Both?"

"Both," I agree. I turn in his arms so my back is pressed to his front because if I don't, we'll spend the whole ride making out and poor Tim will feel awkward. I glance at the pilot, but he's a professional. If he noticed our mid-air make out, he doesn't show it. Soon I'm relaxing into Maddox again. Any awkwardness about Tim is wiped from my brain as the scene around us registers fully for the first time.

I've always been a dusk kind of girl. I love watching the sky paint itself in shades of pink and purple as the day gives way to night. But watching it from the ground has nothing on experiencing it from the sky. This high in the air, we're a part of the sunset. It washes over us, suffusing Maddox's face in warmth. The world is awash in soft pinks and oranges, and my breath catches.

It's breathtaking. I've never seen anything like it.

"This is..." My words trail off. Nothing I could say seems adequate.

"Yeah," Maddox says. "I know exactly what you're feeling."

We fall silent after that, both of us lost in the views and each other as the sun descends sleepily beneath the horizon. We take a few photos of the spectacular view with our phones, more than a few selfies—including some of us kissing, or Maddox kissing my cheek—and the pilot offers to take a nice one of us together. Then Tim lets us know we have another thirty minutes before we'll land. He also reminds us that there's champagne and treats in the picnic basket at our feet. Maddox pours us each a glass, and we munch on cookies and brownies that melt in our mouths as we soak up each other and the impending night.

As the balloon begins its descent, I wonder if the magic we found two thousand feet in the air will last once we're firmly back on the ground. Could we just live up here together? There are no exes, no pressures, no curious reporters and fans, and no worried best friends to drag me back to reality at two thousand feet.

But if Maddox and I are only good in a romantic little bubble, is this worth protecting? Alex and I were great when it was just us. He was funny and sweet, and I felt like I mattered to him. It was once we stepped out of our little college ecosystem and into the real world that we fell apart.

I don't want that again. I want something real. Something that's magical when we're cloistered away from the world, but is also magical when we're moving through the mundanity of daily life.

Our landing is a bit bumpy, but reality always is, right? We thank Tim profusely for the amazing night. When the pilot tells us to come back again, Maddox shoots me a smile and says he's sure we will.

Maddox is already planning dates for us well into the future, and my heart does a little leap.

"That was amazing," I gush once we're back in his car and heading home toward the city. "I've never done anything like that before."

"Me neither." He intertwines our fingers. "That was the best first date I've ever been on."

I giggle at that. It certainly was a better first date than our *practice* dinner. Hell, if Maddox had been this sweet and attentive that night, we could be on our fifth or sixth date by now. But I can't regret how things happened.

"I'm not ready for it to end," I confess. I roll my bottom lip between my teeth. "Do you want to come back to my place? We could grab some takeout or something and hang out."

Maddox's fingers squeeze mine. "Yeah. I'd like that."

My cheeks hurt from smiling when we pull up to my apartment building. Maddox had been telling me stories about all the trouble he and his sister got into as kids. It makes me want to meet her. It also makes me fall a little harder for the tall, tough hockey player. With every new story, it becomes clear that Maddox isn't as tough and grumpy as he pretends. He's kind and loyal and he loves his mom and sister.

We pass one of my neighbors on the way into the building and she gives him an appraising look. She recognizes him but can't place *why* or where she's seen him before. Other than that, we don't encounter another soul. No one pulls us out of our little bubble and we spill into my apartment in a cloud of laughter and casual touches.

Touches that become less casual once the door clicks shut and I engage the lock. It's a force of habit as a single woman living in the city, but with Maddox here, the sharp *click* seems to hold a new weight. It's a reminder that we're alone—really alone—for the first time.

I'm not sure who takes the first step to close the distance between us, but in moments we're colliding in a tangle of lips and limbs. His hands skim along my spine, and mine grip his shoulders, leaving trails of heat wherever we touch. His tongue skates along the seam of my lips before delving inside my mouth. Each stroke and movement is precise and skillful, and I know his talents with that tongue extend far beyond kissing me better than anyone else ever has. It makes my core clench, and I reach up to tangle one hand in his hair, deepening the kiss.

"God, you feel so good," he groans as one hand sneaks under the hem of my sweatshirt and the tee beneath to span the bare skin of my side. "You're so fucking beautiful."

He swallows my moan as I press against him. His touch short-circuits my brain, and all I can think about is feeling more of his warmth against my bare flesh. I let go of his shoulder to wrap my free arm around his neck, and then Maddox lifts me up as though I weigh nothing. My legs go around his waist, and fire flares in my center when it rubs against the hard length of him straining against his jeans.

"Maddox," I groan between fevered kisses. It's just one word, just his name, but he hears the request in it.

"What do you need, baby?"

I point to my room, unable to form words. Well, I could probably form words, but if I open my mouth right now, it'll be to demand that he fuck me, and I'd like to play this a little cooler than that.

Still carrying me, Maddox crosses my apartment. He peppers my neck and lips with kisses as he pushes through my partially closed door and into my bedroom. He only takes a moment to survey the space. It's on the smaller side, but it's tidy.

A soft blue and white shibori patterned comforter covers the queen-sized bed. It contrasts with the light rattan headboard and the plush white carpet. My laptop and notebooks filled with lesson plan ideas clutter my desk, as well as photos of me, Jess, Nevaeh, and a few of my parents. It's cozy and homey and a bit on the eclectic side.

I shift my weight in his hold. He groans and brings his eyes back to me. A wicked grin tilts my lips and I roll my hips again. I want him to make that sound again. I want to feel every hard inch of him pressed against my aching center. This time, we both groan.

"Isla," he warns. "Keep that up, and I'm going to throw you down on this bed and bury myself in you."

I roll my hips again. My breathless words make his eyes flare with heat. "Is that a warning, or a promise?"

One of his hands moves to the back of my neck, squeezing lightly. His eyes don't leave mine. "Are you sure?"

God, yes. I'm very sure. And very glad Louise fit me in for a bikini wax. I'm also so turned on by his touch and his kisses and the feeling of his body against mine that I'm painfully aware of how long it's been since I've had sex. Even the slightest bit of friction has my panties flooding.

Fathomless eyes the color of earth search my face. Whatever he sees has him nodding to himself. Then he carefully lowers my back to the bed. Strong arms cage me in, and his legs force mine to spread wide so he can stand between where they're splayed over the edge of the mattress. He kisses me deeply before his lips move down the column of my neck.

With every ragged breath, my desire rises. His long

fingers drag the zipper of my hoodie down so he can pull the sleeves off of my arms. Once that's off, I sit up to remove my tee, but his hands halt mine. Maddox's eyes burn as he pins me in place.

"Let me."

Wordlessly, I relent. His movements are slow and controlled as he glides the hem of my shirt higher and higher. I arch my back as his knuckles graze my lace-covered breasts. And then my shirt is gone, and Maddox stares at me like I'm the most beautiful thing he's ever seen. And for the first time, I don't feel self-conscious about having a new man see me in such a vulnerable way.

"You're stunning," he murmurs, running his large hands across my bare shoulders and down my sternum. The motions are akin to worship, and my skin pebbles with goosebumps. "The most beautiful woman I've ever seen."

"Maddox." I gasp as his fingers skim my tight nipples.

That devastatingly handsome face of his breaks into a satisfied smile at my breathy plea. I need him to touch me more. I need him to touch me everywhere.

"Patience," he whispers, before pressing open-mouthed kisses to my collarbone. I moan when his mouth moves down to the swell of my breasts and his fingers tug at the cups of my bra. He hums in satisfaction as I spill out of them. My nipples are painfully hard now, demanding his attention. It's attention he willingly gives.

My spine arches as he kisses and nips my right breast before taking the aching bud into his mouth and laving at it with his tongue. "Oh, God."

It's so good. His touch has me on fire with need. My hands snake beneath the hem of his shirt to explore the hard planes of his back. Muscles flex and ripple at my touch, and it's Maddox's turn to sigh as my fingers drag down his spine and back up again.

"Why are you still wearing a shirt?" I ask breathlessly. He chuckles, pressing a kiss to my left breast before rising and tugging off the offending garment.

Holy. Shit.

Maddox Graves is a freaking god. His shoulders are broad, his chest a smooth expanse of muscle and flesh that demands to be touched. I explore the topography of his back and chest with my fingers before they lower and chart the hills and valleys of his abs. I'm an awestruck explorer mapping out a newly discovered land. I've never been with a man who looks like this. He's strength and power personified, and it tickles the primal, lizard part of my brain that screams *this man would make a good protector*.

I might even drool a little.

"No one should be allowed to be this hot," I whisper. His answering laugh is deep and raspy, and I'd press my thighs together if he wasn't wedged between them.

Maddox takes advantage of my arched back and his fingers find the clasps of my bra. He undoes them and pulls the black lace from my body. Heat smolders in his expression as he takes me in. "I agree," he says as he runs his hands over the soft peaks of flesh.

When his gaze rises back to mine, I swallow hard. There's hunger in his eyes, of course, but that's not all that shines out at me. Maddox isn't just looking at me and seeing a body to use and enjoy, he's seeing me. There's genuine affection lighting those chocolate orbs, and my chest fills with warmth.

Maddox holds my eyes while his hands move to the button of my jeans. He holds my eyes as he slides the zipper down and tugs the denim from my hips. Only when I'm before him in nothing but a skimpy pair of black lace panties does his attention dip from my face.

"I'm going to make you feel so good, baby," he promises as he skims my panty-clad mound with his thumb. Even that simple touch has me sucking in a breath as my back arches off the bed. "You're going to look so pretty coming on my face."

And then he's dragging my panties down my legs, and his large hands are spreading my thighs wide so he can lean in and lick my folds with the flat of his tongue.

"Oh, God," I cry. The sudden move sends a zing of pleasure through my core, and I fist the sheets to keep from fisting his hair. He lets out a pleased hum against my pussy before licking me again.

"That's it, baby. Let me hear how much you like when I lick your pussy." He looks up at me with a wicked grin, my arousal already coating his lips and chin. I nearly come from the visuals of it alone. But then he slowly presses one long finger inside of me while he sucks on my clit and I cry out. He rubs my inner walls as he pushes into me before slowly dragging his finger out, only to repeat the movement. My hips buck, and he chuckles the dark, pleased laugh of a man who knows exactly what he's doing and how he's affecting me.

When he adds a second finger, I see sparks. His hands are so big, his fingers so long, he fills me so well. And these are just his fingers. Fuck.

I moan his name as he flicks the tip of his tongue over my clit in a steady rhythm. I'm nothing more than firing neurons and pleasure. My very existence shrinks down to where Maddox touches me and fills me. He hums wordless encouragement as I writhe on the bed, my legs spread and hanging off the edge with his broad body pressing against me between them.

The sounds that fill the room are obscene as he plunges a third finger into my channel and laps up my arousal with his tongue. And when his lips latch around my clit, I cry out. I'm so close. My body tingles and tightens, my stomach hollowing out as my hips move instinctively. Releasing my comforter, I thread one hand in his dark hair.

"That's right, baby," Maddox murmurs against my pussy. "Find your pleasure. Come apart on my face. I could drown in you and die a happy man."

Oh. My. God.

His filthy words flare like a surge of electricity in my mind, igniting a fuse that crackles down my spine, tingles through my belly, and detonates as he absolutely devours me. I try to muffle my scream with my free hand, but it's pointless. Maddox's talented tongue and long fingers make me lose control of my body as the most intense orgasm of my life sweeps through me. He fucks me through it, his fingers moving faster as he sucks hard on my clit until I'm shaking.

"It's too much," I whine when he doesn't relent. Everything is so sensitive. My whole body is flush with endorphins and buzzing with the aftershocks of pleasure. But Maddox doesn't stop. He just chuckles against my pussy before plunging his tongue into me. When I try to wiggle away from him, he loops his arms around my thighs and locks me in place against his mouth. "Oh, God. Oh, God."

He's not going to let up. Pleasure mingles with the burn of oversensitivity until the sharp pleasure-pain gives way to another swell of sensation. Maddox's tongue and mouth bring me to the crest of another wave of bliss and my brain short-circuits.

He's going to make me come again.

I don't even have time to marvel at how that's possible because his tongue is flicking against my swollen clit with just the right amount of speed and pressure, and my soul leaves my body.

Lights dance across my vision as another orgasm rips through me. This one is sharp and forceful, and my fingers clench tightly in Maddox's hair. He grunts, but doesn't stop fucking me with his magical tongue until my pussy stops fluttering through the aftershocks of my second orgasm.

"Holy shit," I gasp as I flop in a boneless heap on my bed. I don't even have the strength to open my eyes, but I feel Maddox's smile as he presses a wet kiss to my lower belly.

"Delicious."

Fuck. Me.

# twenty-seven

## MADDOX

"HOLY SHIT," ISLA SAYS WITH A SHAKY BREATH. HER eyes flutter as she pushes her sweat-dampened hair away from her face. She looks like a goddess. All flushed cheeks, hooded, satisfied eyes, and a lazy smile I want to see more often. I press a kiss to her inner thigh, earning another quiet moan, before rising from my knees to hover over her. I kiss her deeply, making sure she tastes herself on my lips.

I hadn't *planned* to eat her out tonight. Dreamed about it? Sure. But I was fully prepared to take things at a glacial pace to earn Isla's trust. Then she gave me those fuck-me-eyes and opened that sassy mouth of hers, and well, here we are. She's boneless and sated, and my dick is trying to burst out of my pants like the Kool-Aid man busted through all those brick walls in commercials from the 90s.

Isla's arms wrap around my neck and the feeling of her body pressed against mine is unlike anything I've ever experienced. I want to feel every inch of my bare skin against hers, *in* her. But tonight isn't about me and what I want. That doesn't mean I don't have to wrangle every ounce of my self-control when her slim little fingers wiggle beneath the waistband of my pants and stroke along my rock-hard cock.

"What do you think you're doing, Short-Stack?" I ask her as her finger traces the crown of my dick. I'm going for cool and unaffected, but my voice cracks like a teenage boy going through puberty. This makes her smirk adorably.

"You tasted me. Now it's my turn to taste you." She bats her eyelashes at me. She's a goddamn siren.

I let her continue to play with my dick because it feels amazing, but I stop her other hand from unbuttoning my pants. "Not tonight. Tonight is all about your pleasure."

Lower lip out, Isla pouts. She actually pouts when I tell her she won't be wrapping those luscious lips around my dick tonight. I must be out of my mind. But I'm determined.

I have a feeling about something.

Running my thumb over her hard little nipple, I pepper her neck with kisses. My voice is low when I whisper in her ear. "When is the last time a man spent all night bringing you to orgasm because he couldn't get over the sounds you make when you come, or the way your pretty chest flushes pink all the way down to your nipples?"

Her eyes grow even more hooded and her hand wraps around my shaft. She can't do more than that because my pants are too tight, but holy hell, even that feels incredible. But arousal isn't the only thing I see in Isla's hooded gaze. There's surprise and a healthy dose of vulnerability, too.

"Don't get me wrong, beautiful. I can't wait to feel your hot little mouth wrap around my cock. To watch you suck me down as you gaze up at me. I will probably dream of the way your throat will bob when you're trying to suck down every last drop of my cum." Her lips part and she pants as I continue plucking and playing with her nipple. She's so stunning. "But only a selfish asshole would go down on a woman just once. I'm sure you're still feeling sensitive, but after I make sure you're hydrated and comfortable, I'm going to make you come again."

Isla's breathing hard, a look of shock warring with the lust painted in blushing pinks and scarlet across her face. Her hips undulate against me reflexively. She may not entirely believe me, but she's turned the hell on.

"How many times have you come in a single night?" I ask her.

"W-what?"

Oh, this is going to be so fun. Sliding my fingers down from her breast, I push my hand between us and circle her swollen clit. She gasps, bucking into my hand. I use my fingers to punctuate my question. "How. Many. Times. Have you come. In a single night?"

"I... I've made myself come twice a few times," she confesses with a gasp as I press my fingers against her clit. "But if you're asking how many times someone else has made me come? Only once. Before you."

I knew it. I fucking knew it. That worthless, impotent little weasel she was engaged to probably only ever thought of his own pleasure. I won't ask her right now because the last thing I want is for Isla to be thinking about her stupid ex, but I'm curious how often he made her come when they had sex. Did he at least make sure she climaxed every time they were intimate? Or did he just rut into her until he achieved completion, only to flop down beside her and immediately start snoring away?

Nipping at her neck, I make a *tsk*-ing sound. "That's a tragedy, Isla." I part her lower lips with my finger and circle her opening with lazy, indolent movements. "I bet I can make you come at least three more times in the next two hours."

She lets out an incoherent mumble as I press two fingers into her hot, wet, pussy and press on her clit with my thumb. I circle it a few times before dipping my thumb into her slick heat, then bring it back to her clit. I want her messy. I want her dripping. I want her to be so slippery with arousal that she has no other choice but to change the sheets tonight before she goes to bed, no matter how exhausted she is.

"I don't know if I can come again," she tells me with wide eyes. But she will. I can already see the signs. Her hips move faster, her grip on my dick slackens, her chest rises and falls more rapidly. I bet I can pull one more orgasm out of her right now before her body truly needs a break. Not that she'll get much of one. I wasn't kidding when I told her I was going to shoot for giving her five orgasms. I'll stay here all night if that's what it takes.

At least one of them will be from Isla Harding sitting on my face.

"Maddox," she whines, her eyes glazed over with lust. I gently tug her hands out from beneath the waistband of my pants and quickly push them off so I'm in nothing but my boxer briefs. Then I grab Isla's hips and flip her over onto her belly, pushing her into the middle of the bed as I do. She lets out an adorable squeal that turns into a squeak as I playfully swat her ass.

"Do you have a vibrator?" I ask her as I press my hard-on against her backside.

"Huh?"

"A vibrator, Isla," I repeat as I wrap my arm beneath her hips and tug her ass into the air with her knees spread beneath her. It's the perfect angle for my brief-covered cock to rub against the wet heat of Isla's pussy. "Do you have a vibrator? Maybe in your bedside table?"

"Y-yes," she stammers, pressing back into me. "It's in my drawer right there." Sure enough, she points to her bedside table. I grin as I reach over her and pull the drawer open. A bullet vibrator is tucked next to a larger dildo. I consider both but decide on the bullet.

"If it's too much, I want you to tell me. Can you do that, baby?" She shivers beneath me when I turn on the vibrator. She's so responsive. I haven't even touched her with it yet.

She nods. "Mmhm."

Pressing the bullet to her right nipple, I rock against Isla's ass. Her body is caged within mine, and never have I loved being so much bigger than a woman before. She lets out a choked sound of pleasure as I stimulate her nipple and kiss the side of her neck. When she whimpers from the onslaught of sensation, I switch my attention to her other breast.

"Ohmygod," she moans. "Maddox."

The sound of my name on her lips as she moans and mewls like a kitten has me harder than I've ever been. I've never been so turned on, and she's not even touching my dick.

"Do you need to come again, beautiful? Is your clit

aching for my attention?" I nip lightly at the juncture of her neck. The only answer she can muster is a gasp.

"Oh, god." She arches into me, and I seize my opportunity. The bullet buzzes in my fingers as I press it gently against Isla's sensitive clit. She squeals, her arms shaking as she holds herself up. "It's too much, Maddox. It's too much."

"Do you want me to stop?" I ask, pulling the bullet away from her sensitive flesh. "The goal is to bring you pleasure. If this doesn't feel good, I want you to tell me."

"No." Her arms collapse and she rests the side of her face on the mattress, her sweet little ass still in the air. "Please don't stop. It's just... I've never..."

She's never been someone's focus like this. She doesn't know what her body is capable of. She doesn't know what to ask for or what to expect. Tonight I will happily play both teacher and student. I'll teach her that her pleasure is important and that a real man enjoys giving as much as receiving. And I'm planning to learn every single tick and tell, every pleasure point in Isla's body.

Her legs tremble when I hold the bullet against her clit again. I let my body press into hers, lowering her to the mattress so she's lying prone, her legs spread. My dick is aching, it's so hard. It would be so easy to free myself and slide into her warmth. Something to look forward to.

Within another few minutes, Isla is whimpering and gasping as another orgasm rips through her body. She practically convulses beneath me. Her hoarse cries nearly have me coming in my pants like a teenage boy. I toss the bullet aside, working her through her third orgasm with my fingers and the palm of my hand. And once she's spent, I tug her naked body into mine.

"Wow," she murmurs. "I've never come that hard." Her words are slurred and quiet. She's exhausted. Maybe getting to five orgasms is a little ambitious for our first night. But we'll get there. We have all the time in the world. Or we will if I have anything to say about it. For now, I'll take care of her. Make sure she knows she's safe with me.

"I'll be right back," I whisper against the shell of her ear. "You stay here and recover."

Blue eyes find mine when Isla rolls onto her back. "Where are you going?"

"You need water." I gently push her dampened hair from her face. She's so beautiful and real like this. I can't help smiling like an idiot. "And I'm going to get you cleaned up. Do you have washcloths?"

"In the cabinet below the sink," she tells me, pointing to her en-suite bathroom. Then her face softens with a sated smile. "I'm not sure I can walk yet."

Chuckling, I push up from the bed. "If you can, I've failed." And with a wink, I head to her kitchen to get her a glass of water. I'll get her cleaned up, then order Chinese food for delivery. I'm hungry after all our fun, so I can only imagine how ravenous Isla must be. The idea of taking care of her, of fucking and feeding her, of gently washing her sore body expands my chest.

I don't know how her dickhead ex treated her, but I'm determined to treat Isla Harding the way she deserves to be treated. Like a queen. And maybe, if she's not too exhausted after I fill her belly with lo mein and egg rolls, I'll convince her to take her throne so I can enjoy dessert.

# twenty-eight

## MADDOX

"YOU LOOK HAPPY." SEBASTIAN GIVES ME A knowing look when I saunter into the locker room a few minutes before practice. We're gearing up to get on the ice today, and after just over a month of dryland training where we focused on weights and conditioning, I'm looking forward to lacing up. We all are. "I assume your date went well this weekend?"

I chuckle. Navarro's the only one who didn't spend yesterday harassing me. Wright and Byrne both texted me first thing in the morning and didn't shut up until I told them I'd fill them all in at practice. Not that they're getting all the details. I'd never betray Isla's trust and tell them about the things we got up to in her bed. "Yeah, man. It was pretty amazing."

"What was amazing?" Griffin rubs his bleary eyes. He looks like he just dragged himself out of bed. His golden hair is a tousled mess, and his shirt is on inside out. Byrne trails behind him, looking significantly more chipper.

"My date with Isla." I strip out of my street clothes and start putting on my gear.

"Dude, I've been waiting to hear all about it," Griffin says. He winces when Logan tosses his duffel bag on the bench in front of his locker with a loud thud. Of course, Byrne notices.

"Hungover? I told you to slow down last night."

"Whatever," Wright grumbles. He sets his own bag down more gingerly. "I was just trying to enjoy myself before the season starts."

Navarro chuckles. "Enjoying yourself this morning, bud?"

Griffin flips Bash off, wincing again when we all laugh. "You guys suck."

Byrne and Wright invited us all out last night, but Navarro had other plans and I stayed in to work on my ideas for the assembly at Isla's school. I may have also spent a good part of the night flirting with her over text. Not that the guys needed to know that.

"Seriously though," Navarro's voice is muffled as he pulls on his gear. He wears more of it than the rest of us as the goalie. "Was the hot air balloon ride a success?"

Unable to stop myself, I pull out my phone and open up the photos we took so I can show them like some lovesick fool. I'm starting to *feel* like some lovesick fool. I mean, I don't love Isla yet. That would be crazy. But I am kind of crazy about her.

My boys fawn over the photos, making little *aww* sounds. If someone were watching our interaction, they'd probably think the guys were giving me shit, but they're actually happy for me. They like Isla. And more importantly, they can tell I like her. Even though none of them have said anything about it yet, I know they're glad she's nothing like the other women I've dated since joining the team. They were there when Candace gave that bullshit interview. They saw what it did to me. And the thing about being on a hockey team is that the guys become family. You can't spend the better part of a year traveling with a group of guys and *not* grow close like that.

"You guys are so cute together," Wright coos like a weirdo. He clasps his hands under his chin and bats his eyelashes at me.

"So sweet, I have a toothache," Byrne agrees.

I snort-laugh. They can act like little shits all they want, but I know they mean it. They're happy for me.

Navarro rests his hand on my shoulder. "She's good for you. I haven't seen you this relaxed in over a year."

He's right. I hadn't thought about it in those terms, but I do feel looser. Like a Candace-sized weight has lifted off my shoulders. I'm happy and hopeful. Even though I love hockey more than almost anything else and I spend most of my time surrounded by guys that are close as brothers to me, I've been lying to myself about not wanting a real relationship. I glance at my closest friends and the dopey smiles and wistful looks on their faces and wonder if we've *all* been lying to ourselves when it comes to women.

I've been telling myself I don't need anyone, Wright and Byrne tell themselves they only need casual hookups, and Navarro... well, I'm not totally sure what he's been telling himself, honestly. He flirts with women and once in a blue moon he'll hook up with someone, but the guy's always holding himself back. Like he's pining over someone he's never told us about. I know he's afraid to let a woman in, same as the rest of us, but he's more tight-lipped and reserved, and I've never gotten the full story.

Maybe I need to get him drunk and try to pry it out of him. Out of the four of us, he's arguably the best, not to mention the most stable and emotionally intelligent. That means we tend not to worry about him. But maybe we should.

"You gonna post those on your Instagram?" Griffin asks as he laces up his skates.

"I don't know, should I? Would that be too forward? I mean, thousands of people would see it, and I don't know if she's there yet, you know?"

Bash's lips twist to the side as he considers it. "Did she post any of them?"

I hadn't looked. After our date, I'd been so wrapped up in planning for the assembly and figuring out how to blow her away that I'd done little else. "Let's see."

Opening the app on my phone, I type in her username. "Crap. I forgot she set her account to private after people started commenting on her photo of us together."

"So request to follow her," Wright says, pulling out his own phone. He looks over my shoulder to see Isla's user-name, then types it in. "Found her." He taps the follow request button with a grin.

"What's her username?" Logan asks him. Soon he and Navarro have also requested to follow her.

Well, now I'll look like an asshole if I don't also send her a follow request. I tap the button on my screen and stare at it for a second, like my impatience will make her immediately see the requests and accept them. She will accept them, right?

"Dude. Why do you look nervous?" Griffin claps me on the back.

"What if she doesn't want us all following her?"

"Did you guys have a good time?" he asks, rolling his eyes.

"Yeah. Really good."

"Your face is looking a little dreamy there, Graves," Logan says with a smirk. "So is it safe to assume you took your relationship to the next level?"

"I'm not telling you guys what we did," I growl.

Logan holds his palms in the air. "Not asking you to. I'm just saying that Isla doesn't seem like a woman who's into random hookups with no strings attached. So if she let you get any further than the cute little flirting you two were doing at the auction dinner, I think it's pretty safe to assume she has real feelings for you."

He's right, of course. I could tell that much after our first disastrous date. And there is something there between us. I'm not an idiot. I just don't know what she thinks this is. She may not even want a relationship at all, let alone one with me. I know the public attention made her uncomfortable when her photo of us went viral, and that's nothing compared to the attention an actual relationship with me could bring. Thanks to Candace and Georgia and their bullshit stories about how I'm some heart-breaking jerk who loves to win a woman's heart so I can enjoy smashing it into smithereens later. I'll need to talk to her about all of this, but a big part of me wants to hold off until after the assembly at her school.

I've got plans to win her heart. And help a bunch of kids.

"What's taking everyone so long?" Coach shouts, striding into the locker room. "You guys forget how to lace up your skates after a couple of months off? Get moving!"

The whole team replies with a chorus of *Yes, Coach*.

"Seriously," Navarro says as we all tromp down the hallway to the rink, "I know you're gun-shy after everything, but Isla's not like that. I think we can all agree on that. What are you so scared of?"

I don't even have to think about it. The words are out of my mouth in an instant. "I'm scared she'll decide I'm not good enough for her. That she wants more than just some dumb jock."

Logan smacks me upside the head. "Don't be an idiot. You're more than just a dumb jock, and you know it."

"What if I *am* the kind of guy they said I was?" I ask as my blades hit the ice. We make our way over toward our coaches.

"We're starting easy," our assistant coach, Kyle Fry shouts. "Passing and puck control drills today. Navarro and Black, in the crease." Assistant coach Fry claps his hands, and everyone moves. Navarro holds back for a beat to hold my gaze.

"If you were anything like they said, you wouldn't be so worried. And you wouldn't be into an English teacher who doesn't take your shit. I love you, Graves, you know that. So hear what I'm about to say with that in mind. Get your head out of your ass. Love is always a risk. You can run away from it, or you can play to win. No one can make that call but you."

"I'm not in love," I say to his back as he skates toward his goal.

"Dude." Griffin rolls his eyes. "Keep telling yourself that."

"I'm not." The thing is, I could see myself getting there all too quickly.

And that scares the hell out of me.

# twenty-nine

## ISLA

"Oh my God," I mutter to myself with a chuckle when I finally check my phone.

My coworker LaTonya glances at me over a stack of boxes as she wobbles into my classroom. Only her violet braids, forehead, and dark brown eyes are completely visible. I can barely see her nose, the boxes are piled so high. "What?"

I hurry over and grab half of them before she trips over a desk and ends up ass over tits on the floor. It wouldn't be the first time. She's brilliant with math, but as if nature was hell-bent on compensating for her intelligence, she's one of the clumsiest people I know. "You didn't have to bring all of this in by yourself. We're supposed to be helping each other set up our classrooms, not throwing our backs out the week before school starts."

"Oh please. I can handle carrying some boxes." She

rolls her eyes at me as she sets the stack on my desk, trapping her pinkie in the process. "Ouch!"

LaTonya shakes her head as I try to hide my chuckle. She set herself up for that one. But as soon as we're both free of our boxes, she arches one perfect eyebrow and glances at my phone where it sits face down on one of the empty desks. "So what were you *oh my god*-ing?"

My coworkers are bound to find out about Maddox and our... whatever this is eventually, right? The assembly is about two weeks away. I suppose it won't hurt to spill the beans now. Twisting the end of my ponytail around my fingers, I unlock my phone and open Instagram. "I got follow requests from like half of the Minnesota Rogues this morning."

I'd met all of Maddox's teammates at the charity dinner, but mostly in passing. So I was pretty surprised to open my phone to find follow requests not only from Maddox and his closest friends but also the rookie Jess and Nev had been chatting up—Ryder Hanson—and six other guys on the team. Has he been talking about me to them? I know they have practice today, but I wasn't expecting that.

LaTonya whistles. "Seriously?"

I nod, holding the phone up so she can see for herself.

"Girl. Why are all those fine men trying to follow you? Don't get me wrong, I love you, but all you post lately are photos of your lattes and a few random snapshots of pretty scenery. Did you suddenly start posting racy selfies or something? I know we don't get paid a lot, but I have never heard of a single teacher keeping their job if the administration finds out they have an OnlyFans. Even if it's just feet pics. So if that's what you're doing..." Her dark eyes sparkle, her full lips twitching as she tries to suppress a smile. It doesn't last. Soon we're both cracking up. The idea of me posting naked pictures on the internet is so out there that I'm trying to imagine what my angle would be.

"Oh, god. Could you imagine? It would be photos of me fingering books or something. Maybe dressing up in period clothing to look like a character out of *Pride and Prejudice* and showing the barest hint of cleavage while trying to make a sexy face and totally failing."

She laughs even harder. "Do a sexy face right now. Show me what that would look like." So I do. And LaTonya finds this so hilarious that she doubles over in laughter. "Oh girl, you look like you just smelled a fart."

"Crap. That's embarrassing," I say through giggles.

It takes a minute for us both to catch our breath, then I tap the *accept* button on all the requests from Maddox's team. "No porn pics. I'm kinda seeing one of them."

"You're seeing a pro athlete?" Both of LaTonya's eyebrows rise, making her luminous brown skin wrinkle. "Damn, girl. Good for you. You deserve someone strong and sexy after putting up with that entitled man-child for so long."

I cough on a laugh. None of my coworkers liked Alex. They thought he was snobbish and aloof. Of course, they all tried their best to make him feel welcome and to make me feel they accepted him while we were together, but as soon as he broke up with me, the truth came out. They *hated* Alex. Universally.

"You want to see a picture of him?" I ask, already knowing her answer. I'm swiping through my photos from our hot air balloon date before LaTonya even says yes.

"What's his name?"

I hold the phone out to her. "Maddox. Maddox Graves."

"Damn," she says. "I don't know a single thing about hockey, but if all the players look like this, count me in." She flips through more of the photos. "Did this man take you up in a hot air balloon?"

I nod, grinning like an idiot. It was the most romantic date anyone had ever taken me on. And then it was the most erotic. My lower belly clenches just thinking about how Maddox played my body like he was made to do it. My cheeks are warm, and my coworker smirks.

"Oh, he took you on more than one ride that night, didn't he?"

"I can neither confirm nor deny," I say. But I'm not fooling anyone. My cheeks hurt from smiling so wide, and I know they've got to be bright red.

"Riiiight," LaTonya says. "And why is half of his team requesting to follow you now?"

"I don't know. Maybe he was talking about me at practice today? I've hung out with three of them a couple times now, but I only briefly met the rest." I can't deny I'm curious to know what prompted this influx of requests from them.

As if thinking about it summons him, a text from Maddox flashes across my screen.

"Is that him?"

I nod, unlocking my phone.

MADDOX

I made the mistake of showing photos
from our date to the guys. They asked if
you'd posted them on your Instagram
account, and Griff saw your username
when I tried to pull it up. It set off a chain
reaction with half the team wanting to
follow you. They all think you're cool, but
they can be a lot. Sorry.

LaTonya not so subtly reads his text over my shoulder. "Well, that's adorable."

Laughing, I hold the phone to my chest. Because yeah, this text was adorable, but he's sent me some racy ones since giving me three orgasms in one night. And I don't need anyone else seeing a text like that.

My coworker chuckles. "Sorry. I'm being nosey. I'm going to unpack some boxes in my classroom. But I want to hear more about this." She gives me a little wave and a waggle of her eyebrows, and then I'm alone in my classroom. Just me, boxes of supplies, and my thundering heart.

ME

Don't be sorry. I think it's cute.

MADDOX

I think you're cute.

Charmer

So why didn't you post any of the
photos? I'm sure it would make your ex
jealous.

My mind flashes back to seeing Alex's best friend, Jackson, at the charity dinner and all the uncomfortable feelings his appearance dredged up. Would posting romantic photos with Maddox make Alex jealous? Maybe. But I don't want to post something so meaningful for Alex's benefit. I realize I don't give a rat's ass about what Alex thinks of me. Or if he thinks of me at all. Truthfully, I think what I've actually been mourning these past five months is the life I thought I'd have and the dreams I built up when we were first together. Not the man himself. Because he's an ass.

ME

I don't want to make Alex jealous anymore.

Three little dots appear, disappear, and then pop back up a few seconds later.

MADDOX

Oh. I see.

Panic arcs through me like lightning. I reread my text and realize Maddox has probably misunderstood what I mean.

ME

I don't want to make Alex jealous because I don't give a crap about Alex. See, I've gone out on a date with this really great guy, and I don't know where it's going, but he seems to have made me forget all about my ex.

MADDOX

Is that so, Short-Stack?

Yep. And I wanted to post the photos, but I wasn't sure if this guy would be okay with that, and I was too chicken to ask him.

Well, unless the guy is a total idiot, he'd want to show the world that he spent an amazing evening with the most beautiful woman on the planet.

Did you post them?

No. I wanted to talk to you about it first. Dating anyone on the team can mean extra attention and scrutiny, but dating me…

I practically hold my breath, waiting for him to finish his sentence. When it comes, my heart aches for him.

MADDOX

I know you don't believe what my ex-girlfriends said about me, but most people do. Dating me could mean a lot of curiosity and more than a little extra scrutiny. Not sure if it's worth it.

Reading between the lines, I hear what he's not saying. *I'm not sure if I'm worth it.*

I don't give myself any time to think about it. Not that there's anything to think about. I know what it's like to wonder if you're worth the trouble, and I won't let him feel that way. Not on my account.

I pick a selfie where we both look undeniably happy. Our faces are lit with smiles, our eyes sparkle, and I'm leaning back against Maddox's broad chest. He's got his cheek resting on the top of my head. Uploading it to my

Instagram account, I add a caption that reads: *Most romantic night of my life. I don't know what made me more lightheaded—the altitude, or his touch.* And then I hit *share.*

ME

Check my Insta now.

A minute goes by, and just as I'm starting to worry that I did something wrong, my phone rings.

"I made you lightheaded, huh?"

Chuckling, I hum my agreement. "Very. You seem to have that effect on me."

"I want to post one of the photos of us," he says. "I want to show you off. But I also want to keep you to myself a while longer." My heart squeezes at the quiet admission. "Is that selfish?"

"Not at all. That sounds like a good plan." And not just because I'm dreading the attention. But because this is all so very new, I worry the extra eyes will put a strain on something that could be good. As terrifying as it is to entertain that hope.

"How is setting up your classroom going?"

A few posters decorate the walls, and most of my desk is unpacked and organized, but there's still a lot left to do. It'll take me a few days to get things looking the way I want. "I'm off to a good start. I'll probably keep going for another hour, then take a lunch break. How's practice?"

"Done," Maddox tells me. "It was an early start. The guys and I will probably hit the weight room in a bit."

"Are you talking to Isla?" a muffled voice says in the background. It has an instant grin spreading across my face. Maddox says that he is, and Navarro speaks again.

"Tell her, hey. And did you tell her about our first preseason game?"

"Not yet, man. I will."

"You'd better," Navarro warns him. Then louder, he says, "Later, Isla."

"Bye, Bash," I say, even though I doubt he can hear me. It earns a chuckle from Maddox.

"You're supposed to tell me about a preseason game?"

"Yeah. I was hoping you'd come." He sounds like he's not sure if I'll agree or not.

"Of course, I'll come. Just give me the details."

"I will. I'll text you all the information. Hey, I've got to do something. Call you later?"

Disappointment rises like floodwaters in me. I try to push the unwelcome sensation down. I need to get myself under control where Maddox Graves is concerned. He's consumed my thoughts since our date, and I need to focus on the start of the school year. I need to focus on my job and my students.

And I have to remind myself that we've gone on one real date. It's not like we're serious or even exclusively dating right now. At least, we haven't discussed that. I need to suppress my expectations and hopes before I end up hurt. Maddox is sweet and charming, and damn if he doesn't give the most mind-blowing oral, but I've grown a lot since I was a naïve high school girl who fell in love with a boy way too quickly. I won't fall into that same trap with Maddox.

"Isla?"

"Oh, yeah, sorry. Definitely. Talk to you later."

"Yes, you will." We say goodbye, and despite my mind wandering to my insecurities about what this is with

Maddox, I can't wipe the goofy grin off my face. And when he immediately sends me a text that reads, *You take my breath away, too*, I can't help hoping this relationship is different.

Because I may be terrified to give my heart to another person knowing they could break it, but deep down, there's nothing I want more than to be genuinely loved.

Maybe this is it. Maybe it's not. But I'll never know if I don't give him a chance.

# thirty

## ISLA



"Seriously, this is so sweet." LaTonya's voice floats through the open door of my classroom from down the hall, along with a few giggles and the murmurs of a few of my coworkers. "Her classroom is just down here."

That has me straightening. My ears perk up when I hear the familiar rumble of a sexy, deep voice say a simple "Thank you." The scent of pizza precedes Maddox, who walks in with six teachers in his wake. Four of them are female coworkers who definitely take advantage of the fact that they're following behind a hot athlete. They sneak looks at his muscular backside, smirking at each other. Two are male coworkers who have their chests puffed out like they've got to prove their masculinity in the face of a local hockey hero. They may also follow him because Maddox is carrying at least ten extra-large pizza boxes.

Maddox gifts me with a bright smile when he sees me.

It overtakes his whole face, those straight white teeth of his nearly blinding me. "Hey, baby."

*Swoon.*

"What in the world are you doing here? I thought you and the guys were doing weight training." Closing the distance between us, I take some of the pizza boxes off his hands, setting them down on my desk. He follows suit. I take a step toward him, but insecurity makes me freeze. How should I greet him in front of other people? I'm not really sure what we're doing, or if it's more than just having some fun, but he showed up unannounced at my job. That has to mean something, right?

Luckily, Maddox takes my hesitation in stride and decides for me. He wraps me up in a tight hug before pressing a kiss to my forehead and releasing me. "Eh, it wasn't mandatory, and I was distracted thinking about you. When I told the guys I was going to bring you and your coworkers lunch, I had to ban Griffin from coming. He mentioned that teacher you told him about, and I made Navarro distract him because that seemed like a recipe for disaster."

I choke out a laugh. "You have no idea. The teacher I was talking about is sixty."

Maddox's brow rises and his mouth goes slack before he's laughing and kissing my forehead again. "I'm not actually sure if that would deter him."

LaTonya clears her throat behind Maddox and I can feel my cheeks flame hot and pink. She shoots me a knowing look, and I disentangle myself from Maddox's hands and fiddle with the end of my ponytail.

"Oh, uh, sorry. Guys, this is Maddox. Maddox, this is LaTonya, Mike, Kristy, Paul, Kim, Beth, and Sarah." I motion to each of my coworkers. Maddox shakes their hands, telling them it's nice to formally meet them. Since, you know, they've been following him through the school like he's a mama duck and they're his ducklings.

"I have some soda in my car, but couldn't carry them all. I didn't think to grab plates, though. Sorry, that was an oversight." He runs a hand through his dark hair, nervous. It makes me like him even more that he'd be totally at ease around a group of rich, influential people, but with the teachers I work with, that's when his nerves show. Because he cares what they think about him. The realization that he must not care all that much about what the rich and powerful people at the charity dinner thought of him makes me smile like an idiot.

"I think we still have some paper plates in the teacher's lounge. LaTonya, will you check? Can someone also grab napkins and let whoever else is here know there's pizza?" With a bit of reluctance, they disperse, leaving me with Maddox. I go up on my tiptoes and brush a soft kiss against his lips. "This is a really nice surprise. Thank you."

"I hope it's not too much of a distraction, but I wanted to see you."

"Not at all," I assure him. It's like high school all over again. Who would have thought a grown woman could be giddy with butterflies and anticipation? "Let me help you bring in the soda."

He takes my hand in his, interlacing our fingers. We walk in companionable silence. It gives me time to wrap my head around the fact that he's here. He's here, and he brought enough pizza to feed the teachers setting up for the first day of school. It's incredibly thoughtful and sweet.

"If you thought you had a fan club when you walked

in, it's nothing on what awaits you when the rest of the teachers hear you brought free lunch," I say when Maddox opens the back of his SUV revealing three twenty-four packs of different sodas.

He grins at me, grabbing one in each hand and letting me wrap my arms around the last one. "That so?"

"Oh, yeah." I nod. I won't tell him that his ass also has its own fan club. He doesn't need to know that. And that ass is all mine. "I hope you're ready."

Maddox shrugs. "There's only one person I need in my fan club." All of me tingles when his eyes rove over my body with proprietary satisfaction. Damn. I might need to carry around a spare pair of panties because Maddox can wreck them with just one heated look.

"Oh?" I try to ignore the dampness between my legs as we walk back toward the school. I totally don't add an extra, exaggerated sway to my hips, so he has to worry about strolling in with a boner so we're even. Nope. I don't do that at all. "Paul is definitely a Rogues superfan."

Maddox's answering growl is adorable and I can't hold in my giggle. "Careful, Short-Stack. I'm not opposed to spanking your sassy little ass."

A shiver of pleasure skips down my spine like an eager little hussy, ending its journey between my legs. "Don't threaten me with a good time, Graves."

"Temptress," he mutters under his breath as we make it inside the school. There's a lot of excited chatter as we get closer to my classroom; no surprise there. My fellow teachers mill around, along with Craig, our maintenance man extraordinaire, talking excitedly. They quiet as we approach, all eyes on Maddox and me.

"Told you it was him," Paul says to the gym teacher, Archie.

"Dude." Archie's eyes are so wide it's comical. God, it's so hard not to laugh.

"All right, all right," I say. "Clear a path, you gawkers. You'll all meet Maddox, but these cases of soda are heavy, and I really don't want to drop it on my foot." That snaps them all out of their fan-induced stupor, and soon the cases are being taken out of our hands. We all gather in my classroom, but no one touches the pizza.

Maddox runs his hand through his hair again, looking bashful. "Everyone enjoy as much pizza as you want. If we need more, I'll order it, so don't worry about taking too much. I just wanted to show my appreciation for what you all do. Teachers deserve the big bucks more than dumb hockey players," he says with a charming smile. There's a beat of silence, and then everyone's opening boxes and digging in.

"Hockey players aren't dumb," I say, grabbing his hand and resting my head against his arm.

Rich brown eyes peer down at me. They're soft and warm, and I want to burrow into them and never leave. "Maybe not, but what we do isn't nearly as important as what you do."

His words heal something broken in me, or at least start to. I never needed anyone to approve of what I do or praise me for it, but I can't deny how warm and gooey it makes me that Maddox does. "You make people happy," I tell him. "You give people something to cheer for when they may not have anything else to get excited about in their lives. Don't downgrade what you do. I know how hard you work."

Those mahogany eyes of his soften even more, and then he's cupping my face in his large, callused hand and kissing me softly right there in front of everyone I work with. There are a few whistles and cheers, but I don't pay them any mind. My attention is all for the man before me. "Thanks, baby."

For the next hour, we stuff ourselves with cheesy goodness, and all of my coworkers chat with Maddox. His shoulders loosen with each new conversation as the nerves he was battling fall away. Soon, he's laughing and joking around with everyone. Winning them over easily, and not because he's some famous hockey player. He wins them over with his easy smiles, his studious attention to me, and his abundant charisma. He could be a parking cop, and they'd still hang off every word he utters.

Eventually, everyone filters out of the room, offering parting words of thanks and hoping they'll see Maddox around again. Then it's just the two of us, and I wish the afternoon didn't have to end.

"Thanks for visiting me and for bringing lunch for everyone." I wrap my arms around his waist and press my face into the sculpted planes of his chest. "You seriously made my day."

Maddox's arms cocoon around me, and once again I'm struck by how protected and safe I feel when he holds me. I want to chase the feeling, but I'm also terrified of letting myself grow to love it too much. It'll just hurt more when this inevitably ends.

"Kicking me out already?" Maddox arches an eyebrow at me, one corner of his lips quirking.

"Oh, no, I just have to do some more work setting up

my room, and I figured you had more important things to do than watch me."

"I do," he says. "Helping you. Now put me to work, Teach."

Swoon again. I'll have to carry smelling salts around. "You don't have to do that." Even though I want him to.

"I know. I want to. If you don't think I'll just get in your way." He hides a flash of vulnerability with a broad smile, but I catch it.

I rest my chin on his chest and blink up at him. "You're pretty big, but I think I can work around you." He chuckles, and I continue with a smirk. "And I'd love the help. Thank you."

The descent of his lips is slow enough that anticipation builds low in my belly. And when he kisses me, I feel it down to my toes. One of Maddox's large hands braces against the back of my neck, while the other goes to my hip. It's slow, sweet, and so damned hot I consider abandoning my classroom to go back to my place, push him down onto my bed, and have my dirty, wanton way with him.

"If you keep looking at me like that, we won't get much work done."

A sigh escapes me, puffing against his lips. "I know."

He kisses me again. This one is quick and playful. And then my body mourns the loss of his heat. Maddox heads toward a stack of posters piled haphazardly on one of the empty student desks and checks out each one. "Where do you want these?"

And that's how Maddox Graves spends the rest of the day helping me set up my classroom.

# thirty-one

## ISLA

THE WEEK GOES BY IN A BLUR OF SCHOOL PREP AND flirtatious calls and texts with Maddox. He shows up again on Friday to help me finish up all the last-minute little things I didn't get to. The first day of school is Tuesday, so it's crunch time. Maddox also arrives with a food truck in tow, telling everyone that he's booked them for the next three hours, and lunch is on him. He really has a fan club at Center High, now.

A bunch of the teachers post photos to their social media, tagging Maddox and gushing about how sweet he is and how he's shown up twice to help and provide lunch. My coworkers are pretty good at avoiding posting any lovey-dovey photos of Maddox and me, but I'm there in the background of quite a few, and when a reporter from a local news station shows up, I know they've put the pieces together, and she beelines it to where I'm inelegantly scarfing down a street taco. The reporter asks how long

Maddox and I have known each other, if we're dating, and if I'm ready for what a relationship with a pro hockey player will look like once the season kicks off. I'm taken by surprise at first, but Maddox quickly swoops in and turns the whole interview around so that the focus goes to the school and the teachers.

He's amazing, and I spend what feels like every waking moment thinking about him.

That half of the Minnesota Rogues are following my Instagram account doesn't go unnoticed by my friends, and I get quite a few comments, calls, and texts from people I haven't heard from in ages. Even "friends" who likely never spared me a second thought after Alex dumped me. They sure as hell didn't *check in* when my life was imploding, but now that I'm dating a hockey star, they're popping up all over the place telling me how they've *been thinking about me for so long and they've wanted to check in, but things were awkward for a while there.*

Right. I suppose it is awkward to know your friend broke things off with his fiancée two weeks before the wedding with almost no explanation. I don't respond to those people. It seems unlikely that Alex hasn't heard about my relationship with Maddox, but I can't seem to care. The idea of Alex fuming with jealousy doesn't make me all tingly with glee like some evil mastermind the way it used to. Look at me, growing and maturing and stuff.

Maddox and I spend the weekend together. We don't do anything extravagant like another hot air balloon ride, but I almost love the simple things we do more. We sit at coffee shops and get to know each other better, meander around a farmer's market, and eat takeout at my place. I try to get Maddox to tell me what he plans to say at the assembly, but he's adorably tight-lipped.

The first week and a half of school goes by in a blur of early mornings, learning my students' names, and getting back into the swing of things. Maddox and I don't see each other as often during those first two weeks of school because their practice is kicking into high gear to prepare for the preseason on top of my extra hours at school. But we talk and text constantly, and he shows up with dinner a few times. We haven't officially defined the relationship, but I know neither of us is seeing anyone else, and I've caught feelings. Hard.

Maybe that's why I'm a ball of jittery nerves as I get ready this morning. It's the day of the assembly, and for whatever reason, it feels like a defining moment. Today, Maddox will stand up in front of my whole school, and I don't think there will be any hiding our relationship after this. Not that I want to hide it from anyone outside of the media and nosey strangers, but still. There won't be any going back from this, and that old worry that I'm not good enough claws its way up my throat.

Standing in front of my bathroom mirror at an ungodly hour, I take extra care curling my long, red hair. My makeup is impeccable. I spent hours last night choosing my outfit. I look cute, and better than I do most school days, but Alex's voice keeps popping up in my head like some demonic jack-in-the-box.

*Is that what you're wearing tonight? I asked you to make an effort.*

*I really wish you'd straighten your hair. The curls look so... unkempt.*

*That dress is a little tighter on you than it was a few months ago. Have you gained some weight?*

"He was an asshole," I assure my reflection. "It doesn't matter what he thought about you. Especially since he rarely made you come."

Maddox has a huge dick. Not like, *Oh my god, does he have elephantitis?* huge, but definitely *I'm going to get lockjaw from sucking that glorious cock* huge.

"Get it together and stop thinking about penises," I scold my reflection. "You have young minds to mold today. You can't start the morning off horny."

Unfortunately, that part of the self-pep-talk doesn't stick. I am almost always horny since Maddox and I started dating. I used to think I had a low sex drive, but now that I'm dating someone who lights my panties on fire, it was clearly a lack of chemistry and emotional connection.

"Stop thinking about sex, Isla." And with a stupid grin on my face, I get in my car and drive to work.

There's an excitement and energy going into this new school year. Teaching can be a thankless profession, so it means so much when someone says you're doing important work and recognizes you for it. But to have that someone be a professional athlete admired by so many of the staff? It's added a shot of adrenaline to the heart of Center High.

Everyone buzzes about the assembly. Even the students who have never watched a hockey game in their lives look forward to getting out of class for an hour and asking a pro athlete questions. It makes the first half of the day a bit of a bust since no one can seem to concentrate on the material, but I don't scold my students about it. I can't concentrate, either.

When one p.m. rolls around, my chest is a mess of butterflies and nerves. I instruct my class of excited juniors to line up, smoothing my sweaty hands down my jeans.

"Ms. Harding?" One of my students, a super smart girl named Carmen, raises her hand in line. "Is it true you're dating the guy speaking at the assembly today?"

The whole class goes silent, waiting for my answer. Of course, that makes my pasty cheeks flame hot with color, and they all hoot and holler. "Where did you hear that?"

Carmen grins. "My brother is obsessed with the Rogues. He said there are photos of you two together on a few fan sites."

Oh, my god. I hope they're not bad photos. "There are?" I squeak. Not very authoritative, Isla. Carmen just grins and nods. "Are they at least good pictures?"

That has the whole class laughing. Carmen takes pity on me. "Yeah, you looked good in them, Ms. H. One looks like it was in a hot air balloon or something."

My photo from our date made it on some fan site? I had my profile set to private before I posted that, and Maddox didn't post anything from that night. I know the pilot wouldn't have done something like that—not if he wanted to get any future business from high-profile clientele—which means one of my followers posted it. And all of my followers are people I do, or have, considered friends.

Oh well, it's a problem for another day. And it's probably not a problem at all. It just feels strange, and kind of invasive. Sure, you should always assume that anything you post on the internet will make its way to the public for mass consumption, but I've never been in a position where anyone would care about the choices I make with my life.

My students are still watching me with curious expressions, so I shrug. "He took me up in a hot air balloon for one of our dates. It was pretty cool."

"I'd puke if I was that high in the air in an open basket," Brian, one of my students, says as he clutches his stomach.

"That's so romantic," another girl coos, her hands clasped under her chin. "Was it romantic?"

My chuckle is uncomfortable. I am *so* not discussing my dates with my students. "It was. But we're not here to learn about my dating life, right?" I clap my hands after glancing at the clock. "It's time to head to the gym. I know we're all excited, but I expect everyone to be on their best behavior. Let's make sure we represent Center High well. Okay?"

A chorus of agreement fills the room, and then I'm leading my kids through the halls and into the gym. The whole school buzzes with murmuring students and grinning staff. A surge of affection rises in my chest for Maddox. This kind of thing isn't a normal occurrence for these kids, and I love seeing their faces light up with innocent excitement. I know that—at least for the next hour—they'll all get to leave the struggles and stresses of their home lives at the door and just be kids.

The bleachers are full. It wouldn't surprise me to find out we are at one hundred percent attendance today. Teachers line the aisles and the walls of the gym. I'm standing close to the double doors Maddox will enter through, and my eyes stray from my students and to those doors every few seconds. I can't wait to see his face. It's only been a few days since we've been together in person, but it feels like longer.

Feedback screeches through the gym, earning a gasp and boos from the students as Trish White, our principal, takes her place in the middle of the gym. She offers a sheepish smile in lieu of an apology, and motions for everyone to quiet down with her hands.

"Good morning, students. As you all know, we have an exciting assembly planned for you today. I'm sure I don't need to remind you that being here is a privilege, not a right, so I expect you all to be the respectful, exemplary students I know you to be." Kids nod and murmur their agreement to behave as Trish scans the room, her principal face firmly in place. When she feels like everyone is sufficiently calm, her smile grows.

"How many of you are familiar with our local NHL team, the Rogues?" Hundreds of hands shoot up. "Excellent. Well, we are very lucky today to welcome several members of their team."

My eyebrows shoot up at that. Several? Maddox didn't say anything about bringing anyone with him. My eyes jump to the double doors leading into the gym as they open, revealing Maddox, his guys, and a few other members of the team. His rich, brown eyes scan the gym until they land on me and soften. I soften right along with them. I'm practically a puddle of goo when his lips quirk into a smile that's only for me. *What did you do?* I mouth at him.

His smile grows blinding. *For you.* He mouths back.

"Center High, please put your hands together for Maddox Graves, Logan Byrne, Sebastian Navarro, Griffin Wright, Ryder Hanson, Trey Moore, and Javier Martinez."

Trish sweeps her arm out indicating the seven massive hockey players decked out in their best game-day suits.

Maddox brushes the back of his hand against mine as he walks into the gym, which is now thundering with applause and cheers, Griffin winks so exaggeratedly at me I'm sure everyone sees it, Logan and Sebastian offer familiar smiles and nod like we're all in on some inside joke, and the rest of the guys give me little waves.

I can only watch, stunned into silence by the unexpected additions to the assembly lineup. The guys smile and wave, taking the shouting kids in stride like this is normal for them. And I suppose it is. They must be used to this kind of reception. Meanwhile, I'm still struggling to pick my jaw up off the floor, completely overcome with glowing affection for Maddox Graves. When he looks my way again and mouths, *You okay?* All I can do is nod.

The thing is, I'm not sure I am okay. Because I was right. This is a defining moment for Maddox and me. It's the moment I fall a little bit in love with him.

thirty-two

## ISLA

THE GUYS ARE AMAZING. MADDOX IS AMAZING. They spend a solid half an hour answering questions from curious students that range from thoughtful to inappropriate. We have to shut a few questions down, but not that many. All in all, the students of Center High show the Rogues players exactly what I have known from my first day here. They're exceptional teenagers.

When Maddox announces that every single kid will receive family passes to a home game of their choice—plus snacks, shirts, and hats for each attendee—the students go wild. It doesn't matter that most of them have never been to a hockey game. After today, they're fans for life. Maddox also informs the school that the team has donated ten thousand dollars to Center High's after-school clubs and programs.

"I was raised by an amazing single mom," he says, pride glimmering in his rich brown eyes. "So my sister and

I spent a lot of time at after-school programs. We both got opportunities to learn new skills and figure out where we fit into the world at those clubs. All of us at the Rogues believe every single one of you should have the same opportunities." The students cheer and clap, but I'm stunned into open-mouthed silence. When Maddox's gaze slides my way, I press my hand to my heart and hope he can read the thankfulness I know must be etched into my expression.

"Thanks for welcoming us, Center High. We've loved hanging out with you today. I hope we see all of you cheering us on once the season starts at the arena." A cheer goes up and Maddox's smile is blinding. Then he waves his hands in a *quiet down* gesture and says, "We've got some friends stationed at the doors. The Rogues believe that being prepared sets you up for success. At school, at work, and in everyday life. Which is why there are brand new backpacks filled with supplies and gift cards for all of you."

The students really go crazy at this, and my heart is a goner. He did this. I know it was Maddox's doing.

"There's plenty for everyone, so make sure there's no pushing or anything like that, okay?" His brows rise and he looks from section to section. "Okay?" The kids all shout *Okay!* and Maddox grins. "Keep striving for excellence, Center. We believe in you. But more importantly, you've got amazing teachers here who believe in you, advocate for you, and care about you." His eyes find me again, and I feel so seen in that moment that my breath catches and my eyes well with tears. "Go Wildcats," Maddox ends with a shout, and a kid dressed in the Wildcat mascot runs into the middle of the gym as music plays. He does a goofy dance to cheers and jeers as teachers corral their students into some semblance of a line.

Before I can do the same with my students, I'm surrounded by massive hockey players. The guys I don't know all that well all say hi and thank me for the chance to come speak to the kids. *They* thank *me*. As if I were the one doing them a favor and not the other way around. Flustered, I return the thanks, and when they ask if I'll be at their first home game, I say yes without a moment's hesitation. Maddox has dropped hints about wanting me to come, but hasn't officially asked. His teammates have beaten him to it, but when I see his face drop into an irritated scowl at their request, I know it's not because he hadn't wanted me to be there. If I had to guess, he had some grand plan the others just ruined.

Sebastian gives me that gentle smile of his, tugging me in for a hug. It doesn't last for more than a couple of seconds before Griffin yanks me out of his hold and squeezes me so tightly that I squeak.

"Don't crush Isla or Maddox will crush you," Logan says with a chuckle. He helps me escape Griffin's overly enthusiastic greeting, giving me a quick hug of his own.

"All right, all right, that's enough." Maddox pulls me away from all of them, but his eyes dance with laughter. "Hey, Short-Stack. You look beautiful today."

I wrap my arms around his waist and press in for a long hug. A few students in my class hoot and cheer, and a few chant my name, but I can't pay attention to them yet. I let my eyes rove over Maddox's face and whisper, "I can't believe you did all this."

The man simply shrugs. *Shrugs.* As if what he's done here today is no big deal.

It's a very big deal. To me, to these kids, to this school. A very big deal.

"I wish I could say everything I want to say right now, but I have to get my kids back to class. Are you free after school gets out?"

Maddox gives my hand a quick squeeze. "Of course. How about I hang out in the area and pick you up once you're done for the day? We can grab a coffee or something?"

"That sounds great. There's a great little café I always go to like five minutes away."

"Perfect. Text me when you're done?"

I nod. "Yeah. I will." We stare at each other for a few beats before Griffin clears his throat.

"Dude. Don't forget to invite Isla to the barbeque at my house this weekend." Griffin elbows Maddox in the side a little too hard to be considered a nudge.

"I told you I would," Maddox says with a roll of his eyes. "You need to chill the hell out, Wright."

Sebastian chuckles, shaking his head. If these four were actually brothers, Bash would be the oldest. The responsible, conscientious one. Griffin would be the wild youngest child. Maddox would be the second born, and Logan the third. I love watching them interact. Bash rests a hand on Griffin's shoulder. "All right, guys. Let's say hi to some kids, then get out of here. We don't want to disrupt more of the school day than we're supposed to."

"Trust me," I say, "this is the best disruption we've ever had. Thank you guys so much for coming." I flash a bright, grateful smile at all of them. "It means so much to me. And to the kids."

"Anything for our favorite teacher," Logan drawls, earning the attention of a few of my female coworkers. The looks they give him make it crystal clear that *they'd* happily sign up for a chance to be his favorite teacher. Yeah. I'm going to be fending off requests to set them up with Logan for the rest of the week.

It's difficult to tear myself away from Maddox, but my students get rowdy, and I need them lined up so they can pick up their new backpacks on the way back to class.

"All right! I want my class lined up and calm, or I'm switching our next book to something long and dry. I can think of a few really pretentious books that you guys would just *love*." A chorus of groans fills the air as they line up and quiet down. "Aw, come on, people. You don't want to read War and Peace or something?"

"Ms. Harding. No." One of my students shakes his head vehemently. "We're all excited to read *Fahrenheit 451*."

"Okay," I say with a smirk. "Then line up."

"Ms. Harding?" Chris, one of my quieter students, raises his hand. "Are you really friends with all of those Rogues players?" His eyes dart to the guys, who are now all signing things and shaking hands with the students as they wait in line to get their backpacks.

"Well, I don't know all of them very well, but I'm friends with a few of them."

"You totally are dating the big one, aren't you?" A few of the girls giggle when my student, Carissa, asks that.

I try to hide my grin, my eyes instinctively darting to Maddox. He meets my gaze with a blinding smile, and I hope I'm not blushing like an idiot. It wouldn't be very teacherly. "Guys, you know it's not appropriate to talk about my dating life with you."

"That means yes," one of the other students says.

Carissa nods. "Oh, for sure."

It takes all of my self-restraint not to confirm their suspicions. After everything Maddox did today, I want to shout it from the rooftops that I'm seeing him. That this incredibly selfless, sweet man somehow wants me. I want things with us to be official.

But I do what any good teacher would do in this situation. I roll my eyes at my students and pretend I'm completely celibate.

***

MADDOX WAITS FOR ME IN THE PARKING LOT WHEN I finally leave for the day. I have plenty of time to admire his tall, muscular figure leaning against his car as I walk his way. He's backlit, the sun haloing him in the warmth of its late-summer rays, and god, is he a thing of beauty. I've never been so attracted to a man. But the best part of that attraction is that his personality and character are just as beautiful as his appearance.

If only I met him before Alex. Before I was broken. I wish my walls weren't so thick because Alex's casually cruel words hit their mark again and again. Some part of me may always wait for the other shoe to drop, but after what he did today? I'm all in. And I'm going to tell him so.

"Hey, baby, how was the rest of your day?" Maddox scoops me up in a hug as soon as I'm close enough. My feet dangle above the ground, and he chuckles at the squeak that escapes my lips. He makes me feel small and protected, but not in a weird controlling way, and I melt into his hold. Then he's kissing me and my brain short circuits. The kiss is soft and sweet, but there's heat behind it. If we weren't in the parking lot of my school and if there wasn't the possibility of someone seeing, I'd be shamelessly grinding myself against the hard length I feel between us, pressing against the jeans he's changed into. Instead, we break the kiss and he presses his forehead to mine. We're both breathing hard, and I have to remind myself that he asked me a question.

"My day was amazing, thanks to you and the guys." I pull back an inch so I can look him in the eyes. "I can't believe you did that for all of those kids, Maddox." My throat tightens, and I have to clear it. "That was so far above and beyond what I asked you to do."

A slow, sweet smile curves his lips as he brushes a hair from my face. "I *was* those kids, once. And when I told the guys and the team my ideas, it all snowballed from there. But I also know how important those kids are to you, and I wanted to show you how important you are to me."

His last words are soft and adorably hesitant. It's as though he's not sure how I'll react to his confession. Which is crazy, because I'm glowing inside. His words are a ball of light that fills my chest and dispels the shadows that have lurked there for far too long.

I don't know what the future holds for us, but I want to find out. I'm all in.

"Maddox?"

He brushes his thumb along my cheekbone. "Hmm?"

"You're important to me too, and I... I'm not seeing anyone else and I don't want to, and I was just wondering... Well, I was hoping you..." *Ugh.* Eloquent as always,

Isla. I scrunch my nose up and press my lips together. Why is it so hard to tell him I want us to be exclusive? That I want to introduce him as my boyfriend and hold his hand in public without wondering what he thinks we are.

Maddox's face melts into a blinding smile and he flips our position so my back presses against his SUV and his strong arms cage me in. His thumb smooths out the wrinkle between my eyebrows as his eyes dance. The sun makes them sparkle. "Isla Harding, are you asking me to be your boyfriend?"

God, when he says it like that, his tone all teasing and his lips quirked to the side, I want to melt into a puddle and disappear. Because it sounds lame. But yeah. That is what I'm asking. Or would be, if I wasn't such an awkward potato.

"Ugh." I let my head flop forward to rest on his broad chest. He smells so good I just burrow in. This can be my home now. I'll happily die from embarrassment by smothering myself between Maddox's pecs. "Yes," I mumble. His hoodie and body muffle the words. "Yes, I want you to be my boyfriend."

Maddox chuckles, the laugh vibrating through his body and tickling my nose. "Isla." He presses a knuckle beneath my chin, urging me to look at him. I grumble out an unintelligible sound and burrow further into him, which earns another laugh. "Isla. Baby. Would you look at me?"

Reluctantly, I do. I expect Maddox to roll his eyes at me or look exasperated. After all, those are the kinds of reactions I'm used to when I do or say something less than perfect.

But Maddox meets my gaze with such a soft, tender

expression. "I've wanted to ask you to be my girlfriend since our do-over date, but I didn't want to freak you out."

"Really?"

He nods. "Really. You're amazing. Smart, intelligent, passionate, and so damned kind. Say you'll be my girlfriend. I want to show you off at Griffin's barbecue and call you mine. Officially."

That ball of light in my chest flares brighter. I lift onto my toes and tug Maddox's face down with my arms around his neck. My lips feather across his as I fight a smile. "I guess that would be okay. Now let's go get coffee, and then you can tell me all about this barbeque, boyfriend. I'm craving something sweet."

"Mmm. Me too, girlfriend." He nips my bottom lip and grinds his erection into my lower belly. "But what I'm craving will have to wait."

# *thirty-three*

## ISLA

WE HOLD HANDS THE WHOLE DRIVE TO THAT'S Doppio. It's a cute little coffee shop that serves locally roasted coffee but doesn't take itself too seriously. Hence the name. Maddox finds a spot just up the street and opens my door before I can do it myself. Wrapping his arm around me, he pulls me against his side. I sigh happily. Women always talk about how fun it is to have a much taller, larger boyfriend, but I never really got the hype. Until now. Because being tucked into Maddox's side like this is so cozy and comforting. I feel safe and protected.

Maddox changed out of his suit while I finished teaching, but even with his hoodie up and sunglasses on, he's getting more than a few curious looks. We almost make it to the coffee shop when a little blond boy stops dead in his tracks, stares at Maddox with wide gray eyes, then tugs on his mom's jacket and says, "Mom, Mom! Is that Maddox Graves?"

And that's that. Maddox shoots me an apologetic grimace, no doubt recalling our auction date when he blew me off for a solid fifteen minutes to sign autographs and take selfies. But this time it's different. This time I know he wants to say no and run into the coffee shop with me, but how can you ignore the bright, pleading eyes of a kid who can't be older than eight?

"It's okay," I tell him with a chuckle. "Go ahead and sign autographs or whatever. I'll head inside and get us coffees and a table."

He rubs the back of his head, attention bouncing between the growing crowd and me. "You sure?"

"Of course. What do you want?"

"Uh, a black coffee, I guess."

I make a face. "Really? This place has amazing lattes, and you just want a black coffee?"

Maddox chuckles, giving my hip a squeeze. "We stick to pretty strict diets when the season starts. Sadly, I will just have a black coffee."

My nose is still wrinkled when I say, "Okay. See you in there."

He presses a quick kiss to my forehead and watches me walk toward the cafe door before giving his attention to the little boy who jumps in place, he's so excited. "Hey, little man. What's your name?"

"Jude," I hear the little blond boy exclaim. "Could you sign my sweatshirt?"

I'm smiling from ear to ear when I stride into That's Doppio and get in line. The cafe is reasonably busy for being so close to dinnertime, but that's normal. It's a popular place with teachers, students, and professionals alike. The cashier greets me with a smile and asks me how school is going so far before I order my drinks and pay. It's one thing I love about this place. They all know me.

There are a few open tables scattered around the room, so I pick the one most tucked away in a corner. I just have enough time to arrange my cardigan on the back of a chair and set my purse down when the barista calls my name.

Maddox is still scribbling autographs on the sidewalk, so I grab our drinks with a smile, settle in at the table, and pull out my phone. Might as well do some mindless social media scrolling until he gets in. I open Instagram and grin when I see I've been tagged in a photo Griffin insisted we take after the assembly. In it, I'm sandwiched between him and Sebastian while Griffin gives me bunny ears. I'm laughing, and Sebastian is mid-eye roll. He's captioned it with, *Stay in school, kids. You could end up with a teacher like Madds' girl, here.* He follows that pronouncement up with a winky face emoji, and I can't hold in my laughter. He's ridiculous. I'm mid-debate with myself about whether it's wise to read any of the comments when a throat clears in front of me, and an all too familiar voice says my name.

"Isla? I thought that was you."

My happy smile freezes on my face as my eyes rise from my phone. I take in a man with his hands in the pockets of his expensive gray suit. The jacket is unbuttoned, revealing a crisp white shirt and a solid black tie. Full lips I have mapped a million times with my own twist up in a rueful smile, and blue eyes rake over my body with too much familiarity. It makes my skin crawl. At one point, I loved when Alex looked at me like this. Now it just makes me feel cheap and dirty.

"Alex?" My mind stumbles in its attempt to switch

gears from feeling all gooey inside to processing Alex's sudden and unwanted appearance.

His eyes go to the two cups on the table with a frown. When he looks back up at me, his smile seems strained. "You look great. It's good to see you."

I narrow my eyes. I've been obsessed with this place ever since I first student taught at Center. I dragged Alex here exactly one time, and all he did was complain about how noisy it was and how the coffee wasn't strong enough for him. He never came back with me. Which is why all of this is so highly suspicious.

"What are you doing here?"

Alex frowns at my tone. I'm not surprised. The last few times we spoke, it was me calling him, crying, begging him to give us another chance. I was broken and desperate, and I still thought Alex hung the moon.

I don't think that anymore.

"I was in the neighborhood for a meeting and remembered how great this place was from the time we came here."

I want to cough *bullshit* into my hand, but I'm an adult. I still roll my eyes, though. You're never too old or too mature to give a dramatic eye roll. "You hated this place the one time we came together," I say, unwilling to go along with whatever game he's playing.

Alex's frown deepens, but he still pulls out the chair across from me at the four-person circular table and sits his ass down as if I've invited him to join me. He looks constipated. I can't believe I ever found him attractive. "Anyway," he says. "It's pretty crazy we ran into each other, huh?"

"Is it?" I arch a brow. "I wouldn't call this running into

each other. I was just sitting here waiting for my boyfriend when you plopped your ass down uninvited."

When Alex's jaw ticks, I know I'm well and truly pissing him off. This isn't going the way he thought it would, and that brings me great joy. "Boyfriend?"

I snort out an undignified laugh. Of course, that's the part he latches on to.

"You're dating someone?"

As if he doesn't know. He must have heard all about how Maddox and I were acting at the charity dinner from his best friend.

"Yeah," a deep voice rumbles. "She is." Maddox steps beside me and tilts my chin up. He claims my mouth with a searing kiss that leaves me breathless. His molten chocolate eyes hold mine, reading me, making sure I'm okay. Maddox doesn't know the full story of what happened with Alex, but he knows enough. "Sorry that took so long, baby." And then he kisses my forehead, drags a chair beside me, and folds himself into it. Maddox drapes his arm across the back of my chair and nestles me into his side before grabbing his boring cup of plain black coffee.

"It's okay," I reply, my attention only for him. "Your fans are important."

"Not as important as you."

That ball of light in my chest is halfway to going supernova because I know he means it. Maddox isn't just paying me lip service or saying something that sounds good because my ex is sitting across from us, studying this whole interaction with a hilarious frown on his face. Maddox means it.

We stare at each other for a few beats, which I'm sure is super awkward for Alex. To his credit, he lasts a couple of seconds longer than I think he will, then clears his throat.

"You should probably get that checked out," I tell him, sounding infinitely bored.

Alex's forehead creases. "What?"

"You keep clearing your throat. You should get that checked out."

Maddox fake-coughs to cover up a laugh, which Alex does not find amusing. Still, being the bigger man—both literally and figuratively—Maddox reaches a hand out across the table. "I'm Maddox. You are?"

I hide my smirk behind my delicious mocha toffee latte. Alex hesitates for a moment before shaking Maddox's hand and winces when Maddox squeezes. "Alex. I'm Isla's—"

"Nothing." I cut in. "You're not my anything." I haven't told Maddox that Alex and I were engaged, and this isn't really the way I wanted it to come out, but here we are. I suppose there will be no more hiding it after this.

Shifting in his seat, this whole interaction obviously going way differently than he imagined, Alex's jaw ticks. "I'm her ex-fiancé."

Spine stiffening, I glance at Maddox to gauge his reaction. He gives me a squeeze and a quick smile before turning back to Alex.

"Ah. Isla mentioned something about an ex, but she said it was no big deal. One of those relationships you should have ended way sooner, but didn't because you get stuck in a dating rut." He turns to me with a furrowed brow. "I thought you said his name was Leslie or something?"

Oh, god. It's so hard not to laugh at that. Relief floods

my body that Maddox doesn't seem put out even as Alex's face morphs into one of rage before schooling it and leaning back in his chair. All I can do is shrug because if I open my mouth, I'm going to lose my shit.

Maddox tilts his head to the side as though he's really wracking his brain, trying to remember what name I'd given him for my ex. Eventually, he returns my shrug. "Eh, I can't remember. I think we talked about our exes the night I made you come four times in two hours, so I was a little preoccupied."

Oh. My. God. My face erupts in flames and I swat his chest. "Maddox! Jesus Christ, there are families here."

My mischievous hockey player glances around before saying, "No one heard me, baby." He takes a swig of his coffee. His voice lowers. "I think we can break that record tonight."

"Maddox..."

Alex clears his throat for the third time. This time, the sound is decidedly pissed. Maddox turns to him, plastering a concerned look on his face. "Isla's right, man. You should definitely see a doctor. You don't sound too good." He gives my ex a quick once-over. "You don't look too good, either."

"Isla," Alex says, barely ignoring Maddox's jab. "Can we go somewhere and talk? I've been thinking a lot lately about how things ended between us, and it would be good to talk things through. We were always so good together. I hate that I may have hurt you."

May have? *May have?* I want to throw my piping hot latte in his face. I want to punch him. I want Maddox to punch him. A million things I'd love to scream race through my head. But I remain outwardly calm, Maddox's heat grounding me and tethering me. Alex wants an emotional reaction. He thrives off them. His favorite game to play was pushing me and pushing me until I'd blow up, and then he'd press a hand to his chest as though my reaction came out of nowhere, then imply I was crazy or overly emotional.

I won't give him that power over me again.

"Pass," I say, sounding bored. I even fake a yawn while mentally high-fiving myself. Because Alex does *not* like that reaction.

"Pass? What do you mean, pass? You spent months trying to get me to meet with you. You left me messages begging me to take you back, crying and pleading and promising you'd work harder to be the woman I needed. Now you don't want to talk?"

My spine straightens, embarrassment flooding me. I don't want Maddox to think I'm pathetic. I mean, *I* think I'm pathetic when I really let myself dissect the things that happened after Alex left me. It wasn't my finest moment. But I was blindsided and embarrassed. Alex left me to tell everyone the wedding was off a mere two weeks before it was scheduled to happen. But Maddox simply holds me tighter and presses a kiss to my temple. It's a silent promise that he's here with me and in my corner.

I take a steadying breath and roll my eyes. "God, no. The only thing I have to say is thank you."

"Thank you?" Alex stumbles over the words, his brow rising in disbelief.

"Mm hm. You totally saved me from being miserable and sexually frustrated for the rest of my life. Honestly, I'm not sure how long I could have kept lying to you about how big your dick is. I mean, you asked almost every.

Single. Time. We screwed." I pitch my voice low in a horrible impression of my ex. *"It's so big, isn't it, honey? You can barely handle all of this, can't you?"*

Maddox nearly spits out his coffee but manages to hold it in at the last minute. He coughs a few times and pounds his chest. Alex, though? He's less amused.

"Classy as always, I see," he says, standing stiffly. His shoulders nearly touch his ears, and his hands flex at his sides. "And here I was going to give you another chance. Maybe I still would, if you come to your senses. This isn't you, Isla. I could make you something. Make you into *someone.*"

That has Maddox pushing out of his chair. He's got a good six inches on Alex, at least, and some of the color leaches out of Alex's skin. "I'm only going to say this once, Leslie, so listen up." Alex opens his mouth to object to the name, but Maddox silences him with a look. "You can't make Isla into something or someone great because she's already done that herself. She's bold and intelligent and beloved by hundreds of students and teachers alike at her school. She's got my whole damned team wrapped around her finger." Maddox's hand strokes down the back of my head before tangling in my hair at the nape of my neck. "She's got me wrapped around her little finger. The only thing *you* could ever make her is miserable. Now I suggest you get the hell out of here."

Alex scoffs. "I'm not afraid of you. You're nothing more than a Neanderthal who carries around a big stick."

Maddox chuckles at that. "Maybe, maybe not. That doesn't change the fact that I regularly crush men twice your size on the ice. Buh-bye now."

Furious blue eyes swing my way. "Are you serious right now, Isla? You're choosing this guy over me?"

I tug on Maddox's hand, coaxing him to sit down beside me once again. Too many people are looking our way as he and Alex square off, and I don't want this to become an issue for either of us. "Honestly, Alex? It's not even a choice. Have the day you deserve."

Mouth opening and closing, Alex resembles a fish out of water as he struggles to find something to say. When nothing comes and he notices the curious looks being lobbed his way, he turns on his heel and storms out of That's Doppio without another word.

My shoulders sag when he's gone, and Maddox tugs me in for a tight hug.

"You okay, Short-Stack?"

My hands shake and my voice wavers now that the confrontation is over, but I can answer him honestly when I say, "Yeah. I'm good. Listen, I'm sorry I never told you I was engaged, I just…"

"Hey. Nope. You don't owe me anything, okay? You can tell me about it when you're ready." Maddox feathers his thumb over my jaw, studying me. When he's confident that I'm truly okay, he nods to himself. "How about a brownie? My badass girlfriend totally deserves chocolate after that."

I laugh, some of the tension draining out of me. He gets me. He really gets me. "A brownie sounds amazing. But only if you share it with me."

"Anything for you, baby."

I'm watching Maddox's tight ass as he strides up to the counter to order when an older woman leans toward me from the next table over.

"I wasn't trying to eavesdrop," she says apologetically,

"but I couldn't help overhearing some of that." Her soft eyes glance Maddox's way before she looks back at me. "You've got yourself a keeper there, dear. Hang on to that one."

She mirrors the smile that overtakes my face when I say, "Don't worry. I will."

Any man who will stick up for you to your ex, then feed you chocolate without having to be asked, is a keeper for sure.

# thirty-four

ISLA

"ARE YOU SURE YOU'RE OKAY?" MADDOX ASKS FOR the third time since we got in his car. He keeps glancing at me from the corner of his eyes, checking on me. It's sweet.

The smile I offer him is genuine. I was a bit shaken by the whole interaction with Alex, and I'll probably have a small-scale freakout when I get home and have some time to reflect on everything, but I'm surprisingly good. With Maddox there, seeing Alex didn't have the same impact it would have had I run into him a month prior on my own. That would have sent me into a tailspin. This? This is nothing a ten-minute conversation with my therapist can't resolve.

The realization floods my chest with warmth. Maddox is helping me heal. He's changing the way I see myself and the things that went down with Alex.

He's amazing, and I need him.

"About Alex? Yes, I'm okay about that." I roll my lower

lip between my teeth and turn to face Maddox. My eyelashes flutter in time with the butterflies in my chest. "But, Maddox? I do have a problem. I think…" I chew on my lip. "I was hoping you could help me."

Concern bleeds from my boyfriend's pores. He reaches over and intertwines our fingers. "Anything, baby. You know that."

Shifting in my seat, I press my thighs together. Ever since he kissed me possessively in the coffee shop and laid his claim on me, my core has been pulsing. "Anything?"

"Anything."

The words stall in my throat as a sudden attack of shyness seizes me. What if Maddox rejects me? What if telling him exactly what I want turns him off? What if Alex wasn't the one who was mediocre in bed? What if it's me, and having sex ruins this brand new relationship Maddox and I are building?

"Isla?"

No. I will not let Alex-induced doubts impact things with Maddox. I won't. Sucking in a sharp breath, I lay myself bare for him. "Well, the problem is that I'm aching, and I was hoping you could help me. I want you to fuck me, Maddox. Please."

The car swerves slightly within our lane, and his fingers tighten around mine. "Jesus, baby. Are you sure?"

"Yes," I tell him. Because I am. He's been so attentive. So generous with his touch and affection. But I want more than just his fingers and his mouth. I want all of him. I need all of him.

"Fuck," he groans. He sounds pained as he adjusts himself. "I'm taking you to my place."

My stomach flutters. I haven't been to Maddox's home

yet. I think he loves my cozy little apartment, and there's a part of me that worries about walking into Maddox's space. I try not to be judgmental about his money, but my experiences have left me with some pretty negative perceptions of wealth. I know it's silly, but I'm glad I've had the chance to get to know my boyfriend more on my home turf.

But I'm ready to explore his now.

"My car is still at the school," I remind him.

"We can get it tomorrow."

Oh. He wants me to spend the night.

I want that, too. Very much.

It doesn't take long before we pull into a private garage beneath a gleaming building in a trendy part of Minneapolis. It's the kind of place I've never given a second thought to because I could save my whole life and never be able to afford to purchase a unit here. Large, modern balconies dot the exterior, as do huge windows that must boast amazing views of the city.

Maddox grabs my hand as we climb out of his vehicle, and he leads me to a private elevator that requires key card access. It brings us up to a modern lobby where two security guards watch the doors and a wall of monitors. They glance up at us and give Maddox a familiar nod. I give them an awkward wave as Maddox leads me toward another elevator at the far end of the lobby. He scans his key card once again, his foot tapping rapidly on the white marble-tiled floor.

As soon as we're safely inside the elevator and the doors close, he's on me.

Maddox cages me against the wall with his broad upper body and muscular arms. Our chests brush with each ragged inhalation. He stares down at me, pupils blown, and my lower belly clenches. When he removes a hand from the wall to cup my cheek tenderly, even though he looks like he wants to devour me, I swear my knees go weak.

"You're so beautiful," he murmurs as he drops his lips to mine. "So beautiful when you come, too." He presses into me. Everywhere. Plush lips move over mine, his muscular thigh presses between my legs, and his very hard cock pushes into my belly. "I can't wait to watch you shatter around my thick cock, baby girl."

Fuck. Me.

I'm grinding against his thigh when the elevator dings. The loss of contact when he pulls away makes me whimper. It earns me a dark chuckle as he tugs on my hand, dragging me to the lone door on this floor. My pussy aches as he unlocks it. I need him. I must say it out loud because Maddox's fingers tighten around mine.

"Don't worry, baby. I'm going to fill you up the way you need so soon."

The apartment barely registers. There's a vague impression of high ceilings, walls of windows, and lots of muted neutrals before he leads me down a wide hallway and shoves a door open to reveal his bedroom. This room I pay attention to.

Deep gray walls make up the space, except for one to the left, which is solid windows. Gleaming hardwoods reflect the city lights and provide an ambient glow. The bed is huge, though it would have to be to fit a man of Maddox's height. Three industrial-looking black wall sconces are mounted over a slatted wooden headboard stained a rich sienna brown. Cream sheets and a tan comforter that looks like it's made of clouds cover the bed and call my name. A massive cream area rug softens the masculine energy of the room.

It's beautiful and tasteful, but I don't care about any of it. I just need Maddox inside me.

He watches me do a quick inspection of the room and grins wickedly when my hungry eyes come back to him. "Like what you see?" he asks as he prowls toward me.

I can only nod. My voice is stuck in my throat. He's taking up all the oxygen in the room. And when he rips the hoodie over his head, the tee beneath quickly following, my thoughts dry up. Like what I see? How the hell could I not when he looks like that?

"You're wearing too many clothes," he says as he stops before me. Those captivating, warm, amber-flecked eyes of his drag down my body so slowly it almost feels like a physical touch. Almost.

I grin at him. "You should help me fix that."

No sooner have the words left my mouth than he's dragging my shirt over my head and unbuttoning my pants. The long fingers of one hand snake between the waistband of my black panties as the other hand grips the back of my neck. His lips find mine at the same moment his fingers sweep through my dripping folds, and he groans into my open mouth.

"Fuck, baby. You're soaked for me." Thick fingers drag through my wetness again before pressing into my body. I buck into his hand, and he nips at my lower lip. "Have you been drenched all day? Has my poor little Short-Stack been wet and needy this whole time?"

"Yes," I moan. And I have been. I've been wet since he strode into my school and went above and beyond the agreement we made on that first terrible date. I've been wet since he claimed my mouth in front of Alex. I've been dripping as my mind imagined this moment in a thousand different ways.

"We should take care of that then," he says, pumping his finger in and out of me once, twice, three times before he removes it completely. The loss of him has me whining. I've never felt so needy. Then again, I've never wanted anyone the way I want Maddox Graves. It's consuming. Monumental. Life altering.

Whatever I feel for him right now, I know that having sex will amplify it tenfold. I have the distinct impression that the moment Maddox sinks himself into my body, my world will reorient itself, and he'll be that much closer to the center.

That thought should terrify me more than it does.

Deft fingers tug at my remaining clothes, and soon I'm completely bare before him. My entire body flushes with arousal, and I return the favor and drag his pants down his legs. His boxer briefs fall to the floor a moment later.

Maddox's cock is thick and hard. He groans as I stare at it, then hisses when I lean down and swirl my tongue around its crown. I want to take him in my mouth and give him a blow job any porn star would be proud of. But after puking on my high school boyfriend's dick the one time I tried to suck down more than just a guy's head, I've been gun shy. Dick shy?

"I want to suck your cock," I whisper, looking up at Maddox from beneath the fringe of my eyelashes. "Like *really* suck it. Not just the head like I have been doing. But I had a bad experience once a long time ago, and I'm worried…"

"Isla." Maddox interrupts me, his palm cradling my cheek and urging me to look up at him. "Baby, I don't care if you never suck my cock. I don't care if you only ever lick it like an ice cream cone. I never want you to do something that makes you uncomfortable. Understand?"

If I wasn't drenched before, I would be now. "It's not that, it's just…"

He watches me as my words trail off. With soft eyes, he says, "If you want to tell me about it right now, I'm all ears. And if it's something you want to work through, I'm here for you. But baby, you're the one who just had to confront her ex. And as your boyfriend, it's my job to make sure you're okay. Better than okay. Let me make you feel good."

Blinking at him a few times, I wonder how I got so lucky. And I push aside the rogue thoughts warning me that Maddox Graves is entirely too good to be true. "I do want to tell you about it." Even though it's embarrassing as hell. "But not now. Right now, I need you."

The sexiest groan slips past Maddox's lips, and then his hands go to my ass and he's lifting me like I weigh nothing at all. I wrap my arms around his neck and our mouths collide with undisguised need as he holds me to his body. I grind against his abs like a cat in heat, whimpering as my clit pulses.

Maddox's erection rubs against my ass as he carries me over to his bed and gently lays me down. His lips never leave mine. Our connection never breaks. His much larger form covers and cages my body in, and when he braces his knee between my thighs, I unwrap my legs from around Maddox's waist and let them splay open.

"So fucking beautiful," he murmurs as he breaks our

kiss and looks his fill. There's no mistaking the deep hunger flaring in his earthen eyes.

I've never felt so beautiful.

Shivers of pleasure skitter down my spine as Maddox's rough hands explore every inch of my naked flesh. He kisses, nips, and sucks his way down the column of my neck, over my collarbones, and pays particular attention to my aching breasts.

"You're a goddess," he says between kisses. "And you're mine."

God, that possessiveness does it for me. It doesn't send a flare of panic through my chest or a twinge of discomfort because I know he means it in the most reverential way. For some reason, this beautiful, talented, sought-after man seems surprised that I would want to be his.

Madness.

"And you're mine," I reply on a shaky exhalation. My back arches off the mattress as Maddox lightly nips at my breast and his fingers slip between my slick folds. He presses one finger inside of me before withdrawing it and adding another. I cry out when he rubs along my inner walls, stretching me, driving me wild.

"I need to make sure you're ready for me." Maddox's voice is a low rasp. His hard length presses against my hip, and I'm desperate to feel him inside of me. "Don't want to hurt you, baby."

"You won't," I croak. But I've never taken anyone as large as Maddox, so I let myself give in to the pleasure he wrings from my body. I'm so wet that I can hear the slick movements of his fingers as he fucks me with them. The sound is erotic. Reaching down, I fist his cock and rub my thumb along the slit, spreading the bead of pre-cum across its thick head. It's not enough.

My hand falls to my pussy, my fingers skimming across Maddox's hand as he pleasures me. I slip two of my own fingers inside my wet heat alongside his and moan from how full it makes me. He stops licking and sucking my nipples to stare at where our fingers slide together and disappear into my pussy. His gaze is hungry. Wild. And when I draw my fingers out, coated in my slick arousal, and paint the shaft of his dick with it, he practically growls.

"Jesus, baby. That's so hot." His words taper off into a gasp as I palm his length and work him. My arousal makes him slippery and wet, and my hand moves in a fluid dance. His hips buck as I work him. "Shit. Shit, you need to stop, Isla. I don't want to come in your hand. I want to be buried inside you when I explode."

With a devious smirk, I work his dick once more. Maddox grabs my wrist and presses it above my head on the mattress. He slowly withdraws his fingers from my body, which I protest with a whimper, and presses them to my lips.

"Open your mouth, Isla. I want you to taste yourself."

I've never tasted myself, except on his lips, but I obey. I lick and suck my arousal off his fingers without hesitation.

"Good girl," he praises. His chest presses into me as he kisses me, hard. And then he pulls away only long enough to reach for his nightstand. He tugs at the drawer and grabs a condom. I watch with hungry eyes as he rips the little foil wrapper and unrolls it down his length. My legs splay wide in invitation.

"Maddox," I whine. "Please."

"So needy." His eyes twinkle as his face transforms with a devastating smile. "Are you ready for my cock, Isla? Are you ready for me to stretch your tight little pussy and fill you up?"

My stomach hollows out, and I arch my back at his words. I can't help it. My body simply reacts. Never have I wanted someone as badly as I want Maddox Graves. "Yes. God, yes. Fuck me, Maddox."

My clit thrums with pleasure as he bumps the head of his dick against it, rubbing his sheathed length through the wetness of my folds so he can easily slide inside of me. Then he stills and meets my gaze.

"Please."

That's all it takes. One strangled plea, and then he's pressing the head of his cock into me. So slowly, it might as well be torture. Maddox fills me up an inch at a time. He stills as my eyes flutter and roll back into my head. He's so much bigger than anyone I've had sex with before, and while it's not painful, my body needs a moment to adjust to him.

"Are you okay? I'm not hurting you, am I?"

"No," I say with a shake of my head. "More."

Maddox gives me what I ask, and presses in another inch, and then another. I'm panting by the time he's fully sheathed within me. He presses his forehead to mine, still as he lets me adjust. "God, Isla. You feel like heaven."

I need him to move. To fuck me. "Please," I say again. My brain is short-circuiting. All other words seem to be lost to me. "Maddox, please fuck me."

He lets out a masculine groan that goes straight to my clit, and then he moves. He slowly slides himself part way out, and when he pushes back in, he rolls his hips, which rubs his pubic bone over my clit. Encouraged by my cries and mewls, he does it again and again. All the while, his rich, brown eyes hold mine and he kisses me senseless.

It's so much more than I thought it would be. This isn't just fucking. It's not just scratching an itch. Maddox Graves is making love to me. This big, sometimes gruff man stares into my eyes like I'm precious and tells me exactly how he feels with every slow roll and thrust of his hips.

The realization has me spiraling with pleasure. My fingers drag down Maddox's broad back and I wrap my legs around his ass, urging him deeper. Urging him to take me faster. Harder.

"So beautiful," he says before kissing the juncture of my neck and shoulders. "So pretty, filled with my cock."

This man. The combination of his tender looks and touches and his filthy, filthy words has pressure building low in my belly.

"Are you close, sweetheart?"

I can only nod. My body tingles and clenches. I'm so close.

"Good. Such a good girl. *My* good girl." He picks up the pace, thrusting harder and faster, eliciting a gasp from me. "Now come for me, Isla. Come all over my dick. I want you to scream my name."

And god help me, I do. Every muscle in my body tightens before releasing in a wave of euphoria. I scream Maddox's name as my pussy spasms around his hard length. He fucks me through it, and as my orgasm reaches its peak, he stills over me, his face twisting with pleasure. The low, raspy groan as he comes prolongs my climax. Maddox works me through it, his softening cock thrusting lazily inside of me a few more times before he stops and wraps me in his arms. When he pulls out, I whimper.

"Shh, baby. I've got you." He flops down onto his back, dragging my sweaty, naked body into his, and holds me. "I've got you."

He's warm. So warm. His arms are strong, and I feel safe as he holds me. Protected.

I've never felt this way during sex. Or after. I'm overwhelmed as he whispers sweet nothings into my ear and traces patterns over my back.

And as my mind slowly comes back online, I have the unwelcome thought that if this is how I feel after our first time having sex, how much more intense will things be after a few weeks, or a few months? Sex never felt like this in all my years with Alex, and he still broke me in the end.

How much more will I shatter if things with Maddox end badly?

# thirty-five

## MADDOX

Putting a label on our relationship and making it official shouldn't be a big deal. Not much changes in the grand scheme of things. Not really. But the pure satisfaction I feel as I guide Isla into Griffin's crowded backyard with my arm confidently wrapped around her waist can't be denied.

"Hey, you made it!" Griffin throws his arms out in a gesture of welcome. He's got a metal spatula in one hand, a beer in the other, and he's wearing an apron that says *Eat My Meat*. Because of course he is.

"I told you we were coming," I reply.

"Dude, you're like twenty minutes late."

I shrug, a grin tugging at the corners of my lips. "I had to stop and get my girlfriend a coffee. She needed a caffeine fix."

Griffin's gaze bounces between me and Isla, his face

lighting up like a kid in a candy store. "So you two are finally official?"

Isla presses deeper into my side. "Yep. So no more flirting with me, Wright."

That has Griffin laughing. He sets his beer and spatula down and wraps us both in a crushing hug. "I am so happy right now. It's about time this grumpy bastard found someone worthy of him." He lets us go and then turns to the crowd of our teammates, girlfriends, and even a couple puck bunnies the rookies brought with them. "Everyone shut the hell up!" he shouts. "I have an announcement to make. Our own Maddox Graves finally grew a pair and asked our favorite teacher to be his girl. So let's give Isla the Rogues welcome she deserves!"

All the guys raise their drinks and cheer. Someone wolf-whistles and a few guys chant her name. Pink overtakes her cheeks as she covers her face with her hands.

"Oh my god, you guys. Thank you." She's so damned cute when she's embarrassed. "And thank you again to all of you for helping make the assembly at my school such a huge success. You're all amazing." That earns another round of cheers before conversation resumes around us.

"Hotdog, hamburger, or brat?" With my arm still wrapped around Isla's waist, I guide her over to the grill and the massive table covered with food.

"Um, hot dog, please." She tucks a strand of hair that has escaped her ponytail behind her ear while looking at Griffin. "Can you make it a little crispy on the outside?"

Griff chuckles. "'Course. Two brats for you, Madds?"

"To start. I'm not looking forward to burning them off, but it'll be worth it." My phone buzzes in my pocket. I'm tempted to ignore it because I'm here with Isla and my guys, and the only people who ever call me on our days off are all here. With the exception of my mom and sister. When I dig it out of my pocket, I grin. Mira's calling. But not just a voice call. She wants to Facetime. Hitting the green answer button, my sister's smiling face fills the screen. Her dark hair is twisted into a messy braid that hangs over one shoulder, and her face is makeup-free and tanner than the last time I saw her. Freckles skip across her nose and cheeks, and her green eyes dance with her signature mirth.

"Big brother, hey!"

Curious, Isla peeks over my shoulder, and my sister squeals.

"Oh my god, is that her? She's so pretty. Hi, you must be Isla. It is so nice to sort of meet you." Mira does a little wiggle, shaking the phone screen in her excitement.

"Chill, Mi-Mi," I say with a chuckle. "Don't scare her away. I just got her to agree to be my girlfriend."

Isla cocks an eyebrow at me. "Uh, excuse me? Pretty sure I asked you to be my boyfriend, not the other way around."

That makes Mira's day. My sister throws her head back and laughs so loudly it draws Griffin's attention and he wanders over, forgetting about the meat on the grill. "Oh, we're going to be good friends," she says to Isla. "I can tell already."

"I'm sure we will be," Isla replies. "I'm Isla."

"Mira." My sister's cheeks must be hurting with how wide she's smiling. "I'm Maddox's younger, smarter, and hotter little sister."

"Yeah, yeah," I grumble, but there's no heat behind it.

Mira and I are close. Always have been. Shit-talking is practically our love language. "You're also a brat. When are you coming to visit?"

Mira's smile slips. It's slight, and she recovers quickly, but it makes my Spidey sense tingle. I'll have to ask her about it later. "Actually, that was what I was calling about. I'm coming to your first home preseason game. I can stay with you, right?"

"You're coming to our game?" Griffin butts into the conversation, holding his fist out to the camera. "Hell yeah, Mira. Pound it."

My sister laughs, bumping her fist against the camera, and then pulling it away with a little explosion sound. "Hey, Wright. Good to see you."

Griffin grins, running a hand through his blond hair. "You too, Mir. You're looking good. I like the braid. Like a sexy milkmaid."

I elbow my best friend. "Dude. You're an idiot."

But Mira and Isla just laugh. Mira flips her braid off her shoulder and onto her back. "You gonna score a goal for me to make up for that horrible line?"

At least I never have to worry about my sister with these guys. She gives as good as she gets. When you grow up surrounded by a bunch of hockey players a couple years older than you, you learn how to keep up pretty quick. They all flirt and tease her, she humors them for a few minutes, then she puts them in their place. Besides, every single guy on my team knows I'd kick their asses if they tried anything with my sister. She's too good for all of them. Except maybe Navarro, but they've got nothing in common and he's never anything but respectful to her. But

Griffin? He knows I'd bury his body under the ice at the arena if he ever stepped out of line with Mira.

Wright gives her a wink. "Just one? I'll score two for you, Little Gravesy."

The stupid nickname earns a groan and an eye roll from my sister. I glance at the grill to see Isla's hot dog smoking. "Dude, you're burning the meat."

"Shit." Griffin salutes my sister with his spatula. "Later, Mir. See you soon."

"So, Isla." Mira focuses her attention on my bemused girl. "Have you ever been to a hockey game?"

Isla's long ponytail bounces when she shakes her head. "No, but I'm excited. You'll have to give me all the tips about what I should wear."

"Well, you'll definitely need to wear my number," I say before my sister can respond. And hell, my brain fills with images of Isla in my jersey. And nothing else. I need to get her one the next time we practice because now all I'm going to think about is bending Isla over my couch, my name on her back, her sweet little ass in the air, pussy wet and ready for me. There's something primal about fucking your girl while she wears your jersey.

"I think my brother's cave man brain just shorted out," I hear Mira say to Isla. Shaking my head to clear it, I give my girl a smirk.

"Sorry. Just thinking about how you'll look in Rogues yellow and gray."

Isla chuckles, resting her head on my bicep. "You know I'll wear your jersey."

"Gah. You two are way too adorable," my sister says. "Mom is going to flip out when I tell her about this."

"Mira," I warn. My mom will have my hide if I don't tell her about Isla myself. "Let me tell her, okay? Jesus."

My sister smirks. "Fine, fine. Anyway. I was planning to get in two days before your first home game and maybe stay a week?"

"A week? What about that guy you're seeing? You guys just recently moved in together, right? Will he be able to live without you for that long?"

Mira's smile falters again, but it's just as brief as the first time. Her lips pull back in a wide smile that doesn't quite meet her eyes. "Nah. He'll be out of town on business. He won't even miss me."

"Doubt that." This is the first time Mira's lived with a boyfriend. My sister is incredibly driven and determined to make our mom proud. But she's also picked up more than a little of our mom's hopeless romantic gene, and she'll never settle for less than what she believes is true love. She wants a soulmate. Someone who sees her for who she is and loves her unconditionally. That she moved in with Jared tells me she thinks she's found that. Until I met Isla, I would have said all of it's bullshit, but now I'm not so sure. "When do I get to meet him?"

Mira shrugs. Her eyes dart to the side and away from my face. "Oh, uh, I'm not sure. Sometime when you can bring your girlfriend."

Isla's face lights up. "Oh! That would be so fun. I've never been to Chicago."

My sister's smile is tight. "It's a great city. Well, I'll let you guys go. I don't want to interrupt whatever you're all doing. Maddox, I'll chat with you later so we can hammer out the details for my visit. It was so great to meet you, Isla. Love you, Maddy."

"Love you, Mir." I hang up the call, a niggling sense of worry worming its way into my belly. Something's up with my sister.

"She seems sweet," Isla says, looking up at me.

"She is," I reply. "Just don't feel pressured to come to Chicago because she made it sound like you have to." I smile down at my girl, but her own dims at my words.

Looking down, Isla wraps her arms around herself. "Oh, yeah. No, of course. I definitely don't need to come."

Shit. Somehow I just stepped on a landmine I wasn't aware of. Turning my body so we're nearly chest to chest, I gently nudge Isla's chin up with my finger. "Hey. What just happened?"

I can practically see her rebuilding her walls as she shrugs, her shoulders tight. "Nothing. I totally get it if you don't want me to come."

My brow rises at that. "What? No, that's not what I meant at all. I hope you want to come. I just know Mira can be a little pushy and I don't want you to feel obligated, that's all. I want you to come, Isla. Nothing would make me happier."

Her eyes judder between mine, trying to find the lie. When she's satisfied that I'm telling the truth, her shoulders fall. "Sorry. I just…" She inhales deeply. "I'd really love to go with you."

With slow, measured movements, I cup her face in my hands, bringing my nose right up to hers. Our eyes connect and hold before I kiss her slowly. It's purposeful and soft. I need her to know that what I feel for her is deep and real. "Good," I whisper across her lips as I pull back. "I know you were hurt in your last relationship, and I'm just trying not to rush you, Short-Stack. But I need you to know that it's not easy to hold back. I want you with me as often as you'll agree to. Got it?"

Her lips curve against mine. "Got it."

My lips crash against hers in a quick, harder kiss before I return to my full height and wrap an arm around her waist. "Good. Now let's go get some food if Griffin hasn't charbroiled it."

# *thirty-six*

## MADDOX

"You look happy." Bash takes a seat beside me, beer in hand. His gaze follows mine to where Isla sits with a few wives and girlfriends. The sound of laughter has been almost constant from the circle of women, and I've been smiling nonstop. I'm glad she's getting along with my teammates and their significant others. It's important that whoever I end up with feels comfortable with these guys because they're such a massive part of my life. I've known a few players over the years who tried dating women who couldn't stand the team or the other WAGS, and they always ended up completely miserable. When you play a sport with a season as long and grueling as ours is, it's just not possible to separate your life into neat little sections. Everything bleeds together, and disharmony can lead to shit playing and abject misery.

Dragging my attention away from Isla, I turn to

Navarro. "I feel happy. I'm trying not to wait for the other shoe to drop, you know?"

He nods. "Understandable, after everything you went through in your last couple relationships. Isla seems different, though."

"She is. It doesn't mean this will work out the way I hope, but I at least know she'd never turn me into a spectacle if things end between us."

"No," Navarro agrees, "I don't believe she'd do that either."

We fall silent, both of us deep in thought. It's always like this with Bash. He's the most thoughtful of all of us. The one you can just *be* with. When silence stretches between us, it's never awkward. Just companionable. It's not that he has less to say than the other guys, just that he takes more in. I'm not sure if it's something that springs out of being a goalie, or if he's a great goalie *because* he's so observant. Either way, the guy is sharp as a tack and rarely misses anything.

"Her ex showed up at the coffee shop we went to yesterday," I tell him.

One eyebrow arched, Navarro gives me his full attention. "Really?"

I nod. "Yeah, man. It was suspicious as hell. Isla made it pretty clear it's not his normal haunt. I can't imagine it would be *hers* if he was a regular. I think that might have been the first time she's seen him since they split." My mind flashes back to the tremor in her hands once the prick left. She stood her ground, but I know it shook her up.

"She okay?"

"Yeah." I run a hand through my dark hair. "They were engaged."

Navarro's eyebrow climbs higher. "Really?"

"Yep. I figured as much because I kinda came across a few photos of her with a diamond on her finger in her Instagram feed, but she confirmed it yesterday."

Bash barks out a laugh. "Online stalking your girl?"

"Wouldn't you?"

Something flashes across Navarro's face, there and gone before I can read it. "Yeah. If she had social media profiles? I would."

Sensing that my friend won't talk about whatever that was, I forge on. "Right. I don't know the story yet, but the guy was a total douche yesterday. He struck me as one of those manipulative pieces of shit that knows exactly how to twist his words to make sure he never has to take the blame for anything." My lip curls back in a snarl. "He tried to make her feel guilty for dating me."

Navarro's attention zeros in on Isla for a moment before he turns back to me. "None of that really surprises me. She seems way too surprised anytime anyone does anything kind for her. He sounds like a narcissist. People like that are selfish and make everything in the relationship about them." Sebastian takes a sip of his beer, looking again at the girls. "Lots of times, those guys will love bomb their partners, only to use it to control them or to use the nice things they do to hold over their partner's head. She may have a hard time accepting help or gifts without feeling suspicious. Make sure you don't take it personally, if that's the case with her. It's a survival mechanism."

I hate the idea of Isla seeing the world through such a fucked up filter. But I can see it, too. Her hesitation to believe I'd follow through on my end of the deal once she gave the interview after our auction dinner. Her difficulty accepting that I wanted to take her on an elaborate date. I'll have to be careful with that.

"You think he's going to be a problem?" Navarro asks, swinging the conversation back to Isla's ex.

"I hope not. I'd rather not go to jail for assault."

Bash chuckles darkly. "We've all got your back. Hers too."

"Thanks, man. I don't know what I'd do without you guys."

He claps me on the back. "You'd be a hell of a lot grumpier."

He's not wrong. "How're you doing, man?"

Navarro shrugs. "I'm good. Same old, you know?"

"You'll tell me if something's up, right?" Sebastian Navarro is always a little on the quiet and broody side, but he's seemed more in his head than normal lately. I don't know if it has anything to do with me dating Isla, but this new level of introspection seemed to begin around the same time I started trying to make her mine. I know it's not anything about Isla personally, but I worry about him. I'm not the only one with heartbreak in my past, but Bash's is a total mystery.

"Yeah, Madds. I will."

"Good. You'd better. We can't have our goalie in his head and off his game. We need you."

"Who's off his game?" Logan asks as he flops down on Navarro's other side on the outdoor sofa.

"No one," I reply.

"Good." Logan rests his arm across the back of the sofa before turning to me. "D'you think Isla would be pissed if I hooked up with one of the teachers at her school? A few of them gave me their numbers, and they were hot."

Navarro groans as I lean forward in my chair, bracing my arms on my knees. "Don't even think about it, Byrne. Seriously. I will kick your ass."

"What?" He shrugs. "They're adults. I don't see the problem."

"If you didn't see the problem, you wouldn't have asked Graves for his opinion." Navarro shakes his head.

Logan lets his head fall back against the back of the couch. "Fine. You guys are no fun."

"Who's no fun?" Griffin plops himself into the chair across from me, blocking my view of Isla. The rookie Ryder Hanson is with him.

Ryder gives us all nods. "Hey, guys."

"Graves won't let me call any of Isla's coworkers," Logan says over our greetings.

"Aw man. I forgot to ask her which teacher was the dominatrix," Griffin whines.

"I've clearly missed something here," Ryder says with a chuckle.

That has me barking out a laugh, and I decide to take pity on Griffin. "Sorry man, but the teacher she was talking about is like sixty years old."

Griff's nose scrunches up. "Really?"

"Yep."

He tilts his head to the side. "But is she a hot sixty year old?"

Navarro and Hanson groan.

Logan kicks Griffin. "You have issues, man."

"Nah," Griffin shrugs, an impish grin plastered across

his face. "I'm just an equal opportunity lover. The package is important, but it's what's inside that really matters."

"That's surprisingly mature. I think." Navarro's brow furrows.

"Well," Griffin says with a smirk, "a sixty year old's pussy is just as warm and wet as a twenty-two year old's."

"No." Navarro leans over and smacks Wright upside the head. "Just, no." And with that, he stands. "I need another beer. You guys want one?"

"I need brain bleach after that," Logan says with a groan.

Ryder lifts a finger in the air. "I could use another."

Isla's laughter floats through the air, overlaying Logan's grousing, and despite Griffin's ridiculousness, I smile broadly. I wouldn't trade any of this.

Well, I could have done without the visual Griffin just provided, but I wouldn't trade anything else.

<h1 style="text-align:center">thirty-seven</h1>

## ISLA

*WHAT'S SO SPECIAL ABOUT HER?*

*She's a six. He could do better.*

*Omg, I love her hair!*

"Hey." The chair beside me squeals against the tiled floor, announcing Jess's arrival. "You okay?"

"Hmm?" I look up at my best friend with a frown that she mirrors.

"I asked if you were okay. You're making a funny face." Jess snatches my phone before I can lock it and shove it deep inside my pocket. She eyes the photo Griffin posted of us and Sebastian from the day of the assembly, then scrolls through the comments, her brow furrowing deeper the more she reads.

My knee bounces as I watch her, and my bottom lip stings from worrying at it. Why did I have to read the comments? And why the hell didn't I put my phone away before Jess got here?

This began with me opening up my Instagram account to find almost a hundred follow requests. Ninety-nine percent of them were strangers, though there were a few high school classmates I never actually spoke to thrown in for good measure. I denied each one. Even the classmates. I couldn't figure out where this random influx of follow requests came from. But then I remembered what Griffin posted the day of the assembly and navigated over to his profile to see if he'd tagged me. He had. There were a few fans who had been speculating about Maddox and me since I posted that photo of us without setting my profile to private. Looks like they don't need to speculate any longer.

I can't be mad at Griffin for tagging me because I know he's excited that Maddox and I are officially together. And I've seen the comments he gets on his photos. They're almost all positive. Especially from his female fans. I'm pretty sure most of his followers are women. So why would he think I'd receive different treatment?

None of the comments are overtly cruel, but there are a lot of women making bitchy assertions about me being with Maddox for the attention and a lot of men making digs at my appearance. As if they could condense the entirety of my value down to my body or the way I look. It's invasive and uncomfortable, and I've never had so much attention before. I have no idea how to shut those voices out. Especially when they echo things Alex has said.

"Sweet baby Hemsworth," Jess finally says. "How many of these did you read?"

I shrug. "Enough."

"People are assholes, Isla. I'm sorry. Never read the comments, babes."

"I know. I know better. I mean, the internet is a cesspool. But it was hard to look away."

Despite my stomach churning, I take a sip of my latte. Jess and I sometimes meet up at That's Doppio after work, and with the newness of my relationship with Maddox, it's been a while since I've seen her or Nevaeh. We've kept up a steady stream of text conversations, but I've been missing my best friends. Nev couldn't meet up with us today, but with all of this, I'm even more grateful for Jess's presence beside me.

"Has Maddox seen these?" Jess locks my phone before placing it screen-down on the table with a wrinkled nose and a grimace. "Can't imagine he'll be pleased."

I can only shrug because I don't know, and I don't want to ask him. He's seen the ugly side of public attention, so I'm sure he'd sympathize. But what would I even say? *Maddox, strangers on the internet are being mean to me.*

Nope. Can't bring myself to do that.

My bestie sighs and gives my hand a squeeze. "How are things going outside of internet trolls? Tell me all about your first week of official dating."

So I do. I gush about Maddox. I tell her how I'm meeting his sister for their first preseason game at home. How I'm excited to watch Maddox play, but a little nervous for the season to start because I'm not sure what to expect. He'll be gone a lot once things kick off, and I've gotten so used to seeing him most days. I'm trying not to be that clingy girlfriend. Sure, I'm going to miss Maddox like hell, but all of this is still so new that I refuse to let him see how worried I am that the distance will be difficult.

Not to mention the deep, hidden fear that he'll meet someone prettier, smarter, and better than me while he's out on the road. I know Maddox isn't like that; I do. But I still don't understand why a guy like him would choose to be with a woman like me. I'm nobody. Clearly the internet agrees.

"So when is their first home game during the preseason?"

"Well, their first three games are away, then they have two at home, then another away game before the actual season starts." I open my phone and tap on the calendar app. "So the game I'm going to is on the last Wednesday of the month."

Jess grins. She can tell I'm excited to watch my man play for the first time. "And you're meeting his sister? That seems big. Like, serious, big."

Surprisingly, I'm not all that worried about meeting Mira. She seems really cool, and I have a feeling we'll get along well. "Yeah. She's going to come stay with Maddox for a week, so I should have some time to get to know her."

As an only child, I always wanted a sister. Alex didn't have any siblings, so the idea of forming a tight bond with Mira makes me kind of giddy. It's way too soon to be thinking like this, but I have a difficult time reminding myself to be logical where Maddox is concerned.

"Do you get to sit in some fancy box seats or something?" Jess asks. "Is that even a thing in hockey?"

All I can do is laugh, because hell if I know. Maybe tonight I should find a *Hockey For Dummies* book and at least learn the basics. "No idea. All I know is that I've seen photos of my man in uniform, and damn, does he look hot."

Jess shakes her head at me. I know I'm ridiculous, but I'm too happy to care. At least, as long as I'm not thinking about what a bunch of random strangers on the internet think about me.

"So, when are you going to meet his parents?"

"Just his mom," I say. "He doesn't have a relationship with his dad. And I'm not sure. I don't know if I'm ready for that yet, you know?"

Because Alex's family had always been ambivalent toward me. They never even tried to hide it. I'm not sure if it was a me problem, or a them problem, but after the way Maddox gushed about his mom, I know ambivalent won't be good enough for her. If she doesn't like me, it could very well spell the end of things between Maddox and me.

"You need to believe in yourself more, Isla. Alex was a dick, and so were his parents. Don't let them color your current relationship."

It's wise advice, though maybe not so easy to put into practice. "I know, I know."

Jess nods sharply. "Good. Now tell me about the sex."

My cheeks grow hot and I glance around to make sure no one's listening before I say, "Oh, God. Where should I start?" Because it's been five days since the assembly, and Maddox has been insatiable. And even though I refuse to go into graphic detail with my friends, I still have a hell of a lot to tell them about.

"Let's just say that I almost had to ice my vagina the other day..."

# *thirty-eight*

ISLA

THE NEXT WEEK GOES BY IN A BLUR OF SEX AND
sweet moments. Maddox and I spend as much time
together as possible because once the season starts next
week, it won't be as simple as shooting off a text that says
*come over*. I'm trying not to think about him being states
away, but the impending change in our new routine
worries me. How can it not?

Maddox takes me out on dates whenever our schedules
allow. Sometimes it's a romantic dinner or something silly
and fun, like laser tag. But sometimes we hole up at one of
our apartments and spend hours naked, learning each
other's bodies.

Today is a naked day. It's Sunday and our last weekend
day of the off-season. On Wednesday, the Rogues hop in a
plane and travel to Seattle for their first preseason game
against the Seattle Leviathans. Maddox has already given
me two orgasms with his talented mouth, and as I lie on

my back, coming down from the second, I know what I want to do.

I want to give him a blow job. A real one. Like a suck-his-giant-dick-to-the-back-of-my-throat one.

Pushing up onto my elbows, I watch Maddox wipe his mouth with the back of his hand. He gives me a salacious grin that makes my stomach flip. How can he give me two orgasms in half an hour and still turn me on? "Do you remember the other day when I started telling you about my issue with blow jobs?"

That salacious grin twists into something curious. Maddox scoots closer to me and pulls my naked body into his lap so I'm straddling him. His cock juts up between us and I can't help grinding against the length of it. Groaning, he presses his forehead to mine. "Kind of hard to listen to you when you're doing that, Short-Stack."

"Sorry," I say. I'm not, though. Not really. But I *am* stalling. "Right. So, my history with blow jobs is... Well, not great." Maddox lifts one eyebrow but doesn't interrupt me, so I continue. "The first time I ever tried to give my high school boyfriend head, I kinda puked all over his dick."

Maddox is silent for a beat, and then his laughter fills his bedroom. "Oh, baby, no. Really?"

Cheeks flaming, I nod. "Unfortunately. I have an over-active gag reflex. For a while, I was really stressed during grad school and I'd been grinding my teeth at night. I couldn't even wear a mouth guard, because just holding it in my mouth was enough to have me gagging. And it wasn't anywhere near my throat."

Long, strong fingers stroke softly over my shoulders and back, encouraging me to continue with my story. Even if they weren't, it's too late to turn back now. The humiliation train has already pulled out of the station.

"Anyway. My best friends have always been more worldly than me. So, of course, when I got my first serious high school boyfriend, I went to them for advice on how to give good head. Because Brad Johnson was one of the hottest guys in school, and he wanted me. I had to prove I would be the best girlfriend ever."

Maddox's brow rises, but he stays silent. He just watches me with those rich, earthen eyes. His lips twitch like he's holding back a smile, but other than that, he's utterly still.

"Anyway. They showed me a couple of pornos where the girl let the guy shove his penis into her throat, and told me it felt weird to do it, but that guys loved being deep-throated." I suck in a breath, remembering how nervous I'd been that day. "So the next time Brad and I were alone in his parents' basement, I went for it. No one else was home, so I could really go to town and do my best imitation of the porn stars we'd studied."

"Oh no," Maddox murmurs.

I wince. "Oh, yes. Brad was all for it, obviously. I don't know many teenage guys that wouldn't be. Of course, I didn't tell him I'd never gone down on a guy before. I just sucked on him a few times before looking up at him and asking if he wanted me to take him deeper. I thought I was being so sexy and worldly, you know?"

He'd taken my top off and stripped down to nothing but his boxers, which were down around his ankles. I felt powerful and sexy as I leaned down over Brad's dick. "Unfortunately, Brad got a little too excited, and instead of letting me work around him at my own pace, he ended up bucking his hips and shoving his penis down my throat before I was ready. And then I puked. I puked all over his dick, his lap, and his parents' leather couch."

Maddox winces, but he doesn't laugh. His eyes fill with sympathy. "What happened?"

"He broke up with me," I say with a shrug. "It was one of the most embarrassing moments of my life."

"Wow," Maddox says as he hugs me to his naked chest. "I'm sorry, baby. That sounds horrible."

"Not my finest moment," I agree. "I've been too scared to really attempt a full-blown blow job ever since then. Normally, I could half-ass it well enough. But you..." Maddox is so much bigger than anyone I've ever been with.

"Me what?" he asks with a devious grin. He knows what I'm not saying, but he wants me to speak the words. Cocky bastard.

"You're not small. At all. And you're like a master at oral. I want to return the favor."

He laughs at that. Long, loud, and unrestrained. It shakes us both as he holds me. "Sweetheart, I don't need you to return the favor."

That has me raising one eyebrow. "Really?"

"Really. Listen, if this is important to you, we'll try it, okay? But I need you to understand that I don't care if you never suck my dick. It won't change how much I want you."

Heat seeps into every crevice of my chest. His words only make me want to try this more. Because I believe him. Who knows if he'll always feel this way, but he does at the moment, and that's enough for me.

Our eyes lock as I scoot off of his lap. His cock jumps when I press my palms against his chest and push him back onto the mattress. I can do this. I can. My breasts rub against his muscular thighs as I place my hands on either side of his hips and lap at the bead of pre-cum that weeps from his slit. It's salty and musky and *male*. My pussy clenches. Maddox groans as I swirl my tongue around the ridge of his cock head and it emboldens me. Taking the fat crown of his dick into my mouth, I suck lightly. He lets out a strangled curse as I suck again and wrap my fingers around his shaft.

"Feels so good," he mumbles.

I can do this. Filling my lungs with a deep breath, I take more of Maddox into my mouth. My tongue traces the shape of him as I breathe through my nose. I close my eyes and take him a little deeper. His head bumps against the back of my hard palate, and I gag.

"Stop, baby," Maddox says gently as his fingers stroke my hair. "I don't want you to make yourself uncomfortable."

He has no idea how much his words spur me on. I try to relax my jaw and push myself down his length even more. His cock teases the opening of my throat and my throat says, *no thanks*. It's enough that I pull off of him and cover my mouth.

*Oh, shit.*

"Fuck, Isla. Are you okay?" He sounds concerned, but there's humor in his tone, too. He's trying not to laugh, the shithead.

Just a little gagging. No big deal. I nod. "I'm fine. Just relax and let me make you feel good." This is good. This is progress. I can do this. "Lie back down."

He meets the command with an arched eyebrow. "You really want to keep trying?"

"Yes," I say. "I won't be happy until you're coming down the back of my throat."

"Jesus," Maddox mumbles, fisting his very hard dick. "How in the hell am I supposed to say no to that?"

"You're not," I reply with a smirk.

"Seriously, Isla. It's okay. You don't have to do this. I'm happy with you sticking to licking my dick like a lollipop if that's what you need to do."

Letting out a frustrated growl, I grab a pillow and chuck it at his head. "Just shut up and let me blow you!"

Maddox barks out a laugh, but when I skewer him with a glower, he drags the pillow over his face to hide from me. It doesn't work. His whole stupidly ripped body shakes with the force of his laughter.

I'll show him. The shit.

Eventually, I find my rhythm. Tears still stream down my cheeks, but by the fourth gagging episode, I've learned how to breathe through them. I feel powerful. Queasy, but powerful.

"Shit, baby, I'm gonna come." Maddox's grip on my hair tightens, but he still keeps from bucking his hips. Somehow, he's remained still throughout this whole process, leaving me completely in control.

Humming around him, I suck hard as I bob up and down his length. Determined to make this feel amazing for Maddox, I work his head deeper into my mouth. He grunts, I suck, and then he comes with a roar down the back of my throat. Thick, salty cum floods my mouth and throat.

Oh, no. No, this is too much.

I manage to swallow a few mouthfuls, but my stomach rolls. I've dry-heaved one too many times, and I'm afraid this is going to push me over the edge. Releasing Maddox's still-pulsing dick from my mouth, his cum spurts all over my face and gets in my left eye. It stings, and I panic, jerking my head to the side. And then Maddox's dick pokes me right in the eye. I let out an undignified squeal and bat his penis away.

"Oh my god." Maddox sits up and wipes his hot cum off of my face. I can't really see him because I'm blinking like a newborn baby, but I can hear the laughter he's trying to push down. "Are you okay?"

All I can do is nod. I'm still queasy. "Mmhmm."

"Is your eye okay?"

"Shut up."

"Well, that was definitely something." His body shakes with silent laughter. I glare at him through the cum sticking to my eyelashes. It only makes him laugh harder. "Seriously, baby, I know you hate gagging, but I have to be honest. The way your throat strangled me each time... damn, I'm a fan. Five stars. Easily."

"Oh my god, are you seriously leaving a review for how well I suck dick?"

"Absolutely. You have a Yelp page, right?"

My palm connects with Maddox's chest with a sharp *thwack*. "You're the worst. And so was that blow job. It's okay, you can be honest."

His thumb swipes a drop of cum off my cheek, and he presses it into my mouth. I lick it off, even though I'm hesitant to allow anything even close to my mouth right now. "Isla, you pushed through a ridiculous amount of discomfort just to please me. Which, again, you never ever have to do. And yeah, you were a little green a few times there, which was concerning, but that was still hot. For the most part."

It's my turn to laugh. "Next time it'll be easier."

Maddox shakes his head. He flashes me a lopsided smile before murmuring, "You're crazy." Then, reverently, Maddox runs his thumb down the column of my throat.

Maybe I am a little crazy. I'm definitely crazy about him.

# thirty-nine

## MADDOX

"I'm going to miss you," Isla says for the third time. "I wish I didn't have to work so I could be there. But Jess and Nev are going to come over and watch the game with me. They're almost as excited as I am."

I grin, ignoring the amused looks my teammates throw my way. Let them laugh. One day they'll find a woman that knocks them on their asses the way Isla has knocked me on mine, and then they'll get it. She's everything.

"You gonna be wearing my jersey, baby?"

Griffin catches my eye, and at that question, he sticks his tongue out and starts french kissing the air, his arms wrapped around an invisible woman. Bash smacks him upside the head from his seat beside him.

"Of course I am," Isla says. "Gotta support my man."

Logan smirks beside me. I'm sure the shithead can hear her end of the conversation, but I don't care. I'm completely gone for her.

"So, when is your sister coming to town again?" Isla's looking forward to meeting Mira, but I know she's feeling anxious, too. She doesn't need to be nervous, and I've told her that, but I get it. If she had any siblings, I'd probably be worried about making a good impression, too. What Isla doesn't realize is that Mira already loves her just based off the stories I've told and the way my face *gets all gooey* when I talk about my girl. Mira's words, not mine.

"She gets in on Monday. I figured the three of us could go out to dinner?"

"Dude," Griffin says, whacking me on the shoulder. "What about us? We want to come, too." He motions to himself, Logan, and Bash. "It's been too long since we've seen Mir."

"Butt out of my conversation, Wright. We'll all go out after the game. You're not invited Monday night, and if you somehow show up where we are, I'll kick your ass."

"Touchy, touchy," Griffin teases. Isla laughs.

"I want to take you out after Mira leaves. Something fun. There's a fall festival downtown I thought we could go to. They'll have rides and food and entertainment. What do you think, baby?"

Isla does a cute little squeal. "Ohmygod, yes. I have been dying to go to that."

"Great. Then it's a date." I can't wait to walk around and show my girl off. Maybe make out with her at the top of the Ferris wheel.

The tinny voice of the plane's captain crackles over the loudspeaker in the team's jet, letting us know we'll be taxiing to the runway, and to shut off all phones and other electronic devices.

"Gotta go, baby. I'll call you when I land, okay?"

My girl sighs on the other end of the line. "Okay. Be safe. Have fun."

"Bye Isla," my teammates say in unison at Griffin's urging. She giggles and instructs me to tell them she says goodbye, too. We both say our goodbyes three more times, like lovesick teenagers before the flight attendant gives me a look, and I finally hang up the phone.

"Well, that was fucking adorable," Wright says loudly. "Wasn't that just adorable, guys?"

All the guys on the plane coo and give me shit, but I don't care. And when Coach commends me for taking my image-rehabbing so seriously, I just laugh. Let them talk shit all they want. I'm finally really happy.

"Jesus, man," Byrne says, eyeing me.

"What?"

"You're in love with her."

I open my mouth to deny it because that's ridiculous. It's too soon for love, even if I am wild about her. But the words don't come.

Hell, am I in love with her?

Byrne shakes his head, but he's smiling. "Never thought I'd see the day. She's good for you, though. I'm happy for you."

There must be something stuck in my throat because it's feeling a little raw, so I clear it. "Thanks, Byrne. When are you going to give up your *one night* rule and let yourself fall for someone?"

In all the years I've known Logan, he's never dated anyone. Not once.

"Never," he says without pause. "Love's not for me."

Logan's never explicitly told us why he's so anti-love, but his dad was a famous NHL player in his own day, and I know for a fact that the man has been married half a dozen times. Logan never mentions his mom. Seems to me like his parents' shitty relationship put him off as much as my own dad's abandonment put me off.

Still, maybe I'm just riding the high of finding a woman who makes me feel things I've never felt before, but I hope one day he finds someone who forces him to rethink all the rules and bullshit restrictions he's put on himself.

His words echo in my head. *You're in love with her.* Maybe I am. If even closed-off Logan Byrne can see it, it must be pretty obvious. That the thought doesn't scare me is its own revelation.

"Just don't let it mess up your focus on the ice," Logan says. "I think we've really got a shot to go all the way this season."

"I won't." And I mean it. I'm more determined than ever to play my best and win these games. Because my girl's going to be watching at home, and I want to make her proud.

---

MY BLOOD HUMS AS I TEAR DOWN THE ICE. MY blades carve a sharp path toward the goal. I live for this.

We're up two against the Leviathans, despite the solid defensive effort they've mounted. Their goalie is good, but we're on fire.

I pass the puck to Wright, who brings it around the back of the Leviathans' net. He skillfully avoids their left defenseman, pulls back his stick to fake out the goalie, and then passes it back to me. With their goalie distracted by

Griffin's move, I slap the puck in the crease and let out a *whoop* when the flashing red light announces my goal. The fans in the stands boo, but it's music to my ears.

We're up by three, with only four minutes left in the third period. We don't have to hold them off much longer. Even if they score one, they still don't stand a chance and they know it. Their guys are checking us into the boards more and more with every passing minute. If they can't win, they can at least leave us with bruises.

One of their wingers slams hard into Byrne, and I throw myself into the fray as we battle it out for possession of the puck.

The minutes tick down, and the Leviathans make a hard push to our goal. Their wingers crowd Navarro at the net, which pisses me the hell off. I muscle one away, while Wright crowds the other. Their center slaps the puck at the net, but Navarro stops it. Just like he's stopped every other attempt they've made to score.

Byrne chips the puck out of the zone, and we all rush after it as the clock runs down. When the final buzzer sounds, signaling the end of the game, the guys and I head back to the locker room. We're pumped from winning our first game of the year—even if it is just a preseason game —and everyone's talking over each other and celebrating.

"Great game," I shout to my teammates. "You were all beasts out there."

"Hell yeah," Griffin shouts as he pulls his sweaty gear off. "Where are we going to celebrate tonight? Anyone know somewhere that serves good bar food around here?"

A few of the guys call out suggestions as they shower and change back into their game-day suits, but all I can think about is calling Isla. I get cleaned up and ready in record time, and as soon as I'm on the bus, I pull out my phone and find no less than five texts from her. She'd obviously been texting me throughout the game.

ISLA

Oh my god, babe, are you okay? That asshole slammed you into the boards so hard.

You look so hot in your uniform.

Did Griffin just do the Macarena after making a goal?

Hell yeah!! Look at my man scoring a goal! The announcers keep saying you're on fire and they're calling you the Gravedigger. They said you're burying the other team six feet under the ice.

If you were here I would so go down on you. Like, all the way down.

I'm grinning like an idiot when the rest of the guys file in. Griffin flops down next to me and steals my phone. He chuckles as he reads them, somehow keeping the phone out of my reach.

"She liked my celly? Your woman has good taste."

Growling, I rip my phone out of his hand. "Don't read my texts, shithead."

Griffin shrugs, his lips turned up in a smirk. "Fair enough. You going out with us tonight?"

I look down at my phone. "Nah, I don't think so. I'm going to call Isla."

"Ah, I get it. Phone sex *is* pretty hot."

I smack the back of his head, but that's exactly how I'm hoping the call will go. I'm overflowing with energy and adrenaline, and if I can't bury myself in my girl, I can at least get off to the sound of her voice or the sight of her tits if she'll FaceTime me.

"Well, if you change your mind, just text me and I'll tell you where we are."

"Thanks, man, but I'll be good."

Logan's words run on a loop in my head.

*You're in love with her.*

Ignoring Griffin's shit-eating grin, I text my girlfriend.

ME

You alone, baby? Because if you're not, send your friends home. I know we're in different cities, but I still want to celebrate with you.

Her reply is almost instant.

ISLA

Oh yeah? Color me intrigued.

ME

How do you feel about phone sex?

Kicking the girls out now.

Normally, I don't mind life on the road. But right now? Right now I wish I were home because somehow Isla Harding is the only person I want to celebrate a win with. And while phone sex is fun, it's got nothing on savoring her soft body in person, inhaling her scent, and swallowing those sexy little mewls she makes when I push myself deep inside of her.

*You're in love with her.*

Shit. Maybe I am.

# *forty*

## ISLA

When Maddox calls, I'm in nothing but a lacey black bra and thong. My heart pounds as my phone trills. Heat floods my core when I accept his video call.

I can't believe I'm about to do this.

"Hey, baby." Maddox's voice is gruff and low, but there's an intensity to it that dampens my panties.

"Hey, handsome. I miss you."

"I miss you, too." Chocolate eyes flit across my face and the part of my body he can see. They darken when he realizes I'm not wearing much. "Fuck, sweetheart. Let me see you."

"Only if I get to see you too," I reply. The coy tone of my voice takes me by surprise. I've never been much of a seductress, but damn if this man doesn't bring it out in me. I've never had phone sex or gotten myself off on a video call. This is a night of firsts, and apparently I'm determined to do it right.

Maddox hums a low sound of approval and the phone bounces as he switches it to his other hand and begins unbuttoning his shirt. "You want to see me too, naughty girl?"

"Mmhm. Yes, please." I hold the phone a little farther away from my face and trail my fingers down the valley of my breasts. Normally, my own touch provides only a dull sense of pleasure. It's nothing like when Maddox touches me. But with him watching? With the soundtrack of his groans in the background as he stares at the path of my fingers? It's like he's here with me. Like these are his fingers trailing across the swell of my breasts.

"God, you're sexy. I wish I was there. I want to lick every creamy inch of your breasts. Take those pretty little lace-covered nipples in my mouth and suck on them until they're so sensitive you beg me to release you."

I pinch and rub my nipples in time with his dirty talk. When I suck in a little gasp, he groans and rips his shirt all the way off. Gloriously bare skin fills my phone screen as Maddox moves toward the bed. "And then what would you do?"

The phone bounces and jostles as Maddox sets it up on the bedside table. I can see his upper body as he leans against the headboard, down to his knees. He stares at me as his long, powerful fingers undo the buckle of his belt, followed by the fly of his suit pants. "I'd rip those lace scraps off your body, restrain your hands above your head, and lick a path down to that pretty pink pussy."

With every growled word, my pussy throbs. I need to touch myself. So I follow Maddox's lead and set my phone up so he can see me. Then I settle on the mattress, and let my fingers wander. I skim my breasts, my stomach, and my inner thighs.

"You're so sexy," Maddox groans, pushing his pants down just enough so he can pull his thick cock out. When he squeezes the base of it and a bead of pre-cum weeps from the slit, a needy whimper flies out of my mouth. "If you were here, I'd push your perfect mouth around my cock and make you lap up my cum with your tongue." He strokes his cock. "Open your mouth, baby."

I do as he says, wishing he were here to fill it.

"Good girl. Now push two fingers into your wet pussy, then suck them clean. If you can't have my taste on your tongue, you can at least have yours."

With a whimper, I obey. My fingers slip beneath the waistband of my thong and I slowly press two inside my slick channel.

"Pump them in and out a few times," Maddox commands. When I do without hesitation, he hums his approval. "That's right, baby. Fuck yourself with your fingers until they drip. Now put them in your mouth and suck."

Smokey flavor bursts across my tongue as I lap at my own arousal, sucking and licking my fingers like they're his cock. Maddox pumps his thick erection as he watches.

"That's so good, baby. Fuck." Pre-cum beads at his slit, and Maddox works it around the head of his dick with his thumb. It's the hottest thing I've ever seen, and when his head falls back against the headboard, his abs contracting and his Adam's apple bobbing, my pussy floods. "Get naked, Isla."

Releasing my fingers with a wet pop, I hurry to do as he asks. I'm achy and throbbing and desperate for relief.

Maddox tugs his pants and boxer briefs down his thighs and pulls them off. His cock stands tall and hard against his stomach, and my pussy clamps down around nothing.

"I wish you were here," I whine.

"Are you achy, baby?" I nod. "Do you wish I was there to fill your perfect pussy? You want to be stretched out on my cock?"

"God." My chest heaves and my stomach hollows out at his words, making my back arch. "Yes. I need you to fill me."

"Get your dildo out," Maddox says, his voice low and raspy. "But you're not allowed to use any lube. You're going to rub it along your slit until it's nice and slick, do you understand?"

"Yes." I hurry to grab the dildo from my bedside drawer. I know he means the full sized one, not the little bullet. He wants to see me work it in and out of my pussy. And I want to pretend it's him.

"Now spread your perfect thighs and let me see how wet you are." Maddox watches me settle back on the mattress, and when my legs fall open, he hisses, gripping his shaft harder. "Oh fuck, baby, look at you. You're a mess already."

And I am. Arousal coats my pussy and inner thighs. Even through the phone, he can see how wet I am.

"Start to lube that dildo up with your cream, baby. Drag that big fake cock along your slit. Play with your clit. Imagine it's my dick parting your folds. That I'm the one dragging my shaft along your sopping pussy." He strokes faster, his dick growing harder and the head turning a darker shade of deep pink.

Every time the silicone bumps against my clit, I gasp.

Between the sight of Maddox fisting his cock and the sounds it makes as he fucks his hand and the sensation of the dildo slipping through my slick folds, it doesn't take long at all before it's lubed up.

"Now I want you to use one hand to part your folds. Let me see how wet and swollen you are." Maddox tugs on his cock as the muscles in his stomach clench. He hisses when I do as he asks. I bare myself for him, and it's the most erotic thing I've ever done. "Oh fuck, baby. So wet and swollen. Look at your puffy pussy. And you haven't even fucked it yet for me."

My needy core clamps down around nothing at his words. "Maddox, please."

"You need to be filled, Isla?" His voice is almost a growl. It's wild and dangerous, and it makes my sex flood with arousal.

"Yes. Please." What I need is him. The feel of his hard length as he pushes inside me. The heat of his body as he fucks me senseless. I need Maddox's talented fingers and tongue. But this will do. This is one of the hottest things I've ever done.

"Fuck yourself with your toy, baby. Stretch that tight hole. And make sure you play with your clit at the same time. I won't last much longer, but I don't want to come until you're whimpering and crying my name." Maddox works his shaft as he stares at the screen. "Push that cock in your pussy. Now."

The head of the toy slips easily into my entrance and I push it in a couple inches before sliding it out, then work it deeper. Maddox watches with dark, hooded eyes the whole time. The camera is set up so he has a straight shot of my open thighs and the silicone toy as it fills me. Ragged breathing fills my room—both mine and Maddox's—as well as the sounds of him jerking off. It's incendiary, and it doesn't take long before I feel like I'm going to combust.

My walls flutter and tense around the dildo, my spine arches off the bed, and little whimpers fall from my lips every few seconds. "I'm close. So close."

"Beautiful," Maddox grunts as he pumps his dick faster and harder. "Fuck, baby, I can see your cream coating your toy every time you pull it out of your sweet little hole." He grunts, his body tensing. "God, I want to fill you up with my cum. Want to fuck you bare and feel your hot walls clamp around me and milk my cock as you shatter around me."

Oh. My. God. I circle my clit as Maddox's words ricochet through me, setting off sparks that catch and light, and then I'm burning. "Oh," I moan. "Oh god, Maddox. I'm gonna come. Fuck."

"Don't you dare stop fucking that tight little hole, baby." He sucks in a breath as his hands work his shaft faster and faster.

The sight is so erotic, I scream out my release. His name is a plea on my lips. A prayer. A curse. My body tightens as an orgasm tears through me. My pussy clamps down around the dildo and I writhe in front of the camera, falling apart hundreds of miles away from Maddox, but still falling apart together.

His release follows moments after mine and a second, smaller orgasm takes hold of my body when he grunts out a curse, his abs contracting as ropes of cum spray across his stomach and coats his fist.

Our chests rise and fall rapidly as we both struggle to catch our breath. That was... unreal. Hot. One of the most erotic things I've ever done. I hate that Maddox is on the road. Hate that I can't hold him or feel him. But this makes up for it. At least a bit.

"Holy shit," I finally get out after sucking in a shaky breath.

"Agreed." Maddox stares at me, cum still striped across his abdomen, his fist lazily stroking his cock. "That was... You were... Fuck. You're perfect."

My cheeks flush. "I don't know about that."

Maddox grabs the phone so I'm forced to look him in the eyes. The intensity in those earthen orbs makes me shiver in the best way. "You are. Perfect. I can't wait to get home so I can hold you and kiss you and fuck you silly."

The walls of my core flutter and pulse. I'm already ready for more of him. "I can't wait, either. I wish you were here so I could curl up and fall asleep with you." I yawn. It's late, and it's been a long day. Not to mention the fact that my body is pleasantly worn out from what we just did.

"You should get some sleep, baby." His eyes soften at the corners and his full lips curve into an affectionate smile. "Go clean yourself off and go to bed, okay?"

Another yawn grips me, and Maddox chuckles. "I'll text you in the morning. Sweet dreams, sweetheart."

I hate to let him go, but I'm so tired. "Sweet dreams, Madds. I miss you."

"Miss you too, Isla. So much."

I dream about Maddox. He holds me and tells me I'm beautiful. It's the best sleep I've gotten in days.

# *forty-one*

## MADDOX

"Maddy!"

I let out a soft *oomph* as Mira barrels into me, wrapping her arms around my middle in a tight hug. "Hey, Mi-Mi. Long time no see."

"You could have come visit me in Chicago, you know," she says with her face smooshed into my chest. "Then it wouldn't be so long." She releases me with a grin. "Missed you."

"Missed you too, pipsqueak." After grabbing her suitcase, Mira loops her arm through mine as we make our way to the parking garage. "How's the current boy toy? What's his name again?"

My sister rolls her eyes at me, frowning. This is how it always is with us. She dates someone, and I refuse to learn their name because what's the point? They're never good enough for her. "Jared."

"How're things going with him? You're all moved in,

right?" I guess I should meet him, since my sister's living with the guy. He needs to know what's at stake. If he hurts her, he won't just answer to me, he'll answer to every single member of the Rogues. Especially my guys. They're just as protective of Mira as I am.

She clears her throat. "Yeah. All moved in."

"That's all you're going to say? So chatty." She groans as I set her suitcase in the back.

"Oh, come on, Maddy, you don't want to know about my love life. We don't really talk about this stuff. The only reason I found out about Isla was because of social media. I've read more intimate details about your relationships than you've told me personally."

She might have me there. When Candace and I were dating, she liked to be *seen*. I should have recognized it for what it was—a red flag—but I was too wrapped up in her. There were plenty of times when we'd go out and end up being photographed. Now, I wonder if she tipped the paps off about where we were going to be because it happened a lot. And always on the nights when she looked her hottest. I'm sure my mom and sister ended up reading more than they ever wanted to know about my exploits. But I'm not that guy anymore, and Isla isn't like Candace. She doesn't crave the spotlight.

"Yeah, well, don't worry. You won't have to read about my sex life with Isla in the papers. I'm keeping her to myself."

Mira claps her hands and wiggles in the passenger seat after she buckles herself in. "I can't wait to meet her. She seems really sweet."

"She is."

"But you two have definitely made your way into a few articles, Maddy. Sorry to be the one to tell you."

That's news to me. Though, admittedly, I haven't done any googling. "What do you mean?"

My sister rests her hand on my shoulder, understanding softening her features. "Don't worry. It's nothing like when you were with that bitch, Candace. It's just that there are photos of the two of you standing together chatting at that assembly you and the guys did, a few of you together at her school one day, and Griffin posted that photo of her with him and Sebastian calling her *your girl*."

Okay, none of that's so bad. With Candace, there were photos of her draping herself all over me, her tits nearly popping out of her dress. Hell, one time someone caught a shot of us with her hand sneaking down my pants. Coach was pissed about that one, but those kinds of photos never show you what happens after that split second in time. And in the case of Candace's hand down my pants, I put a stop to that before her fingers made it too far past my waistband. Hockey is my passion and my career, and if I'm in the press, I want it to be because they're talking about how well I'm playing, not making claims I get hand jobs on the regular while I'm out at clubs and restaurants.

"People are curious about her. Especially since she's so different from the other women you've dated." Mira watches me closely as she pokes me for more information. "And she *is* different, isn't she?"

"Yeah," I tell her, smiling like a dope as I pull out of the parking garage and head towards my place. "She is. Really different."

Mira leans back in her seat, but never takes her eyes off me. "You seem different, too, you know."

"Do I?"

She nods. "Yeah. You seem more settled. More secure." Her words trail off as she studies me. "Things with her are serious, aren't they?"

If I can't be honest with my sister, who the hell can I be honest with? Mira and I have the same complicated relationship with love because of our upbringing. Even if we deal with things in opposite ways.

So I only hesitate for a moment before I give voice to the truth Logan Byrne, of all people, recognized before I did.

"I think I'm in love with her."

Mira squeals and wiggles around in her seat. "Oh my god, I knew it! Maddox-freaking-Graves, you've finally found your person."

I'm pretty sure I have. It's terrifying as hell, but what's the point in denying it any longer? "I haven't told her yet, so don't be weird, Mir. Seriously. I'll kick your ass if you scare her away. I don't care if you are my little sister."

That has her laughing. "Don't worry, my lips are sealed." She pantomimes zipping her lips, locking them, and then throws away the invisible key. "Does Mom know?"

"Hell, no. Are you kidding? You know she'll show up at my place the minute I tell her, and I'm not ready for that kind of pressure. She'll want to know when I'm going to propose, when we're going to start having babies, how many babies... You know how she is. Isla isn't ready for that kind of chaos."

Mira nods. "Yeah. She keeps digging for info on me and Jared, too, but she's not nearly as bad as all that."

Really? If things with Jared are serious enough for

Mira to live with the guy, the fact that our mom isn't bugging Mira is kind of suspicious. "Does Mom like Jared?"

"I think so." My sister shrugs. "She's never told me she doesn't."

Arching a brow, I side-eye Mira. "She never told me she didn't like Candace, either. But she also never told me she *liked* her. Mom didn't make her feelings known about her until things were over with us."

"What are you saying?" Mira folds her arms over her chest. She's getting defensive. I can see her hackles rising. "You think Mom doesn't like Jared?"

"I don't know," I reply honestly. "I haven't met the guy yet or seen her interact with him. But doesn't it seem a little fishy that she hasn't told you she does?"

My sister falls silent, her lips twisting into a frown.

"Shit, sorry, Mi-Mi. Forget I said anything. What the hell do I know, anyway?"

"Yeah," she says. But she's quieter now. I need to change the subject.

"So I was on the team plane when I told Isla about dinner tonight, and Griffin tried to invite himself along. He and the guys have already demanded that we go out after the game, so prepare yourself. No doubt they'll be as ridiculous as ever."

That has Mira grinning. The guys love her, but the feeling is mutual. She always has fun with them. It's like having a bunch of older brothers around instead of just one. It would probably be overwhelming to some women, but Mira's always thrived under all that attention.

By the time we get to my place and get Mira unpacked, all the talk of our mom and her boyfriend is long forgotten. And when we pick Isla up for dinner, my sister is over the moon. They quickly form a bond, and by the time dinner's over, I'm just sitting back, watching them chatter away about anything and everything, utterly content.

I didn't realize how much hope I was holding onto that they'd get along like this. Mira never liked Candace, and while she made an effort for my sake, I should have seen it. Mira was reserved with Candace. She was guarded. But with Isla? She hasn't stopped laughing, and she keeps looking my way with sparkling eyes.

She doesn't speak the words, but I hear them loud and clear. Isla has Mira's approval. And that means more to me than she could know.

Isla, too, is having the time of her life. I know she was nervous about meeting Mira, but all of those reservations melted away within the first five minutes. They're already thick as thieves, and Mira has convinced Isla not to sit in the private box seats I was planning on putting them in for Wednesday's home game. No, she told Isla that the best way to experience your first hockey game is down in the trenches, right in front of the boards. I can't say I mind. Having Isla front and center like that will only make me play harder.

So as they chat and giggle and make their plans, I work my magic and get them new tickets. I can't wait to show off for my girl.

All is right in the world.

# forty-two

ISLA

I EXPECTED THE ARENA TO BE COLDER. BUT I GUESS when you cram thousands of people into a space—even one with a giant ice rink in the center—it warms things up.

"I can't believe this is your first game," Mira gushes. Her green eyes reflect the sparkling lights of the arena as she takes it all in. Her long, dark hair is braided into loose pigtails and tucked into a yellow and charcoal gray Rogues beanie with a massive yellow pom-pom on the top. She gave me one to match, though my hair is down and in loose curls. I'm already regretting that. Should have let Mira braid mine, too. It's going to be a rat's nest of knots by the end of the game.

We're both wearing a Rogues jersey with Maddox's last name on it. Well, Mira's last name, too, I suppose. Mine is over a hoodie, while Mira just wears a long-sleeved thermal shirt under hers. She looks completely at ease and in her element.

I'm a ball of nerves.

"No need to look so stressed." Mira nudges me with her shoulder. "Maddy's been on fire, so far. And if I know my brother, he'll play even harder since you're here. It's going to be great, you'll see."

"I know," I say, my eyes on the tunnel the team will enter from. "I guess I'm just worried about seeing him get hit in person, you know? It was nerve-wracking enough on TV. He's got a big bruise on his ribs from that hit at the end of the last away game."

Mira shrugs. "At least he has you to kiss it better." She makes a kissy face, complete with obnoxious sound effects, and it helps. There's no way *not* to laugh at her antics.

The guy beside her stares at us for a moment before turning to his buddy and whispering something I can't make out. Hopefully, they don't know who Mira's talking about. I just want to sit here in blissful anonymity while I worry about my boyfriend.

Soon, the arena is packed with loud, excited fans. It's a sea of yellow and gray with a few dots of Boston's royal blue and gold interspersed throughout the crowd. The booming voice of the announcer fills the space, drowning everything else out. He announces the game between the Rogues and the Boston Renegades, then introduces each player that makes up the Renegades, as well as their coaches. The crowd *boos* enthusiastically, some of them heckling the players as they step onto the ice and circle the rink.

Then the lights go down and everyone turns their phone's flashlight apps on, and music blares through the cavernous space. Mira grabs my hand with a squeal and does a little dance in her seat as the announcer begins his introduction for the Rogues. With each new player he announces, my heart beats a little faster. My eyes hungrily scan the tunnel and I stand and cheer alongside Mira when he calls out Griffin and Logan. Maddox must have told them where we're sitting because they skate right up to the rink shield and give Mira and me a wink and a wave before skating off. The guy next to Mira stares at us again.

But then I don't care about anyone or anything else around me. Not Mira, not the guy beside her—hell, I wouldn't care if the president of the United States was in the stands—because the announcer calls out Maddox's name. The crowd goes wild for him, and so does my heart. It's thundering away in my chest. And when he makes eye contact the moment he steps out of that tunnel and onto the ice, I'm a goner.

No one else exists except for my boyfriend when he skates up to the glass, lets his eyes rove over me, winks, and then holds his hand to his heart. He grins at Mira, who's howling with laughter at his antics, then gifts a smile to me before he skates off to join his team. I barely register the announcer calling Sebastian's name or feel Mira bump into me with her shoulder again because I'm stuck in this surreal moment. Even when the people around us whisper my name, I hardly notice.

To be the sole focus of Maddox Graves while he's in his element is heady.

"Oh my god, you two are so fucking adorable I can hardly stand it," Mira crows with her hands interlocked beneath her chin.

Despite the chill in the air, my cheeks heat.

"Seriously," she continues, "he's different with you. You're good for him."

I push out a mumbled thanks, but soon the arena fills with music so loud it's impossible to talk. And I'm glad because my heart is rioting in my chest. Maddox's sister likes me, and he just singled me out in front of thousands of people. He wouldn't have done that if this thing between us wasn't getting serious, right?

As the game begins, I'm focused on only one thing. Maddox Graves. The man who just claimed my heart in front of the world.

---

THE CROWD BOOS AND I WINCE AS ONE OF THE Renegades' players slams Maddox hard into the boards. Neither team has scored, and it's been an incredibly physical game. Our guys grow increasingly frustrated as the second period winds down.

The fans also grow frustrated, and the more beer they drink, the more vocal they are about their dissatisfaction.

"Come on, Wright," Mira shouts as Logan passes the puck to Griffin. He tries to slice through Boston's defense, but they're sticking to the Rogues like glue. Griffin tries to get the puck to Maddox, but it's intercepted. The crowd boos, then grows silent as the Renegades player speeds down the ice toward the goal Sebastian guards. I hold my breath as he swats it away with his stick.

"This is so stressful," I tell Mira. I'm holding onto her arm with a death grip.

"Tell me about it." We both let out a sigh as the second period comes to a close and the guys leave the ice. Maddox glances my way, and I can tell he's frustrated, so I give him a thumbs-up and a goofy smile. His lips twitch at the corners before he disappears down the tunnel.

Mira tries to reassure me. "The Renegades are good. The guys knew this would be a tough game, but I'm not sure anyone expected Boston to come out swinging this hard during the preseason."

"Maybe if our team would get their heads out of their asses, we'd be winning by now," the ruddy-faced man beside her says.

Mira's jaw ticks. She rolls her eyes at me, then turns to the guy and says, "Oh, yeah? And you could do better, right?"

He huffs. "Listen, sweetheart, I'm sure you love watching the guys skate around, but some of us are here for the actual hockey. You wouldn't understand."

*Uh-oh.* I may not know Mira super well, but I know she's fiery as hell and very protective of her brother.

"Listen, *sweetheart*," she says mockingly, "I've been watching hockey games since before I could walk. I understand plenty, and I'm more invested in the Rogues winning than you'll ever be. So why don't you sit down, get another beer, and shut the hell up, okay?"

A guy behind us lets out a low whistle. Our new red-faced friend sputters and huffs out annoyed sounds for a minute, but obviously can't think of anything intelligent to say in response. Mira gives him her back and waves down a vendor selling cotton candy.

WE'RE HALFWAY THROUGH THE THIRD AND FINAL period with nine minutes and forty seconds left on the clock, and both teams seem like they're out for blood. My jaw hurts from clenching it so hard. I still haven't recovered from watching one of the Renegades slam into Maddox directly in front of us. If the people in the seats surrounding Mira and me hadn't realized by that point that I'm Maddox's girlfriend, they sure did after that.

Everyone groans when one of our rookies gets sent to the sin bin for cross-checking.

"They're getting frustrated. It's making them reckless," Mira mutters, more to herself than me. The announcer informs the arena that Ryder Hanson has been given a two-minute penalty. "This isn't good."

It's the opening the Renegades need. With the Rogues down a player during the penalty kill, Boston gets around our d-men, and for the first time in the game, Bash lets a puck slip by him.

"Dammit," I hiss. Poor Sebastian looks pissed at himself, but the Rogues don't give up. The line changes, and Maddox, Griffin, and Logan hop back onto the ice. With clasped hands, I pray to the hockey gods, the ancient Greek gods, hell, I even channel Jess and pray to Chris Hemsworth that the guys can turn this around and take the lead.

Seven minutes left.

Maddox gets control of the puck and speeds down the ice. He's glorious and fierce, and I can't help it. I leap to my feet and shout, "Go, babe, go!" He's quickly surrounded and slaps the puck hard toward the Renegades' net, but their goalie blocks it.

"You know," our pink-cheeked neighbor slurs loudly,

his fifth beer of the night in hand, "Graves has been on fire so far this preseason." The man glares at me. "You his girlfriend or his bad-luck-charm? Because one game with you in the seats, and he's playing like a junior-leaguer."

Heat rushes up my chest and cheeks as people turn to stare at me. This is my nightmare.

"Listen, you sack of shit, blaming an off night on a player's significant other is bullshit, and you know it." Mira stands, her petite frame seeming to puff up with indignation. "So shut your fucking mouth, or I'll shut it for you."

"Mira," I tug on the back of her jersey. Everyone around us stares. "It's okay."

"It's not okay," she says. "Fuck this guy."

"Well, I mean, yeah, he's an asshole. But he's not worth it."

"What did you say?" The drunk fan rises to his feet and squares off with Mira, but his angry gaze is on me. "You think just because you're letting a hockey player fuck you like some common whore that makes you special?"

I want to crawl under my seat and disappear.

"You're just another slutty puck bunny distracting the team in search of your fifteen minutes." He's shouting now, spittle hitting Mira in the face. I'm actively trying to hold her back, because her fists are clenched, and I just know she's about to haul off and hit the guy. Which he totally deserves. But she'll be the one who ends up arrested for it.

A couple of drunk guys two rows back decide to pile on and make their opinions known. They shout at Mira and me to go home, call me names, and blame the fact that the Rogues are losing on our presence. I shouldn't care what any of them have to say. They're drunk, belligerent, and ignorant. But a tear still rolls down my cheek.

I'm so lost in my embarrassment, I don't notice Maddox skate up to the glass until he pounds on it. When I lift my watery eyes to his face, he takes one look at the tear dripping from my jaw, then zeroes in on the jerk next to Mira.

"What the fuck did you say to my girl?" he shouts through the glass. The jerk loses some of his bravado when faced with the murderous attention of Maddox Graves. When the guy doesn't speak, Maddox pounds on the glass. "I'll ask you again, dickface. Why is my girl crying?"

The rest of the Rogues' players notice the commotion, and the Renegades are just as intrigued. Play grinds to a halt as Griffin and Logan skate over to us. The guys who were just shouting at Mira and me and acting like big, tough cavemen fall silent.

"What did he say to you, baby?" Maddox shouts through the glass. When I shake my head, unwilling to repeat any of it, he turns his attention to his sister. "Mi-Mi, what the fuck is going on?"

Mira wraps her arm around my shoulder. "These asshats are calling Isla names and blaming her for the score."

"Bitch," the drunk guy mutters.

"The fuck did you just call my sister?" Maddox pounds the side of his fist against the glass. "You have a death wish?"

The arena is breaking into chaos. Play has completely stopped, and the refs skate over to figure out what's going on. Griffin and Logan try to get Maddox away from the rink shield, but he shoves them away and points to the man beside Mira.

"Say another word to my girlfriend or my sister and I'll lay you out, asshole."

This time, the refs hear his threat. Dragging him away from the glass, they slap him with a misconduct penalty.

"What does that mean?" I whisper to Mira.

She shakes her head, but her expression is proud. She may not be happy about the penalty, but she clearly supports Maddox's actions. "It means he's out for the rest of the game. Normally it's a ten-minute penalty, but there are only six minutes left."

I cover my face and sink as low in my seat as I can manage. If the surrounding fans hated me before, it's nothing compared to the *boos* hurled my way when the announcer calls out the penalty.

Sure, I'm not to blame for being targeted with verbal abuse by drunk strangers, but I still can't help feeling like all of this is my fault. And when the Rogues lose after a brutal game, the fans around me have no problem telling me they feel the same.

My first time at a game, and already I'm bringing Maddox down.

*forty-three*

## MADDOX

"WHAT IN THE HELL HAPPENED OUT THERE?" Coach Cross shouts. The vein in his temple throbs as he paces the locker room. Back and forth, back and forth.

"Look, I'm sorry, Coach, but the assholes sitting next to my girlfriend and my sister were talking shit and calling them vile names. I couldn't let that stand."

"So you threatened a paying fan?" Coach grabs his hair. "Jesus, Graves. What were you thinking?"

The rest of my team watches us like this is some juicy soap opera. They have my back on this—we know anyone who dates or marries us will end up with some level of public scrutiny—but no one gets to make our significant others cry because we're underperforming at a game. "I was thinking I needed to protect two of the most important women in my life, coach. You've got a daughter. I'm sure you understand."

"No, Graves," he shouts. "I don't. Because my daughter knows the score. When I'm coaching, hockey is everything. I don't have a daughter. When I was married, it was the same with my wife. At the arena, I'm not a husband or father. When I'm here, I'm just a coach."

"That's probably why he got a divorce and none of us have ever met his daughter," Navarro mumbles under his breath. And I have to agree. To me, family comes first. The people I love come first. Now, that includes the guys on my team. But a game is a game. Sure, I want to win. And yes, how I play is important to me. This is my career, after all. It's my passion. But hockey *isn't* everything. I'm seeing that with more and more clarity.

"Everyone shower and get the hell out of here," Coach grumbles. "But hear me when I say that this kind of shit will never happen again. Understand?"

"Understood," we say in unison.

"Your sister looked like she was about to punch that guy in the nose," Wright says gleefully as we head for the showers. "She's always been a spitfire."

"She knows how to hold her own," I agree. I never like that she has to, though. I wonder if Isla knows how to defend herself? Something to ask her later. "I should have insisted they sit in the box, but she was so excited to show Isla the whole experience."

"Hey, man." Logan squeezes my shoulder. "That wasn't your fault. Wasn't the girls' fault, either. Sometimes people are the worst. The best thing we can do now is get ready as quickly as possible, meet them out there, and make sure they both have so much fun tonight that they forget the whole thing."

"Yeah, I suppose you're right."

"Nah, I'm Wright," Griffin sniggers. Logan punches him in the arm.

"Moron."

***

ISLA'S QUIET. SHE HAS BEEN SINCE THE MOMENT I emerged from the locker room and wrapped her up in a long, tight hug. She was stiff at first, but eventually melted into my arms. I haven't stopped touching her since. As soon as we sat around the large table at the back of the restaurant we invaded, I pulled her to my side.

"You sure you're okay?" I ask her for the tenth time. The words are a soft caress against the shell of her ear. I know she's feeling out of sorts, and I don't want to draw undue attention to her.

"Yeah," she says. It's not all that believable. "I'm just..." She gnaws on her bottom lip until I pull it away from her teeth with my thumb. "I just feel bad."

"Why in the hell should you feel bad?"

She sighs, and I hate the way her shoulders slump. "I embarrassed you."

What? I rear back like she's slapped me because what in the hell? She thinks she embarrassed me? "Baby, how do you think you embarrassed me?"

"I shouldn't have let those guys bother me," she huffs out. "But I did, and then I caused enough of a scene that you got thrown out of the last few minutes of the game and you guys lost." She peers up at me with sad, sapphire eyes. "Did you get in trouble?"

"No, baby, I didn't get in trouble. Even if I had, it would have been worth it. Besides, *you* are not the reason we lost."

"Nope," Griffin pipes up from across the table. He takes a break from cracking jokes to my sister to quirk an eyebrow at Isla. "We lost because we weren't in sync enough, and Boston's defense was on point tonight."

"He's right," Sebastian agrees with that calm demeanor of his that puts everyone at ease. "Even if Madds hadn't been sent to the sin bin, we probably would have lost. Which is my fault, actually."

Navarro always blames himself when we lose. I suppose that's par for the course with most goalies, but it's still bullshit. He let one shot through, but how many more did he block?

"Not your fault," Logan says, taking a break from flirting with our waitress. He rolls his eyes at Navarro. "The success of the team doesn't rest solely on your self-deprecating shoulders."

"Oooh." Griffin waggles his eyebrows. "Nice vocab word, Byrne. Was that part of your word-of-the-day calendar?"

"Shut the hell up." Logan throws a piece of broccoli at Griffin's head, but Wright dodges it. They both laugh.

Mira shakes her head. "I'm surrounded by children. Giant, six-foot tall children." She turns to Isla and her face softens. "The point is, as much as those shit-for-brains guys around us would love to blame you, that's ridiculous. You are not responsible for anyone else's actions or performance. If Maddy sucks, that's on him. If he's distracted, that's on him. He's responsible for his own damned self."

"She's right," I tell Isla, lightly gripping her chin so she has to meet my gaze and see how serious I am. "Besides, having you there was motivating. Please don't let this turn you off from coming to more of our games."

"I won't," she murmurs, her pretty lips tilting up into the first smile I've seen from her since the end of the game.

I don't care if we're surrounded by my teammates and my sister. It doesn't matter that the other patrons are watching us and some of them have their phones out. None of that matters. All that matters to me is that I help my girlfriend understand how much I want her, and that no bad game will change that. So I dip my face to meet hers and take her pouty lips in a possessive kiss. Her response is instant and perfect. She presses into me, one hand moving to my neck, the other tangling in my hair. And when I open my mouth and encourage her to do the same, she lets out a breathy sigh that I swallow up. Her sexy little noises are for me to hear, and me alone.

Everyone at the table hoots and shouts, even Mira. And by the time Isla and I pull away from each other, she's breathless and pink-cheeked. She glances around the table, adorably embarrassed, then covers her face in her hands.

"Oh my god," she mumbles into her palms.

"Aren't they sickeningly cute?" Griffin asks Mira.

My sister chuckles, her smile stretching wide across her face as she turns my way. "Yeah. Yeah, they are."

After that, Isla relaxes.

"So." Griffin turns to my sister. "Madds said you moved in with your boyfriend. Things are pretty serious, huh?"

Mira shifts in her seat. Her eyes dart to me before returning her attention to Griffin. "Uh, yeah. About that."

Mira clears her throat. "I didn't want to say anything, but since this night has turned into a bit of a downer anyway, I guess it can't hurt."

The table falls silent, and I lean toward my sister. "What can't hurt, Mi-Mi?"

She lets out a nervous giggle. "Um, well, I moved in with Jared, and it… It became clear pretty quickly that our relationship wasn't as strong as I thought."

A frown pulls at Griffin's mouth. "What does that mean, Lil' Gravesy?"

"It means I'm glad I wasn't done unpacking because I need to find somewhere new to live." Mira shrugs, a fake-ass smile plastered on her face.

"What?" My voice is deadly. I'm going to kill her asshole boyfriend. *Ex-boyfriend.*

"Look, don't make it into a whole thing, Maddy. I've taken it as a sign that I should move back home. Chicago's great and all, but I miss Minneapolis and you and Mom." Mira leans to the side and bumps shoulders with Griffin. "Plus, it's been fun hanging out with these weirdos again."

"Did he hurt you, Mira?" Griffin's not amused. In fact, his tone is just as dangerous as mine.

Mira sighs. "No, nothing like that, okay? We just got in a few fights and he made some comments about our future that didn't line up with where I thought we were going, and one thing led to another…" Her lips twist to the side. "Whatever. It doesn't matter. What does matter is that now I need a place to stay. So if you guys know of anyone with a spare room to rent, let me know, okay?"

*Shit.* I should offer a room in my place, but things are going so well with Isla. I don't want to screw that up. But this is my little sister. And she needs help.

Clearing my throat, I glance at Isla before opening my mouth. "Mir, if you need a place to stay…"

"No," she says, cutting me off. "I will not cock block my older brother and his girlfriend right as things are getting serious. Not doing it."

"Mi-Mi," I shake my head.

"Nope. Seriously, Maddy. I didn't bring it up to guilt trip you into offering me a place to live. Just putting it out there in case you know someone who's looking for a roommate."

Griffin's gaze bounces to me before he turns and faces my sister. "I've got a spare room, Little Gravesy. It's a suite, so it has a bathroom and everything. You can live with me."

I open my mouth to say absolutely not, but Mira beats me to it.

"I couldn't do that, Griffin."

"Why the hell not?" he asks. "I've got the room, and you need a place to stay. I'm gone half of the time, anyway, so you'd be doing me a favor. You can grab my mail and shit and make sure the place doesn't burn down when I'm out of town."

"Griffin." Mira shakes her head. "You don't know what you're asking."

"Bullshit, Mira. I know exactly what I'm asking. I also know you're being a stubborn ass."

Bash pinches the bridge of his nose. Logan's attention pings between my sister and my best friend.

"Come on, Mir. We're friends. It would be fun, and you wouldn't even need to pay me rent. I own the place outright, so it's not like I need the money."

Narrowing my eyes, I study my best friend. His typical

flippant attitude is nowhere to be found. His expression is determined. Serious. Maybe my sister living with him wouldn't be the worst thing in the world.

"I think it sounds like a great idea," Isla offers. Her words are soft, but everyone gives her their attention. "Breakups suck, Mira. It would be nice to have a friend around to cheer you up when you need it. Especially one that will be gone sometimes so you can have the place to yourself occasionally."

"See?" Griffin smiles widely. "If Isla thinks it's a good idea, it is."

My sister's lip twitches with a suppressed smile. "If we do this, there will have to be rules, Wright. No walking around naked or banging your puck bunnies on the couch."

Griffin holds a hand to his chest. "I'm wounded that you think so little of me."

"And you definitely won't touch my sister," I add. "Or I'll kick your ass. I don't care if you are my best friend. Keep your diseased dick to yourself."

"It's not diseased," Wright growls. "He's perfectly healthy."

Mira rolls her eyes, but I can see her caving. She's going to agree to move in with him. Hopefully it's not a huge mistake. "You're serious about this?"

"Yeah. I am."

"All right. I'll move in with you. But I'm paying rent."

Griffin runs a hand through his blond hair as a smile crinkles the corners of his eyes. "We'll see about that."

Mira turns to my girlfriend. Most of the tension I've seen plaguing her since I picked her up at the airport has disappeared. "Looks like we're going to have plenty of time to establish our new bestie status."

Isla laughs. She looks so happy. "Can't wait."

With Mira's living situation settled, we sit there for hours, laughing, talking, and eating. Our server doesn't seem to mind because she knows we'll tip well—we always do—and because she's spent the last fifteen minutes perched on Logan's lap.

It's two a.m. by the time we settle up and leave, and Isla's hardly able to keep her eyes open. She's so tired she barely protests when I scoop her up in my arms.

"I can walk," she mumbles. The guys chuckle.

"I know, baby, but I want to carry you. Don't spoil my fun."

She presses her face into my neck and huffs out a silent puff of laughter. "Bossy."

"Stay at my place?"

"Oh, yes, please stay, Isla. It'll be like a sleepover," Mira says. "We can make a big breakfast in the morning and hang out. Please say yes."

"How do you have so much energy?" Isla asks Mira, lifting her head from my chest to look at my sister.

Mira shrugs. "I'm not a teacher, so I don't have to get up as early as you."

"Shit." Isla winces. "I have school tomorrow. I'm going to be so tired."

My sister and I share a grimace. I completely forgot it was a school night for Isla. "Is your car at your place?"

She nods. "I kinda figured we'd end up driving together, so Mira and I took an Uber to the arena."

"All right, then. I'll take you home. You and Mira will have all the time in the world for sleepovers now."

"Mm, okay." She burrows back into my body and closes her eyes. "That sounds good."

Guilt at keeping her out so late nibbles at my chest. I'll just have to bring her coffee tomorrow. And some donuts. Maybe I'll bring enough to stock the teachers' lounge.

"Let's get you home, baby."

# forty-four

## MADDOX

I KNEW THERE'D BE FALLOUT FROM WHAT happened at last night's game, but knowing it's coming and seeing it come to pass are entirely separate beasts.

"Jesus." Mira shakes her head, a frown twisting her lips. "What the hell is wrong with people?" She's reading the comments on an article slamming the Rogues for our loss last night. And unfortunately, Isla's mentioned by name as my unconfirmed girlfriend. Because, of course, they had to cover my altercation with the assholes sitting near her.

"Don't read the comments. You know this."

Her familiar green eyes lift to meet mine. "This is different. You need to know what people are saying about Isla so you can figure out how to best support her. All of this attention is new to her. You may be used to brushing off asshole-ish comments, but she's not."

*Shit.*

Pinching the bridge of my nose, I give my sister a nod. "All right. What are they saying?"

"The kind of garbage you'd expect. That she's a distraction. She's the reason the team lost, and you didn't play your best. People are commenting on her looks, her weight, her hair... basically picking her apart. Then there are the guys commenting about how they'd fuck her, or calling her a gold-digger, or a slut or whatever." Mira's face twists in disgust. "Same shit, different day, Maddy."

Rage bubbles in my gut. I'll never understand what makes people think their opinions matter. Or why these armchair assholes believe they have anything to contribute when they wouldn't last five minutes in a rink. Candace always loved attention. Good or bad, it didn't matter as long as her name and face were splashed across the internet. But Isla? She's different.

Mira's right. I need to help her navigate this, or I could end up losing her.

Maybe we need to keep a low profile for a while. At least until the team is playing more consistently. The last thing I want is for Isla to be subjected to jeering assholes with unwanted opinions.

But shit. I promised I'd take her to that fall festival. She was excited about that.

I'll just have to think of something fun and romantic to do at my place. Hell, we could have a candle-lit dinner and carve pumpkins. Make our own fall festival. One where she's safe and able to let loose.

My phone buzzes with an incoming text.

ISLA

Everyone's looking at me funny. When I grabbed a coffee before school this morning, some guy called me a bitch. What the hell?

My fist clenches and it's a struggle not to crush my phone.

ME

I'm so sorry, Short-Stack. Are you okay? He didn't touch you, did he?

ISLA

No. But it did kinda scare me.

Do you want me to pick you up from work today?

There's a pause as Isla types her response.

ISLA

No, that's okay. Thank you. I'm pretty beat. Would you be mad if I went home and slept today? I know tomorrow is Mira's last day before she goes back to grab her stuff, so I'll definitely hang out tomorrow. I'm just tired.

"She okay?" Mira asks, looking over my shoulder.

I shake my head. "I don't know."

Of course, I won't tell Isla I'll be mad if she doesn't come over tonight as planned. I know this has been a lot for her. But the creeping, crawling sensation of dread that skitters around my stomach makes me consider it.

I don't want her to pull away. I need to ensure that whatever I plan for her in place of the fall festival shows her how much I care. How much I'm falling for her. That I'll do anything to protect her.

ME

Of course, I won't be mad. Are you sure you're okay?

ISLA

Definitely. GTG. The next period is starting.

Okay, baby. Miss you.

Miss you, too.

I stare at my phone for a moment, lost in thought. When my sister's hand rests on my shoulder, I shake my head and snap out of it.

Everything is going to be okay. This is just a little bump.

"All right. Let's make a plan to get you moved in with Wright. Do you need someone to help you pack up a truck in Chicago?"

One of Mira's eyebrows lifts, but she doesn't call me on my abrupt subject change. "Nah. I don't have much. I got rid of a lot of stuff before I moved in with Jared."

"Okay. What day do you want us to move you into Wright's place?"

I can't fully banish the low-level anxiety crawling around my stomach, but I do my best. Everything will be fine.

Things aren't fine. We have our first official home game the week after Mira leaves. When I asked Isla if she wanted to go and sit in the box with the other wives and girlfriends, she declined. Not that I blame her. The bullshit comments about her haven't stopped. In fact, I've made it a part of my daily routine to check her Instagram account just to make sure no trolls have made their way onto her followers list. The last thing my girlfriend needs is some knuckle-dragging dipshit making gross comments about her on her own feed.

She's getting enough of that on everyone else's.

That's how I come across a couple of comments from her ex.

My teammates laugh and talk as we get ready for tonight's game. I'm already dressed and in my skates, so I'm doing my daily scroll through her feed. She hasn't posted anything since the preseason game, but there are new comments on a photo of Isla and her friends from the silent auction dinner and a smiling selfie Isla took in her classroom the day she finished decorating it.

*LawBro19: You always looked beautiful in that dress. Remember when you got it and how I peeled it off of you that night?*

*LawBro19: The room looks great. But you've always had a knack for decorating.*

Blood roars in my ears. *Remember when you got it and how I peeled it off of you that night?* What. The. Fuck? Fighting the urge to chuck my phone against the wall, I click on the username. His bio tells me this is Alex. Isla's ex, Alex.

Why is he commenting on her photos? Especially comments like that?

"You okay?" Sebastian lowers himself onto the bench beside me. His pads bump my knee. "You look like you're about to murder someone."

"Might be," I grumble.

"What's up?"

Unable to form the words, I flip my phone over and point to the comment Alex left about Isla's dress. Bash's brow knits into a frown.

"Deranged fan?"

I shake my head. "No, man. Her ex."

My friend and goalie studies me. He takes in my ticking jaw, the fire in my eyes, and my clenching fist. "Is he bothering her? Do we need to beat this guy's ass?"

I want to. After everything he did to her, he's going to comment trash like this? Why hasn't she blocked him? And why hasn't she deleted the comments?

"I don't know. Maybe? I didn't even realize they were still following each other or in contact. When he showed up the other day, she was pretty shaken. It just doesn't make sense."

Bash claps a hand on my back. "Talk to her. I'm sure there's an explanation. Don't let this psych you out, Madds. We need to win this game."

"Right." I lock my phone and toss it in my duffel bag. "Don't worry. I'll keep my head in the game."

"You better." Bash stands right as Coach storms into the locker room.

"All right, men. Everyone ready? This isn't the preseason anymore. I expect each and every one of you to play like the professionals you are. Play your best, kick some ass, and"—he looks at me—"keep your personal shit off the ice. Got it?"

Everyone shouts their agreement, even me. The problem is that sometimes divorcing yourself from your life when your blades hit the ice is easier said than done.

---

WE LOSE THE GAME BY ONE GOAL IN THE THIRD. Everyone played hard, but that doesn't stop the fans from pitching a fit at the end of the game.

Nothing like skating off the ice to boos and jeers.

Coach rips us new assholes for a solid twenty minutes before storming out of the locker room, red-faced and fuming.

I feel responsible. I had the perfect opportunity to score in the second, and I bounced the damned puck off the iron. If I hadn't missed, we would have tied and had a chance.

"Dude. This isn't your fault." Logan bumps me with his knee while I mope on the bench. I need to shower and change, but can't seem to find the motivation.

"I missed that shot," I growl.

"Yeah, and I missed three," Sebastian says, drying his hair with a towel as he ambles toward his locker to get dressed. "It wasn't our best game. But it's only the first of the season. You can't win them all."

I rake my fingers through my sweaty hair. "Yeah, but people were already giving Isla shit. It's going to be worse now. She wasn't even here, but you know they'll blame her."

"Maybe." Navarro tugs a henley over his head. "But you can't control random assholes on the internet, Madds. The best thing you can do right now is shower, get dressed, and go make sure your girl knows you care about her."

"I know," I say. "I just... fuck. I can feel her pulling away ever since that preseason game and I'm freaking out."

"You've got your issues, and she's got hers. If I had to guess, I'd bet she's freaking out, too. Go to her place. Show up with dinner and ice cream or something. Spend the night making love to her. Tell her you're not going anywhere and that you don't buy into any of the garbage those trolls are saying." Navarro pins me with a serious look. "Tell her you love her."

My heart skips a beat, and I suck in a deep breath. "It's too soon for that."

"Bullshit," Griffin says. "Love doesn't have a timeline." With his hands on his hips, he stares at me. "Is she the first thing you think about in the morning when you wake up and the last thing you think about at night before you start snoring?"

"Yeah," I say. "But I don't snore."

Wright rolls his eyes. "Do you have to keep yourself from beating the crap out of anyone that looks at her the wrong way or hurts her feelings?"

I nod.

"Do you break out in a cold sweat at the thought of her leaving? At the idea of her ending things?"

I nod again.

"Call it whatever you want, Graves, but it sounds a helluva lot like love to me."

Griffin's words slam into me like a freight train running at max speed. Because he's right. I think maybe I do love her.

# *forty-five*

## ISLA

They lost. I shouldn't do it, I know I shouldn't, but I click on the comments of one of the team's social media posts from tonight's game. Some of them are encouraging—telling the guys that it was only the first game of the season and they'll play better in game two—but most post asshole-ish diatribes and express their disappointment. As if every player on the Rogues isn't disappointed too. I may not know all of them super well, but I'm familiar enough with the team to recognize that they're their own harshest critics.

And then there are the comments about me. I knew there'd be some. Mira and I texted throughout the whole game. At the end, she commanded me not to read the comments. But I'm a glutton for punishment. And the things people are saying are nasty.

When a knock on my apartment door startles me out

of my stupor, I'm grateful. My heart is pounding in my chest and I've broken out in a cold sweat. On shaky legs, I head to the door to let Maddox in. I hated saying no when he asked me to go to the game, but it felt like too much without Mira after the last time. He said he understood, but I know he was disappointed. Our compromise was that he'd come spend the night afterward.

"Hey, beautiful," he says when I swing the door open. He looks tired and frustrated. Stress lines his forehead and jaw. But when he smiles at me, all of that melts away.

In two steps, Maddox is in my apartment. He drops his overnight bag on the floor. In two more, he wraps his arms around me, shuts the door with his foot, and lifts me off the ground. A squeak leaves my lips when he squeezes me tightly and presses his face in the crook of my neck.

"God, you smell good."

Some of my anxiety bleeds away. He's here. He's not mad at me. Maddox doesn't blame me for the team's loss like those randos on the internet. "So do you. Like soap and that spicy shampoo you use."

He chuckles against my neck. "You like that?"

"Mmhmm."

We stay like that for another few seconds. Maddox doesn't let me go, and I don't release him. I needed this. I didn't realize how much. A part of me has been worried that Maddox will come to the same conclusion Alex did. That I'm not good enough for him. And with thousands of strangers telling him just that online, I've been waiting for the other shoe to drop.

But he's here. He's holding me like he doesn't want to let me go. That has to count for something.

"I'm sorry about the game," I tell him as he lets my body slide down his. With my feet on the floor, I look up at my boyfriend and study him. He looks tired.

"It's just a game." Maddox shrugs. He turns around to flip the locks on my door. "There'll be more. We won't let it define our whole season."

"Still, I'm sure it was disappointing to lose."

He brushes his knuckles softly over my cheek. "It always is. But losing's part of life, right?"

"Right." When Maddox drops his hand, I take it in my own. "You hungry?"

"I grabbed something on the way over. It's late, and I didn't want you to feel you had to stay up making me something."

"I wouldn't have minded. Can I get you some water at least? Some tea?"

"Water would be great, Short-Stack. Thank you."

He follows me into the kitchen. We're both silent as I fill two glasses with ice and water. We stare at each other as we drink. I hate seeing Maddox discouraged. I want to put that light I love so much back in his eyes. And, after a strange week with less contact and time together than normal, I want to connect with my boyfriend.

Holding out my hand, I give him a soft smile. "Come on, Ogre. Let's go cheer you up."

Maddox's eyebrows rise. "Cheer me up, huh?"

I nod.

"And what exactly did you have in mind?"

"Come with me, and I'll show you."

He chuckles, drops his palm in mine, and lets me lead him down the hall to my bedroom. He takes in the space and my waiting bed with a soft smile. Until his attention falls to my open laptop and the comments I'd been reading beneath an action shot of him during the game. I drop his hand and slam the laptop shut.

"Baby, were you reading the comments?" His brow pinches again, and I hate it.

I shake my head. "Nope."

He knows I'm lying. His long strides eat up the space between us, and he cups my cheeks. "Ignore those assholes, Isla. Their opinions don't matter. And they're wrong, anyway. You and me. That's all that matters."

"You and me," I murmur, nodding.

"I've missed you." He presses a kiss on my forehead. It's lingering and sweet. "This season is going to be so hard. Don't want to be away from you." He kisses my cheeks. First one and then the other.

I sigh, some of my tension dissipating with each new kiss he presses to my face. When I close my eyes, he kisses my eyelids. Then my jaw. Then my lips. When I open for him, his tongue sweeps inside my mouth. Heat pools in my belly and a soft moan escapes my lips, only to be swallowed by his.

We're wearing too many clothes. My fingers go to the hem of his tee and scrabble to tug it up his torso. With a chuckle, Maddox grabs the fabric and tugs it off. As soon as our kiss is broken, it's a race to get naked. Clothes puddle to the floor as our hands explore each other.

Once we're bare, I push Maddox back onto my bed. He falls with a startled laugh. Then his large hands grab me, and I fall on top of him.

"Fuck." He groans as our bodies connect skin to skin. "You feel so good, baby."

"Mm, you do too." My fingers trace the now-familiar

planes of his body as he rocks his hips. The motion draws a gasp from my lips as arousal pools between my thighs. "Oh, god."

Maddox kisses me like he's desperate. His large, calloused hands roam my soft curves and we grow more frantic with every moment.

"Fuck me, Maddox. God, please fuck me."

He hurries to unwrap a condom, rolling it down over the silky skin of his shaft. Within moments, the head of his cock is pressing into me. I gasp at the delicious stretch.

"You feel so good," he praises. In two more thrusts, he's seated fully inside of me and he stills, letting me adjust to him. Until I wrap my legs around his hips and urge him to move. "Impatient?"

"Yes."

Maddox chuckles against my throat, but he obliges me. He feels so good. I can't get enough of him. Each snap of his hips makes me moan. Sweat beads on my skin as we rock together. I need more. I need him deeper.

"Maddox," I whine. "Harder. Deeper. Please."

"You need me deeper, baby?"

All I can do is nod. Then I'm squealing as he pulls out, grabs my hips, and flips me onto my belly.

"Ass in the air, Isla."

"Oh, god." I hurry to comply. I need him to fill me back up. My body is desperate for release, and my soul is desperate for the connection. "Please. Please, Maddox."

"I know, baby. I've got you."

I scream when he slams into me. His palm flattens on my back between my shoulder blades. It pushes my chest into the soft embrace of my mattress. The contrast between his forceful thrusts and the way the memory foam cradles me only pushes me closer to my release.

"That's it, love. You take me so well. Look at your pretty ass bounce when I fuck you."

Oh, god. His mouth.

My orgasm builds. Every muscle in my body tightens.

"I hope you're ready, Isla. Because we won't be done tonight until I've made you come at least four times." When I whimper in response, his deep chuckle vibrates through me. "That's right. We're working up to the five I told you I'd wring out of you that first night."

When his arm wraps around my hips and his fingers press against my clit, I scream. Wave after wave of bliss cause my body to tighten. I'm shaking and crying out his name as he pounds his hips against my ass. He's relentless. It's overwhelming.

It's everything.

"That's my girl," he murmurs against my shoulder as he kisses my feverish skin. His fingers don't stop their ministrations. "Now give me another one."

Ten minutes later, I do. And when he spills inside of me, I fall off that cliff of pleasure for a third time. We both collapse. We're a tangle of limbs and sweat and sated bliss.

My heart feels lighter than it has all week, and I vow that I'm done hiding away. It doesn't matter what anyone else thinks about me or Maddox or our relationship. I can step out of my comfort zones for this man. He's worth the risk. Besides, I'm pretty sure I'm in love with him. And that's not something I'm willing to hide from the world because some strangers on the internet don't like me.

The words bubble up my throat as Maddox holds me.

His fingers trail along my spine and our hearts beat in sync. I want to tell him. To take the risk. I want to be brave.

But as our breathing slows and my eyes grow heavy, I can't quite push the words past my lips.

There's no rush. We have time.

# forty-six

## ISLA

"What are you going to wear?" Jess asks. She and Nev lounge on my bed as I rifle through my closet. I've been trying to settle on an outfit for the fall festival tonight. But nothing is right. It has to be warm but cute. Maybe a little sexy.

I hold up my favorite possibility. "Maybe this?" It's simple, but sexy. A pair of black fleece-lined leggings, an over-sized pumpkin-colored sweater with buttons along the wrists, and a black beanie. Paired with some brown leather ankle-booties and a scarf, it's the perfect combination of functional and cute. And I know Maddox loves my ass in leggings.

"I like it." Nevaeh nods. "You could wear that long gold necklace with it. The one with the triangular pendant."

"Oh, yeah. That would be cute." When neither suggests any further alterations, I head into the bathroom to change, but leave the door open so we can talk.

"So things with you two are getting serious, huh?"

"I think they are," I tell Nev. "I'm still getting used to all the attention being with him brings, but yeah. I'm pretty serious about him."

"Is h*e the one*?" Jess asks.

My lips curve into a smile. It's something I've been thinking about a lot lately. "Yeah. I think he might be."

"And you'll be able to handle all that attention for the long run? Because Maddox may be on the older side for a hockey player, but he's still got some years left in him. Not to mention whatever he does after the NHL. A lot of the guys with his level of popularity can leverage their fame for a sportscaster gig or big time endorsements." Leave it to Jess to ask the practical business questions.

"I'm not saying it'll always be easy, but yeah. I'll do whatever it takes to make this work. I..." Staring at myself in the mirror, I suck in a deep breath. "I love him."

Nevaeh squeals from my bedroom. "Babes, you don't know how happy that makes us to hear that. We were so worried that after everything Alex put you through, you'd never open yourself up to love again."

"I wasn't sure either," I admit. "But Maddox is different." The way he makes me feel... I can push through the little doubts that creep in because of my past with Alex.

"We're really happy for you." Jess grins at me when I stride out of the bathroom. "You deserve someone who treats you like the queen you are." She chuckles, sharing an amused look with Nev. "We never would have guessed any of this would happen when we placed the bid on the date with him."

"Yeah." I laugh. "And I never thought I'd fall in love with the guy who ignored me for the first part of our date.

Life is funny." My best friends wrap me in a hug, squeezing me between them. "Now get the hell out of here. My boyfriend will be here to pick me up soon."

"I see how it is." Nevaeh shakes her head. "We introduce you to your soulmate and you kick us out of your life."

"You look beautiful." Maddox links our fingers as he steers one handed.

I blush. It doesn't matter how many times he says it, my heart still skips a beat. "You look pretty handsome yourself. Are you going to be warm enough, though?"

Maddox wears a button-down shirt and jeans. The sleeves are rolled up to his elbows. He looks hot as hell, but it's chilly out. I glance at the backseat to see if he's stashed a sweater back there.

He clears his throat. "Uh, yeah. About that." Maddox makes a turn leading away from where the festival is being held and toward his apartment.

I laugh. "Did you forget a jacket? That's okay. We can go get one. I don't want you to be cold."

"I didn't forget a jacket." His fingers tighten around mine. "I know we talked about going to the fall festival, but I actually thought we could do something a little different?" His gaze pings my way before returning to the road.

My stomach rolls. "Oh. Okay... Um, what were you thinking?" And why didn't he say something sooner? What's going on? When Maddox hesitates, my stomach twists again. It's more violent this time.

When we stop at a red light, Maddox scratches at the five o'clock shadow covering his chin. "Well, we haven't really gotten to spend much time alone lately, and there's been a lot of scrutiny aimed your way. I know you don't love the public attention, and you know I don't either. So I thought maybe it might be better to do something at my place."

My heart pounds so loudly, I swear I can hear it echoing in the cab of Maddox's SUV. "You don't think we should go out in public right now?"

His throat bobs. He's nervous. "It's not that I think we *shouldn't*, more that I'm not sure it's a great idea. People are still being assholes about everything, and I don't want to give them a chance to say anything else, you know? I don't want to give them any ammo against you."

My stomach drops to the floor of the car.

I've been here before. Way too many times.

"Right."

Maddox glances at me as he pulls into his building's parking garage. "Are you... Are you disappointed?"

Plastering a fake smile on my face, I shake my head. "No, of course not."

"It just pisses me off the way people have been talking about you."

"Yeah, totally." Alex's words play on a cruel loop in my head.

*These are powerful people, Isla. They have certain standards and expectations. I don't want to make you feel like you have to put on an act with them. You'd just be uncomfortable, and I don't want you to feel inadequate.*

Why does it feel like Maddox is using different words to

say the same thing right now? And why does it hurt so much more when he says it?

"Baby, if you really want to go to the festival, we still can. Just maybe let me show you what I have planned at my place first? Then you can decide. Is that okay?" Maddox's dark eyebrows pinch together.

I try to tell myself that this is different. *He's* different. But my head and my heart can't seem to connect. Forcing myself to smile again, I nod. "Sure. Yeah. Of course."

Maddox is silent as he parks his car. I'm still as he climbs out and rounds the car to open my door. It's a struggle to control my breathing. My thoughts spiral. But this isn't my first rodeo. By the time he swings my door open, I've pasted the mask I perfected with Alex onto my face. And when Maddox offers me his hand, mine doesn't even shake as I place my palm in his.

He's tense as we cross the lobby and step into the elevator. I'm silent as the floors tick by on the LED display above us. By the time the elevator doors open, I've replayed the entirety of our relationship up to this point. Did I miss something? Is he ashamed of me? I know he wasn't always, or he wouldn't have stood up for me at that game. But I can't be the only one who's read the comments people are leaving on the team's socials. Of course, he's ashamed of me now. I embarrassed him. I made him look bad.

Maddox Graves is talented, famous, and way too attractive for his own good. He could have anyone he wants. And for a while, that was me. I should be grateful that I got this time with him.

Maddox's fingers splay across my lower back as he

guides me into his apartment. I can feel his eyes on me, so I look up at him with a smile.

"I hired a private chef to make us dinner. There are pumpkins for us to carve. I worked it out with a local movie theater to have someone deliver fresh popcorn at eight so we can have our own theater experience and watch some scary movies." He points at the coffee table. "I got every kind of candy I could think of, and the private chef brought gourmet caramel apples."

The rich scent of something savory and aromatic fills the space. It does smell delicious. And it's clear Maddox put a lot of effort into the evening. Any other time, this would have me swooning. But it's difficult to make myself forget why he went to all of this effort in the first place.

Because my boyfriend is ashamed to be seen in public with me. He's worried about what people will say. How being with me will affect his career.

"Isla? Is it... What do you think?"

Steeling myself, I turn to the man I'm in love with. The man making my heart fracture. "This looks amazing. Smells amazing, too."

Maddox studies my face. His eyes dart across mine, and I wonder what he sees. Does he see a woman whose world is tilting on its axis? Or does he see someone calm and collected? I hope the latter, because I can't bear to let him see how deeply this is affecting me. "Is this okay? I can put dinner in the fridge and we can go to the festival. I just... I thought this might be better given the circumstances."

"You're probably right. We don't want to give people anything new to talk about. Plus, no one's ever hired a private chef to make me dinner before." I rise onto my toes and press a kiss against the scruff of Maddox's jaw. I always feel butterflies when I kiss Maddox. I feel them now. But they're different this time. Their wings drip with dread rather than joy.

Maddox wraps his arms around my waist and pulls me tight against his chest. "You're sure you don't mind the change of plans? I probably should have talked to you rather than springing it on you like this, but I wanted you to see how great it could be if we stayed in." He kisses my forehead. "Are you disappointed?"

*Yes.*

"No. Of course I don't mind. You obviously put a lot of thought into this."

His shoulders lose some of their tension. "I did. Now why don't you go ahead and wash your hands and I'll pull everything out of the oven and set the table."

"Sure. Thanks." I have to force my feet to move across his apartment and into the bathroom. The moment I close the door behind me, I suck in a ragged breath. Rubbing my chest, I stare at myself in the mirror. All of those nights with Alex were good practice because my expression is convincingly placid.

I give myself thirty seconds to drop the mask and feel the full force of my disappointment.

With my palms pressed against the cool marble countertop around the sink, I let my head hang. Every gulp of air feels like work. It scrapes like broken glass down my throat and shreds my lungs. When I look back up at myself, I try to justify all of it.

"He's not Alex. Maddox is protective of you. He didn't tell you because he was trying to protect you. He doesn't want you to have to deal with the trolls. He's not taking you to the festival because he cares about you. Not because he's ashamed of being seen with you."

I stare at myself. The truth of it all stares back.

I'm not good enough. Alex knew it, and now Maddox knows it, too.

But maybe if I don't make a big deal about the change of plans, I can show Maddox what Alex refused to see. That I'm stronger than he ever thought. I can handle whatever Maddox's world throws at me.

It takes longer than I'd like, but I mold my muscles into a mostly-convincing smile. It almost meets my eyes. I take one more deep, fortifying breath, square my shoulders, and step out of the bathroom. I can do this. I can show Maddox that I'm not weak. That I'm not afraid of his world.

He's waiting for me outside the bathroom door. When he wraps me in a tight hug, I have to fight back a sob that tries to claw its way out of my throat.

"Baby, are you sure you're okay? I fucked this up, didn't I?" Maddox's palms cup my cheeks. His eyes are filled with the same affection they've held since we got together. It's confusing as hell because I can't figure out what's happening.

Did he really change our plans to protect me? Or was it to protect himself and his image?

"It just took me by surprise, that's all. I was looking forward to going tonight."

His face falls. "Shit. Of course you were. I'm such a fucking idiot." His thumb traces over my cheekbone. "Forget all of this. Let's go to the festival."

"No." I shake my head. "It's okay. I promise."

He's not convinced, I can tell. "Isla, I'm sorry."

"You have nothing to be sorry for. Let's eat before it's

cold. And then I'm going to carve the best damned jack-o'-lantern you've ever seen."

Maddox's lips twitch. "Is that so? We'll see about that, Short-Stack." He presses a tender kiss to my lips before dropping his hands from my cheeks and intertwining our fingers so he can tug me toward the dining room.

Maybe I was wrong. Maybe he's genuinely just trying to protect me.

I sure hope that's the case, but I can't completely silence the voice in my head telling me Maddox is ashamed of me. That I'm not good enough for him.

The voice sounds a lot like Alex.

# forty-seven

## ISLA

THE REST OF THE WEEKEND WITH MADDOX WENT BY with no issues. We ended up having a good time on our romantic date in, even though I never quite shook off the niggling sense of unease that seemed to cling to my skin. But I spent the night at his house and he woke me up with breakfast in bed and a couple of very nice orgasms. Then we spent all day Sunday together. Things felt normal. Mostly.

Now, here I am, almost halfway through my Monday. The team leaves tonight for three away games that will have them gone until Friday, and as my students race out of my classroom with the bell and I pull out my lunch, I can't ignore this growing sense of dread. Maddox said he'd try to stop by my place after school with some takeout so we could have dinner together before they go. It may be the last chance we have to pencil in some alone time for at least a week and a half.

After the series, Maddox is flying to Chicago so he can help his sister drive her moving truck to Minneapolis. Then we're going to move her in with Griffin.

I can't wait to have Mira here. I always wanted a sister, and I think Mira could grow to feel like one. If things work out between Maddox and me, that is. But I know it will take a bit to get her settled, and the day after they're set to arrive with the truck, the guys have a home game. Well, they have three home games in a row.

Maddox wasn't kidding when he told me dating during the season would be rough. We steal time together as much as possible, but it's never enough. Especially not when I'm feeling less than secure.

It'll be fine. It will all work out.

With a sigh, I push up from my desk, ready to head to the teacher's lounge, when a throat clears from my doorway. I startle at the masculine sound, and look up, hoping to find familiar coffee-colored eyes and dark, wavy hair. Except, that's not what I see at all.

Instead of warm brown eyes, I'm met with the familiar and unwelcome blue gaze of my ex. Unperturbed by my frown, Alex smiles. He holds up a coffee like an offering.

"Hey, Isles. I brought you coffee. You got a minute?"

Confusion and irritation swirl together inside of me. "What the hell are you doing here?"

Alex's practiced smile slips, but he recovers quickly. He takes a few steps inside my classroom with that casual assuredness I used to admire. Now, it only pisses me off. "Come on, sweetheart, don't be like that."

My eyes dart to the hallway behind him to make sure none of my students overhear me. "Don't fucking call me *sweetheart*, Alex. I asked you a question. What are you doing here?"

"Can't a guy miss the woman he was going to marry?" Alex's lips tilt down in a frown. "I wanted to talk, but you blocked my number."

"Gee," I say sharply, "do you think maybe that means I don't want to talk to *you*?"

Alex sighs, and shaking his head, he closes the distance between us. He leans against my desk and holds the coffee out to me. "It's a mocha. Your favorite."

All I can do is stare at the man I gave so many years to. So. Many. Years. "Mocha isn't my favorite."

Alex's frown deepens. The skin between his eyebrows puckers. "Yes it is."

"No," I say with a harsh bark of laughter. "It's really not. My favorite is a flat white with two pumps of vanilla. That's been my favorite since freshman year of college."

"Come on, Isles." Alex sets the cup of coffee down and rolls his eyes. As if I'm being unreasonable. As if he's put out.

That look used to make something inside of me shrivel. He'd level it at me, and I'd curl in on myself. I couldn't understand why I seemed to frustrate him so much.

Now, I can't understand why I didn't walk away. How did I let myself stay with this man for so long, let alone get to the point that we were engaged and two weeks away from being married? Did he really break me down so effectively that I lost the ability to see what was so obvious to my best friends?

Alex was never right for me. He was never good enough for me. And he sure as hell never loved me.

It makes me sad for the woman I used to be. And

angry. I twisted myself into a pretzel to make him happy, and he couldn't even bother to memorize my favorite coffee.

"You've got thirty seconds to get to the point, then you're going to leave. I'm at work, Alex. This isn't the time or the place. Not to mention the fact that I have a boyfriend. It's beyond inappropriate for you to show up here."

"Oh, please." Alex scoffs. "The hockey player? You're serious?"

"Deadly," I growl. "Twenty seconds."

He rolls his eyes again. "Fine. Just hear me out, okay? Please?"

The confusion and irritation I was feeling earlier turns molten in my belly. It bubbles like lava, ready to spill over. To erupt. I want Alex to leave. Seeing him at the coffee shop was bad enough. But to have him show up at my job? I'm pissed. I want to scream.

But I'm at work. I can't scream.

Cracking my neck, I level my ex with the coldest expression I can muster. "Fine. Speak."

## MADDOX

Unease has been eating away at me all morning. I messed up on Saturday. I should have taken Isla to the damned fall festival. I was so worried about how everyone else might make her feel like shit, I didn't realize that my actions would have the same effect.

I tried to make it up to her. I really did. I held her all

night, made her breakfast in bed on Sunday, and made her come several times. I've done everything I can think to reassure her that I'm all in. Because I am. And I'm terrified she's pulling away.

So I picked up an order of her favorite Thai noodles and a Thai iced tea, bought her the most expensive and exotic bouquet of flowers I could find, bribed her teacher friend LaTonya to let me in the school, and now I'm going to spend Isla's lunch hour with her.

And I'm going to tell her how I feel about her.

Maybe professing my love at Isla's school isn't the most romantic way to do it, but I can't wait. I don't want to wait. We'll be apart for almost a week after this, and the idea of getting on the plane without telling her makes my insides squirm. I need her to know that I love her. I need her to know that, no matter how many miles separate us, she's it for me. Maybe it's too soon, maybe it's crazy. I don't care.

I'm in love with Isla Harding.

There's a stupid grin on my face as I reach the last corner before her classroom. I open my mouth to tell her I'm here so I don't startle her when I show up unexpectedly, but the words get stuck in my throat when I hear her speaking in hushed tones to someone. I hang back, waiting to turn the corner because I don't want to interrupt her conversation. She could be speaking with a student, and the last thing I want is to make a scene.

"Just hear me out, okay?" a male voice says. His tone is pleading. "Please?"

There's a beat of silence before Isla replies, "Fine. Speak."

I hold my breath as the male voice begins to speak

again. A voice I've heard before. My grip tightens on the flowers.

"Look, I know I screwed up, okay? I lost sight of what was important."

Isla scoffs. "And that was?"

There's a soft shuffling, followed by a sigh. "You, obviously. I've been thinking a lot about how things ended between us, and I've realized some things. I messed up, sweetheart. I got so lost in all the dinners and schmoozing and I lost sight of us. You always supported me, babe. I can see that now. You always put me first. You took such good care of me, and I took that for granted."

Every cell in my body vibrates with fury. This asshole. He has the nerve to show up at her job and say shit like this? All he's said is that he's sorry he lost her free labor. The man's not sorry that he hurt her. He's not sorry that he let her down. He's sorry she's not there to put him first anymore.

I want to break his nose. I want to storm in there and tell him to get lost. But I don't. I hold my breath and wait for my girl to rip him a new asshole. She did before. I can't wait to hear how she knocks him down a few pegs this time.

So I wait. If she needs me, I'll step in. But if I've learned anything about Isla, it's that she's capable of fighting her own battles. And I need to give her a chance to fight this one.

There's a beat of silence. "That's your apology? That you're sorry you didn't realize sooner how much I was doing for you?" The laugh she lets out is low and bitter. "I've got news for you, Alex. What you should be sorry about is not realizing sooner that you weren't doing anything for me. Yeah, I took care of you. But did you ever take care of me?"

He lets out a sound of protest that Isla quickly cuts off. "The answer is no. You never took care of me. But I've found someone who does. He takes such good care of me, Alex. In ways you could never understand."

Pride fills me at how confidently she says those words. I've been so worried the past few days that I royally screwed up, but here she is, letting me know I haven't completely ruined things. I can't have, if she feels like I take care of her.

Her prick of an ex grunts. "All I ever did was work my ass off so I could take care of you. But none of that was ever good enough for you. You'd still nag me about every little thing. I never spent enough time with you. I never took you out to enough places."

Guilt twists in my belly at that. His words hit a little too close to home after this weekend. But I won't make that mistake a second time.

"Then as soon as we break up, you're dating some hockey player? What the hell, Isles. Did I even mean anything to you?"

"Are you serious?" she asks, her voice barely above a whisper. "I was going to marry you."

"Yeah." Alex chuckles darkly. "Didn't take you very long to move on, did it? You lost your meal ticket when I left, so you set your sights on the first rich idiot you could get, huh? You love to act all superior, don't you? You pretend you don't care about money or status, but as soon as I stopped bringing you around my powerful connections, you showed your true colors. Couldn't stop bitching, then, could you?"

Isla is silent. I want to drop everything in my hands and rush in to her classroom. I want to pull her into my arms and tell her ex that if he ever so much as looks at her again, I'll kill him. But I don't. I'm rooted in place, ears straining to hear whatever he says next.

"I gotta hand it to you. I'm impressed. You really have that meathead wrapped around your little finger. Does he know how much school debt you have? Did you get him to agree to pay for it yet?"

My stomach twists. What the hell? Holding my breath, I wait for Isla to tell him off.

She's silent.

"Don't forget, I know how much you make at this job. You've got to be one car problem away from ruin. It's smart to find a rich jock to take care of you. There's no way the two of you have anything in common. But I guess guys like that are good for at least one thing besides paying the bills, right?"

My body vibrates with rage. How dare he say any of this to her? I can't wait to listen to her eviscerate him.

"At least you're not as stupid as you look," Isla says instead. Her voice is flat. It feels like a slap across the face. "You're right. I put all of those years into you thinking I'd end up married to a rich lawyer. Then you dumped me, and I was back at square one."

*No.*

"All I had to do was act like I was falling apart, and I knew Jess and Nevaeh would start trying to set me up with someone they deemed good enough. I had no idea they'd win a date for me with a rich professional athlete. Talk about luck, right?"

My vision tunnels.

"I'll admit it. At first, I didn't think things would go anywhere with Maddox. He didn't seem all that interested. But with a little luck and some meddling from Jess and Nev, I managed to get his attention. And you're right. He's rich. Way richer than you could ever hope to be. And unlike you, he makes me come. That's all a girl needs, isn't it? Money and a big dick? I should thank you for dumping me. If you hadn't, I never would have landed such a lucrative catch."

Static roars in my ears and my stomach lurches. The words Candace hurled my way when I broke with her clang like dissonant bells in my ears.

I'm going to be sick.

Turning, I stumble down the hallway the way I came. I shove the food and flowers in the first trash can I find.

Isla's flat words play on a loop in my head.

*I should thank you for dumping me. If you hadn't, I never would have landed such a lucrative catch.*

They blend with Candace's parting shots. So similar. So callous.

Candace's words broke my pride. She humiliated me when she sold that phony-ass interview to the tabloids. But Isla's words?

Isla's words break my heart.

*I had no idea they'd win a date for me with a rich professional athlete. Talk about luck, right?*

God, I've been so stupid. So fucking blind and stupid. I should have known all of this was too good to be true. I should have known that the real reason Isla was upset about our change of plans this past weekend was because it meant she'd miss her time in the spotlight. It meant one less chance to publicly claim her rich NHL player boyfriend.

I don't register a single thing but the sharp sting of betrayal as I lurch out of the school and toward my car. I'm so lost in my head and gone to the pain that I don't even remember how I get home.

As I stumble into my apartment, my phone buzzes in my pocket. I pull it out and stare at the screen as my insides scream.

ISLA

I miss you.

I throw my phone across the room with a guttural roar. By some miracle, it doesn't break.

Me? I'm not so lucky.

# forty-eight

## ISLA

I hate him. I hate Alex. I'm full of so much rage that I flay him alive with my eyes while I manage to keep my voice flat and lifeless. I want him to understand how stupid everything he's saying is. How much I think he's an idiot.

So I intone words I don't mean while I roll my eyes and glare. I tell Alex lie after ridiculous lie while I mock him with my eyes.

"I'll admit it. At first, I didn't think things would go anywhere with Maddox. He didn't seem all that interested. But with a little luck and some meddling from Jess and Nev, I managed to get his attention. And you're right. He's rich. Way richer than you could ever hope to be. And unlike you, he makes me come. That's all a girl needs, isn't it? Money and a big dick? I should thank you for dumping me. If you hadn't, I never would have landed such a lucrative catch."

I roll my eyes again and stand with my arms crossed over my chest. It makes me nauseous to even voice such disgusting lies, but Alex needs to understand how absolutely ridiculous his assertions are. I glare at the self-centered asshole I wasted too many years on. He's silent. Fuming.

Alex shifts his weight from one foot to the other, trying to decide how to respond. He clearly didn't expect me to act like this. I'll bet he thought I'd throw myself at his feet and beg him for a second chance.

Moron.

The silence stretches on. I've had enough. "Maddox Graves is ten million times the man you'll ever be, Alex. I wouldn't care if he was broke and waited tables for a living. I don't give a shit about his *fame* or his *money*. Because I'm not a soulless, selfish, grasping little weasel like you."

Alex's jaw ticks. His face flushes a deep, angry red. "You're such a bitch."

I bark out a harsh laugh. "He'd also never call me a name like that."

My ex rolls his eyes.

"It's time for you to leave. Get the hell out of my classroom and get the hell out of my life. I never want to see your face or hear from you again, understand? I'm done with you." I point to the door. "Goodbye, Alex. And good riddance."

"You'll regret this," Alex snarls, snatching the mocha he brought me from my desk and hurling it into the trash. The lid pops off and thick, brown liquid splatters across the side of my desk.

"I regret wasting even a single moment on you," I reply.

"But kicking you out of my life for good? I'll never regret that. Fuck off and have the life you deserve."

With another inarticulate snarl, Alex stomps out of my classroom. When I'm sure he's gone, I sink into my chair. My hands shake as the adrenaline leaves my body and I sit in stunned silence for a few minutes.

I can't believe that just happened. I never thought Alex would have the nerve to show up here and pull a stunt like that.

My mind turns to Maddox. I wish he was here. What I would give to have him pull me into a tight hug right about now... With shaking fingers, I pick up my phone and tap on our text thread. I debate calling him. I want to tell him everything. But after a few moments of consideration, decide against it. Maddox has been stressed, and I know he's feeling pressured to perform by his coach, his teammates, and the fans. I don't want to throw him off before their game tomorrow. Especially not when I took care of things. It's not like there's anything he can do about it either way.

No, I'll wait until after their game tomorrow to tell him what happened. Plus, it will give me some time to calm down and sort through my feelings.

My fingers fly across the screen. I can't tell Maddox what happened with Alex just yet, but I crave that connection with him. It's a quick text, but it'll have to hold me over until he stops by tonight and I can throw myself into his arms.

The bell rings as I hit send, and students fill the hallways.

ME

**I miss you.**

I stare at the screen, willing him to respond, pushing down my disappointment when he doesn't by the time the first students filter into my room. Tucking the phone into my purse, I do my best to push past the drama of my lunch hour. To ignore the growling of my stomach and the nerves that still sing with residual adrenaline.

I just have to get through the next four hours, then I get to see Maddox. Four more hours, and he'll chase away the craziness of the day. Because Maddox Graves is my safe place. And I want nothing more than to hide away in his arms for a few hours.

---

DESPITE MY BEST EFFORTS NOT TO, MY EYES BOUNCE to the time. Again.

Maddox should be here. Should have been here an hour and a half ago. I've texted him three times already, and I'm worried. What if he got into a car accident or something on the way over?

Desperate to make sure he's okay, I call him this time. It goes straight to voicemail.

"Hey." My voice wavers. "It's six o'clock and I'm worried. I know you have to be at the airport at eight. I just want to make sure you're not hurt or something. Please call me back." I suck in a shaky breath. "I miss you."

Once I end the call, I stare at my phone, willing it to light up with his name. It doesn't. Twenty minutes of radio silence later, I text Mira. I wish I had Griffin's number, or any of Maddox's teammates' numbers, because they're more likely to know if he's okay than someone in another state, but I don't.

ME

Hey. Have you heard from your brother today?

Thankfully, her answer comes quickly.

MIRA

No, why? Everything okay?

ME

IDK. He was supposed to meet me at my place almost two hours ago and I can't get ahold of him. I'm worried. I don't have any of the guys' numbers, so I can't check with them.

Don't worry. I'm sure everything is fine. Give me a minute and I'll make a couple of calls, okay?

Okay. Thank you. I'm just so worried.

I know. Just breathe. I'm sure he's okay.

Wringing my hands, I pace my living room while I wait for her to get back to me. My eyes flicker to the door every few seconds.

But he doesn't appear.

A few minutes later, my phone buzzes on the coffee table, and I rush to read the text.

MIRA

Maddy is fine. Griffin said his phone died
and something came up? He promised to
have my brother text you.

Relief floods my body, and I collapse on the couch. He's okay. Thank god.

ME

Thanks, Mira. I feel like I can breathe
again.

MIRA

I'm sorry he worried you. I'll kick his ass
when I see him.

No, don't do that. I just wish I could hug
him right now.

He's lucky to have you.

IDK. I think I'm the lucky one.

You two are so cute. GTG, my asshole ex
is being a dick. Talk soon.

Can't wait for you to move here.

Same, girl, same.

Maddox doesn't call until I'm lying in bed that night. It's after eleven. I've been tossing and turning for an hour. Sleep simply will not come. Which may have something to do with the fact that my eyes keep popping open to check my phone. When it finally rings, I'm so anxious to answer it I nearly drop the damned thing on the floor.

"Maddox, hey. I was so worried about you today."

There's a long pause. "My phone died. Sorry."

Chewing on my bottom lip, I shift onto my side. Is his tone weird? "That's okay. I'm just glad you're all right." I pause for a moment, but when he doesn't say anything, I plow on, needing to fill the strangely awkward silence. "What happened? You were supposed to come over today before your flight."

"Something came up," he says flatly. I wait for him to explain. He doesn't. My stomach flips uncomfortably.

"Are you... Is everything okay? Did something happen?"

The soft rustle of fabric fills the line. "Don't worry about me. How was your day?"

The cold tone of Maddox's voice has my stomach tying itself into knots. I don't understand why he's speaking this way. I don't understand why he seems so reluctant to talk to me. To tell me about his day. Or why he didn't come over. It has me so out of sorts that I don't answer right away.

"Tell me about your day," he prompts again.

My mind goes to Alex showing up out of nowhere. After he left, I made sure everyone knew he was never to be allowed back in the school. I don't know who let him in, but if I ever see him at Center High again, we're going to have issues. I'm tempted to just blurt it all out and tell Maddox what happened because he always seems to put things into perspective for me. And, sure, there's a small part of me that revels knowing that it will probably make Maddox all possessive. Which is hot.

But I'm determined not to throw him off his game. And besides, something is clearly bothering him. I don't want to add my issues on top of whatever it is.

"My day was long," I tell him. It's not a lie. Every hour

felt like two. "Otherwise it was fine. Just another day, you know?"

*Another day, another douchebag.*

Maddox is silent. "Just another day?"

I hum my agreement.

"I'm sure something must have stood out, right? You've got to have some kind of story for me."

My brows knit together. I wish Maddox were here lying beside me so I could read his expression. Because something is up with him. I just can't figure out *what* based on the tone of his voice. I clear my throat. "Is something wrong?"

"You tell me." His voice rumbles through the phone.

"I... I don't know what's happening right now." My lower lip aches from chewing it and my stomach rolls. Whatever is going on, I'm completely lost in the dark. I feel like I've missed something important. "Are you okay?"

"Yeah. Listen, if you don't have anything you need to talk to me about, I gotta go. The guys are making me go out with them."

"Oh." My chest tightens and my eyes fill with tears. "Yeah. Of course."

I want to demand he tell me what's going on. I want to ask him why he's being so short and cold with me.

But I don't. Because I'm terrified I already know the answer.

It's why he didn't take me to the fall festival, despite what he said. It's why Alex left me behind so easily. Maddox just seems to have come to the same conclusion more quickly.

I'm not good enough.

Know what else I'm not? Brave. Which is why I don't

yell at Maddox and demand that he talk to me. Why I don't beg him to be honest.

Because I'm a coward.

And I'm not ready to lose him.

The words *I love you* tingle on the tip of my tongue. Like sweet poison I can't find the strength to expel.

His ragged breathing cuts through the speaker and saws through my chest.

"Maddox?"

He takes long enough to respond that I think he may not answer. "Yeah."

"I..." My damned tongue goes numb. "Have fun with the guys. Talk to you tomorrow?"

"We have a really full day tomorrow. Don't know if I'll have time to call you."

The first tear rolls down my cheek. I want to scream.

But all I can muster is a whisper.

"Okay. Have a good game tomorrow. I miss you."

I hold my breath, waiting for him to reply in kind. He doesn't. He doesn't say anything at all.

He simply hangs up.

# *forty-nine*

## MADDOX

My shoulder throbs as I skate away from the New York Bobcats' defenseman. He pushes up off the ice with a glare.

"What's up with you?" Logan asks me as we grapple with our opponent for the puck. "I've never seen you throw so many hits."

The Bobcats' left defenseman comes barreling toward me. I dodge him at the last second and throw my elbow. He slams into the glass with a satisfying *thud*. I shoot Logan a glare. "Are we playing a game or having a therapy session?"

"Looks like you could use a therapy session," Byrne mutters under his breath. Ignoring him, I focus on the only thing keeping me from screaming. The game. If my mind is on the puck, it can't be on a certain redhead who's been using me just like Candace did. Isla's just a better actress.

We're up five to two with four minutes left in the third. Half of New York's fans have already started leaving the arena. They know as well as we do there's no coming back from that in four minutes. Especially not with the way I'm playing tonight.

I'm exorcizing all these putrid emotions eating away at my insides. Turning them on the Bobcats is a hell of a lot more satisfying than letting them eat me alive.

They'll have plenty of time for that later.

For now, I force them to fuel me.

My world narrows down to my teammates, the ice, and the puck.

Logan chips the puck off the boards, getting it perfectly placed in front of me. I slap it to Wright, who dekes right, then left, then sends it flying with a sharp *crack*. Right past the goalie and into the five hole. The stunned goalie looks down between his legs, as if he can't believe he missed blocking the shot.

The New York fans can't believe it, either. A chorus of *boos* fill the arena as the time ticks down.

Thirty seconds.

Twenty.

Ten.

The buzzer sounds, and the disappointed announcer calls the win in our favor.

I don't feel a thing.

We skate off the ice. My teammates clap each other on the back, shoot the shit, and congratulate one another. Coach keeps his post-game speech brief and tells us we didn't completely disappoint him.

I don't feel a thing.

The guys drag me to some sports bar filled with hockey

fans. We get a mixture of *boos* from the men and hungry looks from the women. I still feel nothing. Going through the motions. That's all I can muster.

"I'm not going to be the responsible one tonight," I tell Navarro. "It's my turn to get shit-faced."

He frowns, his dark eyes seeing too much as he studies me. "What's going on, Graves? You haven't been yourself since we left Minneapolis."

With a roll of my eyes, I bring my second bottle of beer to my lips. "Nothing's going on, man."

Bash tilts his head. "How's Isla?"

As tightly as I grip the bottle, I'm surprised it doesn't shatter in my hand. "She's great. Getting everything she wants in life."

Our goalie's brow furrows. "What's that supposed to mean?"

Some fans cross the bar with their cell phones out. Three women with glassy eyes and way too much cleavage spilling out of their too-tight tops. They survey Navarro and me like we're bars of chocolate and they're on their periods. Hungry. Craving.

Still, I feel abso-fucking-lutely nothing.

I purposefully avoid answering Bash's question and give the three women my attention.

"Hi," the brunette says. Her voice is sultry, and her eyes are hungry as they roam the length of my body. "You guys play for the Rogues, right?"

I nod.

"Do you think we could get a picture with you?"

Sebastian shifts in his seat. He doesn't want to take photos with these women; he wants me to tell him all my secrets. Which is too damned bad because I haven't had nearly enough alcohol for that. He opens his mouth, probably to say no, when I beat him to the punch.

"Sure thing, ladies." I flag down a server. "Think you could take a photo for us?" The guy obliges, and the three women arrange themselves around Sebastian and me. The brunette, after a moment of hesitation, plunks her ass down on my knee.

It takes everything in me not to shove her off and onto the floor. Because Isla might be a fucking fake, but I'm not. I don't want this random woman touching me as though she has any right. But I can't shove her off my lap because Coach would hand me my ass. The last thing I need is for stories to start circulating about how I hurt women or some other bullshit.

The moment the server hands the woman's phone back, I ask her to get off of me. Her cheeks stain pink, but she does as I ask before scurrying away. As soon as she's gone, I down the rest of my beer and flag the server to bring me another.

"What happened, Madds?" Sebastian tries again.

"Just fucking drop it, man. Let it go." Every muscle in my body is tense and ready to get the hell out of Dodge if Bash keeps asking questions. Luckily, he doesn't. Just gives me one of those knowing looks of his.

"I'm here when you want to talk."

A grunt is my only response. Our server sets a fresh beer in front of me, and I swallow the slightly bitter liquid down without another word.

I still don't feel anything, but at least it's becoming the good kind of oblivion.

Until my phone buzzes with a text.

ISLA

That was an intense game. Are you hurt?
You took some big hits. Gave some, too.

Am I hurt?

Hell yeah, I'm hurt. But it's not from the hits I took today.

Sebastian watches me, and I know he didn't miss Isla's text. Hell, the nosy bastard probably read the damned thing over my shoulder. Not wanting to deal with his questions, I type a quick response.

ME

I'm fine.

ISLA

Facetime?

Out with the guys. TTYL.

Oh. Okay. Have fun. Miss you.

I don't respond. Shoving the phone in my pocket, anger begins to overpower the pleasant buzz I'd been working on. My mind replays her callous words, even though I don't want it to.

*I had no idea they'd win a date for me with a rich professional athlete. Talk about luck, right?*

*Luck.* What a fucking crock of shit. She probably planted the idea in their heads. I can't believe I fell for her innocent act. For her good-person act.

"Is everything okay with you two?" Navarro's voice is just loud enough for me to hear over the din of the bar, but quiet enough that no one else will hear it.

I hate the look of concern in his eyes. The pity.

"Don't worry about it," I snap.

Bash frowns, but after considering me for a few moments, he nods. "I'm here when you're ready to talk about it."

This time, when our server comes by, I order something stronger than beer. Turning to my friend and goalie, I give him a brusque nod. "Don't think that's gonna happen, but I appreciate it all the same."

Navarro's lips twist to the side, thinning out into a firm line. "Take it from me, Madds. Sometimes you think it's better to hold things in, but is it? Or will your secrets eat you from the inside out and leave you even more broken than before?"

Fuck. I'm not drunk enough for this.

---

"I'M OUT OF HERE," I SAY TO MY TEAMMATES. WELL, slur is probably more accurate. I'm not sure if what I'm doing can be considered actual speech.

"I'll walk with you," Navarro says, rising from the table as I do. He has to steady me with a hand on my elbow when I wobble.

"Nah. Stay. Have fun."

Sebastian shakes his head. "Coach will kill me if I let you wander, drunk, around a strange city." He nods at the other guys. "See you guys tomorrow morning. Don't get shit-faced and do something stupid."

That's usually my line.

Griffin and Logan roll their eyes. Griffin's chatting animatedly with one of our rookies, Ryder Hanson, while

Logan has two women perched on his lap. I snort. Maybe he's got the right idea. Relationships are pointless and bring nothing but pain. Hot, meaningless sex with a different woman every night could be the answer.

Or it could make your dick fall off.

I laugh quietly.

"All right, Chuckles. Let's get you to bed." Navarro pushes on my shoulders to guide me out of the bar. My laughter cuts off and I scowl at the goalie.

"Don't fucking start calling me that."

He rolls his eyes. "Whatever, Graves. You're a grumpy drunk tonight."

I have a right to be grumpy. Fooled again.

What's that saying? Fool me one, shame on you. Fool me twice and it's clear I'm a stupid fucking idiot?

Surprise, surprise. Maddox Graves has been played again. At least with Candace, I hadn't actually been in love with the woman. Thought I might have been for a while. But in the end, I realized I didn't feel much of anything for her outside of obligation.

Isla?

My chest aches, and I rub absently at it.

I actually love her.

*Loved* her.

Can't keep thinking stuff like that in the present tense. Because with every stumbling step I take toward our hotel, I'm more and more convinced of what I need to do.

I need to break up with Isla Harding, block her number, and pretend she never existed.

"You going to be all right if I leave you?" Bash asks as he deposits me on my bed. "Not gonna throw up and drown in your sleep, are you?"

I grunt. "No."

He pauses by the door, frowning. "You sure you don't want to talk about it?"

"No."

"Okay, Graves. Text me if you need anything, all right?"

He's a good friend. I tell him so, then demand he get the hell out. Once he's gone, I strip out of my clothes and flop down on the king-sized bed. An unwelcome jolt of longing spears my chest when my mind wanders to Isla. To the fake, lying, manipulative woman I thought could be my forever.

I'm a joke. And I'm going to end up alone. It's clear as day.

Might as well make it official.

Fumbling with my phone, I smash my fingers against the screen, pulling up my text thread with Isla. I stare at her last message.

*Miss you.*

Not yet, she doesn't. But she will.

It's probably littered with drunken typos, but I tap out a message with furious, shaking fingers.

ME

It's over between us. You really had me fooled. But you're not the woman I thought you were. I'm looking for more in a partner. More than you and what you can offer. I deserve fucking better. I deserve better than you.

There. I hit send and ignore the violent roiling in my gut. But I do deserve better. I deserve to be loved, dammit. Do I have a sign on my forehead that says *Use Me* or something? Why does this keep happening to me?

Maybe some people just aren't built for love.

Maybe I'm one of them.

Not even thirty seconds later, my phone rings. Isla's name flashes across the screen. I hit deny. It rings again.

The thing is? I don't want to talk to her. *Can't* talk to her. Because as much as I want my love for her to exist firmly in the past, it doesn't. It's still very much a living, breathing, yowling beast inside my chest. Who knows what I'd say if I spoke to her now?

She tries to call three more times, but I deny each attempt. Then the texts come.

> ISLA
>
> What?
>
> Maddox? Did something happen? Please answer the phone.
>
> What do you mean, you're looking for more in a partner?
>
> Please. Please call me back.
>
> I can be better for you. I swear.

That last one makes bile claw up my throat. I don't respond. A minute or two later, she tries calling again. But this time, she calls just once.

Good. She's finally getting the hint. I don't want to talk to her. I don't want anything to do with her.

My phone buzzes, and a notification for a new voice-mail pops up on the screen. I debate deleting it outright, but I'm a glutton for punishment when I'm drunk.

Pressing play, I steel myself to hear her voice.

I expect anger or rage. I expect her to yell at me. To call

me names like Candace did. What I don't expect is to hear panic. Or pain.

Isla's voice shakes and wavers. Sniffles accentuate every few words. Once or twice, she has to fight back a sob.

"Maddox? I... Did something happen? Did I do something? Please call me back. Please. I don't understand what's going on. Whatever it is, we can talk about it. Right? I don't..." Her voice cuts off in a sob. "Maddox, I..." She stifles another cry. "Whatever I did, I'm sorry. I'm sorry. I can be better. Please, just call me back."

The soft sounds of her crying play in my ear. I harden myself to them.

"Please call me back. I lo— I care about you so much. Please don't shut me out. Not like this." Another sniffle. "Call as late as you want. I won't be sleeping. Goodnight, Ogre." The voicemail ends.

She's a good actress. I'll give her that. If I hadn't heard the vile garbage she spewed to her ex, I might even believe her.

I stare at the screen for what feels like an eternity before I do what needs to be done.

I block Isla Harding's number.

*fifty*

## ISLA

I CALL IN SICK FOR THE REST OF THE WEEK. EVERY morning I wake up and tell myself that I need to get out of bed. That my students need me. But I simply don't have the strength.

The night Maddox broke up with me—over text—I spent hours combing through social media posts trying to figure out what had happened. Because *something* had to have happened. He couldn't have just broken up with me out of the blue, right?

That's when I found the photos some female fans posted from a bar. In one of them, a pretty brunette sat perched on Maddox's lap. Her face was bright and happy. Mocking me. Maddox stared at the camera as if daring me to look away.

He's already moved on with someone prettier. Someone new. Of course, he has. I'm just the placeholder.

The woman who's *good enough for now* but not worthy of forever.

I wanted forever with Maddox. I want it still. My stupid, broken heart hasn't been able to accept what my head so easily recognized.

He's done with me. So done, all my calls go straight to voicemail and my texts sit unread.

Rubbing my swollen eyes, I curse the tears that don't seem to stop. They trickle endlessly from my tear ducts. My pillows are perpetually damp. And covered with donut crumbs.

I'm right back to where I was before the auction date. Only it's worse this time. So much worse. Alex crushed my dreams, but Maddox obliterated my heart.

A knock at my door has me groaning. My voice is raw and scratchy from crying and disuse when I shout, "Go away!"

There's a faint jingling of keys, followed by the click of the lock, and then my best friends' voices fill my apartment.

"I swear to god, Isla, you better have changed your underwear today."

Nope. Sure haven't. What's the point?

"Go away," I mumble into my pillow. "I don't want to see anyone."

I hiss like a thousand-year-old vampire when Jess throws the curtains back and light floods my room. "Tough titties, Isla. I swear to Chris Hemsworth, we will not let you wallow this time. Not like we did with Alex."

"Wanna wallow," I grumble. Ice-cold water splashes on my head and body and I scream like a creature of the night. "What the hell?"

"Get your pretty ass up," Nev commands. "We know you're sad and hurting, but babe, you cannot lose a job you love over a man."

I know she's right. Trish has been super understanding about everything. Especially since people are still posting derogatory crap about me online. But her grace can only extend so far. And I can't afford to lose this job.

I've already lost too much.

In a moment that feels entirely too familiar, my besties shove me toward the bathroom and a nice hot shower. It takes all of my energy to strip out of my clothes and get under the spray. At least this time they don't stand in the bathroom with me. But I do leave the door cracked at their request so we can talk.

Ever since the night of Maddox's game, they've been trying to get me to tell them what happened. I haven't been able to bring myself to speak the words. But that was Monday and this is Friday. Apparently, four solid days of wallowing is their limit, this time. If it were up to me, I wouldn't be getting out of bed.

The Rogues get home today. A glance at my phone tells me it's one in the afternoon. Their flight lands at three. Before my relationship imploded for reasons unknown, Maddox had planned to come straight here. I would have seen him in four hours.

Now, I'm not sure if I'll ever see him again.

Another round of tears drip down my face. They mix with the hot spray of the shower as I rub my aching chest.

Everything hurts.

My head, my chest, my heart.

"Are you going to tell us what happened?" Nev asks. Her tone is gentle, but I know I can't put them off forever.

"I don't even know," I admit. My voice breaks. "He was acting all weird on Friday, didn't come over like we'd planned, but wouldn't tell me why, and I didn't even hear from him until I texted his sister in a panic." My stomach lurches. Mira. I wonder if she knows. She's moving here thinking we'll be friends, and now what? Do I reach out to her? Do I simply go into hiding?

Mira and the guys on the Rogues were starting to feel like good friends. Like they could have become even more, with time. So not only have I lost Maddox, but all of them as well.

Fuck, I hate this. Breakups always suck, but this one feels particularly brutal since I don't know what happened. Well, outside of Maddox seeming to move on to another woman.

"He didn't tell you why he was ending things?" Jess asks.

I choke back a sob. "Only that I fooled him into thinking I was good enough and that he deserved better."

My best friends hiss like pissed off snakes.

"That rat bastard," Jess growls. "I'm going to show up at his apartment and break his dick with his own hockey stick."

"Please don't." My forehead falls against the shower wall. The damned thing feels too heavy to hold up. Everything feels too heavy. "I just want to pretend like none of this ever happened."

"That might be a little hard to do," Nevaeh mutters.

"What do you mean? Why?"

She sighs. "I don't know how to say this."

"With words," I snipe. "Spit it out."

"You and Maddox have been the topic of online conversation this week."

Oh, no. How can we be the topic of conversation when I haven't been at any games? When I haven't seen him or spoken to him in almost a week? "What do you mean?"

Nev clears her throat. "Seems Maddox has been starting fights on the ice. Which isn't a thing he normally does. At least, not to the degree he has been this week. He almost got thrown out of their last game."

I shouldn't care after the things he said, but my stupid, traitorous heart lurches. "But why would they talk about me because of that?"

"He's been tagged in a few pictures by female fans. Nothing inappropriate," she hurries to add. "But every time another puck bunny posts a photo with him, people bring you up. They're wondering where you are. Speculating about why you haven't been seen with him. And why Maddox is taking photos with women sitting on his lap."

Oh, god. Will the horrors never cease?

"Okaaaay..."

"Apparently he also got wasted after their last game. When a fan asked about you at a bar afterward, Maddox's teammates had to hold him back from punching the guy."

Not good.

Nevaeh pauses. "There's a lot of speculation about what happened. People are coming up with some wild conspiracy theories."

Great. Do I even want to know? "Like what?"

"Like you ran away and eloped with a player on a rival team, you're secretly pregnant, or maybe you've decided you like girls after Maddox left you unfulfilled. Sexually, I mean."

I almost laugh. "Yeah, Nev. I got that."

"But the worst ones are the theories that you got what you wanted from him, and left. Money, your fifteen minutes of fame. An in to meet someone richer." She pauses before huffing out a breath. "Those are the theories that look like they're sticking."

"So everyone thinks I'm some gold-digging mercenary whore."

There's a long pause. "Pretty much."

"Oh." Suddenly, it's not just my head that feels heavy. It's everything. My back slides down the shower wall until I sit on the cold tile beneath the spray. Every drop that hits my back feels like dull pinpricks.

It shouldn't hurt so much that people keep accusing me of being some shallow gold-digger. I'm not one. I know that. The people who care about me know that. What does it matter if Alex and some randos on the internet believe otherwise?

My thoughts go to Maddox. Does he think I'm a gold-digger? He couldn't, right? I've never said or done anything to lead him to believe otherwise.

"Isla? Are you all right?"

*No. I'm not*

"I know you two were hoping to get me to leave the house today, but I think..." My throat feels raw and there's a lump in the shape of my heart stuck inside it. I clear my throat. "I don't think I'm up for it. Can we just stay here and watch some movies or something?"

There's a long pause while my best friends hold a whispered conversation I don't listen in on. That would require energy I don't have. And the will to do anything other than simply exist.

Even *that* feels like a lot, right now.

"Sure, babes," Nevaeh says. She sounds defeated.

Join the club.

"As long as you promise you'll go to work on Monday."

I have bills to pay. Of course, I'll go in on Monday. What other choice do I have? "Deal."

After crawling out of the shower, I put on some comfy clothes and drag my ass to the couch while my best friends make me tea and lunch. They're worried I haven't been eating. I have. I've eaten half a dozen donuts in the last two days alone.

I give in for the first time in days and tap the Instagram icon on my phone and navigate to the Rogues' profile. Sure enough, comment after comment fill the screen. Some express simple curiosity, some voice ridiculous theories, and some call me all kinds of terrible names and say they're glad it looks like I'm no longer in the picture.

When the acid in my stomach threatens to force its way up my throat, I decide to delete my profile. And then I delete the app.

I don't want to know what people are saying about me.

It was bad enough hearing how Maddox sees me.

Maybe it's just time to admit that I'm just not built for relationships. Love isn't in the cards for me.

Someday, I'll find a way to accept that.

# *fifty-one*

## MADDOX

WE'RE ALL SUITING UP FOR PRACTICE ON SATURDAY morning when Coach storms into the locker room. His face is red with fury, his eyes spit fire, and he's got a stack of papers clutched tightly in his fist. "You got shit for brains, Graves?"

Every eye turns to me, bounces to Coach, then zeroes back in on me. I pause what I'm doing, dropping the laces of my skates to meet Coach's glare. "Excuse me?"

"I told you at the start of the season that everything anyone writes about you reflects on the team. Everything." He throws the papers at me and I instinctively grab for them. They're printed news articles pulled from online blogs, magazines, and news outlets. And all of them feature me in less than flattering ways.

There are articles featuring photos of me with female fans, including the one where the woman had perched herself on my lap. One article talks about how I've become a grade-A agitator in the past few games. How I've started more fights this season than the last two combined, and we're still in the early stages.

And then there's the article that details the fight I almost got in with a fan. What it doesn't say is that the guy asked about Isla and whether she was open for new business now that I seem to have grown tired of her.

I may hate what she's done to me, but that was a bridge too fucking far.

"No one is talking about your playing or the games we've won," Coach continues. Steam will start pouring out of his ears at any moment. "And our legal team just heard that you're being dropped from consideration for that sponsorship deal you've been working on for months."

*Fuck.*

"According to their legal team, you're too volatile. They're concerned about your recent behavior damaging their family-friendly brand."

Well, shit. *Shit!*

"What do you have to say for yourself, Graves?" Coach crosses his muscular arms over his barrel chest.

"Coach, I didn't do anything with any of those women, and as far as the fights go, the fans love it."

"It doesn't matter if you did anything with those women," he shouts. "Don't you get that by now? I don't care if you're fucking half of Minneapolis as long as you keep it out of the tabloids." He pinches the bridge of his nose. "And what about the fight you almost started at that bar, huh? I suppose you have some excuse for that, too."

"That prick said some disgusting things about my girlfr —my ex. I won't stand for that."

Coach throws his hands in the air. "So the twit's not

even your girl anymore and you're trying to start fights over her? Jesus fucking Christ, Graves. How many times do I have to tell you idiots that no pussy is worth hurting your career over!"

"You gotta stop referring to women as *pussy*, Coach," Wright grinds out. "They're fucking people."

"I don't care!" Coach roars. "I care about this team and the game. And that's all any of you should care about, too." His head swivels as he levels all of us with the kind of stare that shrivels your balls before settling it on me. "Pull your head out of your ass and get your act together or you're benched."

"What? That's bullshit, Coach." I stand, the damned news articles crumpling into balls in my fists.

"That's business, son." He turns and storms through the locker room. "You morons have five minutes to get out on the ice or you'll be skating suicides until you puke!"

My teammates pat my shoulder and offer words of support as they file out of the locker room and onto the ice. Except for Navarro, Wright, and Byrne. They hang back.

"What?" I grunt. "Whatever you want to say, say it."

"We're going to your place after practice," Navarro informs me. "We're talking about whatever this is before you leave tonight to get your sister." He waves his hand in my direction when he says *this*. Like I'm some kind of problem to be solved.

My eyebrows rise. "Oh, we are, are we?"

"Yeah, man," Griffin says seriously. "We are."

I stare the three of them down. But if they even have Logan on board with this little intervention, there's no way I'm getting out of it.

"Fine," I grumble. "But my flight is at six, so you have until four to speak your piece."

"That will work," Bash says, clapping me on the back. "Now let's get out there before Coach rips us all new assholes."

I feel like I'm walking toward a firing squad, but I follow them onto the ice.

---

"Spill it," Navarro demands after I hand out the last beer and flop back onto the couch.

"Why do you assume there's anything to spill?"

"You called Isla your ex in the locker room," Griffin says. He frowns deeply. "What the hell happened?"

God, this is humiliating. I don't want to tell them what I overheard. I feel like a big enough loser without them knowing. Pinching the bridge of my nose, I try to get them to back off. "Life happened. It didn't work out. Can we let it go?"

"Listen. You know I'm not a big *relationship* guy." Logan shivers as though someone just walked over his grave. "But even I can admit you've been a surly asshole since we hit the road. Clearly, there's more to it than *it just didn't work out*. You two seemed like you were doing so well. What happened?"

Reluctant to speak, I stare at the three of them for a few minutes. They just stare back. They won't let it go. I sigh, leaning forward so my elbows rest on my knees, and stare at the floor. "My picker's broken."

"What?"

"I keep picking the same kind of woman. My picker is broken."

"What the hell are you talking about?" Logan asks. "Isla isn't like the other women you've dated."

"She is though." My ire rises, and so does my voice. "She's the same as Candace and Georgia and all the other gold-digging women who only want us for what we can give them."

Silence meets my outburst. My three best friends look at me like I've lost my ever-loving mind. And maybe I have. It's Griffin who finally breaks the silence.

"That's the dumbest thing I've ever heard."

I glare at him. What the hell does he know, anyway?

"Isla is nothing like Candace. Nothing. She's smart and cool and she's completely in love with you, you giant idiot."

Scoffing, my lip curls in a sneer. "Is that why I overheard her talking to her former fiancé on Friday about how she lucked out finding a rich guy to take care of her? Is that why she called me a *lucrative catch*?"

Wright's mouth drops open. Navarro and Byrne look just as shocked. Navarro's eyes narrow. "What do you mean, you overheard her?"

"I was surprising her with lunch," I tell him. "I was just around the corner by her classroom when I heard her ex saying all this shit to her. I wanted to storm in there and kick his ass, but I wanted to give Isla the time to defend herself. Instead, she basically confirmed everything the dude accused her of."

"And what did she say when you asked her about it?" Bash asks.

Rubbing the back of my neck, I shrug. "I tried to get

her to admit that she saw him over text that night, but she didn't. That tells me everything I need to know."

Navarro's brow pinches. "So you didn't even talk to her?"

"And say what?" I nearly shout. *Hey, babe. Overheard you talking to your ex today about how you're just using me for my money and my dick. Care to explain?*" I shake my head. "No way."

"Yes, Graves. That's exactly what you should have said." He levels me with a look I can only imagine a disappointed father would wear. Not that I have one to know. Still, it makes the little boy in me shrivel up a bit. "You're in love with the woman, and you didn't even give her a chance to explain the situation? Did you even see her face when she was talking to him?"

"No," I growl. "Didn't need to. Her words were clear enough."

"You're a fucking moron," Griffin says. "A real idiot."

"I know," I shout, rising to my feet. "I am a fucking moron. Because here I thought I'd found someone who actually cared about me. But no. She's just like the rest of them."

"You were triggered," Sebastian says. The look of disappointment he'd been wearing morphs into one of pity. It's even worse. "It's understandable. But you owe it to yourself, and Isla, to have a real conversation about this."

"Why? So I can hear even more of her bullshit? If I wanted to hear more, I would have stuck around for the end of their conversation."

"Wait." Logan leans forward and squints at me. "You didn't even hear the end of the conversation?"

"Why would I want to? I heard enough."

"Did you, though?" Sebastian asks.

"Yeah," I snarl. "I did. Just like I've heard enough from the three of you. You should be on my side."

Logan reaches over and pats my shoulder. "We are, man. Which is why we're telling you to talk to her. Because you were never as happy as when you were with Isla. If there's any chance that things aren't as straightforward as you think they are, maybe this can be fixed. But you won't know until you talk to her. Either way, you both deserve closure."

Closure. Right.

"I'm done. I love you guys, but I need you to get the hell out so I can pack an overnight bag and get to the airport."

"Fine," Griffin says. "But for what it's worth, Isla has never struck me as a woman who cares about money and all that."

I scoff. "She's a good actress."

"Maybe." Griffin shrugs. "Or maybe all of this is a big misunderstanding and you're breaking both of your hearts for no reason."

How has this turned into a *Maddox is an idiot* conversation? I'm the one who was wronged. Isla was playing me, not the other way around.

I thought I'd feel better once I told them what happened. Like it would be a weight off my chest.

So why do I feel like it's even harder to breathe?

fifty-two

## MADDOX

Thank God Mira and I had to drive separately from Chicago to Minneapolis. She knew something was up. Isla texted her the evening I overheard her conversation with her ex, and Mira hates not being in the know. She's like a dog with a bone when there's a mystery to be solved.

I'm tired of talking about Isla. Hell, I'm tired of thinking about Isla. Because it's all I can seem to do. I hate it. And I hate that I miss her so much.

If life were fair, it would be physically and emotionally impossible to miss someone who hurt you. But that's the rub, isn't it? Because even if someone does something that hurts you, it's not like the love you carried for them just ceases to exist. No, they get to hurt you again and again while you try to wrangle your rogue heart and force it to get with the program.

My heart doesn't seem to care that Isla is no better than Candace. It still aches for her.

Smells trigger me. The sound of a stranger laughing when I filled the truck with gas triggered me. Everything reminds me of Isla. Makes me miss Isla.

And I fucking hate it.

The seven-hour drive feels like it takes a week. Without a passenger, there's no one to distract me from my thoughts.

I can't believe I'd been about to tell Isla I loved her. How's that for a cruel twist of fate? I can't believe I actually thought she loved me back.

Mira beats me to Griffin's place. I suppose it's *their* place for now, even though it still weirds me out. I'll need to have another chat with my best friend and remind him what's at stake if he hurts my sister. Not that he would. Wright's a good man. Better than me in a lot of ways.

Maybe he's not the only one on the team whose love life is cursed.

The two of them are standing close together and whispering when I step inside Wright's place. Mira looks my way with a frown.

"What's wrong?" I swear to god, if Griffin has already done something stupid, I will kick his ass into next Tuesday.

Mira crosses her arms over her chest. "I know you've been hurt before, Maddy, so I won't kick your ass, but you're a real moron." She purses her lips before giving her attention to Griffin. "I'm going to grab some things out of my car while we wait for the rest of the guys to get here. Help him pull his head out of his ass, will you?"

Wright nods. His face is more serious than I've ever seen it. "You know I will."

My sister pats my friend on the chest before passing me with a shaking head. It pisses me off. Why the hell does everyone keep acting like I'm the screwup here?

Okay, yeah. So I've been getting some bad press. And yes, losing that sponsorship deal was a blow. Both financially and to my ego. Especially since the reasons they dropped me are usually so out of character for me. But I'm not the one who screwed up. Isla is. She's the one who bragged about using me to her shitty ex. She's the one who ruined our relationship.

Not me.

"The fuck is your problem?" I grumble as Wright stares at me.

His jaw ticks. "Come sit down. We have some things to discuss."

*Great.* Here comes another lecture about how I need to stop instigating fights and taking pictures with female fans until all of this blows over. And from Wright, of all people. I swear to god, the world has gone topsy-turvy.

I follow Griffin into his living room. He sits on an armchair and I fold myself into the couch. Neither of us speaks at first. He just stares at me until I can't take it anymore.

"I know what you're going to say," I growl. "And you can save it. I'll clean up my image again somehow. And yeah, it sucks about the sponsorship, but there'll be others."

My best friend's lips purse, and he shakes his head. "That wasn't what I was going to say at all. Not even close."

Shifting in my seat, I cock a brow at him. "What then? Spit it out, Wright."

"Have you spoken to Isla?" He leans forward, his elbows on his knees. There's something in his expression I don't like.

"No. And I wish you assholes would drop it. There's no point. She's a backstabbing gold digger just like the rest of them." I hate the words even as they spill from my mouth like poison. I hate them for being true, and I hate myself for the hollow pang they elicit in my chest.

Griffin's face contorts into a deep frown. "I can't believe I spent the last couple of months being jealous of you. Fucking idolizing you, man."

"What?" What is he talking about?

"I spent so many years hoping someone would come along and see past my bullshit happy-go-lucky persona and the jokes and the sleeping around. Do you know how long I looked for my person? And every time I thought I found her, my stupid curse twisted everything up." Wright rises from his seat and paces in front of me. He punctuates his words with jerky hand gestures or rakes his fingers through his hair.

"I know you think you're cursed, but what does that have to do with me?"

"Because you had that," he shouts, turning to face me. His hazel eyes are full of emotion. Judgment and pity and anger. It makes no sense. "You fucking had it, Graves, and you blew it."

"How the hell did I blow it?" I push to my feet. My body vibrates with anger at his words. "She betrayed me, Wright. She was using me. None of it was real. I feel like a complete fool."

"You should," he says derisively. "You really should feel like a fool because you had a woman who was head over heels in love with you. She loved you enough to push past her discomfort with the media attention and the bitchy fans, even though they made her feel like she wasn't good enough for you. She loved you enough to put her heart on the line, even though she was scared to be vulnerable with anyone after how her ex dumped her. She loved you enough to stand up for herself and you when that shitty ex caught her off guard and cornered her at work."

*What?*

"She loves you and you didn't even give her a chance to explain what happened. She's spent every day since you dumped her completely clueless about why you did it." His glare causes me to take a step back. "She thinks you dumped her because she's not good enough for you. Told me she knows she's not the prettiest or the smartest or best for your image." He barks out an incredulous laugh.

I'm lost and confused.

"Can you believe that shit? That woman has been sitting at home, crying herself to sleep, and she thinks you dropped her because she wasn't fake and perky enough for you." Griffin shakes his head. "I'd fucking *kill* to be loved the way that woman loves you."

My gut twists. A deep sense of dread churns inside of me.

"And the worst part?" I've never seen my best friend look so disgusted. "All of this could have been avoided if you'd simply brought up what you overheard like an adult and let her explain what happened. But you didn't. You jumped to the wrong fucking conclusion, and you broke her, man." He runs both hands through his hair. "You had the kind of love I've always dreamed about and you walked away from it."

"What the hell are you talking about?" My voice sounds strained and reedy, even to my ears. "Explain, Griff. You're not making any sense."

Griffin sighs. He flops back onto the chair and deflates. "She's not a gold digger. Never was. When I told her what you heard her say, you should have seen her face, Madds. She turned white as a fucking ghost."

I don't like where this is going.

"Seems you missed the first part of that conversation. And the end of it. Her prick of an ex tried to get her back. When he wouldn't leave her alone, she got sarcastic with him."

My stomach churns.

"And then she told him in no uncertain terms that you were ten thousand times the man that human skid-mark could ever hope to be, that she wouldn't care if you were broke as a joke because she loved you, and to get out and never contact her again."

*No. That's not possible.*

"I think I would know if she was being sarcastic," I say. Because he can't be right. So I dig my heels in and ignore the way my stomach rolls. All he has is Isla's word, and right now, that's not good enough. Not after what I heard. She could have made all of this up to get Wright's sympathy and play me for a fool.

Just like Candace.

"You don't believe her." Griffin shakes his head. "I knew you wouldn't. You're dead set on believing no one could love you for who you are and not what you could give them."

"What? That's not true," I splutter.

"It is, man. And I get it, but damn. You're wrong about this one."

"Right," I say derisively. "Because I should just take her word for it."

"Honestly?" Griffin purses his lips and pulls his phone from his pocket. "I think you should. She's never given you a reason not to. But I know you, and I knew her word wouldn't be enough. Which is why I paid her ex a little visit at work."

*Shit.* "And?"

My friend laughs. "The guy almost pissed himself when I strolled into his office. The receptionist was a fan, so he let me right in. He told me where Alex's office was and I just barged right in." His nose crinkles. "The guy was trying to get into this blonde's skirt, man, and it was awkward as hell. Looked like he was having a seizure while he dry-humped the chick."

That has Wright laughing, but I don't join in. I'm too busy holding myself still. I want to shake Griffin and demand he cut the shit and get to the point.

"Anywhooo," he drawls. "After Blondie tried to give me her number as she fled the room, Isla's ex did that whole bullshit routine where he puffed up his chest and threatened that he'd get security. The guy's a serious tool. I don't know what Isla saw in him. She called him a micro-dick when we were talking, and after meeting him, I don't think she was kidding. The dude has total micro-dick energy."

"Griff. Spit it out, man."

"Right." He shakes his head as if clearing it. "After I told Alex that the security guards were huge Rogues fans and that I could shove my hockey stick up his ass without so much as a *you probably shouldn't do that*, I told him he could either tell me the truth about what happened that day, or I'd beat the shit out of him."

"You're lucky you didn't get arrested."

"I'm not a total idiot. I didn't take a video of that part. Just his confession."

I stare at my best friend as he unlocks his phone and pulls up a video. "His confession?"

"Yeah, man. He admits to all of it. Just watch."

So I do. I stare at Griffin's phone and watch Isla's sniveling ex squirm under my teammate's glare and detail how he showed up at Isla's school and tried to get her back. He even admitted that he didn't actually want my girl. He just didn't want anyone else to have her. Couldn't stand the idea that she was happy without him.

Fucker.

Griffin was right. I only caught a small part of their conversation and I totally lost my mind.

And my woman.

I'm such a piece of shit.

Wright watches the emotions play out across my face. Horror followed by anger followed by disbelief before grief wins out. He scoffs. "Yeah. You get it now, don't you?"

I do. Fuck me, I do. "But the things she said…"

"Dude, have you not snapped something sarcastic at someone when they won't leave you alone? You admitted you didn't even see her face when she said it. She was probably making his balls shrivel with her pissed-off glare. But you didn't stop to find out. You just assumed the worst of her and left."

"But I asked her if she had anything to tell me that

night. She didn't bring Alex up. Why would she keep that from me if she didn't do anything wrong?" I'm grasping at straws here, and I know it. But how can I not? The alternative is accepting that I hurt the woman I love and blew up our relationship for nothing.

Because I was too much of a coward to risk hearing that she was using me. Too much of a coward to risk getting my heart broken in a way I couldn't ignore or deny.

Griffin rubs a hand over his mouth as he considers me. Like he's deciding if I can handle more truths capable of digging my grave even deeper. "She didn't want to throw you off your game. She was planning to tell you all about it afterward. But she blamed herself for the bad press you were getting, and all the assholes saying she was the reason you've been distracted got in her head. She thought she was protecting you."

Shit. *Shit.*

"Are you sure that's what happened?"

Wright nods. "Yeah, man. I'm sure."

I'm an idiot. A stupid, cowardly, raging idiot.

Meeting Griffin's eyes, I let him see every ounce of the panic in mine. "She loves me?"

"Yeah, brother. She fucking loves you."

"She's not using me?"

Griffin reaches over and punches me hard in the arm. "No, you stupid asshole. She was never using you. You know she's not like that. We all saw it the first time we met her at Skin and Tonic. She's the real deal, Madds. Once-in-a-lifetime stuff."

She is. I know he's right. She is a once-in-a-lifetime kind of woman. *The* woman. I could comb the globe for someone better and I'd never succeed. Because she's it for me, and I blew it.

"What have I done?" I choke on the words. It feels like there's a boulder lodged in my throat.

"You fucked up," Griffin says. "Badly. The question is, what are you going to do about it now?"

"What can I do?" Hopelessness wraps around me like a shroud. "She'll never forgive me, man. I ghosted her. Threw her aside like she was trash. I'm worse than her ex."

"You might be the dumbest fucker on the planet, but you're not worse than her ex. He never fought for her or tried to make it right. Even when he cornered her in her classroom, he never owned up to hurting her." Wright's hazel eyes bore into me. "But you're going to. You're going to own up to it. And then you're going to beg her to forgive you."

I bark out a laugh. "You make it sound so easy. I doubt she'll even answer if I call."

"Maybe, maybe not." He leans forward. "But we're past the phone call stage. You screwed up too big, Graves."

"Then what am I supposed to do?"

"Grovel big. Show her she means more than your pride or saving face. When you screw up big, you apologize big."

Image after image of Isla spurning my attempts to apologize plays in my mind. Isla slamming the door in my face. Isla dumping coffee over my head. Isla running me over with her car. They get progressively more and more violent and ridiculous with each passing second.

"How in the hell am I supposed to do that?"

For the first time since I walked into his place, Griffin smiles at me. "I've got some ideas. You're lucky I read so many romance novels."

I don't even have time to process that little nugget of information before my sister pushes through the door with a box in her arms.

"We'll brainstorm while we move Mira in."

My sister looks between us. "What are we brainstorming?"

"How Maddox is going to get Isla back."

She grins. "It'll need to involve some form of public humiliation."

"Obviously," Griffin replies with an evil grin.

"Great," I mumble.

But the truth is, I'll do anything to get Isla back. I fucked up. I hurt her. At the first test of my love, I assumed the worst of her, and I hurt her. Badly.

Public humiliation is the least of what I deserve.

"What exactly do you have in mind?"

# *fifty-three*

ISLA

I'm not sure what I expected to happen after Griffin showed up at my house, unannounced, on Sunday, but it wasn't this radio silence. Some stupid, hopeful part of me imagined Maddox calling me or showing up at my door immediately after.

But that's not what's happened.

"Isla?" Trish pops her head in my empty classroom. When she notices that I'm just sitting at my desk, staring off into space, she frowns. She might be my boss, but ever since things imploded with Maddox, she's felt more like how I imagine an older sister would. She was understanding when I told her I needed a few days off. And since I've been back, she checks on me a few times a day.

"Hey," I reply. My voice comes out flat. I hate it. No matter how often I tell myself things will look up eventually, I can't make myself believe it. "What's up?"

Trish wrings her hands as she steps into my classroom. "I need to talk to you about something."

My stomach flips. Am I being fired? Did I speak too soon about her level of understanding? "Okaaay…"

"As you know, the Rogues donated quite a lot of money to our after-school programs." She winces when I flinch. "And since then, we've developed a relationship with the team. They have gotten a lot of positive publicity from our partnership, and would like to do more."

I force myself to smile. "That's great, Trish."

And it is. Really great. But any mention of the Rogues makes my eyes well up with tears. I miss Maddox. And I miss his teammates and Mira. But mostly, I miss Maddox.

"They have a home game on Saturday night, and they'd like to announce our next joint initiative live after the game. Since all of this came about due to your generous idea, the team's owners have requested that you be present."

*Oh, god.*

"Trish, I don't think that's a good idea." Bile climbs up my throat and my hands tremble. Cold sweat beads along my spine. "I feel like I'm going to have a panic attack just thinking about it."

My boss gives me an understanding look and squeezes my shoulder. "I know, and I'm sorry for asking, but we can't risk this falling through. They've offered to replace all of our outdated computers and technology. Not only that, but they'll be providing laptops and hot spots for every single student. They want everyone to have a way to complete assignments and prepare for college."

Despite my nausea, Trish's excitement is contagious.

This is more than I ever could have hoped for when Maddox bribed me to finish our auction date. Things may not have turned out how I wanted with him, but at least some good came out of our relationship.

If I have to be in the same building with him one more time to ensure my students have a shot at a leg up, I can suck it up. It'll just be for a few hours. I'm sure Maddox will be just as motivated to avoid me as I'll be to avoid him.

And when I get home, I'll cry my eyes out, then drown myself in wine and cookie dough ice cream.

"No one else can do it?" I know the answer before I ask, but I have to try.

Trish shakes her head. "I'm sorry, Isla. They specifically asked for you."

My head begins to throb. Right behind my eyes. I rub my temples. "It seems I can't say no. Just email me the details and what I have to do."

"Thank you, Isla. I'm sure you'd rather be anywhere else, but you're doing a great thing. Lives will be changed."

All I can do is nod my head. "I'd do anything for these kids."

"I know," she says affectionately. "I only hope you do something life-changing for yourself when the opportunity arises."

"Of course." I'm not holding my breath. Life doesn't seem to be my biggest fan these days. The most change I can hope for is the kind that involves clean clothes every morning.

Well, most mornings.

Trish gives my hand a squeeze. "Things will get better, Isla. I just know it."

"Thanks." I offer her a strained smile as she waves and leaves for the day.

I'm glad someone thinks things will get better.

I sure as hell don't. Not anymore.

---

ME

Hey. So I have to go to your game on Saturday because of this thing with my school. Could you help me get tickets for my two best friends? I hate to ask, but…

GRIFFIN

But you don't want to see Madds alone.

Pretty much.

Don't worry, Teach. I gotcha covered.

Thank you. Please don't say anything to him.

Your secret's safe with me.

How is he doing? Has he stopped getting himself into trouble?

He's been better. But he'll be okay. He knows what he has to do now.

The more important question is how are YOU doing?

I've been better. I'll be relieved once this whole thing is done and over with on Saturday.

> Mira asked me to find out if she could sit with you and your friends.

MY CHEST SQUEEZES. MIRA WANTS TO SIT WITH ME after everything? A rogue tear slips down my cheek.

"Stupid tears. We've cried enough."

ME

> Of course. I'd love to sit with her if she wants to.

GRIFFIN

> She says, "Hell yeah, I do."

> LOL. Okay then. Sounds fun.

> Well, sounds less tortuous.

> Hang in there, Teach. You let me know if you need anything, okay?

> Thanks, Griffin.

I want to ask him if he told Maddox everything. Did Maddox believe him? Why hasn't he called me? Does he simply not care? Maybe everything between us was all in my head. If that's the case, I might as well give up on finding love altogether. Clearly, I'm shit at seeing things for how they really are.

GRIFFIN

> Night, Isla. See you on Saturday.

ME

> See you then. Night.

I have two days to psych myself up. Two days to build

up my defenses so I don't crumble like a sandcastle in a rainstorm when I see Maddox for the first time since he dumped me. I can do this. Sitting by his sister will be fine, too. Totally fine.

Everything is fine.

I collapse onto my bed and stare at the ceiling.

Who am I kidding? I'm the furthest thing from fine.

Fake it 'til you make it, though. Right?

Right.

fifty-four

ISLA

"I DON'T WANT TO DO THIS." I STARE AT MADDOX'S jersey. It hangs in my closet, taunting me. Laughing at my pain. And the nerves that have me worried I'm either going to puke my guts out or shit myself.

"He probably won't even come near you," Nevaeh says. She means it to be reassuring, but it's not. Because I want Maddox to be near me. I want him to pull his head out of his ass and want me the way I still want him. But Nev's right. He'll probably keep his distance.

"Sure." I settle on a plum-colored sweater, my nicest pair of jeans, and gray suede ankle booties with a slight wedge heel. I *want* to wear a hoodie and sneakers, but since this is for work, I need to look nice. Not like the depressed hermit I've become.

Again.

Don't want to scare the fans.

Jess and Nev keep me distracted while I get ready. They

talk my ear off as we drive to the arena. And they don't leave my side as we push through the crowds. If anyone recognizes me, I don't notice. All of my focus goes to keeping myself calm.

Being back here is harder than I thought it would be. Knowing that Maddox is in this building, getting ready for the game, not missing me, makes it difficult to breathe.

"This was a mistake," I mutter to myself. I'm ten seconds away from turning on my heel and running when I hear someone call my name.

"Isla! Oh my god, I've missed you."

I only get a glimpse of Mira's smiling face before she wraps me up in a tight hug. My body is stiff for a moment, but then I wrap my arms around her, too. Tears threaten my eyes. As I'm blinking through my tears, I notice a beautiful, older, dark-haired woman watching us with a soft smile. Something about her is familiar.

"Hey, Mira. I've missed you too." I pull back from the hug, meeting her gaze. "You all moved in at Griffin's?"

She chuckles. "Yep."

"How's that going so far?"

"Well, we haven't killed each other yet. So I'm counting it as a win." She flashes me a bright grin as her eyes rove over my face. Whatever she sees dims her smile. "How are you doing?"

I shrug. That's all I have to offer because if I open my mouth, I'll start crying.

"Yeah," she says, giving my hand a squeeze. "I figured."

I introduce her to Jess and Nevaeh. They exchange pleasantries and some looks I can't quite figure out, and then Mira looks back at the older woman.

"There's someone I want you to meet."

Looking between the woman and my friend, my stomach twists. Because now I understand why she looks familiar.

"This is my mom, Camila." Mira waves her mom closer. "Mom, this is Isla."

*Oh, god.* I'm meeting Maddox's mother. We're broken up, and I'm meeting his mom.

Swallowing past the lump in my throat, I attempt to smile. "Hi. It's so nice to meet you."

Camila ignores my proffered hand and pulls me in for a hug. She's soft and curvy and the hug she gives me is a true mom-hug. The lump in my throat grows.

"Isla. It's so good to finally meet you. I've heard so much about you." Familiar brown eyes twinkle as she releases me. Maddox's eyes.

God, I miss him.

"Hi," I say, clearing my throat. "Good to meet you, too."

"I'm sorry to spring my presence on you, but it's been a while since I've been to one of my son's games. And I don't see this one enough." Camila hooks a thumb in her daughter's direction. Mira rolls her eyes.

"Mom. I'm back, okay? Don't get your panties in a twist."

Despite my nerves and the crushing regret of everything that's happened the last week or two, I laugh.

"Yeah, and instead of moving back home, you moved in with Griffin Wright. That boy is as sweet as they come, but the two of you lead very different lives."

Mira shrugs and gives me an exasperated look before hooking her arm in mine. The five of us weave through the growing crowds. When I asked Griffin to get tickets for us, I thought he'd get us something toward the back of the arena. But that's not where Mira takes us.

"We're sitting here?" I ask as she leads us into the first row of seats from the boards. My voice is squeaky. "Mira, this isn't a good idea."

She waves dismissively. "This is where the team wanted you. It'll make it easier to get you on the ice after the game when they present you with one of those huge checks for your school."

"But Maddox," I hiss. I'm as quiet as possible so her mom doesn't hear. "Mira, this is too close. He'll be pissed."

And I'll be struggling to maintain my composure the whole game. It will be hard enough to watch him play. But to be this close? Seeing every facial expression when he skates by—every frown, sneer, and grimace—will be too much for me. I already know it.

Mira gives me a sympathetic smile. "He won't be. Trust me. It'll be fine."

"*I* won't be fine," I whisper. She hears me.

"You will. Promise. You're not alone."

"I'm not ready to see him, Mira. I'm not…" My eyes well with tears and I have to clear my throat again. "I'm not okay."

"Man, I want to kick my brother's ass," she mutters, glaring at the tunnel the guys will walk out of soon for warmups. Turning back to me, she grabs my hand once we're settled in our seats. "Don't be mad, but Griff told me what happened. My brother is a dumbass and I get why you're not okay. And he may be my blood, but I'm on your side. So is Griffin. Plus, you've got your friends here to support you. You can do this. You're not alone."

"I don't think you understand," I say as a booming baritone announces the visiting team—the Florida Gators—and the Rogues as they skate onto the ice for warmups. My chest tightens and my hands shake as my eyes find Maddox the moment he emerges from the tunnel.

I'm going to puke.

Turning pleading eyes to Mira, I clutch at her hand. "I'm in love with him."

Mira's face softens. "Yeah, girl. I know. I think the only person who didn't know was my brother. And that's because he's an idiot."

"I can't face him." I start to rise from my seat. "This was a mistake."

"Isla." Mira tugs my arm, and I flop back onto my ass. "Breathe."

But that's the thing. I can't. Because I can feel Maddox's eyes on me. Hell, it feels like everyone is watching me. It's like ants crawling over every inch of my skin. "I need to run to the bathroom. I'll be right back."

I'm fleeing before she can say a thing. The hair on the back of my neck prickles. I'm sure Maddox is watching me run from the arena with a pleased smile. He probably loves seeing me upset and broken.

Careful not to make eye contact with anyone, I hurry into the women's bathroom and close myself in a stall. This was a mistake. I thought I could handle being in the same building as Maddox. But that was before I knew we'd be sitting right against the ice.

Leaning my forehead against the stall door, I try to slow my breathing.

*In for four.*

*Out for four.*

*In for four.*

*Out for four.*

Fans chatter all around, oblivious to the turmoil inside of me. Doors slam, toilets flush, and women laugh.

*In for four.*

*Out for four.*

Why did Trish ask me to do this? And why did I agree? Surely they could have asked someone else.

My mind wanders to Maddox. What must he think of me? Is he mad I'm here, on his turf, after he dumped me? Does he believe I'll throw myself at him and beg him to give me another chance? A part of me wants to. I still don't understand how all of this went so wrong. And if Griffin told him the truth, why hasn't Maddox reached out to me? Should I have reached out to him?

"Isla?" Jess's tentative voice breaks through my spiraling thoughts and the clamor of the bathroom. "Babes, please come out."

Taking one last, deep breath, I steel my spine, wipe the tears from my lashes, and open the stall door.

"Oh, honey." Jess pulls me into a hug. "A few hours, then this will be all over. Nev and I won't leave your side."

"Thanks," I mumble into her shoulder. "I don't know what I'd do without you two."

"Probably sit at home and gorge yourself on donuts until your skin is translucent and your couch is covered in a two-inch layer of crumbs."

A laugh bubbles out of me. "Oh, god. That's horrifying. Don't ever let me get that bad."

"We won't." Her gray eyes shine with promise. "Now. Are you ready to go out there and make Maddox regret the day he let you go?"

"Yes," I lie. With my shoulders back and my chin up, I almost believe myself.

Fake it until you make it... home so you can cry in bed.

I know that's not how the saying goes, but my way is more realistic.

*fifty-five*

## MADDOX

She's been crying.

"Dude. If you don't get your head out of your ass, Coach is gonna bench you." Logan shoulder-checks me.

"Does she look like she's been crying?"

Logan glances over to where Isla sits with my mom, my sister, and her two best friends. She came back from wherever she went and her eyes were red-rimmed and puffy. Maybe it was a mistake to do things this way. I should have showed up at her apartment the minute I learned the truth. But Griffin convinced me that the only way I could win her back is by publicly humiliating myself and making some grand gesture.

So here we are. My nerves are shot and I'm so keyed up, it'll take all my restraint not to start a fight tonight.

"Maybe," Logan answers me. "But you need to focus, Graves. Play well for her. Score as many goals as you can for her."

She won't even look in my direction. Ever since she sat back down, her eyes have been glued on the Gators. Occasionally someone says something, and she responds or smiles in return, but it never reaches her eyes.

I've hurt her. Badly.

Here I was, angry and raw, thinking she'd done me wrong, and all I had to do was talk to her like a rational adult.

I owe her so many apologies.

"You need to stretch," Bash says. Griffin nods his agreement. They've been hovering all week. But they've also done everything I've asked of them and more to set things up for tonight. I couldn't ask for better friends.

They drop to the ice with me as we stretch out our hip flexors and limber up. I watch Isla the whole time.

Is it possible she's even more beautiful than I remember?

We run through our pre-game drills. Passing, shooting, puck handling. Somehow, I get to the end without Coach yelling at me to pay attention. The same can't be said for his pep talk once we're back in the locker room. I can't even begin to tell you what he said.

My mind is elsewhere.

The home crowd roars as the announcer calls our name and the guys skate onto the ice as the customary pyrotechnics display gets the crowd hyped. And when he calls my name and number, I take to the ice with my own internal fireworks display going off in my stomach. I find Isla in the crowd and don't take my gaze off her until we get to the bench. Her sapphire eyes flit between me and the ice. She tries to ignore me, but she can't. Maybe there's hope. Maybe I won't be humiliating myself at the end of the night for nothing.

When our gazes meet across the ice, I try to convey my feelings with a look. *This is for you,* I try to show her. *I'm winning you back. I fucked up, but I'm getting you back.* The corner of my lips quirk when her sky-blue eyes go wide before she looks away.

"Let's kick some ass," I say to the guys. "I have the love of my life to win back."

Griffin claps me on the back. "You've got this, brother."

I sure as hell hope so.

---

THE GATORS ARE MAKING US WORK FOR IT.

We're up by two in the middle of the second period, but both goals were hard fought. Unfortunately for Florida, Sebastian's on fire tonight. He hasn't let a single puck through.

I'm frustrated I haven't managed to sink any. Our rookie, Ryder Hanson, scored the first goal of the night, and Byrne got the second. Now it's my turn.

I hop the boards when Coach calls for a line change, and grin when Wright snipes the puck from Florida's center. He taps it to Byrne who dekes right but passes left, leaving me wide open. The puck smacks against my tape, and I'm flying. When one of Florida's defensemen gets too close, I pass to Wright, get into a better position, and ready myself for the pass. I'm almost perfectly positioned. Until their right wing comes flying across the ice. Frustrated, I skate behind the goal and tap the puck to Byrne. He eyes the net and their goalie shifts, ready to block the shot. But at the last moment, Byrne passes to me without looking my way. Before any of the Gators can stop me, I tip it in the left corner.

*Goal.*

Red lights flash, the horn blares, and the arena erupts in cheers. The guys circle me, cheering and celebrating, but my attention is on Isla. This was for her, and I need her to understand. Tapping my chest twice, I point my stick at her.

*For you*, I mouth.

The crowd goes wild, but I don't hear any of it. I watch as Isla's breath hitches, and I swear I can hear it across the ice. She stares at me, and I hate the confusion in her eyes. Hate that I put it there.

One goal won't be enough to help her start to understand.

Looks like I'm shooting for a hat trick.

We head back to the bench for the next line change and my guys clap me on the back.

"I want to score a hat trick for her," I tell them.

Logan nods. "We'll do what we can to set you up."

And they do. With two minutes left in the period, Florida loses a man to the sin bin for roughing and we strike. Down to four men defending their goalie on the ice, The Gators get aggressive. And sloppy.

We easily maneuver the puck across the blue line and I'm checked hard into the boards. But not hard enough to slow me down. Byrne wrestles the puck from a defenseman, chips it to Wright, who out-skates their players, and taps it to me. Florida is spread too thin, and I slide it past their goalie with a perfect wrist-shot.

Isla's eyes meet mine and I tap my chest twice again before pointing at her with my stick. The cameraman is ready for it this time, and her wide-eyed face fills the jumbotron before cutting back to me. This time I hold up two fingers when I mouth *For you*. The crowd goes nuts. Isla stares at me, her brows furrowing.

Two down, one to go. The buzzer blares, announcing the end of the second period. Isla tracks me with her eyes as I step off the ice and disappear down the tunnel.

"Dude. You're on fire tonight." Griffin slaps my back as we make our way to the locker room. "Just remember. This isn't about you. It's about her."

"I know." All of this is about her. She's the only thing I can think about.

Coach's pep talk is brief, since we're playing so well. He tells us not to get complacent and tells me to stop show-boating. Then he leaves us in peace to rehydrate and rest while the Zamboni crew does their thing.

"Are you ready for this?" Sebastian asks.

I nod. "I'm ready to get her back. Ready to make an ass out of myself? Not so much."

Our goalie chuckles. "It'll be worth it. I know you're nervous, but she can't keep her eyes off you."

"Yeah," Logan agrees. "She's still obsessed with you for some reason."

We all laugh at that. Their teasing eases my nerves. Which is good, because I'm full of them.

The head honchos don't know what I have planned tonight. Sure, they're gifting Center High new computers for the school and all the kids—I didn't even have to lobby as hard as I thought I would for that—but they don't know what I have planned after. I'll probably be in deep shit for it, but it's worth the risk.

She's worth every risk.

"All right, boys. Time to get back out there and shut those Gators out," Coach yells. My teammates cheer.

Time to go out there and win my woman back.

Or humiliate myself trying.

# fifty-six

## ISLA

What is happening right now?

The whole arena buzzes with chatter as we wait for the guys to take the ice for the third and final period of the game. After Maddox's first goal, I had my fair share of gawkers. But after the second goal and having my face plastered across the jumbotron? My name is being whispered all around me.

"What is he doing?" I ask Mira. "He hasn't spoken to me in over a week, and now he's scoring goals for me?" I hate the hint of hysteria creeping into my voice, and that Maddox's mom is hearing this conversation, but I need to know what's going on. The uncertainty of it all is making my stomach eat itself and I'm worried I'll toss my cookies —and the giant pretzel I ate in the first period—all over the plexiglass in front of us.

With my luck, that would make it on the jumbotron, too.

Mira squeezes my hand as the clock ticks down on the intermission. "I know you think he doesn't care, but that couldn't be further from the truth. All I can say is that I hope you give him a chance to make it up to you."

"Make it up to me?" I splutter. "Mira, did Griffin tell him what really happened that day?"

Mira nods.

"But he never called me. He didn't say anything. I sat there, staring at my phone hoping he'd at least text, and *nothing!*"

My friend winces. "Yeah. That may have been Griffin's doing. I should probably kick his ass for it, but his heart's in the right place." She sighs as the clock ticks down to zero and the lights in the arena flash. Mira studies my face before coming to a decision. "Look, all I can say is that he's been miserable without you. A complete ass. Maddy needs you. He cares about you. A lot. And I think you need him too."

The crowd roars as the guys take to the ice. Maddox stares at Mira and me as he skates by, a frown marring his brow.

"He doesn't want me, Mira." No one does for long.

Mira chuckles as she watches her brother watch me. "Come on, Isla. With the way he's staring at you right now, like he wants to scale the glass and steal you away? You can't actually believe that."

I don't respond. Just shrug. Because I desperately want to believe what Mira is saying. I want all of this to have been some awful misunderstanding. For him to leave the ice, drag me somewhere private, and profess his love for me.

But my life doesn't work that way. And hope is dangerous.

The Rogues come out swinging in the third period. My eyes dart across the ice, following the puck. Florida's shots on goal number ticks up as they attempt to score throughout the third, but Sebastian blocks them all. Both teams battle it out and the game gets more physical as the Gators' frustrations grow.

Seven minutes into the third, the Rogues take possession of the puck. I watch, mesmerized, as these massive men fly down the ice. Who knew a bunch of six-foot behemoths could be so graceful? They pass the puck between them like it's nothing. Griffin, Logan, and Maddox evade the Gators wingers, out-skate their center, and barrel through their d-men. Back and forth, they tap the puck, getting closer and closer to the goal. The crowd starts to chant and cheer. And then, with a flick of the wrist so fast I almost miss it, Maddox sinks another goal. Right between the goalie's legs.

The arena erupts into chaos. The red lights behind the goal flash, the siren blares, and the fans are on their feet.

"Maddox Graves scores his third goal of the night with an assist from Logan Byrne and Griffin Wright." The announcer's voice booms over the ice. "He's pulled off a hat trick, ladies and gentlemen! Can you believe that?"

Mira and Camila are cheering like madwomen and hugging each other. Jess and Nev are hooting and hollering. But me? I'm staring at Maddox as he says something to the ref, who nods, then hands Maddox the puck. Then he's flying over the ice until he comes to a sharp stop directly in front of me. We lock eyes, and I swear my heart is trying to beat its way out of my chest.

Maddox searches my face before mouthing *I'm sorry.* He holds the puck to his chest. *This is for you.* And then he tosses the little black disk up over the plexiglass. The man behind me catches it, and Maddox doesn't even have to scowl at the guy to get him to hand it over. I look down at the puck, then back up at the man I'm still hopelessly in love with. He presses a gloved hand to the glass, then gives his mom and sister a wink, and skates back onto the ice to join his teammates.

I... don't know what to think. Or do. Or feel.

Clutching the puck to my chest, I turn to Mira and blink owlishly at her. "What just happened?"

She throws her head back and laughs. "What just happened is my brother scored a hat trick for you." She grins at me. "I know you aren't all that familiar with hockey yet, but that's as good as a love letter from a guy like Maddy."

There's a lump in my throat. I look for Maddox and find him on the bench, watching me. Logan says something to him, but Maddox only gives him a short nod in answer. His attention doesn't waver. Not until he has to get back on the ice.

The Rogues wipe the floor with the Gators, shutting them out completely. But unless Maddox is on the ice, I don't see any more of the game. I'm lost in my head. And his rich, brown eyes.

Until the final buzzer sounds and the announcer tells everyone to stick around for a special presentation on the ice. And then I'm lost in my panic.

"That's your cue," Mira says with a huge smile. "Come on, I'll show you where to go."

People eye us curiously as we make our way through

the crowd. Lots of people stand and head for the exits, but plenty of others stay in their seats, waiting to see what happens next.

A few crew members hurriedly place long mats on the ice so we don't slip once we're out there. Mira leads me toward the tunnel where the guys file through. They smile and wave when they see me. Maddox isn't with them. He must already be in the locker room. I can't deny the pulse of disappointment that reverberates through me at that.

After the show he put on tonight, I thought for sure he'd stick around.

Guess not.

Two guys in suits who are obviously big wigs with the team and a smiley young brunette who introduces herself as the Rogues' social media manager greet me. One man holds one of those ridiculous checks the size of a child. They shake my hand and introduce themselves, but the moment they say their names, I've already forgotten them. I'm too lost in my head to do more than smile and nod.

"Okay," the social media manager says with a huge smile. "Just follow them out onto the ice. They'll say a few things, hand you a big check, and I'll get some video. You'll shake, say thanks, and then you're done. Think you can handle that?"

I glance at Mira, then back at the brunette. "Uh, sure. Yeah. Smile and accept a big check. Got it."

The brunette laughs. "This is going to be the cutest video ever."

*Right.* More like the most awkward video ever. But I don't have time to dwell on how much I'm dreading all of this, because a moment later, the announcer begins to speak.

"Ladies and gentlemen, we have a very special guest with us tonight."

The two men in suits stroll out onto the ice like they were made to command the attention of a crowd of thousands. I hesitate, and the social media manager has to give me an encouraging push to follow them. If it weren't for the camera she then points in my direction, I'd probably turn tail and flee. Instead, I paste a fake-ass smile on my face and pray to Chris Hemsworth that I don't slip on the ice and fall on my ass in front of all these people.

"The Minnesota Rogues are proud to partner with Center High. They're a local high school with big dreams for their students. At the beginning of the school year, we partnered with them to expand their after-school programs. Now, we're excited to provide all new computers for not only the school, but its students."

People in the audience clap. A few get up and leave. Apparently, seeing some random teacher accept a big check isn't all that exciting. If only my nerves would get the memo.

The announcer continues to speak as we find our marks out on the ice. A commotion at the tunnel draws my eye.

"As a thank you to the teacher who made this partnership possible, a few of Ms. Isla Harding's English students have prepared short essays which they will present tonight."

Four of my best students grin at me as they file onto the ice, and my heart swells. Nerves forgotten, I beam as they clutch their printed essays and wave at the crowd.

One of the suits has a microphone now, and says some things I don't really hear. It's all nice stuff. How the Rogues are proud to be investing in Minneapolis's future. That they look forward to partnering with Center High for years to come. And then they flank me on both sides and we pose for photos with the stupid big check.

The announcer thanks the suits, who begin to leave the ice. I go to follow, but the social media manager stops me with a hand on my shoulder.

"Hold on. You won't want to miss this next part," she says with a wink.

The lights in the arena dim, and a spotlight shines on the first of my students. She holds a microphone in one hand and her speech in the other, smiles brightly, and begins to speak.

"Some of you may have heard of our amazing teacher, Ms. Harding." I flush when people in the stands cheer. "Yeah, you *should* know her because she's one of the best teachers around. But you probably know her because she was dating Maddox Graves."

The crowd goes nuts at that, and I can feel my face growing hot. "Teresa," I hiss. "What are you doing?"

My student just winks at me. "Oh, come on, Ms. Harding. We all saw the pics. You two are cute as hell together." She grins when the stands erupt in laughter. "You were happy with him. And then you weren't. Which is why when Mr. Graves asked our class to help him win you back, we said yes."

"Plus, he promised to sign jerseys for us," one of my other students says, leaning toward the microphone. Teresa rolls her eyes and pushes him away. No one is leaving, now. They're all watching this spectacle unfold.

And I'm frozen in place while I try to compute what she just said.

*He asked my students to help him win me back?*

"Mr. Graves said you don't really like being the center of attention like this, but he wanted the world to know how great you are." Murmurs break out in the arena as Rogues players take to the ice. Each holds a paper lantern, complete with flickering tea lights. They encircle the rug I'm standing on, each giving me winks and waves.

I turn to Griffin and mouth *What's going on?* He simply shrugs with an impish grin.

"Mr. Graves asked us to tell everyone what makes you awesome," another of my students, Eddie, says. He holds his paper out. "Our whole class got together and made a list, but it's pretty long. So we're going to give these to you to read later." Eddie and the other students hand me their papers with massive smiles on their faces. "We think there's someone else who should tell the world how great you are."

The spotlight shifts, illuminating Maddox as he steps onto the ice. He's no longer wearing his uniform like the rest of the guys. He's in his game day suit and skates. My students pat me on the shoulder as they file past, leaving me alone in the middle of the ice with a bunch of hockey players and the man who broke—but still holds—my heart.

Maddox murmurs his thanks to my students as they pass him, and he takes the microphone from Eddie. His molten-chocolate eyes fix on me as he skates up. He stops before the mat and clears his throat.

"Eddie's right," he says. His voice is raspy and low. "Even though your students have probably written a much more eloquent speech than I ever could, I'm the one that has something to prove." His eyes scan my face before they drop to my hands, which tremble as I clasp them together over my stomach.

"Everyone here tonight has heard the rumors about me. The stupid Gravedigger nickname and how I always break women's hearts. But until the other week, the nickname was a lie. I hated that name when it was based off of falsehoods." His voice cracks. "But I hate it more now that it's not."

Maddox reaches for my hand. I only hesitate for a moment before placing my palm in his. He takes a step toward me.

"I've been a coward and an idiot. I let my fears and assumptions rule me and I hurt you, Short-Stack. I'm so sorry. I'm sorry for how I acted, baby. It's stupid, but I was so terrified of my feelings for you. No one has ever had the power to break me before you. I've never cared enough about anyone to let that happen. So I lost all sense of reason. The last week and a half I've been miserable. Just ask the guys."

Maddox's teammates grunt their agreement and the crowd laughs.

"The thing is, I don't like who I am without you. You make me want to be a better man, Isla Harding. Ever since our practice date when you ripped me a new one for being rude, you've been it for me. I didn't realize it then, but I almost let the most brilliant, hilarious, beautiful, and loving woman walk away from me that night because I was stuck in my head. Because I was stuck in my fears."

Maddox runs a hand through his hair. He takes another step closer. "Then I did it again the other day. Except this time, it was me who walked away. And it was the biggest mistake of my life."

I'm shaking now. There are still hundreds, if not thousands, of people around us in this arena, but I don't see or hear any of them. Because my whole body is attuned to Maddox. Nothing exists except him.

"Isla, you're too good for me. You know it, I know it, the guys know it. Hell, everyone in this arena probably knows it. You deserve someone who isn't jaded. Someone who doesn't have issues with relationships. Baby, you deserve the best." He takes one final step closer. Our chests are almost brushing. He drops my hand and brings his up to cup my face. When a single tear slips down my cheek, he gently wipes it away with his thumb.

"But the thing is, I'm selfish. And even though you deserve better than me, I can't seem to let you go." He presses his forehead to mine. "So I'm going to tell you how I feel, and I'm going to wish on every single one of these lanterns that you can find it in your big, beautiful heart to give me another chance."

Maddox pulls back and nods at the guys. At his signal, they each release their paper lanterns. They're tethered with a long length of string so they don't set off the sprinklers in the arena, but they still float high enough above us to look like stars.

Or the hot air balloon where I fell for him.

My heart thunders in my chest and more tears pool in my eyes. Maddox looks down at me with so much tenderness.

He's not done with me. He hasn't moved on. In fact, it seems he's been just as miserable as I've been.

"I don't deserve another chance after the way I hurt you. You have no reason to trust me, baby, and I know that. But I'm too selfish not to tell you I love you, Isla Harding. I'm so fucking in love with you."

The crowd roars, and Maddox winces. "I shouldn't have said the f-word. There are kids here."

A giggle bubbles up out of me. Along with more tears.

He loves me?

My knees feel unsteady. I need to tether myself to something. So I reach out and grab hold of the man who was my rock and is asking me to let him be again. My breath comes in short bursts as I cling to his suit jacket. His gorgeous, earthy eyes sparkle under the spotlight. And they're trained on me.

He brushes a thumb over my cheekbone, his forehead still pressed to mine. "I love you, Short-Stack. I got a taste of what life would be like without you this past week, and it was worse than I could have imagined. If you'll let me, I want nothing more than to love you and support you and cheer you on. I want to fall asleep next to you and wake up to your adorable bedhead. And I want you wearing my jersey. Every single game."

Maddox sucks in a deep breath. I hold mine.

"Can you forgive me? Would you give me another chance? I can't promise that I won't mess up again. But I can promise that I will never walk away from you again. I'll fight for you. Always. And I'll love you as long as you'll let me. Even after." He presses a kiss to my forehead as my body quivers with the emotions I'm trying so hard to repress.

I don't need to break down and ugly cry in front of all these people.

"What do you say, baby? Give me another shot? I promise I won't miss this one."

Squeezing my eyes shut so I can have a moment to compose myself, I breathe deeply through my nose. I can't believe this is happening. Never in a million years did I imagine Maddox putting something like this together. He's pushing me outside of my comfort zones, but it's also perfect. I may hate the attention I've gotten because of our relationship, but he's claiming me. Publicly. Telling the world he's not embarrassed of me.

He professed his love for me. In front of an arena full of Rogues fans.

Opening my eyes, I'm met with an achingly familiar face filled with a potent mixture of hope and fear.

My answer is easy.

# fifty-seven

## MADDOX

I'm scared to breathe. Everything feels like it's balancing on the point of a knife. One wrong move, one rogue breath, and all my hopes could topple over and shatter on the ice. The whole arena holds its breath with me.

Isla opens her beautiful blue eyes—eyes I've missed so damn much—and my heart stutters.

This is it. She'll either agree to give me a second chance, or she'll tell me to fuck off and never contact her again. I deserve the latter, but god do I hope it's the former.

"Yes." Her full lips break into a smile so brilliant it melts my insides. "I say hell yes, I'll give you another shot."

My knees nearly buckle.

"But if you ever do something stupid like that again, I'm getting your teammates to beat you up. Got it?"

The laugh that comes out of me is nearly hysterical.

"You got it, Short-Stack. If I ever hurt you again, I'll ask them to kick my butt myself."

"You wouldn't even need to ask," Griffin calls out. "We've got your back, Teach."

It starts with a smile. Then her body shakes. And then Isla's laughing, tears streaming down her face. I hand the mic off to Bash and wrap her in my arms. Where she belongs.

God, I've missed her.

"I love you," I murmur low in her ear. This confession is only for Isla. "I love you so much, baby. I've missed you. I'm so, so sorry."

Isla tilts her chin up to meet my gaze, and I brush a tear away. "I love you too, Maddox. And I'm sorry. I should have told you everything when you called, but I didn't want to ruin your game or make you stress when I was already bringing you grief. But I should have told you. From now on, I won't keep things from you."

My heart squeezes. After everything I did, she loves me. I'm the luckiest bastard in the world. But I hate that she feels responsible for any of this. Yeah, we shouldn't be keeping anything from each other, but this is on me. I don't want her apologizing when I'm the one who nuked our relationship over a misunderstanding.

"You have nothing to apologize for. I'm the one that's sorry. I should have brought it up and talked to you about it instead of jumping to conclusions. Yeah, I've been hurt before, but that's no excuse. You're not like the women who hurt me, and you don't deserve to be treated with suspicion. Forgive me?"

"I forgive you," she whispers. Our lips are millimeters

apart, and I feel the words as much as hear them. "Now kiss me, Ogre."

So I do. I kiss the hell out of Isla Harding in front of my teammates, my mom and sister, and thousands of cheering fans. We kiss until we're both breathless and the cheering becomes hoots and wolf-whistles.

Panting, I force myself to pull away. "Want to get out of here?"

"Please," the love of my life says.

She doesn't need to ask me twice. I bend down and scoop Isla up. She squeals and wraps her arms around my shoulders, pressing her face into my neck as the fans go nuts. I give a quick salute to my teammates—my brothers —and glide quickly over the ice. I need to get Isla home.

There's a lot to make up for. Conversations need to be had.

But first, I'm going to worship Isla's body and make her come so many times, she won't be able to walk tomorrow.

WE CAN'T GET OUR CLOTHES OFF FAST ENOUGH.

The moment we step inside my apartment, her fingers grasp at my suit jacket. They shake when she undoes the buttons of my shirt. She's just as frantic as I am.

"I didn't think I'd ever get to touch you again," she murmurs, more to herself than me.

Guilt lances through my heart. "Fuck, baby. I am so damn sorry. I can't say it enough."

"I know," she says. "But talk is cheap, Maddox. I want you to show me."

Oh, sweet Isla. I will show you. Again and again.

With a groan, I tug her pretty purple sweater over her head. It leaves her in a sexy black lace bra that gives me a perfect view of peaked, rosy nipples. Her chest rises and falls harshly, those crystalline blue eyes of hers fixed on my face as I drink her in. My fingers skim over her flushed skin. They blaze a path from her shoulders over her collarbone, then down the valley between her breasts. She's so soft. Inviting.

She's home.

Silently, I drag one strap over her shoulder and down until the lacy cup falls and exposes her breast for me. The hard bud of her nipple begs to be touched. I drag my thumb over her puckered flesh, and Isla gasps. Her eyes flutter shut as she gasps.

"Maddox. Please."

"Are you aching for me, baby?" I bend down and trail nips and kisses down the column of her neck. She tilts her head, giving me better access. "Do you need relief only I can give?"

"Yes." She grips my biceps as I pull the second cup down. "I need you."

I need her too. With an intensity that should scare the hell out of me. But it doesn't. Not now that I know she's willing to give me a second chance. "You have me. Always. I'm yours, Isla."

Wide blue eyes meet mine. Her pupils are blown wide and little pants slip past her bee-stung lips. "Promise?"

With a growl, I pick her up and carry her to the bedroom. "Yes. I'm yours, Isla Harding. And you are mine." I lay her down on the bed and drink in the sight of her. She's flushed and turned on, squirming and needy. "You. Are. Mine."

Then I'm ripping the jeans off her body and peeling delicate lace from her flesh until she's bare beneath me.

"Beautiful. You're so beautiful."

A tentative smile curves Isla's lips. "And you're wearing too many clothes."

It's a problem I remedy as quickly as possible. Isla watches me with unguarded hunger. She presses her thighs together, needing relief. Relief I'm more than happy to give.

I drop to my knees before tugging her ass to the edge of the mattress. She lets out an adorable squeak, which quickly turns into a moan when I push her thighs apart and give her a long, slow lick from slit to clit.

"Oh, god. I've missed your talented mouth."

Grinning against her pussy, she writhes when I chuckle. The vibration goes straight to her clit, which I suck between my lips. "Gonna show you how sorry I am, baby. How much I love you."

"Yes, yes, yes," she chants as I push one finger, then two, into her drenched pussy. When I curl them, she cries out. I rub that magical spot inside of her again and lap up her arousal as it floods my face. Soon, she's writhing and moaning in earnest. Her spine arches, the muscles in her thighs tighten, and her fingers grip my hair painfully.

"That's it, my love. Soak my face like the good girl I know you are."

"Oh, fuck," she whines. She's so close.

I bring my left hand to Isla's lower belly and splay my palm across her heated flesh. And as I suck her clit and curl my fingers against her g-spot, I push down on her lower belly.

"Oh my god," Isla cries. She thrashes as her body goes

taut. I lash at her clit with my tongue and press harder on her abdomen.

"Come for me," I command. And come she does.

Isla cries out as a gush of hot liquid soaks my face. I work her through it, pleased as hell with myself. She shakes and shivers, her perfect, curvy body nearly convulsing with pleasure that drips down my chin and splashes over my chest.

"That's my good girl," I purr against her fluttering pussy. Her eyes are wide as I rise from my knees. She takes in the wetness coating my face and tracks my hand as I wipe my mouth with the back of it.

"Oh my god, I'm so sorry." Her cheeks flame pink with embarrassment. "I've never... I don't know what..."

I silence her with a kiss. My fingers tangle in her hair, and I give the barest tug to ground her. "Why the hell would you apologize for doing exactly what I hoped you'd do?"

She looks bewildered and embarrassed. "I..."

"You squirted all over my face like I asked you to. Fuck, that was hot." I rest my forehead against hers and give her a chance to read the truth in my expression. "One down, baby. Before the night's over, I'm going to make you come at least three times. At least."

She squeals when I slide an arm beneath her and drag her up the bed.

"I need to be inside of you." I smash my lips to hers and let our tongues tangle before I drag myself away and stand.

"What are you doing?" Her slim fingers grip my wrist.

"Just getting a condom, Short-Stack."

"I..." Isla sucks her bottom lip between her teeth. She

squirms in my bed. "I've got an IUD. And all my tests have been clear."

Staring into her vibrant azure eyes, I swallow roughly. "Baby, are you saying you want to have sex without a condom?" I need to hear her say it. This isn't the kind of thing you make assumptions about. Especially not when trust is a tentative thing between us.

The pretty pink in her cheeks darkens. "Yes. If you want to."

"I'm all clear," I tell her, abandoning my plans to grab a foil packet out of my bedside table. Instead, I turn back to Isla and cage her in with my arms. "And I've never had sex without a condom." Not even when I was with Candace. Some part of me never trusted her enough. But Isla? Hell yes, I want to be bare inside of her.

Her lips part enough to let her tongue run across them. "Then fuck me bare, Maddox."

Her words unleash something wild in me, and I pick her up, settling on the mattress with Isla in my lap. I groan when she straddles me. Her pussy's so warm and wet. And she grinds it across my rock-hard shaft. "Damn, baby. You feel so good."

"I'd feel better if you were inside me," she whines.

This woman. I chuckle, taking her lips with mine. "So impatient."

She opens her mouth to reply, but whatever she was going to say gets lost in a gasp as I lift her hips, line myself up, and pull her down onto my cock.

Holy shit. She feels like heaven. Warm and soft and wet, I never want to leave the satiny embrace of her pussy.

"Maddox," she says in a breathy exhalation. Her arms

wrap around my neck as she buries her face in my shoulder. "Oh, god."

It takes all of my self-restraint not to rut into her like a wild beast. I've missed her. I've missed this. But we'll have plenty of time for wild sex. What we both need right now is to reconnect. This incredible woman needs to know beyond a shadow of a doubt that I love her and I'm never leaving her again.

"You okay, sweetheart?"

She nods against my shoulder. Isla's hips begin to move, her body seeking friction and relief. She grinds her clit against my pelvis and moans. "So good."

I couldn't agree more. My fingers skim across her back as I hold her. Goosebumps erupt in their wake. And when I can't stay still any longer, I gently grip her chin and silently ask her to look at me. "I love you."

"I love you, too."

Our bodies find a slow, sensual rhythm. We stare into each other's eyes. When we kiss, it's deep and drugging. The sensation of her soft breasts pressed against my much harder chest, of our sweaty skin sliding together, and my fingers gripping the softness of her hips is more profound than anything I've ever experienced. This isn't just sex. This is making love.

With every rock of our hips, we profess our devotion. Every breathy moan is a promise for our future together. Every soft cry is an apology. Each kiss breathes new life into the relationship I thought I'd lost.

"You're everything," I whisper against Isla's lips. My hips buck a little faster. I'm so close, but I refuse to come until she's ready to fall over the edge with me.

"Maddox," she cries.

"That's it, baby." I reach between us and press my thumb against her clit as she grinds against me. Her arousal drips down my balls. She's close, too. Shifting, I angle my hips to give her better friction. Isla's breathing turns ragged, and she arches her back. It presses her perfect tits up, and I bend down to take a nipple into my mouth. Swirling my tongue over the tight bud, I nip at her before licking it better.

"Oh!"

Her inner walls tighten and ripple around my cock. "That's it, baby. That's it."

I continue to lavish Isla's breasts with attention as I grip her hips and grind her clit against my pubic bone with every stroke. Her breathing speeds up, and my balls tighten.

"Maddox, I'm so close."

"Let go, Isla. I want to feel your pussy milk my cock as I fill you with my cum." I punctuate every few words with harder thrusts. The head of my cock drags against her inner walls and I have to grit my teeth to keep from shooting off before her. "I want you to scream my name as I paint your insides."

"Oh god!"

And that's all it takes for her to clamp around me like a vise. Her inner walls flutter and contract. I've never felt anything like it, and when she tilts her head back and screams my name, I'm gone. My balls tighten almost painfully, and every muscle in my body flexes as I pound up into her relentlessly. My cock jerks and I fill her with rope after rope of hot cum.

"I love you, I love you, I love you," I chant as we writhe against each other.

"I love you too." She stares at me as we both gasp for air. Her expression is soft and vulnerable. Just like the next words that leave her lips. "This is real, right?"

My arms tighten around her. "Yeah, baby. This is real."

It's my fault she feels the need to ask. And it's my job to make sure I reassure her every single day that she's it for me. I look forward to the challenge.

Isla Harding is everything. She's my present and my future. She's wrapped up in every dream and goal for my life, now. She's a part of me. The best part.

"This is real."

I'll make sure she feels the truth of that vow down to the very marrow of her bones.

# fifty-eight

## ISLA

The next few months fly by in a whirlwind of stolen moments between games, phone sex when Maddox is away, and finding our new normal. It's been an adjustment. Ever since that night when Maddox publicly professed his love, we've gotten a lot of attention.

A lot.

It's gotten to the point that Maddox asked me to move in with him last week. His building has a doorman and security. Mine... Well, mine doesn't, and I've had more than my fair share of paps and obsessed fans ambush me on my way out the door in the morning. As much as I hate to admit to my protective boyfriend that it freaks me out, it does. He told me he's been wanting to ask me to move in with him for a while. This just gave him a reason.

My apartment was packed up a few days later thanks to help from Maddox, Griffin, Jess and Nev, Mira, and Camila. Maddox's mom is great, and Mira is starting to feel like a sister. They all helped move my things into Maddox's apartment yesterday.

Well, our apartment, now.

Everything has changed so much in such a short time.

We're celebrating our cohabitation tonight. The guys have a rare three day break in between games, so Maddox rented out a restaurant for us and all our closest friends. Normally, we'd just book a big table, but with all the fan and media curiosity about our relationship, this is the only way either of us will be able to truly enjoy ourselves.

"You rented out Rêveur?" I ask with a laugh as he pulls up to the scene of our first—sorry, our *practice*—date. "How did you manage that?"

He gives me a wink as he turns off the car. "I have my ways."

I giggle as he opens my car door and helps me climb out. "You offered box seats to the owner, didn't you?"

"And two jerseys signed by all the guys on the team, yeah." The grin he gives me melts my insides. The way his chocolate eyes crinkle in the corners tells me he's truly happy.

He smiles like that a lot these days.

So do I.

It hasn't all been sunshine and roses since we made up. We bicker and argue like every couple does. But the beautiful moments far outweigh the annoying ones, and I've never been happier.

I love him so much, and I no longer doubt he loves me. Maddox makes it clear every single day that he chooses me. That he's proud of me. And of being seen with me. He shows me off every chance he gets, and his Gravedigger moniker is rarely uttered these days. Now people love to give him a hard time for how often he gushes about me and our relationship. He's unapologetic about being my biggest fan, and I'm equally unapologetic about being his.

As long as it's not an afternoon game during the school week, I go to every single one of Maddox's games with Mira. I wear his jersey and cheer like a madwoman.

My boyfriend holds my hand as we stroll into the restaurant. We're greeted by Kacey, the same hostess who seated me the night I first met Maddox. Her eyes grow wide when she spots us, and a huge smile lights up her face.

"Welcome back to Rêveur! The rest of your party has already arrived. Please follow me." She gives me a wink.

"Surprised to see us here together again?" I tease.

She shakes her head. "Nah. I'm a hockey fan, so I saw the post-game spectacle a few months ago."

Maddox chuckles. "Is there anyone who hasn't seen it by now?"

"I got to tell my friends that I witnessed your first date." She snickers. "Who would have thought it would lead here?"

"Yeah." Maddox squeezes my hand. "I was a dick that night, that's for sure."

"Well, I'm glad to see it didn't get in the way of true love." She gives us both a broad smile as we make it to the massive table full of the people who've become like family. "Please let me know if you need anything." She starts to walk away before pausing. She hesitates for just a moment before saying, "Do you think I could get a photo with you two? Is that weird? I just feel like a fangirl after everything."

I laugh. It's still completely bizarre that anyone would

ask for a photo with me, but it happens occasionally. With Kacey, it's a no-brainer. She was so sweet that day. "Of course."

We take a quick photo with just the three of us, then Maddox ropes all of his teammates into taking a photo with the star-struck hostess. She nearly floats away from our table.

Maddox and I exchange hugs and greetings with everyone before settling down in our seats. The table is raucous and full of laughter. I grin when I spot Nev flirting with Sebastian, who smiles politely at her, but it's obvious she's not going to snag the goalie. His heart is elsewhere. I can tell. I just don't know who holds it. Jess tries to flirt with Griffin, but he's too busy joking around with Mira and making her cackle loudly. When it's clear Jess isn't going to get anywhere with Wright, she turns her attention to Logan.

It's chaotic and wild. It's perfect.

A voice greets us right as my stomach rumbles.

"Good evening and welcome to Rêveur. My name is—"

"Alex?" Jessica's incredulous voice cuts through the din, and my head whips up.

Alex? As in my ex-fiancé, Alex?

"Jess?" Alex's blue eyes are full of shock as he stares at my best friend. Then his gaze shifts as he takes in Nevaeh and the table full of hockey players. His face pales when he sees Griffin before his eyes land on me. And Maddox's arm around my shoulders. His voice comes out in a croak. "Isla?"

I'm gaping like a fish. I know I am. But I mean, what the hell? What is Alex doing here, waiting tables? The last I heard, he'd gotten that prestigious position at the law firm he'd been grasping at. "Alex? What... What are you doing here?"

"I—" His face blanches even further before a furious blush overtakes his face. He opens his mouth, shuts it, then opens it again. Then, he turns on his heels and sprints out of the dining room.

Silence stretches over the table until Sebastian turns to Nev and says, "Wait, was that Isla's ex?"

Nevaeh nods.

The table is silent for a few beats, then everyone's talking over each other.

I turn to Maddox, my eyebrows hitting my hairline. "What just happened?"

"I have no idea." His nose scrunches. "I thought he was a lawyer."

"Me too," I say.

Kacey, noticing the commotion, comes back over to our table. "What happened? Is everything okay?"

"Um, we're fine, but I think we're going to need a different server."

Kacey frowns, her attention swinging to the doors leading into the kitchen. "What happened to Alex?"

"He's probably massaging his bruised ego in the bath-room," Griffin offers.

Our hostess waits for an explanation. Griffin grins.

"You know. Because he's Isla's asshole ex-fiancé, and the last thing any of us knew, he was claiming to be some hot-shot lawyer."

"No way," Kacey says, her eyes going wide. She turns to me. "That guy's your ex?"

I nod.

"I hate that guy!"

The whole table laughs at her frank statement, and Mira leans forward. "Do you know what happened?"

Kacey cackles like she's a super villain who's about to ruin someone's life. And maybe she is about to ruin Alex's, but I have a feeling she's about to make mine better. "Oh, yeah. I know what happened. A few of us made it our mission to find out after he started, because he's such an insufferable asshole. He acts like he's better than everyone, even though he's working the same job as the rest of us."

"Well, don't leave us hanging, Kace," Griffin says with a wink. Kacey blushes at the nickname.

"Apparently, a few months after getting some fancy job at one of the biggest law firms in town, Alex's boss walked in on him boning his much-younger wife against the boss's desk." My jaw drops and Kacey shakes her head. "Can you believe that guy? He wasn't even banging her in his own office. He did it in his boss's because he thought banging the boss's wife in a corner office with a view of the city would somehow manifest the success he thought he deserved in life." Kacey snickers.

I'm just gaping at her. I wish I could say I can't believe Alex would do something like that, but the fact of the matter is, I can. He was probably banging other people's wives while we were together, too.

"Needless to say, he got fired, and now he's been blacklisted. Apparently, he couldn't even get a job as a public defender. So here he is. Well, for now. He'll probably get fired from this job too, after the stunt he just pulled."

"Oh my god," I murmur. I can't believe any of that just happened. "What an asshole."

Maddox chuckles, squeezing my shoulder. "What an

asshole, indeed. Good to see Karma getting it right, occasionally."

"Here, here," my besties agree, raising their water glasses.

"Let me just grab a pencil and a pad and I'll be right back to take your order," Kacey tells us.

"You good?" Maddox asks me. He studies my expression, looking for any signs of distress.

But I don't feel distressed. I don't feel anything at all for Alex Jones, outside of a deep sense of gratitude that I didn't end up married to him.

To think, if he hadn't dumped me, I'd probably be at home tonight, miserable and alone, while he was off screwing some busty blonde at a *work dinner*. The thought is truly horrifying. I suppose, in a way, I owe Alex my thanks. If he hadn't been such a colossal asshole, I never would have met Maddox. I wouldn't be living with the sweetest grump that ever lived or sitting around a table filled with hockey players who have my back like brothers, or a woman I hope will become my sister-in-law one day.

"I'm good," I answer honestly. Leaning into Maddox's arm, I sigh deeply. "I'm so good."

Maddox flashes me an indulgent smile before pressing a searing kiss to my lips. Everyone at the table cheers.

Who could have predicted any of this when Jess and Nev won that date auction? They thought they'd bid on a night of no-pressure fun to help me out of my post-Alex shell. In their minds, they won a fun night out on the town for me.

In reality? It was love I won that night.

And when Maddox looks at me like I'm the best thing that's ever happened to him, I know this is a love I'll keep winning. We both got a taste of what it would be like to lose each other, and neither of us will ever let that happen again.

Leaning against Maddox's strong chest, I say a silent thanks to Alex, my best friends, and I even take a page out of Jess's book and thank Chris Hemsworth. However it happened, I found the kind of love most people spend their whole lives hoping for.

I can't wait to see what comes next.

# *epilogue*

A FEW MONTHS LATER...

## ISLA

"I can't believe they won!" Mira grips my hands tightly in hers, bouncing up and down with me.

Maddox blows me a kiss as he skates off the ice, and even after all these months together, I still swoon. Mira chuckles when Griffin gives her a wink. The two of them have become close since Mira moved in with Griffin after a surprise breakup with her ex-boyfriend. If I didn't know that Maddox's best friend was allergic to relationships and that his sister would never agree to something casual, I might suspect them of having a thing for each other. They're constantly sharing looks and inside jokes.

But they're polar opposites in the way they approach life, so I know I'm wrong.

"Come on," I say, grabbing Mira's hand and dragging

her toward the area designated for family. "Let's not make them wait."

We have plans to celebrate tonight. The Rogues are having a phenomenal season, and we're all excited about the possibility of going all the way. No one would be surprised if they end up being serious contenders for the Stanley Cup.

Dodging pissed-off Scorpions fans who look ready to sting, we make it to the family area and spend the next forty-five minutes chatting while we wait for the guys. I practically leap into Maddox's arms when he walks out in his game-day suit.

God, he looks good in these things. I swear, his game-day suits are the best aphrodisiac.

"I'm so proud of you," I squeal before peppering my boyfriend with kisses. "You played so well tonight." I look over Maddox's shoulder and grin at the rest of the guys. "You all did."

"We were extra motivated," Griffin says with a grin. "Gotta have a reason to hit the town and celebrate."

"Hell yeah," Logan agrees. "So what are we waiting for?"

"Do we still want to do the High Roller?" Sebastian asks. It's a five hundred foot tall observation wheel that's supposed to have amazing views of Vegas. It looks like a Ferris wheel, but it's not quite the same.

I can't wait. I've been looking forward to this the whole trip. There's something about being so far above the ground with Maddox. It's like flying, only better.

"Let's do this," Mira shouts! She hops on Griffin's back with a cheer, and he gives her a piggyback ride out of the arena where a couple of cars wait to take us to tonight's destinations. The guys went all out and booked drivers for the whole weekend.

Sometimes I forget they lead very different lives than I ever did as a single teacher.

The drive to the High Roller doesn't take long. The guys bought out an entire cabin just for us.

It takes about fifteen minutes for the pod to reach the top of the observation wheel, and the view is stunning. I've got my nose pressed against the glass, taking it all in, loving it.

"Isla, check out the view behind you," Sebastian says from across the cabin.

Not wanting to miss a thing, I turn.

Sebastian's right. The view leaves me absolutely breathless.

"Baby." Maddox is down on one knee in the center of the cabin. His earthen eyes glitter as they reflect the lights of the strip. Or maybe it's the light reflecting off the tears pooling in his eyes. His smile is blinding as he watches me process what I'm seeing.

Maddox is down on one knee. He's holding an emerald velvet ring box containing the most stunning vintage-looking diamond ring. He's staring at me like I am his entire world.

My hands tremble as I cover my mouth. "Oh my god," I whisper.

"Isla Rosemary Harding, the first time I met you, I thought you were the most beautiful woman I'd ever seen. Which was inconvenient, because I was determined to dislike you."

Mira and the guys chuckle. My breath comes out in short little gasps.

"But when you put me in my place and refused to take my shit, I grew to admire you. And when you gifted me with the privilege of seeing the world through your eyes and getting to know the real you, I fell in love. Every day, I ask myself how I got this lucky. And every day I decide it doesn't matter. All that matters is that I get to live life by your side."

A tear slips down my cheek. Maddox reaches up to wipe it away, but he remains kneeling.

"Baby, I'm so in love with you. And maybe this is fast, but I don't care. Because I've never been as sure about anything as I am about you. I want to share my life with you. Go on adventures and have some babies that look like mini-Islas. I want to grow old and wrinkly with you and wake up each and every morning with your head on my shoulder."

The tears fall in earnest, now. My whole body shakes.

Is this really happening?

"Isla, baby, will you marry me?"

"Yes," I cry, throwing myself at Maddox the moment he's on his feet. He spins me around as his lips crash against mine. My tears of joy wet both of our cheeks, but he doesn't seem to notice or care. "I love you so much. Yes, I will marry you!"

Our friends cheer and clap, shouting their support and congratulations. Maddox lets me down and slips the ring on my finger. It's a perfect fit. Just like us.

"You guys want to get married tonight?" Griffin asks with a twinkle in his eyes. "There have to be at least a dozen chapels on the strip."

"No way," Maddox says with a laugh. "My mom would kick my ass." He turns to look down at me, and the love in his eyes is staggering. "Plus, I'm going to give Isla whatever fairytale party she wants."

The thing is? I don't need some massive party. It's not the cake or the dress or the flower arrangements that make this a fairytale.

It's Maddox. It's the way he loves me and the way I love him. It's all the magical little moments that led up to this moment.

Looking up at my fiancé, I rise onto my toes and press a tender kiss to his lips.

"You're the fairytale, Maddox."

He cocks one eyebrow. "Oh yeah? I thought I was your ogre."

I laugh. "You are. But maybe even an ogre can be a prince charming."

Maddox wraps me up in his arms and everything else fades away. "Well, I do plan on living happily ever after with you."

"God, you're cheesy."

"You love it," he says with a smirk.

"I do," I reply.

I really, really do.

# *acknowledgments*

If you got this far, that means you finished The Love You Win. So first and foremost, thank YOU for giving this little (chunky) book a chance. I hope you enjoyed it, and I hope you'll check out the next book in the Going Rogue series. Ryder and Lexi's book is one of my favorite things I've ever written, and I'm so excited to share it with you.

I want to take a moment to thank some people that have been in my corner for a long time on my writing journey. They've seen all the iterations of me and my writing, and they've cheered me along from the start. So Mal, Jennica, Ashley, and Kim, thanks for listening to me blather on about plot bunnies, encouraging me when I was down, and cheering me on. You all make even the smallest victory feel like it's monumental.

To my beta readers, Kim and Raquel, thank you for helping me shine Maddox and Isla's story up and for being so encouraging. My editor, Jennifer- thanks for fitting me in and always helping me tame my commas. My PA, Mal- thanks for sticking by me through thick and thin, even when I'm stressed and radio silent. You are such a fantastic friend. I don't know what I'd do without you. My illustrator, Andra- I mean, this cover. What can I say besides you are amazing and thank you so much?

And finally, to my kids, who definitely may not read this book but who always deserve the biggest shout out.

You two are the reason I do everything. All the hard things, all the risks, every time I push myself, I do it for you. I love you both so stinking much. I hope I make you as proud as you both make me.

I hope I haven't forgotten anyone. If I did, I'm sorry. And thank you!

See you all next book.

Xo,

Piper

# about the author

*Piper Hale is a Midwestern girl who loves golden-retriever heroes, imperfect heroines, and some coffee with her sugar. She lives with her two crazy (but amazing) kids in the middle-of-the-map USA.*

*Piper grew up listening to her dad's silly stories at bedtime, became a voracious reader as a child, and never forgot her high school creative writing teacher, who told her she had what it took to write romance. Even if she didn't give it a go until the pandemic.*

*These days, you'll find Piper writing contemporary romance that's sassy, sexy, and chock-full of cinnamon rolls.*

For an up-to date list of Piper's books, please click here or visit
https://linktr.ee/piperhale